D0591440

ANTHOLOGY OF
KOREAN LITERATURE

ANTHOLOGY OF KOREAN LITERATURE

From Early Times to the Nineteenth Century

COMPILED AND EDITED
BY PETER H. LEE

UNIVERSITY OF HAWAII PRESS
HONOLULU

UNESCO COLLECTION OF REPRESENTATIVE WORKS

In agreement with the Republic of Korea, this book has been accepted in the Translations Collection of the United Nations Educational, Scientific and Cultural Organization (UNESCO).

Library of Congress Catalog Card Number 81-69567
ISBN 0-8248-0739-1 (cl.)
ISBN 0-8248-0756-1 (pa.)
Printed in the United States of America

Publication of this book has been assisted by the Andrew W. Mellon Foundation.

Paperback edition 1981
04 03 02 01 00 99   11 10 9 8 7

University of Hawai'i Press books are printed on acid-free paper and meet the guidelines for permanence and durability of the Council on Library Resources.

FOR DONALD KEENE

Contents

Preface

The purpose of this anthology is to make available to the general reader a representative selection of Korean literature from about A.D. 600 to the end of the nineteenth century. The aim has been to present poetry and prose written in Chinese and Korean, ordered chronologically—with a few exceptions such as "foundation myths" and "biographies"—and to present them in accurate and readable translation. The contents were selected for their literary merit in consultation with leading scholars in Korea, who have also been helpful in other ways throughout the preparation.

Translations are intended to be literary, and classical allusions are worked into the texts whenever possible to keep the notes to a minimum. Texts derive from the latest authoritative editions; when the works exist in manuscript, authentic copies have been consulted. Some of the translations were made at my request; others were drawn from published materials, with slight revisions. Translations unattributed in this volume are my own.

Introductions to the chapters are intended to be informative, but in some instances brief interpretive remarks have been added to enhance appreciation of the selection. For those who wish to delve more deeply, complete translations of certain classic fiction and *p'ansori* are listed in the Bibliography.

I have attempted to include most forms and modes of classic Korean literature except for literary criticism and drama. Traditional literary criticism concerns mostly poetry written in Chinese by Koreans. A typical essay consists largely of quotations and terse comments on specific lines from poems, with arguments for and against the use of certain words, phrases, allusions, images, and rhymes, as well as information regarding the biographical origins of the poems. These random remarks, which recall the method and tone of the Chinese "talks on poetry" *(shih-hua),* have little meaning apart from the original. The chapter on *sasŏl sijo* presents a traditional preface to illustrate the close alliance between poetry and music in Korean society, where poems were meant to be sung.

As for Korean drama, no text survives from early times. More information exists about the court masks and other dramatic performances during the Yi dynasty. A sixteenth-century record, for example, reports that on New Year's day at court, actors presented a play on the levy of a cloth tax on shamans and another on a covetous magistrate. These may have been simple morality plays. The texts of the popular mask and puppet plays, in my judgment, have little merit as written literature.

I would like to thank the translators; Kim Kyu-t'aek and Paek Sŭng-gil of the Korean National Commission for UNESCO, which sponsored the project; Chŏng Pyŏng-uk of Seoul National University, for his advice and friendship; and Stuart Kiang and James J. Y. Liu, for their help.

PHL

Introduction

The legend of the first Korean king, Tangun, who ascended the throne in the second millennium B.C. and is affectionately known today as "Grandpa Tangun," was first written down in Chinese in the thirteenth century by Iryŏn, the Great Master of Sŏn (Zen) Buddhism. Blending native shamanistic beliefs and the Chinese concept of the trinity of Heaven, Earth, and Man, the story offers an instance of the integration of the indigenous and foreign, low and high, folk and literate, that was to characterize much of later literature in Korea. Existing on several cultural levels, Korean literature thus includes folk literature, literature written in Chinese, and literature in the vernacular.

As Latin was the written language of Italy till the thirteenth century, so classical Chinese was the primary written language of Korea till the fifteenth. In the absence of a writing system of native origin, an ingenious system was devised by the Silla people to transcribe the current spoken language using Chinese logographs. Some graphs were used for their original meaning, and some were borrowed for their phonetic values to transcribe particles and inflections. The system came to be widely used from the sixth century on; and it was through it that the extant Old Korean poems, or *hyangga,* were preserved.

Most Old Korean poems, which again illustrate the convergence of native and foreign cultures, were written or rather sung by members of the *hwarang* and by Buddhist monks. The *hwarang* was an indigenous institution which recruited men of ability for national service and educated them as soldiers, statesmen, and poets. Monks provided the guiding spirit in this training, as, for example, Wŏn'gwang's "Five Commandments for Laymen" shows; some monks were believed to be reincarnations of Maitreya, a patron saint of the institution. Silla Buddhism, which was introduced from China and made the state religion in 527, was closely related to the state and the ruling house. The king enforced the rules of discipline and protected the clergy, and the clergy in turn prayed for the country and helped the administration implement its policies. As royal chaplains and advisers, politicians and diplomats, compilers and exegetes, eminent monks played a crucial role in the development and preservation of the native tradition. Although the selection of poems may reflect the compiler's taste, it was fortunate for Korean literature that learned monks like Iryŏn acted as custodians of the native culture.

Some *hyangga* gain their resonance through verbal felicity and symbolism. The "Ode to Knight Kip'a," for example, begins with a symbolic equation between the moon that pursues the white clouds and the speaker seeking the depths of his friend's mind, and concludes with a correspondence between the knight and the pine that "scorns frost, ignores snow." Like the pine tree, encompassing the past, present, and future through its roots, branches, and leaves, the knight represents the principle of growth and order: an emblem of continuing society and culture. "Requiem" uses the very old trope comparing the generations of man with the scattering of leaves. The devotional poem by Kyunyŏ recalls the canticles in its imagery and symbolism. As passion's flame scorches and destroys the fabric of human nature, so the ignorant mind suffers the blight of affliction. Only the Buddha's sweet rain of truth, like God's love and grace, can cause the withered soul to yield the grass of spiritual regeneration. If the rain falls over the dried, ignorant soil of the mind, the blight will be dispelled, the grass will grow, and the soil will bear the golden fruit of knowledge. This harmonious state of the mind is expressed by the single beautiful metaphor of "a moonlit autumn field," the full moon standing for enlightenment.

The interplay of Buddhism and native beliefs continued to inspire popular culture during the Koryŏ dynasty (918–1392). Along with the lantern festival of Buddhist origin, there existed various folk arts and customs, epitomized in the harvest festival which was held in the eleventh month to give thanks to native gods in song, dance, and drama. Koryŏ lyrics, a blend of folksongs and art songs rooted in the indigenous culture, were composed and sung to musical accompaniment whenever men and women got together to be entertained with poetry. The refrains in these songs reflect the association of verbal and musical rhythms and were used by the poets, together with nonsense syllables and onomatopoetic representations of the sounds of the drum, to create tension, suspense, and the quality of incantation.

These nameless poets explored the joys and torments of love in a frank and powerful language, singing of the sadness of parting, revulsion at betrayal, renewed desire, and grief at abandonment—all convincingly dramatized by the skillful use of inherited materials. They were all at war with time, the greatest enemy of love, because time is mutable and illusory like the ceaseless flow of the river or the changeless yet constantly changing fire. In "Ode on the Seasons," the speaker likens the stage of her love to the four seasons; in "Spring Overflows the Pavilion," the speaker laments a blighted spring in her heart, and in "Winter Night" she compares the agony of desertion to a stormy night that scatters sleet and snow. But the poets say they can make the river stand still, they are content to be dissolved by fire, and are able to transform the icy bamboo hut into a love grotto. Whatever the reasons, the flowering of women's songs in the thirteenth and fourteenth centuries gave dignity and power to vernacular poetry, and the women poets and professional entertainers, like their sisters in the Yi dynasty, left some of the most moving love lyrics in the language.

With the establishment of the Yi dynasty in 1392, Buddhism, which had been the state religion for the previous eight hundred years, gave way to Confucianism as the official political and moral philosophy. The central figure in the first half of the fifteenth century was King Sejong (1397–1450), who ascended the throne at the age of twenty-one. A true humanist, versed in the arts and sciences from philology to music and literature to medicine, he established the Academy of Worthies as a royal research institute in 1420 and assembled young scholars there. He inspired the imagination and loyalty of these dedicated men by his erudition and example, taste and tact. It was his great achievement to channel the ideals and aspirations of the age and to give to diverse activities a strong sense of national purpose.

His greatest gift to his people was the invention of the Korean alphabet (1443–1444), which provided for the first time a set of twenty-eight (now twenty-four) phonetic letters with which thought and speech could be expressed in writing. The first literary work to use the new alphabet was the *Songs of Flying Dragons,* a eulogy cycle compiled from 1445 to 1447 to praise the founding of the new dynasty by the king's grandfather. Employing all the literary devices and encomiastic topics known to the tradition, the *Songs* follow a biographical pattern adorned with motifs drawn from folklore, myth, and history to create an exemplary hero eminent in arms and letters. They are a mirror for princes, a handbook of education, and a *summa* of Confucian humanism.

The civil service examination system, which had been in use from the mid tenth century, stressed learning as the most suitable preparation for public service. Books bind men of all times together—indeed, they are "the key of remembrance." Candidates were therefore tested in the Confucian classics, histories, and literature and wrote prose and verse in Chinese. Thus was created an aristocracy of culture, based not on blood lineage but on literary accomplishment. The topical training, with an emphasis on the dialectical and rhetorical "places" in these texts, stressed rhetorical skills. The pervasiveness of such education is reflected in the phrases that live in the language and the speech of men who never read books, as later verse and prose seem to show. Compared with some five thousand collected works in classical Chinese by individual authors from the tenth to the nineteenth century, the latest anthology of *sijo,* a vernacular form, lists a total of 3,335 poems—an indication of the prevalence, authority, and prestige of written Chinese as the usual means of expression and communication among Korean men of letters. Most of these works were produced in the Yi dynasty, Korea's Confucian era that lasted 518 years. Some authors wrote both in Chinese and in Korean, and it is no surprise that the great contributors to the development of vernacular genres—the *sijo,* the *kasa,* and prose narrative—were also scholar-officials.

Both of these genres of poetry, one lyrical and one narrative, came into being at about the same time. The *sijo,* the most enduring classic poetic form, is a three-line poem, each line consisting of four rhythmic groups, a minor pause occurring at the end of the second, and a major at the end of the fourth. The introduction of a deliberate twist in phrasing or meaning in the third line is often a test of the poet's originality. The interplay of sound, rhythm, and meaning is the soul of the *sijo* and the basis of its organic structure. It is admirably suited to the native sensibility and adaptable to a wide range of topics—it was a rare Korean who would not try his hand at the *sijo,* some of which are still being discovered. The *sijo* were sung and orally transmitted until the texts began to be written down from the eighteenth century onward. It is an oral art even today for both the lettered and unlettered. Its themes range from praise and satire, court and country, love and friendship, to time and change. The favorite topics during the Yi dynasty included the relative merits of engagement and withdrawal—or society and nature—contemplated in a Confucian-Taoist double vision.

The *kasa,* on the other hand, like the Chinese rhymeprose, is narrative and discursive, without stanzaic divisions, and variable in length. It also is suited to various moods and subjects: journeys in and outside the country, pledges of loyalty to the king, the sorrow of unrequited love, the hardships of exile, praise of a life of retirement and reflective leisure, and the pleasures of the farmer's life, patterned after the seasonal cycle, as in "The Farmer's Works and Days," written in a realistic language close to the life of the common people. Women writers from the upper classes also used the form to express the sorrow of their restrained life. These and other variants with stanzaic divisions and a refrain, together with the earlier *kasa* by men of letters, were all meant to be sung. Some later examples became favorite reading among women in this century.

Prose narrative in the Yi dynasty takes the form of tales, romances, and fables written in Korean and in classical Chinese. Kim Si-sŭp combines magic and poetry to create a world of dream and fantasy in his tale of Student Yi and his ghost-wife, modeled on the Chinese tale of wonders. Hŏ Kyun, in his tale of exploits and adventures that test and reward the hero Hong Kiltong, touches on a social issue, the discrimination against illegitimate children. In Kim Man-jung's *A Dream of Nine Clouds,* built on the familiar romance pattern, the hero is banished to earth, savors its pleasures, and returns to the Buddhist paradise as an enlightened one. After experiencing the ideal life of a Confucian official, he realizes that Confucianism teaches man how to live but does not tell him what life is—the hero's ultimate quest. As in the apprenticeship novel, the lessons of the world mature the hero and make him see wherein salvation lies. The story indicates that an age of reason and rules was also an age of questioning, one in which Buddhism was still a living force not only among the people but also for kings and ministers. Like nature poetry written in the first person singular, the utopian visions of these writers make clear the failings of actuality and form a commentary on contemporary affairs.

Other prose narratives of the Yi dynasty include portraits and satires. Characterized by anecdotal charm, the intimate and engaging portraits of historical individuals from every walk of life are full of concrete details and realistic scenes. Such portraits, scattered in some 560 collections of random jottings or miscellanies written in classical Chinese, rely on the plain style and witty dialogue, as do satires from the eighteenth century. The portraits also include satiric deflation of certain social types, but fuller treatment of the prevalent evils of the literati came from members of the class themselves. As a champion of practical learning—practical as opposed to the metaphysical speculations of Neo-Confucian philosophy—and concerned with improving the welfare of the country and its people, Pak Chi-wŏn elucidates, through the mouth of the enlightened pioneer Master Hŏ, the most significant certainty of the time: the idle and impractical nobility must wake up from their conservatism and self-indulgence. The man of authority, too engrossed in bookish learning and empty rituals to earn a living, is also the butt of other humorous and pungent satires. Because of the standard education of the time, every schoolboy was familiar with the classical references in "The Story of a Pheasant Cock," which mixes high and low styles and strives to speak with the voice of a woman.

Women have not been silent in Korean literature—we have only to recall the authors of Koryŏ lyrics, the *sijo,* and the *kasa.* Some secretly taught themselves Chinese, much as Lady Mary Wortley Montague taught herself Latin, and some were gifted poets in Chinese forms. These women writers all had love of learning, intelligence, and independence of mind. Princess Hyegyŏng's chief claim to renown is her diary, *A Record of Sorrowful Days.* Written in a graceful and sonorous court language seldom surpassed, her prose transforms her tragic life into a work of art. The author of "Viewing the Sunrise" excels in descriptive prose verging on lyricism, while that of "Lament for a Needle" shows feminine charm and inimitable style. These writers made prose speak the language of verse, so that their works in the apostrophic style could easily be chanted and memorized by a growing female readership. Although they do not plead for feminine individualism and equality, they earned their fame through their use of the vernacular, for the refinement of Korean prose.

The Song of a Faithful Wife, one of the most popular pieces in the *p'ansori* repertory, is a fitting memorial to the classic Korean literary tradition. This verse narrative, performed by a single entertainer, embodies motifs from folklore, romance, and high literature. Transmitted orally, it grew in size during performances over the years until it was set down by a master of the genre in the nineteenth century, the golden age of vigorous popular arts. Whatever her charms, Ch'un-hyang, or Spring Fragrance, is one of the most memorable characters in Korean literature. She is admired for various qualities: her learning, intelligence, and courage; her combination of propriety and earthiness; her constancy which proclaims the victory of true love. Even under a heavy cangue in the dark prison, a streak of light flashes from her radiant personality. She endears herself to countless readers and spectators even today, is worshiped in a shrine, and has haunted the imagination of modern poets. As writers in the twentieth century absorb the new and reanimate the old, they will surely encounter Spring Fragrance in the creative roots of the people.

Three Kingdoms and Unified Silla

57 B.C. – A.D. 935

FOUNDATION MYTHS

The ancestor of the Shang was born from a swallow's egg and that of the Chou after his mother stepped into the footprint of a deity. Tangun, the legendary founder of Korea, the land of Bright Morning, was the son of a heavenly god and she-bear. He is said to have ascended the Korean throne in 2333 B.C., and the modern Korean calendar begins from that year.

Particularly noteworthy in the legend of Tangun is the she-bear, which represents endurance undergoing trials in the dark cave. Contrarily, the tiger, as in Western folktales, represents the untamed forces of nature. The herbs given to transform them were sacred plants in shamanism. The bear's trials may thus be a symbolic record of initiation rites, consisting of isolation, observance of taboo, and final metamorphosis.

From the fourth century onward, three aristocratic kingdoms flourished on the Korean peninsula. The legend of King Tongmyŏng concerns the northern kingdom of Koguryŏ, that of Pak Hyŏkkŏse, the southern kingdom of Silla, and that of Suro, the confederation of Karak. Birth from an egg is a recurrent motif in these legends. The egg descends from heaven or is born of a woman miraculously impregnated; it is either worshiped or abandoned. The exposed child may then be protected by birds and beasts. Other motifs include rebirth, sibling rivalry, castration, journey, and escape. As oral correlatives of ancient customs and beliefs, they may have served social and religious functions in the community, and variations on the motifs—together with such archetypes as the cave, water, and light—compose the biographical patterns of legends, folktales, and lives of ancient heroes.

"Husband Yŏno, Wife Seo" is the only extant version in Korea of a sun myth. Seo is a personification of the sun, and her migration to Japan and similar stories current there deserve further study.

These tales were recorded for the first time centuries later; the story of Tongmyŏng by Yi Kyu-bo in pentasyllabic old-style poetry in 1193, and the other stories by the Great Master Iryŏn in his collection in 1285. Hence the versions may not be the same as the earliest forms of the tales.

TANGUN

[from *Samguk yusa*]

The *Wei shu*[1] tells us that two thousand years ago, at the time of Emperor Yao, Tangun Wanggŏm chose Asadal as his capital and founded the state of Chosŏn.

The *Old Record* notes that in olden times Hwanin's illegitimate son, Hwanung, wished to descend from heaven and live in the world of man. Knowing his son's desire, father surveyed the three highest mountains and found Mount T'aebaek the most suitable place for his son to settle and help man. Therefore he gave [Hwanung] three heavenly seals and dispatched him to rule over the people. [Hwan]ung descended with three thousand followers to a spot under a tree by the Holy Altar atop Mount T'aebaek, and he called this place the City of God. He was the Heavenly King Hwanung. Leading the Earl of Wind, the Master of Rain, and the Master of Clouds, he took charge of some three hundred and sixty areas of responsibility, including agriculture, allotted lifespans, illness, punishment, and good and evil, and he brought culture to his people.

At that time a bear and a tiger living in the same cave prayed to Holy [Hwan]ung to transform them into human beings. The king gave them a bundle of sacred mugworts and twenty cloves of garlic and said, "If you eat these and shun the sunlight for one hundred days, you'll assume human forms." Both animals ate [the spices] and avoided the sun. After twenty-one days the bear became a woman, but the tiger, unable to observe the taboo, remained a tiger. Unable to find a husband, the bear-woman prayed under the altar tree for a child. [Hwan]ung metamorphosed himself, lay with her and begat a son called Tangun Wanggŏm.

In the fiftieth year of the reign of Emperor Yao, Tangun made the walled city of P'yŏngyang the capital and called his state Chosŏn. He then moved his capital to Asadal on Mount Paegak, also named Mount Kunghol, or Kŭmmidal, whence he ruled for 1,500 years. When King Wu of Chou enfeoffed Ch'i Tzu to Chosŏn in the year *kimyo*, Tangun moved to Changdang capital, but later he returned and hid in Asadal as a mountain god at the age of 1,908.

---

1. "Book of Wei"; otherwise unknown.

PAK HYŎKKŎSE, THE FOUNDER OF SILLA

[from *Samguk yusa*]

In olden times Chinhan had six villages, each belonging to a separate clan whose ancestor was said to have descended from heaven. . . .

On the first day of the third month of the first year, *imja*, of Ti-chieh of the Former Han [69 B.C.], the ancestors of the six villages, together with their children, gathered by the shore of the Al River. They said, "Because we have no ruler above to govern the people, the people are dissolute and do only what they wish. We should seek out a virtuous man to be our king, found a country, and lay out a capital."

When they climbed to a height and looked southward they saw an eerie lightning-like emanation by the Na Well under Mount Yang, while nearby a white horse kneeled and bowed. When they reached the spot they found a red egg; the horse neighed and flew up to heaven when it saw men approaching. When the people cracked the egg open, they discovered within a beautiful infant boy with a radiant visage. Amazed by their discovery, they bathed the infant in the East Spring, then he emitted light. Birds and beasts danced for joy, heaven and earth shook, and the sun and moon became bright. They named the child King Hyŏkkŏse, or Bright, and titled him *kŏsŭrhan*, or king.

The people congratulated one another and said, "Now that the Son of Heaven has come down to be among us, we must seek a virtuous queen to be his mate." That day a hen dragon appeared near the Aryŏng Well in Saryang district and produced from under her left rib an infant girl. Her features were unusually lovely, but her lips were like the beak of a chick. Only when the girl was given a bath in the North River in Wŏlsŏng did the beak fall off. The river was then called Palch'ŏn. The people erected a palace at the western foot of Mount South and reared the two wondrous babes together. Since the boy had been born from an egg in the shape of a gourd, *pak* in Korean, they gave him the surname Pak; the girl was named after the well where she was born.

When the two reached the age of fifteen in the first year, *kapcha*, of Wufeng [57 B.C.], the boy became king and the girl became queen. They named the country Sŏrabŏl, Sŏbŏl, Sara, or Saro. And because of the circumstances surrounding the queen's birth, the country was also called Kyerim, or Forest of the Cock, to commemorate the appearance of the hen dragon. According to another story, the country was so called because a cock crowed in the woods when Kim Alchi was found during the reign of King T'arhae. Later, Silla became the offical name of the country.

After a sixty-one year reign Hyŏkkŏse ascended to heaven, and after seven days his remains fell to earth. His queen is said to have followed him. The people wished to bury them in the same tomb, but a large snake appeared and stopped them. So the remains of each were divided into five parts and buried. Called Five Tombs or Snake Tomb, it is the present North Tomb at Tamŏm Monastery. The heir apparent succeeded Hyŏkkŏse as King Namhae.

THE LAY OF KING TONGMYŎNG

[*Tongmyŏng wang p'yŏn*]

In the third year of Shen-ch'üeh of Han,[1]
In early summer, when the Great Bear stood in the Snake,
Haemosu came to Korea,
A true son of Heaven.
He came down through the air
In a five-dragon chariot,
With a retinue of hundreds,
Robes streaming, riding on swans.
The atmosphere echoed with chiming music,
Banners floated on the tinted clouds.
From oldest times men ordained to rule
Have come down from heaven,
But in daylight he came from the heart of the sky—
A thing never before seen.
In the mornings he dwelt among men,
In the evenings he returned to his heavenly palace.
The ancients have told us
That between heaven and earth the distance
Is two hundred thousand million
Eighteen thousand seven hundred and eighty *li*.

1. 59 B.C.

A scaling-ladder could not reach so far,
Flying pinions could not bear the strain,
Yet morning and evening he went and returned at will.
By what power could he do it?
North of the capital was the Green River,
Where the River Earl's three beautiful daughters
Rose from the drake-neck's green waves
To play in the Bear's Heart Pool.
Their jade ornaments tinkled,
Their flowerlike beauty was modest—
They might have been fairies of the Han River banks,
Or goddesses of the Lo River islets.
The king, out hunting, espied them,
Was fascinated and lost his heart,
Not from lust for girls,
But from eager desire for an heir.
The three sisters saw him coming
And plunged into the water to flee,
So the king prepared a palace
To hide in till they came back:
He traced foundations with a riding whip:
A bronze palace suddenly towered,
Silk cushions were spread, bright and elegant,
Golden goblets waited with fragrant wine.
Soon the three maidens came in,
And toasted each other until they were drunk.
Then the king emerged from hiding;
The startled girls ran, tripped and fell.
The eldest was Willow Flower,
And it was she whom the king caught.
The Earl of the River raged in anger,
And sent a speedy messenger
To demand, "What rogue are you
Who dares behave so presumptuously?"
"Son of the Heavenly Emperor," replied Haemosu,
"I'm asking for your noble daughter's hand."
He beckoned to heaven: the dragon car came down,
And straightway he drove to the Ocean Palace
Where the River Earl admonished him:

"Marriage is a weighty matter,
Needing go-betweens and gifts.
Why have you done these things?
If you are God's own heir,
Prove your powers of transmogrification!''
Through the rippling, flowing green waters
The River Earl leapt, changed into a carp;
The king turned at once into an otter
That seized the carp before it could move.
The earl then sprouted wings,
Flying upward, transformed into a pheasant;
But the king was a golden eagle
And struck like a great bird of prey;
The earl sped away as a stag,
The king pursued as wolf.
The earl then confessed that the king was divine,
Poured wine and they drank to the contract.
When the king was drunk, he was put in a leather bag,
Set beside the girl in his chariot,
And sent off with her
To rise to heaven together;
But the car had not left the water
Before Haemosu woke from his stupor
And, seizing the girl's golden hairpin,
Pierced the leather and slid out through the hole,
To mount alone beyond the crimson clouds.
All was quiet; he did not return.

The River Earl punished his daughter
By stretching her lips three feet long,
And throwing her into the Ubal stream
With only two maidservants.
A fisherman saw them in the eddies,
Creatures disporting themselves strangely,
And reported the fact to King Kŭmwa.
An iron net was set in the torrent,
And the woman was trapped on a rock,
A monster of fearful appearance,
Whose long lips made her mute.

Three times they were trimmed before she could speak.
King Kŭmwa recognized Haemosu's wife,
And gave her a palace to live in.
The sun shone in her breast and she bore Chumong[2]
In the fourth year of Shen-ch'üeh.[3]
His form was wonderful,
His voice of mighty power.
He was born from a pottle-sized egg
That frightened all who saw it.
The king thought it inauspicious,
Monstrous and inhuman,
And put it into the horse-corral,
But the horses took care not to trample it;
It was thrown down steep hills,
But the wild beasts all protected it;
Its mother retrieved it and nurtured it,
Till the boy hatched. His first words were:
"The flies are nibbling my eyes,
I cannot lie and sleep in peace."
His mother made him a bow and arrows,
And he never missed a shot.

Years passed, he grew up,
Getting cleverer every day,
And the crown prince of the Fu-yü[4]
Began to grow jealous,
Saying, "This fellow Chumong
Is a redoubtable warrior.
If we do not act soon,
He will give trouble later."
So the king sent Chumong to tend horses,
To test his intentions.
Chumong meditated, "For Heaven's grandson
To be a mere herdsman is unendurable shame."
Searching his heart, he sought the right way:
"I had rather die than live like this.

2. Chumong means "able archer."
3. 58 B.C.
4. The eldest of Kŭmwa's seven sons.

I would go southwards,
Found a nation, build a city—
But for my mother,
Whom it is hard to leave.''
His mother heard his words
And wept; but wiped her glistening tears:
''Never mind about me.
Rather I fear for your safety.
A knight setting out on a journey
Needs a trusty stallion.''
Together they went to the corral
And thrashed the horses with long whips.
The terrified animals milled about,
But one horse, a beautiful bay,
Leapt over the two-fathom wall,
And proved itself best of the herd.
They fixed a needle in his tongue
That stung him so he could not eat;
In a day or two he wasted away
And looked like a worn-out jade.
When the king came around to inspect,
He gave this horse to Chumong,
Who took it, removed the needle,
And fed the horse well, day and night.
Then he made a compact with three friends,
Friends who were men of wisdom;
They set off south till they reached the Ŏm,
But could find no ferry to cross.
Chumong raised his whip to the sky,
And uttered a long sad plaint:
''Grandson of Heaven, Grandson of the River,
I have come here in flight from danger.
Look on my pitiful orphaned heart:
Heaven and Earth, have you cast me off?''
Gripping his bow, he struck the water:
Fishes and turtles hurried, heads and tails together,
To form a great bridge,
Which the friends at once traversed.
Suddenly, pursuing troops appeared
And mounted the bridge; but it melted away.

A pair of doves brought barley in their bills,
Messengers sent by his mysterious mother.
He chose a site for his capital
Amid mountains and streams and thick-wooded hills.
Seating himself on the royal mat as King Tongmyŏng,[5]
He ordered the ranks of his subjects.
Alas for Songyang, king of Piryu,
Why was he so undiscerning?
Was he a son of the immortal gods,
Who could not recognize a scion of Heaven?
He asked Tongmyŏng to be his vassal,
Uttering rash demands,
But could not hit the painted deer's navel,[6]
And was amazed when Tongmyŏng split the jade ring;
He found his drum and bugle changed
And dared not call them his;[7]
He saw Tongmyŏng's ancient pillars,
Then returned home biting his tongue.[8]
So Tongmyŏng went hunting in the west,
Caught a tall snow-white deer,
Strung it up by the hind feet at Haewŏn,
And pronounced a great malediction:
"Let heaven pour torrents on Piryu,
And wash away his capital.
I will not let you go
Till you help me vent my wrath."
The deer cried with sounds so piteous
They reached the ears of Heaven.
A great rain fell for seven days,
Floods came like Huai joined with Ssu;
Songyang was frightened and anxious.
He had thick ropes stretched by the water,
Knights and peasants struggled to clutch them,
Sweating and gaping in fear.

5. Chumong becomes Tongmyŏng, "Eastern Light."
6. In an archery contest, Songyang and Tongmyŏng were to shoot a painted deer from a hundred paces.
7. Tongmyŏng did not have musical instruments and had one of his officers steal some from Piryu.
8. Songyang claimed he was the senior ruler, because his palace was older; Tongmyŏng confused him by building a palace of decaying wood.

Then Tongmyŏng took his whip
And drew a line at which the waters stopped.
Songyang submitted
And thereafter there was no argument.
A dark cloud covered Falcon Pass,
The crests of the ridges were hidden,
And thousands upon thousands of carpenters
Were heard hammering there.
The king said, "Heaven for me
Is preparing a fortress up yonder."
Suddenly the mist dispersed
And a palace stood out high and splendid,
Where Tongmyŏng ruled for nineteen years,
Till he rose to heaven and forsook his throne.[9]

TRANSLATED BY RICHARD RUTT

KING SURO, THE FOUNDER OF KARAK

[from *Samguk yusa*]

Since the creation of heaven and earth there had been no name for
the country of Karak or its ruler. The nine chiefs ruled over a hun-
dred households with a population of seventy-five thousand, who
lived on the hills and plains and plowed fields and dug wells.

In the eighteenth year of Chien-wu, *imin*, of Emperor Kuang-wu
of the Later Han [A.D. 42], on the day of the lustration festival, a
strange voice called out from Mount Kuji in the north. Two or three
hundred people gathered there. They heard the voice but could not
see the speaker.

The voice asked, "Is anyone here?"
The chiefs replied, "Yes."
"Where is this place?"
"This is Kuji."

The voice continued, "Heaven commanded me to come here to
found a country and be your king, so I have come. Dig the earth on
the peak, sing this song and dance with joy to welcome your great
king:

9. Died at the age of forty.

O turtle, o turtle!
Show your head.
If you do not,
We'll roast you and eat you.''

Overjoyed, the chiefs sang and danced and looked up to the sky. A purple rope descended to earth; at the end of it hung a golden chest wrapped in red cloth. The chest contained six eggs round as the sun. The people venerated the wondrous eggs, wrapped them in cloth and brought them to the house of Ado, where they placed them on a bed. When they returned at dawn, twelve hours later, and opened the chest, the eggs had hatched into six handsome boys. The people put them on the bed and bowed to them. The boys grew day by day, and after ten days the boy who had hatched first reached nine feet in height. He was like King T'ang of Yin; he had the dragon-face of the founder of the Han, eight-colored eyebrows like those of Emperor Yao and double pupils like those of Emperor Shun. On the fifteenth day of the month he ascended the throne. His taboo name was Suro, or Surŭng, and the name of the country became Great Karak, or Kaya. This was one of the six Kaya confederations. The other five boys became the rulers of the other five. . . .

Suro had a temporary palace built, which was roofed with uncut thatch in the interest of simplicity. The earthen platform of the palace was only three feet high. Then, in the first month of his second year, *kyemyo,* Suro declared, "I wish to establish a capital." He went south and surveyed the contours of the land. Looking back at his subjects he said, "This place is as small as a bean patch, but the hills and streams are beautiful and plentiful. It is fit to house the sixteen arhants or the seven sages. Proper reclamation will make this a fine place." Before returning to his residence he marked out sites for the outer walls, some fifteen hundred steps round, and for palaces, halls offices, armories, and storehouses. Workers and artisans were conscripted, and construction went on from the twentieth day of the first month to the tenth day of the third month. The palaces and houses were built during the farmers' slack season, which lasted from the tenth month to the second month of the following year, *kapchin.* Suro chose an auspicious day and moved into his new palace, where he conducted the affairs of state.

About this time the queen of King Hamdal in the country of Wanha conceived and gave birth to an egg. Out of the egg came a boy named T'arhae. T'arhae crossed the sea to Karak. He entered the palace and nonchalantly announced that he had come to take over the throne.

The king replied, "Heaven has commanded me to be king. I am to pacify the country and unite the people. How can I go against the mandate of Heaven and yield my throne and my people?"

T'arhae proposed to settle the question with a contest in magic, and the king agreed. In the batting of an eye T'arhae became a hawk, whereupon the king became an eagle. T'arhae changed into a sparrow; the king changed into a falcon. Finally, both resumed their human forms.

T'arhae said, "I was a hawk before an eagle, a sparrow before a falcon. I escaped death because in your virtuous wisdom you do not wish to take life. I am not your equal."

T'arhae departed and boarded a Chinese ship in a nearby port. Fearing that T'arhae would foment rebellion, the king sent five hundred ships in pursuit. When T'arhae's ship fled toward Silla, the king's ships returned.

On the twenty-seventh day of the seventh month of the twenty-fourth year of Chien-wu, *musin* [A.D. 48], the nine chiefs proposed to the king at the morning audience, "Since you are a heavenly being, we can find no one worthy to be your queen. Please choose the most beautiful and virtuous of our daughters."

The king replied, "My coming here was ordained by Heaven, and Heaven will choose my future queen as well. Please don't worry." He then ordered Yuch'ŏn to sail to Mangsan Island with a light boat and a fast steed, and bade Sin'gwi to go to Sŭngch'ŏp.

Unexpectedly, a ship with red sails and a red flag approached from the southwest. Yuch'ŏn brandished torches, and the passengers were eager to come ashore. Sin'gwi galloped off to relay the news to the king. The gladdened king sent the chiefs to receive the princess in a splendid boat and escort her to the palace.

"He and I have never met," the princess said. "Am I to follow you so easily?"

When her words were conveyed to him, the king thought them proper. He had a canopy built on a hill sixty feet southwest of the palace, and he waited there with his officials. The princess had her boat moored at Pyŏlp'o Ford and walked up to the hilltop, where she removed her silk trousers and offered them as a gift to the mountain spirit. Her retinue consisted of some twenty people, including Sinbo and Chogwang, and their wives, Mojŏng and Moryang, and slaves; they had brought numerous precious goods as well. As the princess approached the temporary quarters, the king went out to welcome her and lead her in. The king bestowed proper gifts on her retinue and had the soldiers guard their residences. . . .

In the bed chamber, she said calmly, "I am a princess of the Indian kingdom of Ayodhyā. My surname is Hŏ, my given name Hwangok [Yellow Jade]. I am sixteen years old. In the fifth month of this year, my father and mother told me of a dream they had, wherein the supreme deity appeared and said, 'The king of Karak, Suro, has been sent by Heaven. He is a holy man. He is still unmarried, so send your daughter to be his queen.' He then returned up to heaven. His words still ring in my ears: 'Take leave of your parents and go there.' So I started on my voyage, with steamed dates and heavenly peaches to sustain me. Thus it is that I stand before you now."

"Because of my divine nature," the king replied, "I knew you were coming, and I refused my officials' proposal. Now the wise and chaste princess has come. Great is my fortune."

The king passed two nights and one day with her. When the time came to return her escort, the king gave each of the fifteen sailors ten bags of rice and thirty rolls of hemp.

On the first day of the eighth month, the king and queen returned to the palace in a royal carriage, accompanied by courtiers in carriages and followed by a train of wagons laden with exotic goods.

The king's exemplary rule was not harsh, but majestic. His administration was not strict, but well ordered. In that year [A.D. 48] his queen dreamt of a bear, conceived and gave birth to a son, who was Heir Apparent Kŏdŭng.

On the first day of the third month of the sixth year of Chungp'ing of Emperor Ling [189], the queen died at the age of 157. The king spent many days mourning her death, and at last died ten years later, on the twenty-third day of the third month of the fourth year of Chien-an, kimyo, of Emperor Hsien. He was 158.

HUSBAND YŎNO, WIFE SEO

[from *Samguk yusa*]

In the fourth year of King Adalla [*r.* A.D. 154–184], there lived on the east coast a couple named Yŏno and Seo. One day the husband went to the sea to gather seaweed. Suddenly a rock, or a fish, carried him off to Japan. The people there thought him extraordinary and made him their king. Wondering why her husband did not come back, Seo searched for him and found a pair of shoes on a rock. No sooner had she climbed on the rock than it carried her away to Japan. The Japanese saw it, thought it strange, and reported the matter to the king. The couple was thus reunited.

At this time, the sun and moon lost their light in Silla. The astrologer divined that the spirits of the sun and moon had left Silla for Japan, thereby causing the strange phenomenon.

King Adalla then sent an envoy to Japan to find the couple. Yŏno declared, "My coming to this country must be a wish of Heaven. How can I leave? Here is a roll of fine silk cloth woven by my wife. Take it home and offer it as a sacrifice to Heaven. Everything will be all right again." The envoy reported the matter to the king, who offered the sacrifice to Heaven. As expected, the sun and moon shone again.

The king placed the silk cloth in his storehouse—called Kwibigo, or the Queen's Storehouse—as a national treasure. The place where he worshiped Heaven was named Yŏngil, Welcoming the Sun, or Togiya, the Field of Prayer.

OLD KOREAN POETRY: *HYANGGA*

From early days on, poetry and music played an important part in the daily lives of the Korean people. This love for song and dance impressed the ancient Chinese, as is attested by their early records. Unfortunately, little of the earliest flowering of Korean poetry has survived, owing to oral transmission and the lack of a unified writing system. Later, when a system of writing was devised, some of the more personal lyrics were found to be unsuitable for public performance, perhaps because of a change in taste.

The lyrics of the twenty-five extant *hyangga*—fourteen in the *Memorabilia and Mirabilia of the Three Kingdoms* (*Samguk yusa,* 1285) and eleven in the *Life of the Great Master Kyunyŏ* (1075)—were transcribed into Chinese logographs chiefly on the basis of phonetic values, in a system known as *hyangch'al,* somewhat like the method used in the *Man'yōshū* (*c.* 759). Twenty of the twenty-five *hyangga* are Buddhist in inspiration and content, reflecting the current trends in Silla and early Koryŏ Buddhism.

Kwangdŏk (fl. 661–681)

PRAYER TO AMITĀBHA

O Moon,
Go to the West, and
Pray to Amitābha
And say

That there is one who
Adores the judicial throne, and
Longs for the Pure Land,
Praying before Him with folded hands.

Can the forty-eight vows be met
If this flesh remains unannihilated?

Siro (fl. 692–702)

ODE TO KNIGHT CHUKCHI

All men sorrow and lament
Over the spring that is past;
Your face once fair and bright,
Where has it gone with deep furrows?

I must glimpse you,
Even for an awesome moment.
My fervent mind cannot rest at night,
In the hollow rank with mugwort.

Sinch'ung (fl. 737–742)

REGRET (737)

You said you would no more forget me
Than pines would wither before the fall.
O that familiar face is there still,
The face I used to admire.

The moon in the calm lake
Complains of the transient tide.
Your face I see no more!
The vain world harasses me.

Master Wǒlmyǒng (fl. 742–765)

REQUIEM

On the hard road of life and death
That is near our land,
You went, afraid,
Without words.

We know not where we go,
Leaves blown, scattered,
Though fallen from the same tree,
By the first winds of autumn.

Abide, Sister, perfect your ways,
Until we meet in the Pure Land.

Master Ch'ungdam (fl. 742–765)

ODE TO KNIGHT KIP'A

The moon that pushes her way
Through the thickets of clouds,
Is she not pursuing
The white clouds?

Knight Kip'a once stood by the water,
Reflecting his face in the blue.
Henceforth I shall seek and gather
Among pebbles the depth of his mind.

Knight, you are the towering pine
That scorns frost, ignores snow.

Hŭimyŏng (fl. 742–765)

HYMN TO THE THOUSAND-EYED GODDESS

Falling on my knees,
Pressing my hands together,
Thousand-Eyed Merciful Goddess,
I implore thee.

Yield me,
Who lacks,
One among your thousand eyes,
By your mystery restore me whole.

If you grant me one of your many eyes,
O the bounty, then, of your charity.

Priest Yŏngjae (fl. 785–798)

MEETING WITH BANDITS

My mind that knew not its true self,
The mind that wandered in the dark and deep,
Now is started out for bodhi,
Now is awakened to light.

But on my way to the city of light,
I meet with a band of thieves.
Their swords glitter in the bushes—
Things-as-they-are and things-as-they-are-not.

Well, bandits and I both meditate on the Truth;
But is that sufficient for tomorrow?

Ch'ŏyong (fl. 875–886)

SONG OF CH'ŎYONG (879)[1]

Having caroused far into the night
In the moonlit capital,
I return home and in my bed,
Behold, four legs.

Two were mine,
Whose are the other two?
Two were mine,
No, no, they are taken.

Great Master Kyunyŏ (923–973)

from ELEVEN DEVOTIONAL POEMS

To the majestic assembly of Buddhas
In the Dharma realm,
I fervently pray
For the sweet rain of truth.

Dispel the blight of affliction
Rooted deep in the soil of ignorance,
And wet the mind's field of the living
Where good grasses struggle to grow.

Ah, the mind is a moonlit autumn field
Ripe with the golden fruit of knowledge.

---

1. Ch'ŏyong, one of the seven sons of the Dragon King of the Eastern Sea, married a beautiful woman. Seeing that she was extremely beautiful, an evil spirit transformed himself into a man and attacked her in her room while Ch'ŏyong was away. But Ch'ŏyong returned, and witnessing the scene, he calmly sang the following song, which so moved the evil spirit that it went away. The Ch'ŏyong mask was later used to exorcise evil spirits, usually on New Year's Eve.

BIOGRAPHIES

Biographies by Ssu-ma Ch'ien, Grand Historian of the Han, had as lasting an impact on Koreans as on his own people. Looked upon as exemplars of biography, they were read by Koreans for their "vivid sketches and moving anecdotes, which give insight into the personality and essential worth of the subject"—in short, for pleasure and profit. Like the Chinese models, biographies in the *Historical Record of the Three Kingdoms* (1146) contain anecdotes—usually in chronological order—sayings, letters, speeches, and other writings, as well as the historian's personal comments.

The first two biographies in our selection deal with persons of humble origin—the poor but good Ondal who marries a princess, and the beautiful and chaste wife of Tomi. These two combine fact and fancy, incorporating a tradition already rich in fictional elements. The following three lives of eminent Silla monks are examples of hagiography. Prenatal wonders, feats of endurance, wondrous miracles, and communication with supernatural beings help create glittering examples to confirm the faithful and glorify the world of the Buddha. Descriptions of the subjects' physical appearance are rare, as they are in saints' lives in the West. The life of Wŏn'gwang is from the *Lives of Eminent Korean Monks* (1215), and those of Wŏnhyo and Ŭisang are from Iryŏn's collection (1285).

ONDAL

[from *Samguk sagi*]

Ondal was a man who lived at the time of King P'yŏngwŏn [559–590] of Koguryŏ. He had an absurd countenance but was goodhearted. Being very poor, he would beg food to support his mother and walked through the streets in rags and worn sandals. People called him Foolish Ondal.

At the time the king's young daughter was given to crying, and the king used to joke, "You do nothing but cry and hurt my ears. You can't be a nobleman's wife when you grow up, so I shall marry you off to Foolish Ondal.''

When the princess reached the age of sixteen, the king wished to give her in marriage to a man of the noble clan of Ko. "You used to tell me that I am to marry Ondal, but now you won't keep your word," the princess said. "Even a lowly man will keep a promise, so much more should a king. 'The king does not joke,' the saying goes. I cannot obey your misguided command.''

The king grew very angry. "If you will not listen to me, you will not be my daughter. Why live with me? Go where you please!'' he retorted.

Thereupon the princess tied ten precious bracelets around her wrist and set forth from the palace. She asked the way to Ondal's house, and upon reaching it she bowed to Ondal's blind old mother and sought to learn where Ondal might be.

"My son is a humble rustic," the mother replied, "you could have no business with him. You are fragrantly scented, your speech is refined, and your hands are soft as cotton. You must be a noble person. Where do you come from? My son went to the mountain some time ago to peel elm bark for his food, and he has not yet come back.''

The princess went to look for Ondal at the foot of the mountain. There she found him carrying elm bark on his back. She told him why she had come.

He put her off, saying, "This is no place for a young girl. You can't be human; you must be a fox or a demon. Stay away from me.''

He turned his back and walked away. The princess followed him and spent the night by the brushwood door. The following morning she went into the cottage and related her story to Ondal and his mother. Ondal was still suspicious, and his mother broke in, "My son is a rustic, hardly a fitting husband for you, and our humble dwelling is hardly the place for you to make your home.''

The princess replied, "'Even a peck of millet is fit to be pounded, even a foot of cloth is fit to be sewn,' the old saying goes. If we're of one mind, why must we be rich to be married?''

She then sold her bracelets and bought a house and land, slaves, cattle, and utensils, and furnished the house with necessities. When Ondal went to buy a horse, the princess said, "Don't buy the horse in the market. Get one abandoned by the state stable because it is either sick or thin. If you can't find such a horse, buy a good one and later exchange it for a state horse." Ondal did as he was told, and the princess devotedly looked after the animal; it soon grew fat and strong.

It was the custom of Koguryŏ to hold a hunt on the third day of the third month on the hill of Lo-lang, and to sacrifice a boar and deer to Heaven and to the deities of the mountains and rivers. That day the king too went hunting, followed by his ministers and soldiers from the five districts. Ondal went along on the horse the princess had reared. He was constantly at the head of the chase and caught the most game. Surprised, the king summoned him, asked his name, and praised him.

Shortly thereafter Emperor Wu [560–578] of the Later Chou invaded Liao-tung, and the king met the invaders on the plains of Paesan. Ondal fought courageously in the vanguard and killed several tens of the enemy. Seizing an opportune moment, Koguryŏ troops launched a fierce attack on the enemy forces and routed them. When rewards were being distributed, everyone recommended Ondal for the highest honors. The king was greatly pleased and declared, "He is my son-in-law." At last he received Ondal with due ceremony and conferred on him the rank of *taehyŏng*. Thereafter Ondal enjoyed the king's favor, and his fame increased from day to day.

Upon the accession of King Yangyang [590–618], Ondal reported to the throne, "Silla has usurped our territory north of the Han and established towns and counties. Our people, bitterly resentful, are unable to forget the country of their parents. Please don't say your subject is foolish and unworthy, but rather grant him an army. He will then recover the land we have lost." The king granted this boon. Before leaving for battle, Ondal vowed, "I'll not return until I've regained the territory west of Kyerip county and Bamboo Ridge." He was slain by an arrow during the battle with the Silla forces at the foot of Adan Fortress.

At his funeral, the carriage could not be moved an inch. The princess arrived and touched the coffin, saying, "Life and death have been decided. Let's return home." Only then did the hearse move. The king heard the news and mourned his subject's death.

TOMI

[from *Samguk sagi*]

Tomi was a native of Paekche. He was a righteous man of humble birth, with a beautiful and chaste wife, and those who knew him spoke well of him.

King Kaeru [128–166] heard of the couple and summoned Tomi. "Generally, women consider chastity and purity to be their foremost virtues," he said, "but if they are tempted with clever words in the dark when no one else is around, few will remain unmoved."

Tomi replied, "One cannot fathom another's mind, but your subject's wife would remain true even on pain of death."

Wishing to test the wife's virtue, the king detained Tomi on some pretext and sent a trusted attendant on horseback to Tomi's house to announce a royal visit. That night the king himself arrived and said to Tomi's wife, "I've long heard about your beauty and I like you. I won you from your husband in a wager. Tomorrow I'll make you my consort, so from now on you're mine."

"The king would not tell a lie, so how could I disobey you? Please enter the room first. I'll change my clothes and follow you," the wife said to the king. She then sent in a female slave disguised as herself.

Later, when the king realized that he had been deceived, he grew angry. On trumped-up charges the king had Tomi's eyes gouged out and had him dragged to a skiff and set adrift on the river. Then he had Tomi's wife sent in and tried to violate her. She declared, "Now that I've lost my husband, I cannot live alone. Still more, since I am to serve your majesty, how could I go against your will? But at the moment I am menstruating, and my body is unclean. Please allow me to wait another day, and then I'll be yours."

The king believed her. The wife then seized the opportunity to escape and reached the shore, only to find that there was no boat. She cried to Heaven, and an empty skiff appeared. She jumped aboard and reached Ch'ŏnsŏng Island, where she found her husband. He was still alive, and the couple dug up tree roots to still their hunger. Eventually the couple boarded a boat that took them to the foot of Mount San in Koguryŏ. The people there took pity on them and provided them with clothes and food. They lived on, and eventually died far from home.

WŎN'GWANG

[from *Haedong kosŭng chŏn*]

Sŏk Wŏn'gwang's secular name was Sŏl or Pak. He was a resident of the capital of Silla. At the age of thirteen he had his head shaved and became a monk. His Sacred Vessel was free and magnificent, and his understanding beyond the ordinary. He was versed in the works of the metaphysical school and Confucianism, and he loved literature. Being lofty in thought, he had great disdain for worldly passions and retired at thirty to a cave on Samgi Mountain. His shadow never appeared outside the cave.

One day a mendicant monk came to a place near the cave and there built a hermitage for religious practice. One night, while the master was sitting and reciting scriptures, a spirit called to him, "Excellent! There are many religious people, yet none excels you. Now, that monk is cultivating black art; but because of your pure thought my way is blocked, and I have not been able to approach him. Whenever I pass by him, however, I cannot help thinking badly of him. I beseech you to persuade him to move away; if he does not follow my advice, there will be a disaster."

The following morning the master went to the monk and told him, "You had better move away to avoid disaster; if you stay it will not be to your advantage."

But the monk replied, "When I undertake to do something opposed by Māra himself, why should I worry about what a demon has to say?"

The same evening the spirit returned and asked for the monk's answer. The master, fearful of the spirit's anger, said that he had not yet been to the monk but that he knew the monk would not dare disobey. The spirit, however, remarked, "I have already ascertained the truth. Be quiet and you shall see."

That same night there was a sound as loud as thunder. At dawn the master went out and saw that the hermitage had been crushed under a landslide.

Later the spirit returned and said, "I have lived for several thousand years and possess unequaled power to change things. This is, therefore, nothing to be marveled at." He also advised the master: "Now the master has benefited himself, but lacks the merit of benefiting others. Why not go to China to obtain the Buddha Dharma, which will be of great benefit to future generations?"

"It has been my cherished desire to learn the Way in China," replied the master, "but owing to land and sea obstacles I am afraid I cannot get there." Thereupon the spirit told him in detail of matters relating to a journey to the West.

In the third month, spring, of the twelfth year of King Chinp'yŏng [590], the master went to Ch'en. He traveled to various lecture halls, received and noted subtle instructions. After mastering the essence of the *Tattvasiddhi,* the *Nirvāṇa Sūtra,* and several treatises from the *Tripiṭaka,* he went to Hu-ch'iu in Wu, now harboring an ambition which reached to the sky. Upon the request of a believer, the master expounded the *Tattvasiddhi,* and thenceforth requests from his admirers came one after another like the close ranks of scales on a fish.

At that time Sui soldiers marched into Yang-tu. There the commander of the army saw a tower in flame. But when he went to the rescue, there was no sign of fire, and he found only the master tied up in front of the tower. Greatly amazed, the commander set him free.

It was during the era of K'ai-huang [590–600] that the *Mahāyānasaṁgraha* was first spread, and the master cherished its style; he won great acclaim in the Sui capital.

Now that he had further cultivated meritorious works, it was incumbent on him to continue the spread of the Dharma eastward. Our country therefore appealed to Sui, and a decree allowed him to return to his country in the twenty-second year, Kyŏngsin, of King Chinp'yŏng [600] together with the *Naema* Chebu and the *Taesa* Hoengch'ŏn, who at that time served as envoys to China. On the sea, a strange being suddenly appeared out of the water and paid homage to the master, saying, "Would the master please erect a monastery and expound the truth there for my sake, so that your disciples can gain outstanding rewards?" The master complied. Because he had returned after an absence of some years, old and young alike rejoiced, and even the king declared his pious respect and regarded him as the "Mighty in Kindness."[1]

One day Wŏn'gwang returned to his old retreat on Samgi Mountain. At midnight the same spirit visited the master and asked him about his experiences abroad. The master thanked him and said,

---

1. An epithet for Śākyamuni.

"Thanks to your gracious protection, all my wishes have been fulfilled."

"I will not abandon my duty to protect you," the spirit replied; "you have an agreement with the sea dragon to erect a monastery, and now the dragon is here with me."

The master then asked where the monastery should be built. The spirit replied, "North of the Unmun, where a flock of magpies are pecking at the ground. That is the place."

The following morning, together with the spirit and the dragon, the master went to the place and, after the ground was cleared, found the remains of a stone pagoda. A monastery was erected there, named the Unmun monastery, and there the master stayed.

The spirit continued to protect the master invisibly, until one day he returned and said, "My end is drawing near, and I want to receive the Bodhisattva ordination so that I might qualify for eternity." The master administered the rites, and they vowed to save each other from endless transmigration.

Afterwards, the master asked if he might see the spirit's manifestation. The latter answered, "You may look to the east at dawn." The master then saw a big arm reach through the clouds to heaven. The spirit spoke, "Now you have seen my arm. Although I possess supernatural power, I still cannot escape mortality. I shall die on such and such a day in such and such a place, and I hope that you will come there to bid me farewell."

The master went to the place as instructed and there saw an old black badger whimper and die. It was the spirit.

A female dragon in the Western Sea used to attend the master's lectures. At that time there was a drought and the master asked her to make rain to alleviate the disaster in the country. The dragon replied, "The supreme deity will not allow it. If I make rain without his permission, I sin against the deity and have no way of escaping punishment."

The master said, "My power can save you from it."

Immediately, the morning clouds appeared on the southern mountain and rain poured down. But thunder from heaven broke out, indicating imminent punishment, and the dragon was afraid. The master hid her under his couch and continued to expound the scriptures.

A heavenly messenger then appeared, saying, "I am ordered by the supreme deity. You are the protector of the fugitive. What shall I do if I am unable to carry out my orders?"

The master, pointing to a pear tree in the garden, replied, "She has transformed herself into that tree. You may strike it."

The messenger struck it and then left. The dragon then came out and thanked the master. Grateful to the tree that had suffered punishment for her sake, the dragon touched the trunk with her hand and the tree revived.

In his thirtieth year [608] King Chinp'yŏng, troubled by frequent border raids from Koguryŏ, decided to request help from Sui to retaliate and asked the master to draft the petition for a foreign campaign. The master replied, "To destroy others in order to preserve oneself is not the way of a monk. But since I, a poor monk, live in Your Majesty's territory and waste Your Majesty's clothes and food, I dare not disobey." He then relayed the king's request to Sui.

The master was detached and retiring by nature, but affectionate and loving to all. He always smiled when he spoke and never showed signs of anger. His reports, memorials, memoranda, and correspondence were all composed by himself and were greatly admired through the whole country. Power was bestowed on him so that he might govern the provinces, and he used the opportunity to promote Buddhism, setting an example for future generations.

In the thirty-fifth year [613] an Assembly of One Hundred Seats was held in the Hwangnyong monastery to expound the scriptures and harvest the fruits of blessing. The master headed the entire assembly. He used to spend days at the Kach'wi monastery, discoursing on the true Way.

Kwisan and Ch'wihang from Saryang district came to the master's door and, lifting up their robes, respectfully said, "We are ignorant and without knowledge. Please give us a maxim which will serve to instruct us for the rest of our lives."

The master replied, "There are ten commandments in the Bodhisattva ordination. But, since you are subjects and sons, I fear you cannot practice all of them. Now, here are five commandments for laymen: serve your sovereign with loyalty; attend your parents with filial piety; treat your friends with sincerity; do not retreat from a battlefield; be discriminating about the taking of life. Exercise care in the performance of them."

Kwisan said, "We accept your wishes with regard to the first four.

But what is the meaning of being discriminating about the taking of life?''

The master answered, "Not to kill during the months of spring and summer nor during the six maigre feast days is to choose the time. Not to kill domestic animals such as cows, horses, chickens, dogs, and tiny creatures whose meat is less than a mouthful is to choose the creatures. Though you may have the need, you should not kill often. These are good rules for laymen." Kwisan and his friend adhered to them without ever breaking them.

Later, when the king was ill and no physician could cure him, the master was invited to the palace to expound the Dharma and there was given separate quarters. While expounding the texts and lecturing on the truth, he succeeded in gaining the king's faith. At the first watch, the king and his courtiers saw that the master's head was as golden as the disk of the sun. The king's illness was immediately cured.

When the master's monastic years were well advanced, he went to the inner court of the palace by carriage. The king personally took care of the master's clothing and medicine, hoping thus to reserve the merits for himself. Except for his monastic robe and begging bowl, the master gave away all the offerings bestowed upon him to the monasteries, in order to glorify the true Dharma and to lead both the initiated and the uninitiated. When he was near the end, the king tended him in person. The king received his commission to transmit the Dharma after the master's death and thus to save the people. Thereupon the master explained the omens to him in detail.

In the fifty-eighth year of Kŏnbok,[2] seven days after the onset of his illness, the master died, sitting upright, in his residence, after giving his last commandments in a lucid, compassionate voice. In the sky northeast of the Hwangnyong monastery music filled the air, and an unusual fragrance pervaded the hall. The whole nation experienced grief mingled with joy. The burial materials and attending rites were the same as those for a king. He was ninety-nine years old.

Years later, a baby died in the womb. According to the popular belief that if it were buried beside the tomb of a virtuous man the family's descendants would not die out, the family of the dead baby buried it there secretly. The same day, the earth shook and threw the baby corpse out of the tomb.

2. The fifty-eighth year of Kŏnbok did not exist. Wŏn'gwang died in 640.

His reliquary on Samgi Mountain still stands today. . . .

The eulogy says: Formerly the master Hui-yüan [334–416] did not neglect worldly texts. During his lectures he illustrated his points by quotations from Chuang Tzu and Lao Tzu in order to make people understand the mysterious purports. The commandments for laymen laid down by the master Wŏn'gwang were really the result of his all-embracing knowledge and demonstrated the efficacy of his technique of preaching the Dharma according to the receptivity of his listeners. Discrimination in the taking of life is none other than T'ang's leaving one side of the net open and Confucius' not shooting at roosting birds.[3] As for his ability to move heavenly deities and dismiss heavenly messengers, he must have possessed unimaginable spiritual power.

WŎNHYO

[from *Samguk yusa*]

The secular surname of Master Wŏnhyo, the holy monk, was Sŏl. He was born under a śāla tree in Chestnut Valley, north of Pulchi village and south of Amnyang county. The master's house was said to be southwest of the valley. One day, as she was passing under the tree, the master's mother felt labor pains and gave birth to him. It was too late to return home, so she hung her husband's clothes on the tree and spent the night under it. That is why the tree is called the śāla, and its unusually shaped fruit the śāla chestnut.

An old record says that long ago an abbot gave his slave two chestnuts for supper. When the slave complained to an official about his meager rations the official thought it strange and had the fruit brought to him. Upon inspection, he found that a single chestnut filled a wooden bowl. The official promptly decreed that subsequently only one chestnut should be given. It is from this story that Chestnut Valley got its name.

When the master became a monk, he turned his house into a monastery, calling it Ch'ogae. He built another monastery near the tree and named it Śāla. The master's childhood name was Sŏdang, or

3. *Analects*, VII, 26.

Sindang. On the night he was conceived, his mother dreamed that a shooting star entered her bosom. At the moment of the master's birth, five-colored clouds hovered over the earth. This was in the thirty-ninth year of King Chinp'yŏng [617], *chŏngch'uk*, the thirteenth year of Ta-yeh. Wŏnhyo was a clever and versatile child who needed no teacher. The *Lives of Eminent Monks of T'ang* and the "Accounts of Conduct" describe his wanderings and religious accomplishments, so I will omit them here and include only some anecdotes from our own sources.

While young the master often had spring fever; once he walked through the streets singing: "Who'll lend me an axe without a handle?[1] I'd like to chisel away at the pillar that supports heaven." The people did not understand his cravings.

King T'aejong heard of Wŏnhyo and said, "This monk wants to marry a noble lady and beget a wise son. If a sage is born the country will benefit greatly." At that time a widowed princess lived alone in the Jasper Palace. The king dispatched attendants to bring Wŏnhyo to the palace but Wŏnhyo met them halfway, having already come down from Mount South as far as Mosquito Stream Bridge. There he deliberately fell into the stream and doused his clothes. The attendants took him to the palace, where he changed his clothes to dry them and spent the night. The princess conceived and gave birth to a son, called Sŏl Ch'ong. Clever and intelligent, Sŏl Ch'ong was versed in the classics and histories and became one of the Ten Worthies of Silla. He annotated in the Korean language[2] the customs and names of things of China and Korea, and the six classics and other literary works. These are recommended to any scholar who wishes to elucidate the classics.

After breaking his vow and begetting Sŏl Ch'ong, Wŏnhyo put on worldly clothes and lived in the style of a "Humble Householder." One day he met an actor who danced with a gourd mask, which struck him as uncanny. He made himself a gourd mask and called it Unhindered[3] after a passage in the *Flower Garland Sūtra*, which says that "All unhindered men leave birth and death through a single path," and then composed a song and sang it until many people knew it. He toured the villages singing and dancing, so that even usurers and bachelors soon knew the name of the Buddha and called

1. *Book of Songs*, 101, 158, where the axe stands for a matchmaker.
2. Through the unique system of transcribing Korean words by Chinese logographs.
3. Without hindrance to achieving enlightenment.

on Amitābha in order to be reborn in his Pure Land. Wŏnhyo's native valley was then renamed Buddha Land, and his monastery was called Ch'ogae, or First Opening. He gave himself the name Wŏnhyo, which means "dawn" in dialect but also indicates that it was Wŏnhyo who made the Buddha-sun shine brightly in Korea.

When he wrote commentaries on the *Flower Garland Sūtra* in the Punhwang monastery, he stopped at the fourth chapter on the "Ten Transferences." As he was so busy with public affairs, he was called the one in the first bodhisattva stage. Also, induced by a sea dragon, the protector of the faith, he received royal orders while traveling to compile commentaries on the *Vajrasamādhi Sūtra*. He placed his inkstone and brush on the two horns of the ox he rode, and soon the people called him Horn Rider. To this day "horn rider" symbolizes the subtle purport of the two enlightenments—original and actualized.

When Wŏnhyo died his son, Sŏl Ch'ong, pulverized his remains and cast them into a lifelike image. This he enshrined and worshiped in the Punhwang monastery.

One day, as Sŏl bowed down, the image turned its head to look at him. Its head is still turned to one side. The site of Sŏl's house is said to be near a cave monastery where his father had once lived.

The eulogy says:

> Ox-horns revealed the mystery of *samādhi,*
> The dancing gourd met the wind in myriad streets.
> He slept a spring sleep in the moonlit palace and left;
> The closed Punhwang monastery casts no shadow.

ŬISANG

[from *Samguk yusa*]

The surname of the Dharma Master Ŭisang was Kim. In the capital, at the age of twenty-nine, Ŭisang had his head shaved in the Hwangbok monastery and became a monk. Shortly afterwards, he thought to travel to China to gauge the extent of the transformations that the Buddha Dharma had brought about there. As it happened, he went with Wŏnhyo to Liao-tung [650] but was detained by the Koguryŏ frontier guard as a spy. After spending dozens of days in confinement, he was set free to return home.

In the beginning of Yung-hui [650–655] Ŭisang sailed on the ship of the returning T'ang envoy, and so was able to visit China. At first he stopped at Yang-chou. There the governor of the prefecture, Liu Chi-jen, invited him to stay at the government offices and entertained him in grand style. Afterwards Ŭisang went to the Chih-hsiang monastery on Mount Chung-nan and had an audience with Chih-yen [602–668]. The night before Ŭisang arrived, Chih-yen had a dream: a tall tree with luxuriant leaves shot out from Korea and covered China. In the top of the tree was the nest of a phoenix. Chih-yen climbed to the top of the tree and found a brightly glowing pearl that shone far and wide. After he had awakened, Chih-yen marveled and pondered over the dream. He sprinkled and swept his abode, and waited. Soon Ŭisang arrived. Chih-yen received his guest with special courtesy and addressed him calmly, "Last night, in a dream, I received an omen of your coming." He then invited him into his chambers and carefully explained the mysteries of the *Flower Garland Sūtra*.

At that time T'ang Kao-tsung was planning to invade Silla, and Silla officials Kim Hŭmsun [or Inmun], Yangdo, and others in the T'ang capital told Ŭisang to return home. He did so in the first year of Hsien-heng [670] and informed the Silla court of danger. . . . In the first year of I-feng [676]Ŭisang returned to Mount T'aebaek and built the Pusŏk monastery in accordance with a royal command. There he preached Mahāyāna Buddhism and was rewarded for his prayers.

When Fa-tsang sent a copy of the *T'an-hsüan chi* together with his personal letter to Ŭisang, Ŭisang ordered ten monasteries to study it. . . .

Ŭisang wrote the *Pŏpkye tosŏ in* [Diagram Seal of the Dharma Realm] and the *Yakso,* which encompasses the gist of the One Vehicle and is worthy of being a touchstone for a thousand generations. Everyone, both high and low, made an effort to carry them with him. The *Diagram* was completed in the first year of Tsung-chang [668], the year Chih-yen died. . . . Ŭisang was thought to be a reincarnation of the Buddha. He had ten disciples who distinguished themselves as Great Masters, and the biography of each has been recorded. . . .

Ŭisang is said to have walked on air while climbing around the pagoda of the Hwangbok monastery with his devotees. The monks therefore did not install a ladder. When the devotees also began to circle the pagoda three feet from the ground, Ŭisang looked back at them and remarked, "Ordinary people would think it strange if they saw us. Walking on air cannot be taught to the masses."

The eulogy says:

> Parting thorns and braving smoke and cloud, he crossed the ocean.
> The gate of the Chih-hsiang monastery opened, and he received the auspicious and precious.
> He planted the luxuriant Hua-yen tree in his home country,
> Now spring prevails on Mounts Chung-nan and T'aebaek.

FA-TSANG'S LETTER TO ŬISANG

The monk of the Ch'ung-fa monastery in the Western Capital of T'ang, Fa-tsang, sends a letter to the attendant of the Buddha and Dharma Master of the Great Flower Garland School in Silla.

More than twenty years have passed since we parted, but how could affection for you leave my mind? Between us lie ten thousand miles of smoke and clouds and a thousand folds of land and sea; it is clear we will not see each other again in this life. How can I express, adequately, how I cherish the memory of our friendship? Owing to the same causes in our former existence and the same karma in this life, we were fortunate; we immersed ourselves in the great scripture, and we received its profound meaning by special favor granted us by our late master.

I hear with even greater joy that you have, on your return to your native country, elucidated the *Flower Garland Sūtra,* enhanced the unimpeded dependent origination [*pratītyasamutpāda*] in the Dharma realm. Thus Indra's net is multimeshed and the kingdom of the Buddha is daily renewed; you have widely benefited the world. By this I know that after the death of the Tathāgata, it will be because of you that the Buddha-sun shines bright, that the wheel of Dharma turns again. You have made the Dharma live for us. I, Fa-tsang, have made little progress and interceded even less for others. When I think of you and look on this scripture, I am ashamed that it was me that our late master transmitted it. But, according to my duty, I cannot abandon what I have received. I only hope to be part of the future causes, direct and indirect, by relying on this karma.

Our teacher's discourses and commentaries, though rich in meaning, are terse in style and difficult for posterity to approach. Hence I have recorded his subtle sayings and mysterious purport, with a commentary on their meaning. Dharma Master Sŭngjŏn has made a copy of my writing and will introduce it to your country upon his return to Silla. I beg you to scrutinize its good and bad points; I shall be happy if you would kindly revise it and enlighten me.

If we are reborn in the future, meet again in the Assembly of Vairocana Buddha, receive the boundlessly wonderful Dharma, and practice the immeasurable vows of Samantabhadra, then evil karma will be overthrown in a day.

It is my earnest hope that you will not forget our friendship at various places in our former existence, that you will instruct me in the right path, and that you will inquire after my destiny either through a person or by letter.

First month, twenty-eighth day [of 692]

With respectful salutation

FA-TSANG

POETRY IN CHINESE

In the mid seventh century a national academy was established in Silla, and by the mid tenth century, with the institution of the civil service examination system, every educated man in Korea was read in the Confucian classics, histories, and literature. The amount of poetry written in Chinese in all known genres of Chinese origin is staggering. Poems were produced on every conceivable occasion; Yi Kyu-bo, for example, left some 1,500 poems. Great masters of the T'ang and Sung as well as pre-T'ang poets were studied and imitated; writers also profited from the study of others whom they had no intention of imitating.

Perhaps the most renowned scholar, statesman, and poet of Silla, Ch'oe Ch'i-wŏn went to China in 868, where he passed the T'ang civil service examination in 874, and held a number of posts. When, in 885, he returned home, he found Silla in its decline and withdrew from public service to spend his last years in a monastery. Considered to be a master of poetry and parallel prose in Chinese, he is included in the "Monograph on Bibliography" in the *New History of T'ang,* and his collected works were compiled in 886 and published in both Korea and China.

In this and in later sections, I have chosen poems that are brief and translatable, relatively free of allusion, and on themes each writer seems to be better suited to than others.

Ch'oe Ch'i-wŏn (857–?)

ON THE ROAD

Whirling east and west on a dusty road,
A lonely whip, a lean horse—so much toil!
I know it's good to return home;
But even if I did, my house would still be poor.

AT THE UGANG STATION

Dismounting on the sandbar I wait for a boat,
A stretch of smoke and waves, an endless sorrow.
Only when the hills are worn flat and the waters dried up
Will there be no parting in the world of man.

IN AUTUMN RAIN

Although I painfully chant in the autumn wind,
I have few friends in the wide world.
At third watch, it rains outside.
By the lamp my heart flies myriad miles away.

NIGHT RAIN IN A POSTAL STATION

In a hostel an autumn rain stops;
A quiet night, a lamp on the cold window.
Sighing I sit sunk in sorrow—
Just like a monk in meditation.

ON SEEING A FELLOW VILLAGER OFF IN SHAN-YANG

We enjoyed a brief spring together on Mount Ch'u;
Now you leave and tears soak my kerchief.
Don't think me strange gazing windward dispirited,
It's hard to meet a friend this far from home.

INSCRIBED AT THE STUDY ON MOUNT KAYA

The wild rush of water down jumbled rocks
    makes the mountains roar
So human speech can't be made out
    even from an inch.
The constant fear that distinctions
    might reach our ears
Makes the running water cage in
    the whole mountain!

TRANSLATED BY RICHARD J. LYNN

Koryŏ Dynasty
918 – 1392

KORYŎ SONGS: *CHANGGA*

The following examples of Middle Korean poems known as *changga* or *pyŏlgok* are characterized by a recurrent refrain which reflects their folk and musical origins and their oral transmission. Consisting of pure onomatopoeia of drum sounds or nonsense jingles—omitted in translations—the refrain sets up a mood or tone which carries the melody and spirit of the poem (as in "Ode on the Seasons") or links a poem comprised of parts with differing contents ("Song of Green Mountain"). The refrain attests, therefore, to the association of verbal and music rhythms in the *changga*.

The theme of most of these anonymous poems is love. They were sung to musical accompaniment—some settings are still preserved—chiefly by women entertainers, known as *kisaeng*. The last poem in the section, "The Song of the Gong," is a poem of praise, approximating the "myth of the impossible." The last stanza of the poem is a folk saying which also appears in "Song of P'yongyang." The use of similar popular and proverbial expressions is commonplace.

THE TURKISH BAKERY

I go to the Turkish shop, buy a bun,
An old Turk grasps me by the hand.
If this story is spread abroad,
You alone are to blame, little actor.
I will go, yes, go to his bower:
A narrow place, sultry and dark.

I go to the Samjang Temple, light the lantern,
A chief priest grasps me by the hand.
If this story is spread abroad,
You alone are to blame, little altar boy.
I will go, yes, go to his bower:
A narrow place, sultry and dark.

I go to the village well, draw the water,
A dragon within grasps me by the hand.
If this story is spread abroad,
You alone are to blame, O scooper.
I will go, yes, go to his bower:
A narrow place, sultry and dark.

I go to the tavern, buy the wine,
An innkeeper grasps me by the hand.
If this story is spread abroad,
You alone are to blame, O wine jug.
I will go, yes, go to his bower:
A narrow place, sultry and dark.

ODE ON THE SEASONS

With virtue in one hand
And happiness in the other,
Come, come you gods,
With virtue and happiness.

The river in January
Now freezes, now melts.
Born into this world,
I live alone.

You burn like a lantern
In the February moon.
Your bright figure
Shines upon the world.

In the beginning of March
Plums are in full bloom.
Others envy
Your magnificent figure!

In April the orioles
Come singing on time.
But you, my clerk,
Forget bygone days.

On the feast of the irises
I brew healing herbs.
I offer you this drink—
May you live a thousand years.

On a June day I am like
A comb cast from a cliff.
Once I followed you,
I thought you looked after me.

For the feast of the dead,
I prepare dainties of land and sea,
And pray in this mid-year day,
That we may be always together.

This is the full moon
Of the mid-autumn festival.
This will be the festive day
If only I am with you.

On the double ninth,
We eat yellow flowers.
O fragrance of chrysanthemums,
The year's end draws near.

In October
I'm like a sliced berry.
Once the branch is broken,
Who will cherish it?

On a long November night
I lie on a dirt floor
With only a sheet to cover me.
O troubled heart, a night without you.

In December I am like
Chopsticks carved from pepperwood
Placed neatly before you:
An unknown guest holds them.

SONG OF P'YONGYANG

Although P'yongyang is my capital,
And the walls have all been repaired,
If I must part from you,
I'll stop spinning and weaving
And follow my love with tears.

Were the pearls to fall on the rocks,
Would the thread be broken?
If I parted from you for a thousand years,
Would my heart be changed?

Not knowing how wide the Taedong River is
You pushed the boat off, boatman!
Not knowing how loose your wife is
You had my love board the ferry, boatman.
Once he has crossed that Taedong River,
He will pluck some other flower.

SONG OF GREEN MOUNTAIN

Let us live, let us live,
Let's live in the green mountain,
With wild grapes and thyme,
Let's live in the green mountain.

Cry, cry birds,
You cry after you wake.
I've more sorrow than you
And cry after I wake.

I see the birds passing,
I see the passing birds on the water.
With a mossy plow
I see the passing bird on the water.

I have spent the day
This way and that.
But where no man comes or goes,
How am I to pass the night?

At what place is this stone thrown?
At what person is this stone thrown?
Here where no man loves or hates,
I cry being hit by a stone.

Let us live, let us live,
Let us live by the loud sea,
With seaweeds and oysters and clams,
Let's live by the sea.

Turning the corner of the kitchen,
I have heard,
I have heard the stag fiddling,
Perched on a bamboo pole.

I've seen strong wine brewing
In a round jar.
A gourd-shaped leaven seizes me.
What shall I do now?

WINTER NIGHT

After a rain comes a thick snow.
Do you come, who made me
Lie awake half the night,
Through a pass in the wood,
Through a path to sleep at dawn?

Fires of hell or thunderbolts
Will soon consume my body.
Fires of hell or thunderbolts
Will soon consume my body.

Would I seek another in your place?
I've made no vows,
Not this, not that,
But to go wherever with you!

WILL YOU GO?

Will you go away?
Will you forsake me and go?

How can I live if you
Forsake me and go away?

I could stop you but fear
You would be annoyed and never return.

Go, then, I'll let you go.
But return as soon as you leave.

SPRING OVERFLOWS THE PAVILION

Were I to build a bamboo hut on the ice,
Were I to die of cold with him on the ice,
O night, run slow, till our love is spent.

When I lie alone, restless, vigilant,
Only peach blossoms wave over the west window.
You have no grief, welcome the spring breeze.

I have believed those who vowed to each other:
"My soul will follow yours forever."
Who, who persuaded me this was true?

"O duck, beautiful duck, why do you come
To the swamp, instead of the shoal?"
"If the swamp freezes, the shoal will do."

A bed on Mount South, a jade pillow, gold brocade,
And beside me a girl sweeter than musk,
Let us press our hearts together.

O love, let's be forever together.

SONG OF THE GONG

Ring the gong, strike the chimes!
In this age, calm and plenty,
Let us live and enjoy.

On a brittle sandy cliff,
Let us plant roasted chestnuts, five pints.
When the chestnuts shoot and sprout,
Then we'll part from our virtuous lord.

Let us carve a lotus out of jade,
And graft the lotus in the stone.
When it blossoms in the coldest day,
Then we'll part from our virtuous lord.

Let us make an iron suit of armor,
Stitch the pleats with iron thread.
When it has been worn and is spoilt,
Then we'll part from our virtuous lord.

Let us make an iron ox, and put him
To graze among the iron trees.
When he has grazed on all the iron grass,
Then we'll part from our virtuous lord.

Were the pearls to fall on the rocks,
Would the thread be broken?
If I parted from you for a thousand years,
Would my heart be changed?

PROSE ESSAYS

Since the compilation of the collected works of Ch'oe Ch'i-won (886), the first extant collection of an individual author, most learned men in Korea left volumes of verse and prose in Chinese. Their prose writings are usually classified as admonition, disquisition, dirge, appreciation, proclamation, announcement, memorial, proposal, letters, and description (or records). The present selection includes two pieces by Yi Kyu-bo, one by Monk Sigyŏngam, and one by Yi Che-hyŏn.

Yi Kyu-bo (1168–1241) passed the state civil service examination in 1190 and rose to be First Privy Councilor. Yi styled himself as master of the lute, poetry, and wine; his prose has the charm of variety, as his pen name "White Cloud" seems to imply.

Monk Sigyŏngam (*fl.* 1270–1350), teacher of the National Preceptor Pogak (1329–1392) and specialist in the *Laṅkāvatāra Sūtra*, left only thirteen prose works. His essay on the virtues of the bamboo reflects the Zen (Sŏn in Korean) point of view.

Yi Che-hyŏn (1287–1367) placed first in the state examination of 1301. In 1314 he went to the Mongol capital, Peking, to join the Korean king who was in residence there and befriended a number of scholars and artists, especially the famous calligrapher and painter Chao Meng-fu (1254–1322). He made several trips to Peking and was versed in the state of arts and letters in fourteenth-century China.

Poems by Yi Kyu-bo and Yi Che-hyŏn are represented in the next section.

Yi Kyu-bo (1168–1241)

ON DEMOLISHING THE EARTHEN CHAMBER
[*Koe t'osil sŏl*]

On the first day of the tenth month, I came home and saw my sons digging a hole in the earth and building a hut like a grave. I feigned stupidity and asked, "Why are you digging a grave within the premises of the house?"

They replied, "It is not a grave, but an earthen chamber."

"Why have you made it?" I asked.

"It is good to store flowers and melons during the winter," they replied. "Womenfolk may come here and do their spinning and weaving without their hands getting chilled and chapped; even in winter it will be as warm as spring here."

I grew doubly angry and said, "That it is hot in summer and cold in winter is the regular course of the four seasons. If the opposite comes about, it will be strange and uncanny. The ancient sages taught man to wear fur garments in winter and hempen ones in summer. This is sufficient for our needs. Building an earthen chamber to turn cold into heat is to resist the ordinances of Heaven. In addition, it is inauspicious for men to dwell in holes in winter like, snakes or toads. As for spinning and weaving, a proper season is set aside for them. Why should they be done in winter? Also, it is natural for flowers to bloom in the spring and fade in winter. If we reverse the process, we will surely go astray. To grow unseasonable things for untimely pleasures is to usurp the prerogatives of Heaven. All this is not what I intend. If you don't destroy the earthen chamber at once, you will not be forgiven and will receive a good flogging from me."

My sons feared my anger and leveled the earthen chamber and made its lumber into firewood. Only then was my mind at peace.

QUESTIONS TO THE CREATOR

[*Mun chomul*]

> I raise this question because I dislike
> such species as flies and mosquitoes.

I said to the Creator of the universe: "When Heaven gave birth to man, it created men first, and then the five grains so that man would have things to eat. Then it created mulberry and hemp so that man would have clothes to wear. This would indicate that Heaven cherishes man and desires that he live. But it is also true that Heaven created evil things. It created savage animals, such as bears, tigers, wolves, and jackals, and such vermin as mosquitoes, gadflies, fleas, and lice. Inferring from the existence of creatures that do great harm to man, it would seem that Heaven detests man and wishes him dead. Why is Heaven so inconsistent in its love and hate?''

The Creator replied: "You ask about the birth of man and other things. But from the remote beginning they came into being of themselves according to the spontaneous workings of Nature. Heaven itself does not know why, nor do I. Man's birth occurred of itself, not because of Heaven. The five grains and the mulberry and hemp came to the world of themselves, not because of Heaven. If so, how could heaven discriminate among benefits and harms and manage good and evil? He who has the Way accepts good when it comes, without rejoicing, and accepts evil without dread. Because he takes all things as nothing, nothing can harm him.''

I asked the Creator: "In the beginning primal material force divided itself into three powers: Heaven above, Earth below, and Man between. Since one principle runs through the three, is it possible that there are evil things in Heaven?''

The Creator replied: "Have I not said that nothing can harm a man who has the Way? Could Heaven be less than a man with the Way and harbor anything harmful?''

"Then, once man attains the Way, can he reach the Jade Palace of the Taoist trinity?''

"Yes.''

"Now you have clearly dispelled my doubts . . . But I am unclear on one point. You say Heaven does not know, nor do you. Heaven is nonaction, and therefore it is natural if it does not know. But how could the Creator not know?''

The Creator replied: "Have you seen me create anything? Things come into being of themselves and change of themselves. How could I fashion things, and how could I know? I do not even know that you call me Creator.''

TRANSLATED BY UCHANG KIM

Monk Sigyŏngam (fl. 1270–1350)

A RECORD OF THE BAMBOO IN THE BAMBOO ARBOR OF THE WŎLTŬNG MONASTERY

[*Wŏltŭngsa Chungnu chukki*]

In the southwest corner of Wŏltŭng monastery on Mount Hwa is Bamboo Arbor; on a hill to the west stand thousands of bamboo, girding the back of the monastery. An old abbot, the Great Sŏn Master, used to love the grove. One day he gathered friends in the arbor and, pointing to the bamboo, said, "Please tell me the good qualities of bamboo."

One said, "Bamboo shoots are delicious. When the buds sprout, the joints are close together and the inside is soon filled with meat. Then you chop them down, cut up the meat, boil them in a sacrificial vessel, and roast them on the stove. Their aroma is sweet, their taste crisp. They fill your mouth and stomach. You will lose your taste for beef and pork fed on grain and look askance at the strong smelling meat of wild game. Eat bamboo shoots every morning and you will never tire of them. Such is the flavor of bamboo."

Another said, "The bamboo is strong, yet not strong; pliant, yet not pliant. It is fit to be used by men. Bend it, and you can make a basket, a hamper, and a box. Cut it fine and bind it, and you have screens for the door; cut and weave it, and you have a mat for the hall; split and sharpen it, and you have a box for clothes, a basket for cooked rice, a strainer for wine, a fodder-tub for the ox and a water bag for the horse, as well as a round or square basket, wine skimmer, and wattle. Such are the uses of bamboo."

Still another said, "When the young sprouts come up, they cluster in rows, the small ones, the large ones, the early, the late, all in due order. At first, they are tender, then they become tapered. When their tortoise-shell skin peels, their jade-red stalks grow tall. Then they shed their powder, the skin becoming white, and the white nodes are distinct. Their leaves like emerald smoke do not scatter, but cold winds rise from them. Their branches seem to murmur; their shade is deep. By evening their shadows play in the moonlight, and their chill figures are crowned with snow—such is the best time to enjoy them. From spring till the twelfth month you can chant verses here every day, dispel melancholy, and play with zest. Such is the elegance of bamboo."

A fourth said, "A bamboo a thousand fathoms high is called *hsin;* one whose girth is several fathoms round, *shih;* one whose top is speckled, *chih;* dark-bodied ones, *yu;* prickly ones, *pa;* and hairy ones, *kan.* The staff from Ch'iung-chou in Szechwan, the flute from Ch'i-chou in Hupei, the large-leaved ones from the Yangtze and the Han, the *tao* from Pa and Yü in Szechwan, the winter-sprouting ones from Li-p'u in Kwangsi, the speckled ones from the rivers Yüan and Hsiang, and the large ones called *yün-tang* growing in the marsh, and the flavorless *mo-yeh*—the names and appearances may differ from place to place. But their leaves do not fall even if the sea freezes, or dry up when it is hot enough to melt gold. Green and luxuriant, they do not change with the seasons. Therefore, the sage praised them and accomplished men emulated them. They do not alter their determination according to time and place. Such is the integrity of bamboo."

Sigyŏngam said, "If I love the bamboo for its flavor, its usefulness, elegance, and integrity, all I get is externals, not its essence. When I look at the grace and height of a shoot since its sprouting, I realize how the embedded seed, once awakened, makes sudden progress. I look at it growing tougher as it ages, and I understand how cultivated power increases gradually. Its hollowness indicates that nature is empty. From its upright appearance, it is possible to deduce the true form of things. The transformation of its roots into a dragon I compare to a man's becoming a Buddha. And feeding the phoenix with its fruit is its way of benefiting man. My love of the bamboo stems not from what the four gentlemen have said, but from my own observations."

The master remarked, "How profound! You are indeed a devoted friend of the bamboo."

I hasten to write these remarks down on the board as a model for future lovers of bamboo.

Yi Che-hyŏn (1287–1367)

DESCRIPTIONS OF THE CLOUD BROCADE TOWER
[Ungŭmnu ki]

One need not go to remote places in search of beautiful scenery among mountains and streams. There are places of great natural beauty even in the midst of a capital city or a large town where people crowd together. Even if Mounts Heng and Lu, Tung-t'ing Lake, or the Hsiao and Hsiang rivers were right before their eyes, those who compete for a name at court or wrangle for profit at the marketplace would not recognize their beauty. For one who pursues deer does not see the mountain; one who carries off gold does not see others; and one who can discern the tip of a fine hair overlooks a cartload of faggots. If a man is preoccupied with one thing, his eyes have no time for other sights.

Amateurs and those who travel at their own leisure pass through guardhouses at river crossings and choose their abodes in country villages. Then, roaming over hills and valleys and content in themselves, they recall Hsieh Ling-yün, who opened roads and frightened people, and Hsü Fan, who sought out his own home but was shunned by brave men. I say that both men were elegant!

To the south of the capital, there is a small lake, its area about ten thousand square feet. Along the shore, the houses of the commoners are joined together like scales on a fish or teeth on a comb. On the road that loops around the lake there is no end of passersby—some with loads on their backs or heads, some on foot, some mounted. Looking at their comings and goings, few would suspect that in the midst of this hustle and bustle there is a place secluded and rare, affording leisure and a broad view.

In the summer of the year Chŏngch'uk [1337], Lord Hyŏnbok, Kwŏn Yŏm [1302–1340], seeing the lotuses in full bloom on the lake, at once fell in love with the place, bought a piece of land on the eastern shore, and built on it a tower about sixteen feet high and thirty feet across. There are no cornerstones, but the pillars have been treated to keep them from rotting. The roof is not covered with tiles but thatched with grass, yet it does not leak. The roofbeams are light and unplaned, yet straight. The walls have no paint, yet they are neither gaudy nor shabby. Whatever the external dimensions of the tower, its distinction is that it embraces the lotuses of the whole lake in its view.

The lord invited his father, Great Lord Kilch'ang, his brothers, and other relatives to a feast in the tower, and they passed so pleasant a time that the lord neglected to return home after sunset. One of his sons was good at large characters, so the lord had him write two logographs, CLOUD BROCADE, which were then hung up as the name of the tower.

I went there to see for myself. The place is beautiful indeed and worthy of its name: the fragrance of pink flowers and the green shadows of leaves cover both the lake and its shore; dewdrops shaken by the breeze fall into the water, gently rippling it. Not only this. The peaks of Dragon Mountain, now blue, now green, their shadows changing with the light of morning and day, come up to the eaves of the tower.

Sitting in the tower, one can also observe the various aspects of a commoner's life and enjoy the sight of passersby—the loaded and the unencumbered, pedestrians and cavaliers, those who run and those who rest, onlookers and those who beckon, friends standing and talking to each other and those who bow to their elders. While all this can be viewed and enjoyed, the passersby see only the lake and do not suspect there is a tower, much less someone watching them from it.

Natural beauty is not found only in remote places, but it cannot be discovered easily by the eyes and minds of seekers after office and profit. Perhaps heaven makes natural beauty and earth hides it so that men cannot find it easily.

Lord Hyŏnbok carries the seal of a myriarch and belongs to a family that married into the royal house. He is still under forty years of age. Whether in deep sleep or a drunken dream, he will enjoy fame, wealth, and honor. But he delights in the good and the wise. He does nothing that would frighten the people or make braves shun him. He always lives in a secluded and empty place where the eyes of courtiers and merchants cannot reach. He delights his parents, and their happiness is passed on to friends; he enjoys happiness, and his happiness gladdens others. This is indeed praiseworthy!

The retired gentleman Ikchae hereby writes this description of the tower.

TRANSLATED BY UCHANG KIM AND PETER H. LEE

POETRY IN CHINESE

Chŏng Chi-sang (d. 1135)

PARTING

After a rain on the long dike, grasses are thick.
With a sad song I send you off to the South Bank.
When will the Taedong River cease to flow?
Year after year my tears will swell the waves.

AFTER DRINKING

Birds mumble in a pink rain of peach petals,
Emerald mists on the blue hills lap the cottage.
A black gauze cap worn aslant seems untidy;
Drunk on the flowery bank I dream of the south.

Ch'oe Yu-ch'ŏng (1095–1174)

HARMONIZING WITH SECRETARY CHŎNG ON THE NINTH DAY

Yellow flowers and scarlet leaves—again this year
Old zest shakes us as we sit at an elegant feast.
Drinking done, we madly sing and lean on the dawn moon;
This feeling worth a decade rises above the world.

UPON FIRST RETURNING HOME

The village is desolate, people have changed,
Grass nearly engulfs the leaning walls and house.
Only the well in front of the gate remains—
Its sweet, cool taste has not changed.

Yi Il-lo (1152–1220)

CICADA

You drink wind to empty yourself,
Imbibe dewdrops to cleanse.
Why do you get up at autumn dawn
And keep crying so mournfully?

ON THE RIVER ON A SPRING DAY

High high azure peaks—a bundle of brush tips,
The broad river, far and hazy, spreads beyond the pines.
Files of dark clouds—an array of strange letters,
A vast blue sky—a scroll of despatch.

MOUNTAIN DWELLING

Spring is gone, but flowers linger;
The sky is clear, but the valley remains dark.
A cuckoo cries in broad daylight—
Now I know I live in a deep valley.

WRITTEN ON THE WALL OF THE CH'ŎNSU MONASTERY

I wait for a guest who does not come;
I look for a monk who is also out.
Only a bird beyond the grove
Welcomes me, urging me to drink.

TRANSPLANTING BAMBOO ON BAMBOOS-ARE-DRUNK DAY[1]

Then and now are like badgers from the same hill,
Heaven and earth are only inns.
Only this gentleman gets stinking drunk,
Staggers, not minding where he's going.
Rivers and hills may have different names,
But the scenery won't change.
Why sober up or come to your senses,
I'll take up the spear and move you!

TRANSLATED BY RICHARD J. LYNN

---

1. Bamboos-Are-Drunk Day, or Day-When-Bamboos-Are-Befuddled, occurred on the 13th day of the 5th month (or 8th day of the 8th month), the day traditionally designated for transplanting bamboo.

Yi Kyu-bo (1168–1241)

THE COCK

The cock
Likes to peck for worms.
I cannot stand to watch it;
I shout to scatter his flock.
Don't scorn me for what I have done.
I like every living being to live.
Old and retired, I am idle—
No plans for an audience or an early meal.
What need have I of a cock to announce the dawn?
I like to sleep, I want to avoid the bright morning.

Yi Che-hyŏn (1287–1367)

ANCIENT AIRS (Four Poems)

A young gentleman travels afar,
His saddle and red horse glowing.
A pining girl on a jade tower
Fights to keep tears from falling.
Unable to forget the thought of him,
She rouses herself to fly, but has no wings.
The cold bell strikes painfully late,
When will the east dawn?

*

The coldest winter, heaven and earth frozen,
Dragons and snakes asleep in the dark palace.
The way of the world is full of ups and downs,
A superior man can withstand hardships.[1]
The empty window fronts a row of peaks,
White clouds sail across the clear sky.
I rebuke and send off visitors,
Strum the lute, my eyes following the geese.[2]

*

A dear friend of the hills
Sends me a letter—
You wish to become an immortal,
Because this world is but a grass hut.[3]
You don't want a carriage and gown,
But then it's also hard to live among trees and rocks.[4]
Come down, friend, drink my wine,
Let life and death take their course.

*

Lowering the curtain nine out of ten days,
I rejoice that I'm free on a clear morning.
By chance I go out to a broad street,
Rest the horse, watch the bustling crowd.
How heedless, seekers of fame and profit,
How confused, the rich and idle!
Back home, I face the yellow scrolls,
Chuckle to myself and feel happy.

1. *Analects*, XV, 1.
2. Hsi K'ang (233–262), "Eighteen Poems Presented to Hsi Hsi on His Joining the Army," 14.
3. *Chuang Tzu*, 14.
4. *Mencius*, 7A, 16.

Yi Saek (1328–1396)

A RETURNING SAIL AT CHINP'O

A fine rain—spring freshets swell,
Clear frost—reeds announce autumn.
Where does a returning boat moor?
A single skiff on the vast sea!

MOON VIEWING AT COLD COVE

At sundown the sand looks whiter,
Clouds shift, the water becomes clear.
A lofty man enjoys the moon—
All he lacks is a purple panpipe.

Chŏng Mong-ju (1337–1392)

SPRING MOOD

A fine spring rain doesn't form drops,
At night I hear a faint drizzle.
Snow melts, the southern stream swells;
Grass pushes out new shoots.

Sǒng Sǒng-nin (1338–1423)

TO A MONK GOING TO THE DIAMOND MOUNTAINS

Twelve thousand jagged peaks—
Some high, some low.
Observe, sir, when the sun rises,
Which peak first turns crimson.

Chǒng To-jǒn (1342–1398)

PLUM

You engraved jade to make a dress,
Drank ice to nurture your spirit.
Every year girdled with frost and snow,
You don't know the splendors of spring.

Yi Ch'ǒm (1345–1405)

IN RETIREMENT

Back of the house, mulberry shoots sprout,
West of the dikes, shallots open leaves.
Spring water fills the pond;
Children know how to pole a boat.

Kil Chae (1353–1419)

IMPROMPTU

The clear spring is cold to wash my hands,
Thick trees are tall to cover my body.
A capped boy comes and asks about some lines—
He is worthy to roam with me.

POEMS IN CHINESE BY ZEN MASTERS

National Preceptor Chin'gak (1178–1234)

LIKE THE SUN

Cut down being and nonbeing
    The All enfolds.
A dot of Buddha nature—
    It shines like the sun.
You may grasp it right away
    But can't escape a stick.
How can you then sit idly
    And have a moment to think?

NIGHT RAIN

For no reason it rains,
    whispers of reality.
How lovely it sings,
    drop by drop.
Sitting and lying I listen
    with emptied mind.
I don't need ears,
    I don't need rain.

Master Paegun (1299–1375)

CLAY OXEN

Two clay oxen fight each other,
Then they jump into the sea, bellowing.
Past, present, and future rush after
But can't find them in the roiled water.

IN THE MOUNTAIN

Yellow chrysanthemums and green bamboo,
    they don't belong to others.
Bright moon and clear breeze
    are not for the sphere of the senses.
They're all treasures
    of my house—
Fetch them home freely
    use them, get to know them!

TO A FRIEND SEEKING POTALAKA

The body of the Buddha is everywhere,
Does the Goddess of Mercy live in the eastern sea?
Every green mountain is a place of awakening;
Why must you seek Mount Potalaka?

National Preceptor T'aego (1301–1382)

NOTHINGNESS

Still—all things appear.
Moving—there is nothing.
What is nothingness?
Chrysanthemums bursting in the frost.

HERDING THE OX IN THE HIMALAYAS

Chew the glossy, tender leaves—
You'll know the sweet and the sour.
Snow lies thick in the hottest summer,
Spring lingers in the coldest winter.
You wish to lean, then lean;
You wish to lie down, then lie down.
Seeing this, Shih-te roars with laughter,
And Han-shan opens his mouth wide.

AT DEATHBED

Life is like a bubble—
Some eighty years, a spring dream.
Now I'll throw away this leather sack,
A crimson sun sinks on the west peak!

Royal Preceptor Naong (1320–1376)

IN THE MOUNTAINS

With the true emptiness of nonaction,
I nap on a stone pillow among rocks.
Do you ask me what is my power?
A single tattered robe through life!

Yi Dynasty

1392 – 1910

SONGS OF FLYING DRAGONS (1445–1447)

The *Songs of Flying Dragons,* a eulogy cycle in 125 cantos comprising 248 poems, was compiled to praise the founding of the Yi dynasty by General Yi Sŏng-gye (1335–1408). Written by the foremost philologists and literary men of their day, the *Songs* were the first experimental use in verse of the Korean alphabet invented in 1443–1444. They are also a manifesto of the policies of the new state, a mirror for future monarchs, and a repository of heroic tales and foundation myths of China and Korea.

The organization may be summarized as follows:

I.	1–2	proem
II.	3–109	celebration of military and cultural accomplishments of the six dragons, especially the founder
	110–124	admonitions to future monarchs
III.	125	conclusion

Each canto, except for cantos 1, 2, and 125, consists of two poems, the first relating generally to the great deeds of Chinese sovereigns and the second to those of the Yi kings.

The poems below portray Yi Sŏng-gye as a paragon of the Confucian soldier-statesman. Topics analogous to those in Western epic include the description of the hero's weapons and horse, the use of portents, epic games (hunting trips, contests, and a polo match), and the conflation of the hero with his people. The Confucian heroic ethos is seen as comprising *fortitudo et sapientia,* valor and virtue, as in the dynastic hymns in praise of the Chou founders in the *Book of Songs* and in such Western epics as the *Aeneid.*

SONGS OF FLYING DRAGONS

[*Yongbi ŏch'ŏn ka*]

2   The tree that strikes deep root
Is firm amidst the winds.
Its flowers are good,
Its fruits abundant.

The stream whose source is deep
Gushes forth even in a drought.
It forms a river
And gains the sea.

27   His arrow was huge beyond compare—
His father saw it and abandoned it.
On the same day he rejoiced
In him whose genius astounded the day.

32   Heaven sent a genius
In order to save the people.
Hence he shot with twenty arrows
Twenty sables in the bush.

43   On Mount Chorae he struck two roebucks
With a single arrow.
Must one paint
This natural genius?

44   It was a polo match played by royal order—
He hit the ball with a "sideways block."
People on nine state roads
All admired his skill.

70   Heaven gave him courage and wisdom
Who was to bring order to the country.
Hence eight steeds
Appeared at the proper time.

86 He shot six roebucks,
   He shot six crows,
   He flew across
   The slanting tree.

88 He hit the backs of forty tailed deer,
   He pierced the mouths and eyes of the rebels,
   He shot down three mice from the eaves,
   Were there any like him in the past?

89 Seven pine cones,
   The trunk of a dead tree,
   Three arrows piercing the helmet—
   None like him in the past.

53 He opened the four borders,
   Island dwellers had no more fear of pirates.
   Southern barbarians beyond our waters,
   How could they not come to him?

73 Because robbers poisoned the people,
   He initiated a land reform.
   First he drove away the usurper,
   He then labored to restore the state.

76 Kind and selfless to his brothers,
   He covered their past misdeeds.
   Thus today we enjoy
   Humane manners and customs.

79 He was consistent from beginning to end,
   Meritorious subjects were truly loyal to him.
   He secured the throne for a myriad years.
   Would his royal works ever discontinue?

80 Though he was busy with war,
    He loved the way of the scholar.
    His work of achieving peace
    Shone brilliantly.

81 He did not boast of his natural gifts,
    His learning was equally deep.
    The vast scope of royal works
    Was indeed great.

82 Upon receiving an old scholar
    He knelt down with due politeness.
    What do you say about
    His respect for scholarship?

112 When you are wrapped in a dragon robe,
    When you wear the belt of precious gems,
    Remember, my Lord,
    His fortitude and tenacity.

113 When you sup on northern viands and southern dainties,
    When you have superb wine and precious grain,
    Remember, my Lord,
    His fortitude and fervor.

114 While the stately guards stand row upon row,
    While you reign in peace and give audience,
    Remember, my Lord,
    His piety and constancy.

115 When you have men at your beck and call,
    When you punish men and sentence them,
    Remember, my Lord,
    His mercy and temperance.

116   If you are unaware of people's sorrow,
       Heaven will abandon you.
       Remember, my Lord,
       His labor and love.

117   If a deceitful minister flatters you,
       If you are roused to pride,
       Remember, my Lord,
       His prowess and modesty.

118   If a king loses his inward power,
       Even his kin will rebel.
       Remember, my Lord,
       His fame and virtue.

119   If brothers are split,
       A villain will enter to sow discord.
       Remember, my Lord,
       His sagacity and love.

120   If a ruler taxes his people without measure,
       The basis of the state will crumble.
       Remember, my Lord,
       His justice and humanity.

121   If your advisors wrangle before you
       In order only to assist and secure the Throne,
       Remember, my Lord,
       His goodness and justice.

122   If a small man wishes to curry favor
       And preaches "No leisure for culture,"
       Remember, my Lord,
       His effort and erudition.

123   When slanderers craftily make mischief,
      When they grossly exaggerate small mistakes,
      Remember, my Lord,
      His wisdom and justice.

124   If perverse theories of the Western barbarians
      Threaten you with sin or allure with bliss,
      Remember, my Lord,
      His judgment and orthodoxy.

125   A milennium ago,
      Heaven chose the north of the Han.
      There they accumulated goodness and founded the state.
      Oracles foretold: a myriad years;
      May your sons and grandsons reign unbroken.
      But you can secure the dynasty only
      When you worship Heaven and benefit the people.
      Ah, you who will wear the crown, beware,
      Can you depend upon your ancestors
      When you go hunting by the waters of Lo?

EARLY YI ROMANCE

Kim Si-sŭp (1435–1493), a child prodigy, had a checkered life as an eccentric monk and writer of verse and prose. At the news of Sejo's usurpation of the throne from his young cousin Tanjong (1455), Kim had his head shaved and became a wandering monk. From then on he was known for his odd behavior, which hid his brilliance. In 1465 he built a study on Mount Kŭmo near Kyŏngju, where he wrote the *New Stories from Golden Turtle Mountain* in classical Chinese. The five stories in this collection are in the tradition of the *ch'uan-ch'i* (tales of wonder) and concern love affairs between mortals and ghosts and dream journeys to the underworld or to the Dragon Palace. The story of Student Yi, set in the Koryŏ capital of Kaesŏng, shows a number of features common to the type: exchange of poems—a common activity of characters in East Asian romance since the Chinese *Visit to the Fairy Grotto* (*Yu hsien-k'u*, written before 733), a ghost-wife, and a didactic comment at the end of the tale. Kim's extensive use of allusions evinces his wide reading—especially of the *New Tales Written While Cutting the Wick (Chien-teng hsin-hua)* by Ch'ü Yu (1341–1427), to whom he is indebted. Kim's collection was popular in Japan, where it was published several times; it is said to have influenced the *Tales of Moonlight and Rain* by Ueda Akinari (1734–1809).

Kim Si-sŭp (1435–1493)

STUDENT YI PEERS OVER THE WALL
[Yisaeng kyujang chŏn]

In Songdo there was a man named Yi who lived by the Camel Bridge. He was eighteen, cultured and handsome, and had innate talents. As a student at the National Academy, he would read poetry even on his way to school.

In a nobleman's house in Sŏnjuk village there lived a Miss Ch'oe.

She was about fifteen, beautiful, skilled in embroidery, and she excelled at poetry. People used to praise the two young people:

> Free and elegant, the son of Yi,
> Lovely and virtuous, the daughter of Ch'oe.
> His talent and her face,
> One look will ease your hunger.

Yi would pass by Miss Ch'oe's house, books tucked under his arms. The north wall of her mansion was ringed with graceful drooping willows, under which Yi would rest.

One day he peered through the wall. Beautiful flowers were in bloom and birds were vying clamorously. To one side, through clusters of flowers, a small tower could be seen. A jeweled blind was half raised, and silk curtains hung low. A beautiful girl sat within. Tiring of embroidery, she had halted her needle in mid course. Resting her chin in her palm, she hummed:

> Alone by the gauze window, my embroidery lags;
> In a clump of flowers, the oriole trills.
> For no reason I resent the eastern breeze;
> Sunk in thought I quietly stay my needle.
> Who is that pale young man on the road,
> Among drooping willows, with his blue collar and
>   broad belt?
> Were I to turn into a swallow in the hall,
> I'd lift the beaded curtains and cross over the wall.

Hearing this, Yi became anxious to display his skill at versemaking. But the walls were high, and the garden deep and secluded. He had no choice but to turn back frustrated. Before leaving he wrote three stanzas of verse on a slip of paper, tied the paper to a tile, and threw it over the wall. The poems read:

> Twelve peaks of Witches' Mountain, lapped in mist,
> Their pointed edges dewy, purple, and blue-green.
> Don't prey on King Hsiang's dream on a lonely pillow,
> Let's meet on the Sun Terrace as clouds and rain.

> As Ssu-ma Hsiang-ju enticed Cho Wen-chün,
> So my love is already deep.
> Pink peach and plum blossoms on the wall—
> Where do they fall, scattered by the wind?

Will we be together, will we not?
In vain my sorrow turns a day into a year.
You pledged love with your poem;
When will I meet my fair love?

Miss Ch'oe asked her maid Hyanga to retrieve the message. She read the poems over and over and was delighted. She then threw back over the wall a slip of paper bearing nine words: "Have no doubt, Sir! Let us meet at dusk."

Yi set out for the house at dusk just as the girl had asked. Suddenly he saw the branch of a peach tree beckoning to him above the wall. He drew near to examine it closely and found a bamboo chair suspended from a rope swing. He climbed over the wall.

The moon was rising over the eastern mountain; flowers cast shadows on the ground, and their pure fragrance was lovely. Yi thought he had entered a fairyland. Though he might chuckle to himself about the affair, he realized it had to remain a secret. He was apprehensive. When he looked around, he found the girl and the maid sitting on a mat in a secluded corner among the flower bushes; they wore flowers in their hair. Catching sight of Yi, the girl smiled and sang two leading lines: "Between peach and plum boughs brilliant flowers, / On the bridal pillow the delicate moonlight." Yi capped the verse: "If someday our secret leaks out, / How sad the heartless wind and rain."[1]

The girl grew pale and said, "At first my desire was to serve you, keep house for you, and be happy with you forever. But how could you say such a thing? Though I am a woman, my mind is calm. How could you, a man, compose such lines? If what happens in my room someday leaks out, my family will censure me. But I shall accept the blame myself. Hyanga, please go within and bring wine and fruit for our guest."

The maid went. There was quiet all around, no sound of voices anywhere. Yi asked, "What place is this?"

"We're beneath a small tower in the north garden," Miss Ch'oe answered. "Because I am their only daughter, my parents love me deeply. They built this tower by the lotus pond so that my maid and I might enjoy the lovely springtime blossoms. My parents live apart, so they can't hear us talking and laughing." She then poured a cup of "green bubble" wine and sang a poem in the old style:

1. Commentators say "the heartless wind and rain" refers to the anger of parents.

Over the carved rail I look upon the lotus pond;
Among the pond flowers, lovers whisper.
Light, light scented mist, mild, mild spring.
Let's write a new song, sing of love.
The moon shines through the flowers and on to the mat;
Pull the long branch—a shower of pink petals.
The wind stirs a pure fragrance that seeps into my robe;
Miss Chia steps forward to do a spring dance.[2]
Her silk blouse skirts a wild rose,
And rouses the parrot dozing among the blossoms.

Yi harmonized:

I stumble into Peach Blossom Spring, with flowers
    everywhere;
I cannot express all that is in my breast.
The cloud of your hair, golden hairpin placed low;
Your cool spring blouse, newly made of green silk.
The east wind first breaks a row of lotus stems;
Don't let the branches shudder before wind and rain.
A fairy's sleeves whirl, shadows sway;
Among the cassia shadows the moon goddess dances.
Sorrow always comes before a good thing is complete;
Don't teach the parrot a new tune.

When Yi had finished, Miss Ch'oe said, "What has happened to-day has certainly not happened by chance. Follow me, and let us embrace."

With these words, she entered through the north window, and Yi followed. There they climbed a ladder into the tower. Inside there stood a stool and a desk with writing materials neatly arranged. On the wall was a painting of a mountain range rising above a misty river, and another of a dense bamboo grove and old trees—both were famous paintings. Above each was an unsigned inscription. The first read:

Whose brush has the extravagant power
To paint a thousand hills above the river?
Majestic Fang-fu, thirty thousand fathoms high,
Its peaks shimmer through haze and smoke.

2. A reference to Chia Ch'ung's (217–282) daughter, who stole her father's exotic perfume when she had an affair with Han Shou.

Its power stretches for hundreds of miles.
Nearby, steep peaks are green knots.
Boundless blue waves touch the far sky,
At dusk I gaze into the distance and think of home.
This painting makes me lonely and desolate,
Like a boat on the Hsiang in the wind and rain.

The second read:

The wind sighs through the dark bamboo grove;
A tall old tree seems to groan.
The wild root is coiled and moss-covered,
The old trunk, gnarled, resists wind and thunder.
My heart treasures the painter's brushstrokes;
With whom can I talk about this wonderful place?
Wei Yen and Wen T'ung have long since gone;
How many can fathom the secrets of heaven?
Forgetting all cares, we face the bright window,
I am one with the wonderful brushstrokes.

One wall was covered with pictures of the four seasons, each with an anonymous quatrain. The writing was elegant and refined in the style of Chao Meng-fu. The first scroll read:

The lotus curtain is warm, its fragrance trails.
Outside the window, a rain of pink blossoms.
My dream is broken by the bell of the fifth watch;
On the magnolia-covered hillside a shrike screams.

On a long day a swallow enters my room,
Weary and mute, I stop my sewing.
Butterflies flit in pairs among the flowers,
Chasing the falling blossoms in the garden's shade.

A chill passes through my green silk skirt,
Heartbroken I face the spring wind in vain.
Who can measure the throbbing of my heart?
Among a thousand flowers mandarin ducks dance.

Spring colors sink deep into the humble house,
Deep red and light green on the gauze window.
Fragrant garden grasses suffer a spring sorrow.
I'll lift the beaded curtains and view the falling blossoms.

The second scroll read:

> Thick ears on early wheat, a young swallow darts aslant,
> In the south garden the pomegranate tree blooms.
> Leaning against the green window a girl weaves,
> Cutting purple silk to make a new skirt.
>
> The season of golden plums, a fine rain on the screen;
> Orioles twitter in the shade, swallows fly in through the
> curtains.
> A year gone, its view is old—
> Flowers fall, and only bamboo shoots grow.
>
> Should I hit the oriole with a green plum?
> The wind blows at the southern eaves, the sun sets late.
> Lotus leaves exude fragrance, the pond is full.
> In deep green waves, cormorants bathe.
>
> The pattern on the bamboo couch resembles waves,
> On the screen are the Hsiao and Hsiang, and a wisp of
> cloud.
> She cannot bear being lazy and wakes from her day-
> dreams;
> Through the half-open window slant the rays of the setting
> sun.

The third scroll read:

> Chill, chill, the autumn wind; a cold dew forms:
> The graceful autumn moon, the blue autumn pond.
> Wild geese return cackling in ones and twos;
> At the golden well a rustle of paulownia leaves.
>
> Chirp, chirp, a hundred insects under the couch;
> Upon the couch a fair lady sheds a glistening tear.
> Miles away her lover fights at the front;
> Tonight at the Jade Gate Pass the moon is bright.
>
> She wants to make new clothes—the scissors feel cold;
> She calls her maid to bring the iron.
> She hadn't noticed the fire was out,
> She plucks the zither and scratches her head.

> The lotus dies in the pond; plantains turn yellow.
> The first frost coats the duck-painted tiles.
> She cannot hold back old sorrow or new grief;
> Crickets still cry in her secluded room.

The fourth scroll read:

> A plum branch casts its shadow upon the window,
> On the windy west veranda the moon is bright.
> The fire in the brazier is not yet out—she stirs it with
>   tongs,
> Then calls to her maid for another pot of tea.
>
> Startled by night frost, the leaves shiver,
> The whirlwind chases the snow to the veranda.
> She dreams all night of her love,
> As he wanders along the icy river, the old battlefield.
>
> The sun in the window brings the warmth of spring,
> Her grief-stricken eyebrows show traces of slumber.
> A small plum branch in the vase half opens its buds,
> Demure, silent, she stitches a pair of ducks.
>
> Frosty winds ravage the northern forest,
> A hungry crow, alarmed, caws at the moon.
> Before the lamp she sheds lovesick tears
> That spoil the cloth and rust her needle.

To one side there was a small, separate room, with curtains, a mattress, a blanket, and pillows, all neatly arranged. Outside the curtains there was musk incense and an orchid-oil lantern burning bright as day. Their lovemaking was delicious.

Yi stayed several days, then quoted Confucius, "'While father and mother are alive, a son does not wander far afield. If he does, he should let them know where he goes.'[3] It has already been three days since I left home. They must be waiting for me at the entrance to the village. This is not the way of a son."

Miss Ch'oe sympathized and sent him away over the wall. From that time on Yi went to her every night.

One evening, Yi's father said to him, "Your leaving in the morn-

3. *Analects*, IV, 19.

ing and returning in the evening was to study the way of goodness and righteousness as taught by the sages of the past. But now you go out at dusk and return at dawn—what is this all about? You are behaving frivolously, climbing over people's walls and breaking their trees. If this becomes known, everyone will blame me for not raising you strictly. And the girl—if she is of noble birth, your reckless behavior will sully her reputation and bring censure down upon you. This is a serious matter. Go at once to the south and take charge of the servants on the farm. And don't come back!''

The very next day Yi went south to Ulchu. Miss Ch'oe waited for him every evening in her garden, but he did not return for several months. Assuming that he had been ill, she sent Hyanga to make secret inquiries of Yi's neighbors. A neighbor said, ''Young Yi offended his father. It has been several months since he went south.''

On hearing this, Miss Ch'oe fell ill; she lay in bed tossing and turning and could not get up. She took no food, her speech grew delirious, and, due to her grief, her skin lost its color. Her parents thought this strange and inquired about her illness, but she would not speak. They rummaged through her box and found the poems she had exchanged with Yi. They beat their breasts and exclaimed, ''We nearly lost our daughter! Who is this Yi?''

The matter had come to light, and Miss Ch'oe could dissemble no longer. Her voice was unsteady and her speech halting as she said, ''Father and Mother who raised me with love, how can I hide my secret? I believe that the love between man and woman is the most important human emotion. The *Book of Songs* says 'The plum falls; let those gentlemen that would court me come while it is auspicious,'[4] and the *Book of Changes,* 'The influence shows itself in the thighs!'[5] I am frail as the willow, but I did not heed the warning about the falling mulberry leaves, yellow and sere.[6] I did not guard my chastity and so I am mocked by those close to me. Like the creepers that feed on other trees, I have behaved like a girl in a Chinese romance.[7] My guilt is obvious, I have dishonored my family's name. After getting to know that mischievous man I grew fond of him, and my sorrows

4. *Book of Songs,* 20.
5. Hexagram 31, which warns against acting impulsively.
6. *Book of Songs,* 58.
7. In the original, an allusion to Ch'ü Yu's (1341–1427) story in *Chien-teng hsin-hua,* in which the student Wang meets a girl at a pond by the Wei River.

multiplied. In my weakened condition I have tried to bear the pain and live alone, but every day my longing grows deeper, and my pain is twice as intense. I have reached death's door and soon will be a poor spirit. If my father and mother honor my wish, my life will be preserved; but if they reject my earnest plea, I must surely die. I shall roam with my love again by the Yellow Springs before I marry another.''

Seeing the girl's resolve, her parents ceased their questioning. Now stern, now cajoling, they tried to reassure their daughter. They then secured a matchmaker and proposed marriage to the Yi family.

The elder Yi asked about the lineage of the Ch'oe family. "My son may be young and unbalanced, but he is well educated and carries himself like a man. Someday he will succeed in the examinations and be well known. As yet, though, it is too early to think of finding him a wife.''

When the matchmaker reported back to to the Ch'oe family, the elder Ch'oe sent her back again with a message: "My friends all praise your son's surpassing talents. Even though he has not yet passed the examination, I know he will not be content to live in obscurity. I think it would be well to quickly set an auspicious date to unite our two families.''

To this the elder Yi replied, "I too have studied the classics since my early years, but have grown old without achieving my goal. My slaves have left and my relatives are of little help. Life is hard for us, and we're not well placed. Why would a powerful family like the Ch'oe consider the son of a poor scholar as a possible son-in-law? This must be the work of some meddler who wishes to flatter my house and deceive yours.''

Through the matchmaker the elder Ch'oe replied, "The wedding presents and gowns are all ready. Please choose an auspicious day for the ceremony.''

Only upon hearing this did the elder Yi reconsider. He at once sent for his son and asked his opinion. Beside himself with joy, the son wrote a poem:

> The broken mirror becomes round again—at last we meet;
> Magpies in the Milky Way will grace the auspicious moment.
> Now the old man in the moon ties the knot;
> Don't resent the cuckoo calling to the east wind.

Miss Ch'oe was relieved to hear the good news. She wrote:

> Bad ties have become good,
> Old vows are now fulfilled.
> When shall we pull a small carriage?[8]
> Help me rise, girls, and put the flowery hairpin in place.

An auspicious day was chosen, and at last the ceremony took place. Their love, once ended, began anew. After becoming husband and wife, they loved one another deeply but still accorded one another the respect that a host might accord a guest. None could equal in constancy these paragons of conjugal bliss.

The following year Yi passed the final civil service examination and rose to a high rank. His fame spread at court.

In 1361, the Red Turbans occupied the capital, and the king fled to Pokchu in the south. The bandits burned houses and massacred people and cattle. Defenseless families fled east and west seeking refuge. Although Yi hid his family deep in the mountains, one armed bandit followed them. Yi managed to escape, but his wife was caught.

When the bandit was about to have his way with her, she rebuked him, "Kill me and eat me, you tiger and devil. I'd rather be food for a wolf than the mate of a dog or pig!" In rage the bandit killed her and hacked apart her body.

Yi hid in the wilderness, barely surviving. He heard at last that the bandits had been subdued and made his way to his parents' home, but it was burned to ashes. Next he went to his wife's home. Every wing was deserted; only mice squeaked and birds cried. Unable to bear his grief, he climbed the small tower and stifled his sobs with deep sighs. He sat there till dusk, thinking of the happy days that now seemed but a dream.

At about the second watch, when the beams reflected the wan moonlight, Yi heard footsteps approaching down the corridor. He turned and saw his wife. He knew she was no longer of this world, but he loved her so much he did not doubt her presence. He asked her, "Where did you flee to save yourself?"

Clasping Yi's hands, she wept loudly and poured out her tale: "As the daughter of a good family, from childhood I received instruction from my family. I became skilled in embroidery and sewing, learned

---

8. Alludes to a story about the wife of Pao Hsüan of the Later Han, who helped pull her husband's small cart.

poetry and calligraphy, and the way of goodness and constancy. I knew only the ways of a woman. When you peered through the wall of red apricot blossoms, I offered my love to you. Then we exchanged smiles before the blossoms and pledged ourselves to a lifelong union. When we met again behind the curtains, our love could not be contained in a hundred years. To speak of these things brings unbearable sorrow. I wanted to live with you forever, but I met calamity and found myself face down in a ditch. I resisted a wolf's advances to the end, but I was torn to pieces and left abandoned in the mire. It was surely Heaven's command, but how could a human heart bear this?

"After we separated in the mountains, I became a bird that had lost its mate. Our house was destroyed, my parents were lost. A tired homeless spirit, I lamented. Integrity is great, and life is light; it was fortunate that my frail body escaped shame, but am I not to be pitied? Only my rotten entrails remain to harbor resentment. My bones lie exposed in the wilderness, and my innards abandoned in the ground. Were the joys of the past my compensation for the sorrow of that day?

"Now that the warm spring wind has visited the deep valley, I have returned to the earth to fulfill our vows for a time. You and I are bound by the karma of three lives and I wish to make up for our long separation. If you have not forgotten our vow, I will serve you as long as I can. Will you let me?"

Overjoyed and filled with gratitude, Yi answered, "That has been my wish from the beginning."

They abandoned themselves to their feelings. When their talk touched on the family fortune, Yi's wife said, "Nothing was lost— it is buried in a mountain valley."

"What about our parents? Where are their remains?"

"They were abandoned in a certain place."

When they had finished talking they went to bed and took great pleasure in each other, as in the past.

The following day, Miss Ch'oe went with Yi to look for the hidden treasure and found several ingots of gold and silver and some valuables. They gathered up the remains of their parents and buried them side by side at the foot of Mount Ogwan. They planted trees, offered sacrifices, and completed the rites.

From that time on, Yi did not seek office and lived with his wife. The servants who had fled returned, but Yi took no interest in daily affairs and shut the gate to relatives and guests who came on ceremonial occasions. He exchanged cups with his wife, harmonized with her in poetry, and enjoyed only her company.

One evening a few years later, Yi's wife said, "We pledged our love for three lives, but worldly affairs intruded. Before we tire of our joy, a sad parting must come." Then she sobbed.

Surprised, Yi asked, "Why do you say such a thing?"

"I cannot escape the underworld," she answered. "The Heavenly Emperor, knowing that our ties were unbroken and that I had not sinned in the previous life, allowed me to return here to share your sorrow for a time. But I can tarry no longer in this world to tempt men."

She called her maid to bring wine and bade Yi drink. Then she sang a new song to the tune of "Spring in Jade Pavilion":

> Arms in the battlefield as far as one can see,
> Jade smashed, flowers blown away, a drake has lost his mate.
> Who will bury the scattered remains?
> A wandering soul, its blood defiled, has none to whom she can plead.
> I can't become a fairy on Witches' Mountain.
> The broken mirror breaks again—Oh, my grieving heart!
> Once parted, we shall be endlessly apart,
> With heaven and earth torn asunder.

Choking with tears at every phrase, she could not finish. Yi was also unable to contain his grief. "I would rather go with you to the Nine Springs than suffer this separation. After the invasion, families and servants had fled in all directions and my parents' remains were scattered in the wilderness. Who would have buried them had it not been for you? You have fulfilled the ancient sage's teaching through your inborn filial devotion and deep humanity. I am deeply moved and overwhelmed by shame. Why should we not live a hundred years here, and become dust together?"

"For you, life still remains," she answered, "but my name has been logged in the roll of departed spirits, and I can remain here no longer. To persist in my love for a mortal would defy the laws of the underworld. Then not only would I be punished, but you would be as well. My remains are still scattered in a certain place. If you would favor me, place them beyond the reach of the elements."

The couple gazed into each other's eyes, as tears streamed down their faces.

"Take care, my love," she said, and gradually disappeared, leaving no trace.

Yi gathered her remains and buried them beside her parents'. The rites concluded, Yi fell into a deep despondence, became ill, and died within a few months.

Hearers of this story were all moved by it, and by the couple's constancy in particular.

SIJO, I

The following short poems are examples of the *sijo,* the most popular, elastic, and mnemonic poetic form of Korea. Dating from the fifteenth century, the *sijo* is a three-line poem, each line consisting of four rhythmic groups, a minor pause occurring at the end of the second, and a major at the end of the fourth. An emphatic syntactic division is usually introduced in the third line, often in the form of exclamation, presenting a leap in logic and development. Some interjections postulate a dialogue, attesting to the poet's openness to the world and his ability to ask.

The diction of *sijo,* despite some loanwords from Chinese, is native in the frequency of use of given words. In addition to high-frequency words, certain epithets and phrases are used for poetic amplification, serving to establish a community of mind and of imagination between the poet and his audience. While some epithets are dictated by seasonal, topical, and structural requirements, others are necessitated by the brevity of the form itself. Indeed, the frequency of certain images and microthemes helped the Korean singer to act as the memory of society.

Hwang Chin-i (*c.* 1506–1544) and Chŏng Ch'ŏl (1537–1594) stand out from among a host of sixteenth-century poets. Generally regarded as Korea's greatest woman poet, Hwang Chin-i's works on the mutability of love are acclaimed for their depth of feeling, meditative rhythms, and rich symbolism. Chŏng Ch'ŏl wrote moral verse and invectives, as well as poems on wine, music, and love. He is represented here by poems expressing a longing for his lord in exile and the nobility of a mind in adversity. Chŏng Ch'ŏl is also the author of three *kasa* (narrative poems), given later.

U T'ak (1262–1342)

East winds that melt the mountain snow
Come and go, without words.
Blow over my head, young breeze,
Even for a moment, blow.
Would you could blow away the gray hairs
That grow so fast around my ears!

*

Sticks in one hand,
Branches in another:
I try to block old age with bushes,
And frosty hair with sticks.
But white hair came by a short cut,
Having seen through my devices.

Yi Cho-nyŏn (1269–1343)

White moon, white
Pear blossoms, the Milky Way
White across the sky.
An ignorant bird
Repeats and repeats its song,
Not noticing
The sorrow of spring.
Too much awareness is a sickness;
It keeps me awake all night.

Chǒng Mong-ju (1337–1392)

Were I to die a hundred times,
Then die and die again
With all my bones no more than dust,
My soul gone far from men,
Yet still my red blood, shed for you,
Shall witness that my heart was true.

Hwang Hǔi (1363–1452)

Spring has come to a country village;
How much there is to be done!
I knit a net and
A servant tills the fields and sows:
But who will pluck the sweet herbs
That grow on the back-hill?

King Sǒngjong (1457–1494)

Stay:
Will you go? Must you go?
Is it in weariness you go? From disgust?
Who advised you, who persuaded you?
Say why you are leaving,
You, who are breaking my heart.[1]

---

1. Addressed to Yu Ho-in (1445–1494), assistant section chief of the Ministry of Works and the king's favorite courtier.

Kim Chŏng-gu (fl. 1495–1506)

Who says I am old?
Is an old man like this?
Heart welcomes sweet flowers,
Laughter floats over fragrant cups:
What can I do, what can I say?
My hoary hair floats in the spring wind.

Song Sun (1493–1583)

I have spent ten years
Building a grass hut;
Now winds occupy half,
The moon fills the rest.
Alas, I cannot let you come in,
But I shall receive you outside.[1]

*

I discuss with my heart
Whether to retire from court.
My heart scorns the intent:
"How could you leave the king?"
"Heart, stay here and serve him,
My old body must go."

*

Do not grieve, little birds,
Over the falling blossoms:
They're not to blame, it's the wind
Who loosens and scatters the petals.
Spring is leaving us.
Don't hold it against her.

1. Also attributed to Kim Chang-saeng (1548–1631).

Yi Hwang (1501–1571)

The green hills—how can it be
                    that they are green eternally?
Flowing streams—how can it be;
                    night and day do they never stand still?
We also, we can never stop,
                    we shall grow green eternally.

Yu Hŭi-ch'un (1513–1577)

A little bunch of parsley,
                    which I dug and rinsed myself.
I did it for no one else,
                    but simply to give it to you.
The flavor is not so very pungent;
                    taste it, once more taste it, and see.

TRANSLATED BY RICHARD RUTT

Hwang Chin-i (c. 1506–1544)

I will break the back
          of this long, midwinter night,
folding it double,
          cold beneath my spring quilt,
that I may draw out
          the night, should my love return.

TRANSLATED BY DAVID R. MCCANN

*

Do not boast of your speed,
O blue-green stream running by the hills:
Once you have reached the wide ocean,
You can return no more.
Why not stay here and rest,
When moonlight stuffs the empty hills?

*

Mountains are steadfast but the mountain streams
Go by, go by,
And yesterdays are like the rushing streams,
They fly, they fly,
And the great heroes, famous for a day,
They die, they die.

*

Blue mountains speak of my desire,
Green waters reflect my lover's love:
The mountains unchanging,
The waters flowing by.
Sometimes it seems the waters cannot forget me,
They part in tears, regretting, running away.

Kwŏn Ho-mun (1532–1587)

Nature makes clear the windy air,
And bright the round moon.
In the bamboo garden, on the
Pine fence, not a speck of dust.
How fresh and fervent my life
With a long lute and piled scrolls!

Sŏng Hon (1535–1598)

The mountain is silent,
The water without form.
A clear breeze has no price,
The bright moon no lover.
Here, after their fashion,
I will grow old in peace.

Chŏng Ch'ŏl (1537–1594)

Snow has fallen on the pine-woods,
        and every bough has blossomed.
I should like to pluck a branch
        and send it to where my lord is.
After he has looked at it,
        what matter if the snow-flowers melt?

*

Could my heart but be removed
               and assume the moon's bright shape
To be hung there bright and shining
               in the vast expanse of heaven,
I could go where my dear lord is,
               and pour my light upon him.

TRANSLATED BY RICHARD RUTT

*

A dash of rain upon
The lotus leaves. But the leaves
Remain unmarked, no matter
How hard the raindrops beat.
Mind, be like the lotus leaves,
Unstained by the world.

*

Let forty thousand pecks of pearls
Rest on the lotus leaves.
I box and measure them
To send them off somewhere.
Tumultuous rolling drops—
How zestful, graceful.

*

Boys have gone out to gather bracken;
The bamboo grove is empty.
Who will pick up the dice
Scattered on the checkerboard?
Drunk, I lean on the pine trunk,
Let dawn pass me by.

*

Milky rain on the green hills,
Can you deceive me?
Sedge cape and horsehair hat,
Can you deceive me?
Yesterday I flung off my silk robe—
I have nothing left that will stain me.

Yi Wŏn-ik (1547–1634)

What if the willow has ten thousand strings;
Can these tie down the spring breeze?
What if the bees and butterflies search out nectar;
Can they stop the falling blossoms?
What if we feel secure in the time of our love;
What will become of it if she leaves?

Im Che (1549–1587)

Green grass covers the valley.
             Do you sleep? Are you at rest?
O where is that lovely face?
             Can mere bones lie buried here?
I have wine, but no chance to share it.
             Alone, I pour it sadly.

TRANSLATED BY RICHARD RUTT

Myŏngok (late sixteenth century)

They say dream visits
are "only a dream."
My longing to see him
is destroying me.
Where else
do I see him but in dreams?
Darling, come to me
even if it be in dreams:
let me see you, let me
see you time and time again.

PROSE PORTRAITS

From the thirteenth century on, men of letters and affairs kept diaries and recorded anecdotes, observations, and comments on various subjects. Students of the humanist tradition, their interests were encyclopedic, and their habits of mind leisurely. Collections of these jottings, known as *chapki* ("literary miscellany"), include character sketches, poetry criticism, and miscellanea.

The *chapki* portrait galleries resemble the early seventeenth-century English character books, but with some difference in procedure and aims. The writers who created Theophrastian characters in England attempted to reveal a class through an individual's characteristic actions, each portrait delineating a type dominated by a single vice or virtue. Our examples usually deal not with personified abstractions ("He is the sort of man who . . .") but with historical individuals. If a writer is to achieve brevity in depiction, he must present a telling detail—in word, deed, or gesture. He is not recounting a person's life, yet he should be able to reveal what sort of person his subject is. The following examples show a keen eye for the single action that reveals the qualities of a man's mind and character.

Ŏ Suk-kwŏn (fl. 1525–1544) was an interpreter of Chinese and went to Ming China seven times. He is remembered for his two books, and the present selection is from the *P'aegwan chapki* (The Storyteller's Miscellany), often considered a masterpiece in the form.

Ŏ Suk-kwŏn (fl. 1525–1554)

THE STORYTELLER'S MISCELLANY
[from *P'aegwan chapki*]

Before taking the civil service examination, Kim Su-on [1409–1481] studied behind closed doors. One day he stepped out into the courtyard to urinate; only then did he notice the fallen leaves and realize that autumn had come. Our elders studied as diligently as he did. Later, when he was seriously ill and about to die, he told his juniors,

"All of you should take heed not to study the *Doctrine of the Mean* and the *Great Learning.* I'm in agony, for I see only phrases from these two books!"

*

Chŏn Im [?-1509], Magistrate of Seoul, received official preferment after passing a military service examination. He was rude and fierce of character. Once, seeing that the horse he rode had boils on its back, he cut into the back of his aged servant, saying, "You did not protect the horse from boils; now feel its pain." Later, when he was critically ill, he arose and became violent. He stared and bent his bow, yelling angrily, "What ghosts are you that dare kill me?" He then stomped with rage for a long while.

*

The Third Minister without Portfolio Cho Wŏn-gi [1457-1533] was frugal by nature. He once asked a furrier to make him a cape. Usually tailors use the thicker fur to make the outside, and the thinner fur to line the interior. On seeing this, Cho remarked, "What an unskilled worker you are. We wear capes to keep warm, but you sew the thin fur on the inside and thick fur on the outside; this is no way to keep warm." He then told him to reverse the procedure.

He also could bear the cold; even in cold winter he wore only a coat and a lined jacket. Once he observed someone wearing socks in spring and asked, "Why do you wear them?" The man replied, "Without them, the cold air might enter my stomach!" Cho laughed and said, "The stomach is far from the feet. How could cold feet possibly harm the stomach?" When he died, his sons Hŭngjo, Hŏnjo, and the others stayed in the same household with no thought of setting up separate houses. People praised them.

*

In the beginning, Cheju Island was inhabited not by men but by spirits who emerged from the ground. This was at Mohŭng Cave, north of Mount Halla. The eldest spirit was named Yang Ŭlla, the second Ko Ŭlla, and the third Pu Ŭlla. Ko Hu, a descendant of Ko Ŭlla, bore the title *sŏngju* and was an able statesman of Silla. Throughout Koryŏ and to the present dynasty, descendants of the Ko clan have passed the civil service examinations and become ministers.

During the era Cheng-te [1506-1521], one Ko filled a post in the

Palace Guard. When a certain military official named Yi returned from a trip to Cheju, Ko asked him if he had seen the cave. Yi replied, "I saw it and urinated into it." Ko was speechless.

*

Buddhists consider compassion and nonkilling as their path. Once a mendicant monk in Hwanghae province encountered mounted hunters pursuing a boar. The animal ran in rage. The monk confronted the animal, saying, "Poor thing, poor thing." Then he pointed to the south with his staff and said, "Run quickly to the south." The boar, however, attacked the monk and gored him.

KASA, I

The *kasa* originated as song lyrics written to prevailing *kasa* tunes. It is characterized by a lack of stanzaic division, varying length, a tendency toward description and exposition, at times also lyricism, and by its verbally and syntactically balanced parallel phrases. Its structural norm is a group of two four-syllable words—or alternating groups of three and four syllables—which form a unit and are repeated in parallel form. Emerging as a new genre toward the middle of the fifteenth century, the form was perfected by such masters as Chŏng Ch'ŏl (1537–1594) and Hŏ Nansŏrhŏn (1563–1585).

"The Wanderings," written on the occasion of Chŏng Ch'ŏl's appointment as governor of Kangwŏn province, is a description of the eight famous scenes in the Diamond Mountains. His "Hymn of Constancy," literally the "Fair One," addressed to the king while in exile, is an allegorical poem in the tradition of the *Li sao* (Encountering Sorrow). "Little Odes on Mount Star," written to praise the elegant life of Kim Sŏng-wŏn (1525–1598), which centered on the Sŏha Hall and Sigyŏng Arbor on Mount Star in South Chŏlla province, catalogs the delights of the four seasons and claims that the expansive landscape reflects Kim's own liberality, freedom, and unworldliness. Unlike seventeenth-century English country-house poems, it omits descriptions of buildings or of their pedigree. Kim's estate is Nature itself, mirroring the state of his mind.

Hŏ Nansŏrhŏn, the elder sister of Hŏ Kyun, the author of the *Tale of Hong Kiltong,* was an accomplished poet in Chinese and Korean, and her "Woman's Sorrow" is a dramatic narrative on the sorrow of unrequited love.

Chŏng Ch'ŏl (1537–1594)

THE WANDERINGS (1580)
[*Kwandong pyŏlgok*]

I lay sick among rivers and lakes,
resting in bamboo groves.
Then the king made me governor
of Kwandong, eight hundred *ri* long.
O royal favor, unfathomable grace.
I rush through the Prolonging Autumn Gate,
bow toward the South Gate,
bid my lord farewell and withdraw,
and find a man holding a jade tally.
I change horses at Flat Hill Station and follow the Black River.
Where is the Striped Toad River? Here Pheasant Mountain rises.
O waters of the Luminous Ether, whither do you flow?
When a lonely subject leaves the court,
there is nothing left to him but growing old.

After a sleepless night at Ch'ŏrwŏn,
I climb to Broad North Arbor,
scanning the first peak of Three Peaked Mountain.
Magpies chattering at the palace site of Kung Ye,
do you know the rise and fall of changing ages?
May we witness again
the noble mien of Chi Ch'ang-ju!
Oh my Hoeyang, my town, Hui-yang of the Former Han.

My hostel is quiet, it is the third month.
A path along the Flower River stretches to the Diamond Mountains.
I fling off coat and sack and let my staff lead me on a stone path
along Hundred Rivers Canyon
to Myriad Falls Grotto.
There, silver rainbows, dragons with jade tails,
turning and coiling, spurt cataracts,
rending the hills ten miles away.
Listen to the thunder; look, there is snow.

At the top of Diamond Terrace,
home of immortal cranes,
awakened by spring breeze and jade flute,
noble birds in white and black silk
soar into mid-air
to frolic with Lin Pu, master of the West Lake.
Looking downward the peaks like incense burners,
I am at the True Light Temple on True Rest Terrace.
I can see it all, the true shape of Mount Lu!
Ah extravagant celestial creator! What abundance of strange forms!
Some fly, some dash—some stand, some soar—
as if planting lotus, bundling white jade,
sifting the Eastern Sea from its bed,
and heaving up the North Pole!
Lofty Height Viewing Terrace and lonely Cave Viewing Peak
shoot into the blue and speak to the Maker
from eons constant and unbending.
Ah, it could only be you,
could we match your steadfastness?

From Open Mind Terrace I view All Fragrance Castle
and count twelve thousand peaks in the clear air.
If we could gather the air's vitality, pure yet clean, clean yet pure,
on every peak and every crest
and bring it back to create a man!
O multitudinous, baffling shapes,
come into being of themselves when heaven and earth first opened.
Now that I look at them they seem to have feelings.

Who has ever stood on the crest of Vairocana Peak?
Which is higher, Mount Tung or Mount T'ai?
Who said the kingdom of Lu was small?
Who said all under heaven appeared to him small?[1]
Ah, how could we know its limits?
Better descend, if you cannot gain the summit.

1. Mencius, 7A, 24.

Through a narrow path along the Grotto of Perfect Penetration
I find Lion Peak.
Giant boulders in front form the Fiery Dragon Pool.
A thousand-year old dragon, coiling round and round,
floats day and night and reaches the open sea.
When will you gain winds and clouds, and send rain for three days
to yellowing leaves on a shadowy cliff?
Seeing Maha Chasm, Maitreya on a cliff, and Goose Gate Hill,
I cross a rotting log bridge to Buddha's Head Terrace,
a cliff hanging in air over a thousand fathoms deep.
The Milky Way unrolls its filaments
showing the warp and woof of its hemp cloth.
Twelve cascades on Nature's map; but I can see a few more!
Had Li Po been here and compared two views,
he would not have bragged of the waterfall at Mount Lu.

Why linger in the mountains? Let's go to the Eastern Sea.
A bamboo sedan-chair climbs slowly to Mountain Glare Tower.
Crying birds and crystal torrent hate to part.
Unfurl banners and flags, five colors brave the sky;
beat the drum and play the flute, music rolls away clouds and seas.
A horse familiar with singing sand beach carries the drunken poet,
with the sea by his side to look for clusters of wild roses.
Gulls, don't fly away! How do you know if I'm your friend or not?

Circling around Gold Orchid Cave I climb to Clustered Rock Arbor
and see four pillars of the palace of the White Jade Tower.
Work of a master artisan, the touch of a magic axe.
What is meant by its six-sided shape?

Leaving Kosŏng behind, I reach the Three-Days-Cove.
The six red letters are still on the cliff,[2]
but where are the four knights of Silla?
After three days here, where did they go?
Were they staying at Sŏnyu pool, or by Yŏngnang Lake?
Were they sitting at Clear Torrent Arbor, or on Myriad View Terrace?

2. Supposed to have been written by four knights of Silla.

Pear blossoms fall, a cuckoo calls sadly.
Along the east bank of Mount Nak I climb to Ŭisang Terrace
and get up at dawn to await the rising sun.
On the horizon lucky clouds appear;
six dragons uphold and push the sun.
When the sun left the sea, the whole world shimmered in its light;
now that it shines in midair, I can count the tiniest hair.
May the clouds never cover the sunlight.
Yes, Li Po is dead, but his poems endure. How subtly
he sang of this magnificence between heaven and earth.

Continually treading the azaleas on Steep Hill Mountain
the noble carriage with feathered top rolls down to Mirror Cove.
Behind old pines rimming like hedges I scan a ten-mile long beach
like ironed and stretched white silk;
the water is calm and clear, I can count the grains of sand.
I row a solitary boat and climb to an arbor beyond River Gate Bridge,
the ocean is forever placid, leisurely in temper, vast in boundary,
unmatched anywhere in the world in its natural splendor.
People still tell the tale of Hongjang.[3]
Kangnŭng Province, famed for virtue and good customs—
flagpoles for filial sons adorn the valleys.
Truly the people of Yao and Shun still seem to linger here.

The Fifty River flows to the sea, below Pearl House and West Bamboo
Tower, mirroring the green of the Great White Mountains.
Would that I could make it flow to the Han below Mount South.
Official's journeys have limits; only landscapes are infinite.
My heart is full; I'll brave the wanderer's sorrow—
Should I board the celestial raft to the Dipper and Herdboy?
Should I go to Cinnabar Cave to find the four immortals?
To fathom the roots of *Ti* Star the poet asks:
"Heaven lies beyond the seas; What lies beyond heaven?"
Who enraged the already angered whale?
It blows and spews, how giddying its tumult!
The silver mountain is leveled; it crashes in every direction.
What a sight—snow falls in the boundless sky of the fifth month!

3. Refers to a romance between the famous female entertainer Hongjang and the governor of
Kangnŭng.

Unawares night falls, winds and waves lull.
As I wait for the moon from the east
the horizon seems to draw near.
Lustrous moonlight a thousand feet long
appears only to hide itself again.
I roll up again a pearl bead screen and sweep the jade stairs;
while I sit erect awaiting the morning star,
someone sends me a spray of white lotus.
O let this world be revealed to all!
Holding a cupful of enchanting wine
I ask the moon: "Where are the heroes,
who are the four immortal knights?"
No one listens; I am not answered.
I have miles to travel in this magic mountain of the Eastern Sea.

I doze and fall asleep, my head on the pine trunk.
A voice whispers to me in my dream:
How could I not know you? You are a good fairy from Elysium
who misread the word in the Book of the Yellow Court,
banished from heaven to the world of men.
But linger on, friend, taste my immortal wine.
Pouring from the Dipper, filling from the Ocean,
he himself drinks and offers me a cup.
One cup, two cups, we drink by turns
until the gentle warm breeze lifts me by the arm
and I can stride into the great void.
Let us divide this wine among the four seas.
Let the whole world drink and be in wine.
Then let us meet again and exchange cups.
Words spoken, he soared skyward on a crane's back.
Only a jade flute rings in the void.
Was it yesterday or the day before?
Awakening, I look downward.
I know not the sea's depth nor its breadth.
Only the bright moon is shining
on a thousand hills and myriad villages.

HYMN OF CONSTANCY

[*Sa miin kok*]

When heaven created this body, I was born to serve you.
It is a lifetime affinity, Heaven, too, knows it.
I stayed young and you loved me alone.
Nothing can match my constancy and your love.
My lifelong wish was to be with you always.
Why in our old age do we yearn for each other?
Yesterday I repaired with you to the Moon Palace.
But for some reason, I came down to the lower world.
My hair, well-combed then,
has been disheveled for three years.
I've rouge and powder,
but for whom should I make up?
My mind, tied in knots of grief, piled fold upon fold,
only produces sighs, only brings tears.
Life has an end; only sorrow is endless.

Fickle time flows, flows by like water;
cold and heat come and go, as if they know time.
Much to hear and see, everything stirs deep feeling.
In an instant spring winds hollow out piled snow,
and two or three plum sprays blossom outside my window.
They are calm and easy, why do they send hidden fragrance?
At dusk the moon rises and shines on my pillow.
Is it feeling and welcoming? Is it my lord, is it not?
Were I to send him a plum branch,
what would he think when he saw it?
Flowers are gone, and a green shadow adorns the ground.
Gauze curtains are forlorn, embroidered canopies raised in vain.
Pulling a lotus curtain aside, I set a peacock screen.
My grief is enough—O long cruel day!
Cut the silk stuff with mandarin-duck designs,
loosen the thread of five colors,
and size it with a golden measure:
I make his clothes with skill and style, every detail proper.
On a coral carrier in a white jade box
I'd offer him this garment, gazing toward his far abode—

Mountains are rugged, clouds are ominous,
Who will risk these thousand miles?
Would he open the box and welcome it as if it were me?

When frost falls overnight and wild geese pass crying,
I stand on a high tower rolling up the crystal screen:
The moon rises over the eastern hill, and stars glitter in the north—
Is it he? I rush out to meet him: Only tears blind my eyes.
Let me seize a handful of clear light
and send it to your phoenix tower.
Hang it atop the tower, please, let it shine over eight corners,
and make every deep hill and valley bright as day.

Now the whole world is frozen; white snow is everywhere,
both men and birds have vanished from sight.
When the south bank of the Hsiao and Hsiang
is as cold as it is now,
how cold must he be in that high tower?
Would I might catch spring, make it shine on him!
Would I might offer him the sunlight
that once shone on my cottage eaves.
Tucking in my red skirt, rolling up my green sleeves,
I lean on tall bamboo at sunset.
A thousand thoughts are too many.
The day was short; but at night I sit up
with a mica-inlaid harp by the hanging blue lamp,
chin in my hand, leaning on a wall, hoping to dream of him.
O cold is the mandarin-duck embroidered quilt,
long is the night.

Twelve times a day, thirty days in the month,
in vain I try, not to think, but to bury this grief,
tangled in knots and piercing me to the marrow.
Not even ten renowned doctors can cure my sickness.
This is all, alas, all due to my lord.
Better to die and become a butterfly,
stop at each flower, rest upon each branch,
with scented wings, and light upon his cloak.
He may not remember me:
yet I will follow him.

LITTLE ODES ON MOUNT STAR

[*Sŏngsan pyŏlgok*]

An unknown guest in passing
stopped on Mount Star and said:
"Listen, Master of Mist Settling Hall
and Resting Shadow Arbor,
despite the many pleasures life held,
why did you prefer to them all
this mountain, this water?
What made you choose
the solitude of hills and streams?"

Sweeping away the pine needles,
setting a cushion on a bamboo couch,
I casually climb into the seat
and view the four quarters.
Floating clouds at the sky's edge come and go
nestling on Auspicious Stone Terrace;
their flying motion and gentle gestures
resemble our host.
White waves in the blue stream
rim the arbor,
as if someone stitched and spread
the cloud brocade woven by the Weaver Star,
the water rushes in endless patterns.
In other mountains without a calendar
who would know the year's cycle?
Here every subtle change of the seasons
unrolls before us.
Whether you hear or see,
this is truly the land of the immortals.

The morning sun at the window with plum trees—
the fragrance of blossoms wakes me.
Who says there is nothing
to keep an old hermit busy?

In the sunny spot under the hedges
I sow melons, tie the vines, support them;
when rain nurtures the plants,
I think of the old tale of the Blue Gate.
Tying my straw sandals, and grasping a bamboo staff,
I follow the peach-blossom causeway
over to Fragrant Grass Islet.
As I stroll to the West Brook, the stone screen painted by nature
in the bright moonlit mirror accompanies me.
Why seek Peach Blossoms Spring? Arcadia is here.

The casual south wind
scatters green shade;
a faithful cuckoo, where did he come from?
I wake from dozing
on the pillow of ancient worthies
and see the hanging wet balcony
floating on the water.
With my kudzu cap aslant
and my hemp smock tucked into my belt,
I go nearer to watch the frolicking fishes.
After the rain overnight,
here and there, red and white lotus;
their fragrance rises
into the still sky
filling myriad hills.
As though I had met with Chou Tun-yi
and questioned him on the Ultimate Secret—
as though an immortal Great Unique
had shown me the Jade Letters[1]—
I glance toward Cormorant Rock by Purple Forbidden Shallows;
a tall pine tree screens the sun,
I sit on the stone path.

1. Supposed to have been found by the legendary Yü the Great.

In the world of man it is the sixth month;
here it is autumn.
A duck bobbing on the limpid stream
moves to a white sand bar,
makes friends with the gulls,
not bothering to return to the water.
Free and leisurely,
it resembles our host.

At the fourth watch the frost moon rises
over the phoenix trees.
Thousand cliffs, ten thousand ravines,
could they be brighter by daylight?
Who moved the Crystal Palace from Hu-chou?
Did I jump over the Milky Way
and climb into the Moon Palace?
Leaving behind a pair of old pines on the fishing terrace,
I let my boat drift downstream as it pleases,
passing pink knotweeds and a sandbar of white cloverfern.
When did we reach
the Dragon Pool below Jade Ring Hall?
Moved by a sunset glow,
cowherds in green pastures by the crystal river
blow on their pipes.
It might awaken the dragon sunk deep at the pool's bottom.
Emerging from mists and ripples,
cranes might abandon their nests and soar into midair.
Su Shih in his poem on Red Cliff
praises the seventh moon;
but why do people cherish the mid-autumn moon?
When thin clouds part, and waves grow still,
the rising moon anchors herself in a pine branch,
How extravagant, Li Po drowned
trying to scoop up the reflected moon.

North winds sweep away
the heaped leaves on empty hills,
marshal the clouds,
drives the snow.
The Creator loves to fashion—
He makes snowflowers of white jade,
devises thousands of trees and forests.
The shallows in front freeze over.
A monk crosses over
the one-logged bridge aslant
a staff on his shoulder.
What temple are you headed for?

Don't boast of the recluse's riches
lest some find out this lustrous, hidden world.
Alone, deep in the mountains,
with the classics, pile on pile,
I think of the men of all times:
many were sages, many were heroes.
Heavenly intention goes into the making of men.
Yet fortunes rise and fall; chance seems unknowable.
And sadness deep.
Why did Hsü Yu on Mount Chi cleanse his innocent ears?
When he threw away his last gourd,
his integrity became even nobler.

Man's mind is like his face—
new each time one sees it.
Worldly affairs are like clouds—
How perilous they are!
The wine made yesterday must be ready:
Passing the cup back and forth,
let's pour more wine till we're tired.

Then our hearts will open, the net of sorrow unravel to nothing.
String the black zither and pluck "Wind in the Pines."
We have all forgotten who is host and who is guest.
The crane flying through the vast sky
is the true immortal in this valley—
I must have met him on the Jasper Terrace under the moon.
The guest addresses the host with a word:
"You, sir, you alone are immortal."

Hŏ Nansŏrhon (1563-1589)

A WOMAN'S SORROW

[*Kyuwŏn ka*]

Yesterday I fancied I was young;
But today, I am aging.
What use is there in recalling
The joyful days of my youth?
Now I am old, to recount
My sad story chokes me.
When Father begot me, Mother reared me,
When they took pains to bring me up,
They dreamed, not of a duchess or marchioness,
But at least of a bride fit for a gentleman.
Through the retribution of karma
And the ties chanced by a matchmaker,
I met as if in a dream
A valiant man known as frivolous,
And I served him with care, as if trodding on ice.
When I reached fifteen, counted sixteen,
The inborn beauty in me blossomed,
And with this face and this body
I vowed a union of a hundred years.

The flow of time was sudden;
The gods too were jealous of my beauty,
Spring breezes and autumn water,
They flew like a shuttle.
And my face once young and fair
Has become ugly to look at.
I know my image in the mirror;
So who will love me now?
Blush not, my self, and reproach no one.
Do you say a new customer showed up
At a tavern where men cluster?
When flowers smiled in the setting sun,
He left home for no fixed place
On a white horse with a gold whip.
Where does he stop to enjoy himself?
How far he went I don't know;
I'll hear no word from him.
Our ties are broken,
But I still think of him.
I don't see him at all, but I still yearn for him.
Long is a day, cruel is a month.
The plum trees by my window,
How many times have they fallen?
The winter night is bitter cold,
And snow, or some mixture, descends.
Long, long is a summer's day,
And a dreary rain comes too.
And spring with flowers and willows
Have no feeling for me.
When the autumn moon enters my room
And crickets chirp on the couch,
A long sigh and salty tears
In vain make me recall the past.
It is hard to bring this cruel life to an end.
But when I examine myself, I shouldn't despair so.
Turning the blue lamp around,
I play "A Song of Blue Lotus,"

Holding the green zither aslant,
As my sorrow commands me.
As though the rain on the Hsiao and Hsiang
Beat over the rustling bamboo leaves,
As though the crane returned whooping
After a span of a thousand years,
Fingers may stylishly pluck
The old familiar tune;
But who will listen in the room
Except for the lotus-brocade curtains?
I feel that my entrails are torn to pieces.
I would rather fall asleep
To see him at least in a dream.
But for what enmity
Do the leaves falling in the wind
And the insects piping among the grasses
Wake me from sleep?
The Weaver and Herdboy in the sky
Meet once on the seventh day of the seventh moon—
However hard it is to cross the Milky Way—
And never miss this yearly encounter.
But since he left me alone,
What magic water separates him from me,
And what makes him silent about his comings and goings?
Leaning on the balustrade, I gaze at the path he took—
Dewdrops glitter on the grass,
Evening clouds pass by, birds sing sadly
In the green bamboo grove.
Numberless are the sorrowful;
But can there be anyone as wretched as I?
Love, you caused me this grief;
I don't know whether I shall live or die.

A TALE OF ADVENTURE

Hŏ Kyun (1569–1618), the author of *The Tale of Hong Kiltong*, was the third son of Minister Hŏ Yŏp. Hŏ Kyun rose to a high position at court but was implicated in an attempted coup, through his association with a group of discontented illegitimate sons, and was executed.

The hero of the story, which was inspired by *The Water Margin*, the late fourteenth-century Chinese novel about Sung Chiang and his band of outlaws, wishes to rectify discrimination; but the central concern of the story is pedigree. The hero tries to correct social ills single-handedly, but does not repudiate the nobility and what it stands for. He desires to be accepted as a legitimate member of the literati and to share their privileges. Even his utopia built on a remote island is a replica of the Confucian society—perhaps a good place, but it is no place. His idea of a better society is one free of the discrimination based on blood lineage. It is therefore fitting that only on the island kingdom is the hero able to offer sacrifices to his parents as a full-fledged member of the Hong family. The story could be considered a pseudo-autobiography, even though it is not written in the first person.

Hŏ Kyun (1569–1618)

THE TALE OF HONG KILTONG
[*Hong Kiltong chŏn*]

During the reign of King Sejong in Chosŏn there was a minister whose name was Hong. Scion of a long-established and illustrious family, he passed the civil examinations at an early age and went on to attain the post of Minister of Personnel. He enjoyed a good reputation both in and out of government circles and his name resounded throughout the country as a man in whom loyalty and filial piety were combined.

Early in life he had two sons. The first son, named In-hyŏng, was born to his official wife, who was of the Yu clan, and the other son,

Kiltong, was the child of his maid-servant Ch'unsŏm. Minister Hong once dreamed of Kiltong's birth: sudden thunderbolts resounded and a green dragon with flailing whiskers leaped at him; he woke frightened, only to find it was but a passing spring dream. In his heart he was overjoyed; he thought: "Surely this dream must herald the birth of a lovely son!" And with this thought he rushed to the inner room where his wife rose to meet him.

In joy he took her jade hands to draw her near to him and press his love upon her, but she stiffened and said, "Here, you, a minister of state, forget your dignified position and take to the vulgar antics of a giddy youth! I will not submit to it."

So saying she drew her hands away and left the room. The minister, disconcerted and unable to endure his exasperation, returned to the outer room where he deplored his lady's lack of understanding, when the maid-servant Ch'unsŏm came to serve him tea. Quietly, he drew the girl to him and led her to a room, where he made love to her. Ch'unsŏm at this time was eighteen. Having once given her body to the minister, she never left his gates again and had no thoughts of accepting another lover. The minister, delighted with her, made her his concubine. Indeed, from that month she began to show the signs of pregnancy and in the ninth month gave birth to a child of jade-fair beauty whose frame and vigor were like no other and whose mien and spirit betold a brilliant hero. The minister was happy, but still saddened that the child had not been born to his proper wife.

Kiltong grew steadily and when he was eight years old he could already grasp a hundred things from hearing only one. The minister was more devoted to this son but, owing to the boy's ignoble birth, felt compelled to rebuke him promptly whenever the child called him *father*, or his brother *brother*. Even after Kiltong had reached the age of ten he could not presume to address his father and brother as such. Moreover, he was scorned even by the servants. This grieved him deeply and he could not still the turmoil within himself.

Once, at the full moon of the ninth month, a time when the bright clarity of the moon and the brisk coolness of the wind conspire to engage a man's passions, Kiltong in his study set aside his reading and, pushing the table away, lamented, "When one born to a man's role cannot model himself after Confucius and Mencius then he had best learn the martial arts. With a general's insignia tucked into his waistband he should chastize the east and subjugate the west, render meritorious service to the state, and illuminate the generations with his name. That's the glory of manhood. But why have I been left disconsolate, why my heart rent that I may not name my own father and brother? Have I not cause for grief?" Kiltong stepped down into the garden and set about practicing his swordsmanship. The minister, also out enjoying the moonlight, caught sight of his son pacing the garden and called him over to ask the reason.

"What's gotten into you—not asleep so late at night?"

Kiltong answered respectfully, "I have always enjoyed the moonlight, but there is something else tonight. While Heaven created all things with the idea that mankind is the most precious, how can I be called a man when such value does not extend to me?"

The minister knew what he meant, but scolded, "What are you talking about?"

Kiltong bowed twice and explained. "Though I grow to manhood by the vigor your excellency has passed to me, and realize the profound debt I owe for your gift of life and mother's upbringing, my life still bears one great sorrow: how can I regard myself as a man when I can address neither my father as *father* nor my brother as *brother*?" He wiped off his flowing tears with the sleeve of his jacket.

The minister heard him out and though he felt compassion for his son, he could only rebuke him severely for fear an expression of sympathy might give him license. "You're not the only child born to a maidservant in the home of a minister. How dare you show such willful arrogance? If ever I hear such talk as this again, I will not allow you in my presence!"

Kiltong dared not utter a word but could only sink to the ground in tears. The minister ordered him away and Kiltong returned to his quarters where he was overcome with sorrow. He was by nature uncommonly gifted and was a boy given to thoughtfulness and generosity. So it was that he could not quiet his heart or manage to sleep at night.

One day Kiltong went to his mother's room and in tears said, "We are in this world as mother and son out of the deep ties we had in a former life. My debt to you is immense. But in my wretched fortune I was born ignoble and the regret I harbor is bottomless. When a man makes his way in the world he cannot submit to the scorn of others. I cannot suppress this spirit innate in me and have chosen to leave your side, Mother. But I beg you not to worry about me and to take care of yourself."

Astonished, his mother replied, "You are not the only boy born humbly in a minister's home. How can you be so selfish? Why do you tear at your mother's heart so?"

Kiltong replied, "Long ago, Chi-shan, the illegitimate son of Chang Chung, left his mother when he was thirteen. In the Yün-feng Mountains he perfected the Way and left a glorious name to posterity. Since I have decided to follow his example and leave the vulgar world, I pray you wait in peace for another day. From the recent behavior of the Koksan woman, it appears she has taken us for enemies out of fear that she might lose the minister's favor. I'm afraid she plots misfortune for me. Please don't let my departure worry you so."

But his mother was saddened.

The Koksan woman, originally a kisaeng from Koksan named Ch'onan, had become the minister's favorite concubine. Since she was extremely arrogant and quick to carry false tales to the minister about anyone who displeased her, she was at the center of countless difficulties in the household. Ch'onan had no son of her own and, having seen the affection shown Ch'unsŏm by the minister after Kiltong's birth, she plotted with all her spite to eliminate the boy.

Then one day, her scheme conceived, she called in a shaman and said, "I must have this Kiltong out of the way to find any peace in life. If you can carry out my wishes, I shall reward you handsomely."

The shaman listened and replied with pleasure. "I know of an excellent physiognomist living outside Hŭngin Gate who with only one look at a person's face can divine the good and evil of both past and future. What we should do is call the woman in, explain your desires to her, and then recommend her to the minister. When she tells him about events of the past and future just as if she had seen them herself, he is sure to fall under her influence and could be made to get rid of the child. Then if we only wait for the opportune moment and do thus-and-so, how could we fail?"

Ch'onan was very pleased. Straightaway she gave the shaman fifty *yang* in silver and then set her off to call in the physiognomist. The shaman bowed low and left.

The next day when the minister was in the women's quarters talk-ing about Kiltong with his wife, praising the boy's uncommon vir-tues and regretting his low birth, a woman suddenly appeared in the courtyard below and bowed to him. Thinking it strange, the minister questioned her.

"Who are you? What do you want here?"

"I practice physiognomy for my living and just happened to be passing by Your Excellency's gate."

This reminded the minister of Kiltong, for he wanted to know the boy's future. He called the boy immediately and showed him to the woman. She looked him over for some time and in her astonishment almost blurted out, "I see in your son's face a hero, unchallenged by history and peerless in his own age! Only his lineage would be a drawback—there should be no other cause for concern!" But instead she only faltered and stopped.

The minister and his wife were puzzled and asked, "Whatever it is, we want you to speak directly with us."

The woman, feeling compelled, asked that the others retire. "From what I see, the boy cherishes elaborate and untamed dreams. The lustrous ether of the hills and streams radiates from between his eyebrows—a royal countenance. Your Excellency had best watch him carefully, for your household will surely be visited with ruinous misfortune when he grows up."

After a moment of stunned silence, the minister finally gathered himself and said, "Though I know man cannot escape his fate, I still forbid you to reveal this to anyone." With this command he gave the woman a little silver and sent her away. Not long after, the minister moved Kiltong into a cabin in the mountains where he could keep careful watch over his movements.

Unable to overcome the even greater sadness he felt at this turn of events and seeing no way out, Kiltong occupied himself with study-ing the military arts, astronomy, and geography. The minister was disturbed when he learned of this. "If the boy uses his native talent to further ideas that go beyond his station, the physiognomist will have been proven right. What am I to do?"

In the meantime, Ch'onan maintained her secret contacts with the shaman and physiognomist and through them managed to keep the minister stirred up. Intent on getting rid of Kiltong, she secured at great expense an assassin named T'ŭkchae and explained the circumstances to him. She then approached the minister. "It was uncanny that day the way the physiognomist could perceive events. What do you think? What are you going to do now about Kiltong's future? Even I was surprised and frightened. Doesn't it seem the only choice is to have him put out of the way?"

The minister worked his brows as he listened. "The matter is in my hands and I want you to refrain from involving yourself in it." He dismissed her but was left troubled and confused. Finding it impossible to sleep at night, he soon grew ill. His wife and son In-hyŏng—the latter now an assistant section chief in a ministry—were greatly worried and at a loss for what to do.

Ch'onan, who had been attending the minister, one day remarked, "The minister's critical condition is brought about by the presence of Kiltong. Now this is the way I see it. If we just do away with the boy, not only will the minister completely recover, but the whole household too will be assured of security. How is it you haven't considered this?"

"You may be right, but who could possibly do such a thing that violates the most solemn strictures of moral law?" the wife asked.

"I have heard there is an assassin called T'ŭkchae who claims he can kill a man as easily as picking something out of his pocket. Give him a thousand *yang* and then let him sneak in at night to do the job. By the time the minister finds out, there will be nothing he can do about it. I suggest, my lady, you give this serious thought."

The wife and her son broke into tears as they replied. "Painful as it may be, such a move would not only serve the good of the country, but help the minister and indeed protect the Hong family. Yes, do as you have planned!"

Highly pleased, Ch'onan called T'ŭkchae in again and explained in detail what she had been told. Ordered to do his work with dispatch that very night, T'ŭkchae agreed and waited for dark to come.

The story goes on: When Kiltong considered the sorrow and pain of his present situation he had no wish to remain any longer, but his father's strict commands left him with no choice. He passed the nights without sleep. On this night, he had lit the candle and to steady his wits had turned to the *Book of Changes,* when suddenly he heard a raven cry three times as it passed. Kiltong thought this ominous and said to himself: "This bird usually avoids the night. Crying out in passing like this must surely bode ill." He spread out the eight trigrams and studied them and was alarmed at what they portended.

He pushed his desk aside and, employing his knowledge of magic, made himself invisible and watched and waited.

It was during the fourth watch that a man carrying a dagger stealthily opened the door and entered his room. Kiltong, making sure he was unseen, chanted a mantra. A cold wind suddenly filled the room and in a moment the house had vanished—in its place was only the fresh beauty of a vaulted mountain recess. Terrified by Kiltong's marvelous powers, T'ŭkchae concealed his dagger and sought to escape. But the road ahead was suddenly cut off when a lofty, bouldered cliff rose to block his way. Trapped, he groped frantically about him. Just then he heard the sound of an eight-holed flute and, pulling himself together, looked up to see a young boy approaching astride a donkey.

The boy stopped playing the flute and began to rebuke T'ŭkchae. "Why would you want to kill me? Do you think you can harm a guiltless man for no good reason and still avoid the retribution of Heaven?"

He chanted one more mantra, a black cloud formed, and sand and stones flew through the air. When T'ŭkchae managed to gather his wits and look about he discovered Kiltong before him. "Even with his marvelous powers, how could this child be any match for me?" thought T'ŭkchae and flew at him.

"Though this is your death, bear me no malice! It was Ch'onan who swayed the minister through a shaman and a physiognomist to have you killed. Don't hold it against me," he cried as he leaped, dagger in hand.

Kiltong could not control his rage. Blinding T'ŭkchae with magic, he snatched the dagger away and denounced the would-be killer under the blade of his own knife.

"If your greed allows you to murder so easily, then I can kill your brutish sort without a second thought," Kiltong said and sent T'ŭkchae's head flying across the room with a single sweep of the blade. Still overcome by anger, Kiltong went that same night and seized the physiognomist and pushed her into the room with the dead T'ŭkchae. "What have you against me, to plot my murder with Ch'onan?" He chastized her; then slit her throat.

Was it not a terrible thing?

Kiltong had killed them. Now he looked up into the night sky where the Milky Way trailed to the west. Moved by the clarity of the moon's thin light, Kiltong, in his rage, thought to kill Ch'onan. But the thought of the minister's love for her dissuaded him; he threw away the dagger and resolved to seek an exile's life. He went directly to the minister's room to take formal leave of him.

Startled to hear the footfalls outside, the minister opened his window and discovered Kiltong there. He called him in and asked, "What are you doing up and about so late at night?"

Kiltong prostrated himself and answered, "I have always intended to pay back the life's debt I owe you and my mother, if only one ten-thousandth part. But someone of evil design in the household has deceived your excellency and attempted to kill me. Though I have escaped with my life, I know I cannot remain here and serve your excellency any longer. So I have come now to bid you farewell."

The startled minister asked, "What calamity could have occurred that would force you to leave your childhood home? Where do you intend to go?"

Kiltong answered, "By the time day breaks you will have learned the circumstances as a matter of course. And, as for me, why worry about the whereabouts of this cast-off child? It's my lot to wander aimlessly as a cloud." In twin streams his tears poured forth; his words faltered. The minister was moved to pity at the sight and began to offer counsel.

"I can appreciate the grief you must be suffering. I am going to give you my permission to address me and your brother as *Father* and *Brother* from this day on."

Kiltong bowed twice and said, "Now that my father has cleared away this one small sadness of mine, I know I could die without regret. I sincerely wish you a long, untroubled life, my father." Again he bowed twice to take his leave, and the minister, unable to stay his son, could only ask him to take care.

Kiltong then went to his mother's chambers to inform her of his departure. "Though I am leaving your side now, there will be a day when I can come back to serve you. I pray take care of your health while I am away."

As she listened, it crossed her mind there might have been some calamity but, seeing him bow now in departure, she grasped his hands and cried, "Where will you go? Even in the same house it has always seemed difficult to accept the small distance that has separated our quarters. But now how am I to endure, having sent you off to an unknown place? I only pray you will return soon so we can be together again." Kiltong bowed twice in taking his leave and, passing through the gate of his home, headed aimlessly toward the shrouded mountain recesses.

Is this not a pitiful thing?

The story goes on: Extremely apprehensive at receiving no word from T'ŭkchae, Ch'onan inquired into what had happened. She learned that Kiltong had disappeared without a trace and that the bodies of T'ŭkchae and the woman had been found in the room. Stricken with terror, she flew to inform the minister's wife of what she had found out. The lady, equally alarmed, called in her son, the assistant section chief, to tell him what she had heard.

When all this was finally reported to the minister, he went white with shock and said, "Kiltong came to me last night and with heavy heart bade me farewell. I thought it very strange at the time—but now, this!"

In-hyŏng dared withhold no longer what he knew of Ch'onan's involvement in the affair. Greatly angered, the minister had Ch'onan driven out of the house and the bodies quietly removed. He then called in the servants and ordered them never to speak of the matter.

The story continues: After leaving his parents and going out through the gates of his home, Kiltong wandered aimlessly until one day he happened upon a place where the scenery surpassed anything he had ever seen. He ventured further, looking for a house, and discovered a closed stone portal at the base of a huge boulder. Opening the door with care, he stepped through it and saw hundreds of houses set out neatly across a wide and level plain. A great number of men were gathered before him, enjoying themselves at a feast; this valley was a bandit's lair. Suddenly they caught sight of Kiltong and were pleased to see from his appearance that he was a man of no mean quality.

"Who are you?" they questioned him. "Why have you sought out this place? The braves you see gathered here have not yet been able to settle upon a leader. Now, if you think you have courage and vigor enough to join our ranks, see if you can lift that rock over there."

Sensing good fortune in what he heard, Kiltong bowed and said, "I am Hong Kiltong from Seoul, the son of Minister Hong by his concubine. But when I could no longer endure the scorn I suffered there, I left and have since been roaming the four seas and eight directions until I chanced upon this place. I am overwhelmed with gratitude that you speak of my becoming your comrade. But what trouble should it be for a man to lift a rock like that?'' With this, he hoisted the rock, which weighed one thousand catties, and walked some ten paces.

The assembled braves praised him with a voice. ''Here is a real man among men! Not one man in all our thousands could lift that rock, but beneficent Heaven has today given us a general!'' They seated him at the place of honor and each in turn pressed wine upon him. Swearing oaths of fealty in the blood of a white horse, the assemblage raised its unanimous approval and celebrated the day long.

Kiltong and his men practiced the martial arts until, after several months, they had quite refined their tactics.

Then one day some of the men approached Kiltong. ''For some time now, we have wanted to raid the Haein temple at Hapch'ŏn and strip it of its treasures, but we have been unable to carry out our plan for lack of a clever strategy. Now, as our general, what do you think of the idea?''

Kiltong was pleased and answered, ''I shall send out an expedition soon and you should be ready to follow my commands.''

In black-belted blue ceremonial robes, Kiltong mounted a donkey and prepared to leave camp with several followers in attendance. As he started out, he said, ''I am going to that temple now and shall return after looking over the situation.'' He looked every inch the scion of a high minister's family.

When he arrived at the temple, he first called the abbot to him. ''I am the son of Minister Hong of Seoul. I have come to this temple to pursue my literary studies and shall have twenty bushels of white rice shipped in for you tomorrow. If you are tidy about preparing the food, I will be glad to join you and your people for a meal at that time.'' Kiltong looked over the temple and left its precincts, having made promises for another day with the overjoyed monks.

As soon as he got back, Kiltong sent off some twenty bushels of white rice and called his men together. ''Now, on a certain day I wish to go to the temple and do such-and-such.'' When the appointed day arrived, Kiltong took some tens of his followers and went ahead to the Haein temple. He was received by the monks, who all came out to meet his party.

He called an elder to him and asked, "With the rice I sent, were you able to make enough food?"

"Enough, sir? We have been overwhelmed!"

Kiltong took his seat in the place of honor and bade the monks share his company, each having been given a tray of wine and savories. He then led the drinking and pressed each monk in turn to join him. All were filled with gratitude.

Kiltong received his own tray and, while eating, suddenly bit with a loud crack on some sand he had secretly slipped into his mouth. The monks, startled at the sound, begged his forgiveness, but Kiltong feigned a great rage and rebuked them, saying, "How could you be so careless in preparing my food? This is indeed an insufferable insult and humiliation!" So saying, he ordered his followers to bind the monks together with a single rope and sit them on the floor. The monks were in a state of shock, no one knew what to do. In no time, several hundred fearsome bandits came swooping into the temple and set about carrying off all its treasures. The helpless monks could only look on, screaming their laments.

Soon after, a temple scullion on his way back from an errand, saw what had happened and hurried off to notify the local government office. When he heard about this, the magistrate of Hapch'ŏn called out his militia and charged them to capture the bandits.

The several hundred troops who dashed off in pursuit soon came upon a figure in black robes and a nun's pine-bark cap who called to them from a promontory: "The bandits took the back road to the north. Hurry and catch them!" Believing this to be a helpful member of the temple, the soldiers flew like the wind and rain down the northerly back road, only to return empty-handed at nightfall.

It was Kiltong who, after sending his men along the main road to the south, had remained behind to deceive the troops in this clerical disguise. Safely back in the bandit lair, he found the men had all returned and were already sizing up the treasures. They rushed out to meet him and shower rewards upon him but Kiltong laughed and said, "If a man hadn't even this little talent, how could he become your leader?"

Kiltong later named his band the "Save-the-Poor" and led them through the eight provinces of Korea, stopping in each township to confiscate the wealth unjustly gained by magistrates and to succor the poor and helpless. But they never preyed upon the common people nor ever once touched the rightful property of the state.

So it was that the bandits submitted to Kiltong's will.

One day Kiltong gathered his men around him to discuss their plans. "I am told the governor of Hamgyŏng province with his rapacious officials has been squeezing the citizenry to a point where the people can no longer endure it. We cannot just stand by and do nothing. Now, I want you to follow my instructions exactly."

Thus the braves slipped one by one into the Hamgyŏng area and, on an agreed night, built a fire outside the South Gate of the provincial capital. When the governor, in a state of alarm, called for the fire to be extinguished, the yamen clerks and the city's populace all rushed forth to put it out. Meantime, several hundred of Kiltong's bandits poured into the heart of the city and opened the warehouse to uncover the stores of grain, money, and weapons, which they carried out the North Gate, leaving the city to churn in chaos. These unexpected events left the governor helpless. When at dawn he discovered the warehouses stripped of their grain, money, and weapons, he paled in consternation and bent all efforts toward the capture of the bandits. The notice he forthwith posted on the North Gate named Hong Kiltong as leader of the Save-the-Poor Party and responsible for looting the city stores. Troops were dispatched to bring in the outlaws.

While Kiltong, with his band, had made a good haul of the grain and such, he was still concerned lest they be apprehended on the road by some misadventure. Thus he exercised his occult knowledge and ability to shrink distances, bringing them back apace to the lair where they ended the day.

Another day, Kiltong again gathered his men around him to discuss plans. "Now that we have looted the Haein temple at Hapch'ŏn of its treasures and robbed the governor of Hamgyŏng of his grain and money, not only have rumors about us spread across the country but my name has been posted at the provincial offices for all to see. If I don't take steps I am likely to be caught before long. Now, just watch this trick!"

Whereupon, Kiltong made seven straw men and, chanting mantras, invested them with such spirit that seven Kiltongs all at once sprouted arms, cried aloud, and fell into animated chatter with one another. From appearances alone, no one could tell which was the real Kiltong. They separated, each going to a province and taking several hundred men under his command. And now no one knew where the real Kiltong had gone.

Eight Kiltongs roamed the eight provinces, calling wind and commanding rain as they exercised their magic. In night sorties that left no trace they made off with grain stores in every township and even managed without any difficulty to snatch a shipment of gifts bound for officials in Seoul. Every township of the eight provinces was in turmoil, sleep at night was impossible, and travelers disappeared from the roads. Chaos covered the country. At last one governor reported the situation to the throne: "There is an accomplished bandit known as Hong Kiltong, who strikes without warning and can with ease summon up the wind and clouds. He has looted treasures from every township and raised such a furor with his antics that even gift shipments cannot be sent up to the capital. If this bandit is not caught, the whole country will fall under his threat. Thus I humbly beg the throne to charge the Gendarmerie of the Left and the Right to capture this man."

When he heard this, the king was alarmed and summoned the captains of his gendarmerie. Reports continued to arrive from the rest of the eight provinces, and when the king opened and read each one he discovered that the names of the bandits were all the same Hong Kiltong and that the raids had taken place all on the same day at the same time.

Astonished, the king said, "The dauntlessness and wizardry of this bandit are unchallenged even by the rebel Ch'ih-yu. But still, no matter how marvelous the fellow is, how could he, with his one body, be in eight provinces and stage his raids in one day and at the same time? This is no common bandit—it looks as though he will be a difficult one to capture."

The captains of the Left and Right were to dispatch their troops with orders to apprehend the bandit, but Yi Hŭp, the captain of the Right, memorialized, "Though your servant is without particular talent, he begs the throne rest assured that he himself can capture and deliver up the bandit. Why, then, should the gendarmeries of both the Left and Right be dispatched?"

The king approved and pressed the captain to depart with all haste. Yi Hŭp took his leave and, commanding a host of government troops, deployed them widely with instructions to gather again on a certain day in the county of Mun'gyŏng. Yi Hŭp himself took only a few gendarmes with him and scouted the countryside incognito.

Late in the afternoon of another day the party sought out a wine shop where they stopped to rest. Presently a young man rode up on a donkey and, exchanging courtesies with the captain, sighed and said, "The *Book of Songs* says: 'Everywhere under Heaven is no land that is not the king's. To the borders of all those lands none but is the king's slave.'[1] Even though living here so far out in the country, I am still concerned for the country!"

The captain feigned surprise and said, "What do you mean by that?"

The boy answered, "Could I not be sorely troubled when people are being victimized by that bandit Hong Kiltong? He roams the eight provinces and mounts raids at will, but no one has yet been able to catch the marauder."

The captain responded, "You impress me as a brave and spirited young man who speaks with directness; how about joining me in capturing that bandit?"

"I have long wanted to catch him but could not find a man of courage to share my purpose. How fortunate to have met like this! Still, I know nothing of your ability—why don't we find a quiet spot and stage a contest between us?"

They went together to another place, where they climbed to the top of a boulder and sat down.

"Kick me as hard as you can with both legs and try to knock me off this boulder," said Kiltong as he moved out to the very edge and sat down again.

The captain thought: "No matter how powerful he is, he is sure to fall off if I give him one good kick." And, summoning all his strength, he kicked Kiltong with both legs at once.

But the boy just turned to him and said, "You are indeed a strong fellow. Though I have tested a number of men, none has been able to move me. But you, indeed, have nearly shaken me. If you will come along with me, I know we can catch Hong Kiltong!" With this, the boy led him into the deep recesses of the surrounding mountains.

As he followed his guide, the captain thought: "Until today I had

1. Poem 205 (Waley, p. 320).

always thought my strength worth boasting about. Seeing this boy's prowess, could one remain unawed? With just his help alone, I am sure to capture Hong Kiltong." A moment later, the boy turned and said to the captain, "This cave leads into Kiltong's lair. I am going in first to take a look around—you should wait for me."

The captain was suspicious at heart, but he bade the youth bring his captive back quickly and so he sat down to wait. Suddenly many tens of screaming warriors descended on him from the hills around. The captain attempted to escape but was easily overtaken by the bandits and bound.

"Are you not Yi Hŭp, Captain of the Gendarmerie? We have come to arrest you under orders from the king of the underworld." Collared in chains and driven like the wind and rain, the captain was frightened beyond his wits. It was not until after they had arrived at another place, where he was forced to his knees amidst fierce cries, that he could begin to grope toward consciousness and take in his surroundings. It was a grand palace; he saw countless yellow-turbaned warriors ranked to the left and right, and a sovereign sitting upon his dais in a hall beyond.

"Contemptible wretch!" the lord roared. "How dare you presume to capture General Hong? For this we are going to condemn you to the underworld!"

His senses nearly recovered, the captain pleaded, "Worthless though I am, I have been arrested for no real crime. I beg you, my lord, spare my life and allow me to leave."

But the response from the dais was a burst of laughter. "Take a good look at me, you knave! I am Hong Kiltong, leader of the Save-the-Poor Party, the very man you seek. Since you had set out to capture me, I decided to test your courage and determination. So I lured you here in the guise of a blue-robed youth, that you might have a taste of my authority."

Whereupon, Kiltong ordered his attendants to loosen the captain's bonds and seat him near at hand in the great hall. Pressing wine on his guest, the general said, "You can see how futile it is to scout around for me—you had better just report back. But do not let on that you have seen me, for they are sure to hold you responsible. I urge you not to say a word of this." After pouring another cup and offering it to his guest, Kiltong ordered his attendants to free the captain and send him off.

At this, the captain thought: "Whether this is real or a dream, I do not know. Yet somehow I have come here and have learned to appreciate Kiltong's marvelous powers." But no sooner did he turn to leave than he suddenly found himself unable to move his four limbs. When he calmed his spirit sufficiently, he considered his plight and discovered he was wrapped inside a huge leather sack.

After extricating himself with some difficulty, the captain found three more sacks hanging on the tree beside him. He opened them one after the other, and discovered there the three retainers with whom he had set out originally. "What has happened? When we set out we had agreed to meet at Mun'gyŏng—how did we get here?" So asking each other, they looked around and saw they were on Mount Pugak, overlooking Seoul.

"How did you three get here?" the captain questioned his men, as the four stood looking in amazement down at Seoul.

"We fell asleep back in the wine shop. Then we were suddenly carried here, shrouded in wind and rain. There is no way to account for it."

"No one is going to believe this absurd story—you must say nothing to the others about it. This Hong Kiltong really has powers beyond believing—how could we ever capture him by human means? But if we return empty-handed now, we could never escape punishment. Let's wait a few more months before reporting back."

With this, they descended the mountain.

In spite of royal commands throughout the eight provinces ordering his capture, there was no second-guessing Hong Kiltong's stratagems: now riding about the thoroughfares of Seoul in a one-wheeled chaise, and now—with solemn prior announcement—appearing in various townships in the guise of a Royal Inspector aboard a two-horse carriage. To top it off, after ferreting out and summarily executing corrupt and covetous magistrates, the self-appointed Royal Inspector was even making official reports to the throne.

At this, the king, now in a towering rage, demanded, "That cur can wander the provinces indulging in such antics and yet no one is able to capture him. Just what do you intend to do about it?" Even as he called his counselors and ministers into conference, reports continued to arrive at court from the various provinces—each of them about the work of Hong Kiltong. Examining each as it came in, the king became distressed. He looked round at his officers and asked, "Maybe this fellow isn't a human after all—his behavior is more like that of a demon! Does any one among my ministers know something about his origins?''

One of the officers stepped forward and addressed the throne. ''This Hong Kiltong is an illegitimate son of the Hong who was once Minister of Personnel, and is half-brother to Hong In-hyŏng, now an assistant section chief in the Board of War. All the facts might be brought to light were you to detain the father and son for a personal royal interrogation.''

Further incensed, the king responded, ''Why is it only now that you tell us of this?'' He forthwith ordered the father's arrest through the State Tribunal and meanwhile had In-hyŏng brought in for questioning. Pounding his writing desk with awesome rage, the king roared, ''We have learned that the bandit Kiltong is your half-brother! How is it you have failed to restrain him and are content to stand by while the state is thrown into turmoil? If you do not bring him in now, the loyalty and filial piety of you and your father will go for naught in our eyes. Apprehend him immediately and remove this affliction from Korea!''

Awe-stricken, In-hyŏng removed his cap and bowed his head deeply. ''My low-born younger brother was with us until he killed a man and fled, some years ago now, leaving us unable to learn of his fate. As a result, my aged father has sunk into a critical illness and can reckon his remaining life only in mornings and evenings. Kiltong, with his disregard for mortality, has burdened Your Majesty with deep concern, for which we deserve death without mercy ten thousand times. But if Your Majesty, in the warmth of your compassion, would grant our humble petition and forgive my father for his crime, allowing him to return home to recover his health, I intend, even at the risk of life, to capture Kiltong and thus atone for the sins of this father and son.''

The king, having heard him out, was deeply moved. He forgave the old minister and appointed In-hyŏng governor of Kyŏngsang province. ''If you, my minister, had not the power of a governorship, I fear you would not be able to catch Kiltong. I am giving you a year's time in which you should be able to apprehend him easily.''

In taking his leave, In-hyŏng bowed over and over again, expressing his gratitude for the king's benevolence, and that same day he set out for Kyŏngsang. Upon assuming his new office, he had notices posted in every township urging Kiltong to turn himself in. They read:

The life of men in this world is governed by the five relationships; and these relationships are realized through the constant virtues of humanity, righteousness, propriety, wisdom, and faithfulness. But if one, ignorant of this, disobeys his sovereign's commands and behaves in a manner disloyal and unfilial, how can he be countenanced by the world? Kiltong, my brother! You should be aware of these things; come to your older brother voluntarily and let yourself be taken alive. Our father is sickened to the bone because of you, and His Majesty is deeply anxious—so extraordinary is your sinfulness. I have therefore been especially appointed to the governorship with orders to apprehend you, in failure of which the fair virtue amassed by generations of the Hong family will overnight be brought to naught. Would this not be sorrowful? Kiltong, my brother! If you consider this and surrender straight off, as I pray you do, your crimes should indeed be lessened and you would preserve our family. I do not know your heart, but it is imperative that you give this serious thought and present yourself.

Posting this notice in every township, the governor suspended all other official activity, awaiting only the surrender of Kiltong. One day a youth astride a donkey followed by tens of attendants appeared outside his residence to request an audience. But when the youth entered the receiving hall on command and made his obeisance, the governor studied his eyes carefully: it was Kiltong for whom he had been waiting so long.

With joyful astonishment he dismissed his officers and, embracing the boy, said in a tear-choked voice, "Kiltong! After you left home, our father, not knowing whether you were alive or dead, was taken by an illness that invaded his very breast. Not only have you thus compounded your unfilial behavior, but you have become the cause of great distress to the state. What can you be thinking to behave in a manner so disloyal and unfilial and, more, by turning to banditry, to commit crimes that are without parallel in the whole world? His Majesty, enraged by this, has ordered me to bring you in. Your crimes are beyond denial. You must go immediately to Seoul and submit quietly to the royal judgment."

As he finished speaking the tears rained from his eyes. Kiltong lowered his head and replied.

"At this pass what else could I presume to say but that I am determined to save my father and brother in their peril? Yet, would we have come to this, I wonder, had his excellency, our father, in the first place allowed this humble Kiltong to address him as Father and you as Brother? But, at this point events of the past have become meaningless; now you must have me bound and sent up to Seoul.'' Kiltong said nothing further.

Though the governor, on the one hand, saddened when he heard this, he nevertheless composed an official report to the throne. After having Kiltong shackled in fetters and cangue and locked inside a barred wagon, he assigned more than ten strapping officers as escorts to push on day and night for Seoul. The people of each township along the way, knowing of Kiltong's prowess and having heard of his capture, choked the roads to gape at the prisoner as he passed.

But by now, a different Kiltong had been arrested in each of the eight provinces and sent up to Seoul. The court and citizens of the capital were lost in helpless confusion—there was no one equal to the situation. When the astounded king convened his full court to conduct a personal interrogation, the eight Kiltongs were brought forward only to argue among themselves.

"You're the real Kiltong, not me!" So they fought on, making it impossible to guess which one was the real Kiltong. Puzzled, the king forthwith summoned the former Minister Hong and said, "The saying goes, 'No one knows his son better than the father.' I want you to pick out your son among these eight.''

The old minister respectfully bowed his head in remorse. "My low-born son, Kiltong, can be distinguished by the red birthmark he has on his left leg." And, admonishing the eight Kiltongs, he said, "Remember that you are in the presence of His Majesty and that your father is here below. You have committed crimes unheard of even in remote antiquity: do not try to avoid your just fate." With this, he vomited up blood and collapsed in a faint.

The king, in alarm, commanded his Royal Physicians to save the minister, but they could effect no improvement. The eight Kiltongs, seeing the old man's condition and tears streaming from their eyes, each produced from his pocket a pellet of medicine and put it in the minister's mouth. The old man recovered his senses before the day was out.

The eight Kiltongs addressed the king. "In view of the many boons granted my father by the state, how could I dare give myself over to improper behavior? But in origin I am the child of a lowly serving woman who could not call his father Father or his brother Brother. To my lifelong regret, I chose to leave my home and join a party of bandits. Still, I never once abused the common people but confiscated only the wealth of magistrates amassed through exploitation of the people. And now, when ten years have passed, I shall leave Korea, for I have a place to go. A suppliant at Your Majesty's feet, I beg you end your concern over me and rescind the orders for my arrest.''

As they finished speaking, the eight Kiltongs tumbled over all at the same instant—close scrutiny showed them all to be only straw men. Astonished anew, the king reissued his orders, this time with the aim of capturing the real Hong Kiltong.

The story goes on: Divesting himself of the straw men, Kiltong continued to wander about. Then one day he posted a notice on the four gates of Seoul which read: ''Wondrous is he, for there will be no capturing Hong Kiltong. Only if he be appointed Minister of War can he be apprehended.''

When the king had read the text of Kiltong's notice, he called the ministers of his court into conference.

The various ministers chorused: ''To appoint that bandit now as Minister of War, after having failed in all attempts to arrest him! What an embarrassment if such news were heard in neighboring countries!'' The king concurred in this and settled with pressing the governor of Kyŏngsang province, In-hyŏng, to capture Kiltong posthaste.

When the governor saw these stern royal instructions he was struck with fear and trembling, lost for a way out of his dilemma. But then one day Kiltong appeared out of thin air and, bowing before him, said, ''This time I truly am your brother, Kiltong. I want you to worry yourself over me no longer: have me bound and sent up to Seoul.''

At this, the governor tearfully grasped Kiltong's hands. ''Oh, irresponsible child! As much as we are brothers, I cannot but grieve at your failure to heed the guidance of your father and brother, putting the whole country into chaos. But still, you are to be commended for having surrendered to me voluntarily.'' He quickly examined Kiltong's left leg, and when he found the identifying mark there, he promptly bound his prisoner—taking special care to pinion all four limbs—and put him into the barred wagon.

Even engirded tightly as an iron drum by tens of select and strapping officers, and driven like the wind and rain, Kiltong's countenance did not change an iota. After several days the party arrived in

Seoul. But just as they reached the palace gates, the iron bands broke away and the wagon flew into splinters, while Kiltong, with a twist of his body, flew up into the air like a cicada throwing off its shell and disappeared in a flutter, wrapped in clouds and mist. The officers and soldiers were left dumbfounded, able only to gape mindlessly into the empty air.

They had no choice but to report these facts to the throne. Upon hearing this, the king responded in great consternation, "I have never heard of such a thing—even from greatest antiquity!"

Then one of his ministers proposed, "Since it is this Kiltong's expressed desire to serve one time as Minister of War and then leave Korea, why don't we grant his wish this once? If so, he would come to express his gratitude and then, grasping the opportunity, we could capture him."

The king approved and immediately appointed Kiltong Minister of War, posting notices to this effect on the four gates of Seoul.

Kiltong soon heard of this and promptly made an impressive appearance on the main thoroughfare of the capital, riding in high dignity on a one-wheeled chaise and wearing the silk cap and formal gown, and a belt of rhinoceros horn, appropriate to his new office. The officials of the Ministry of War, hearing that the new Minister Hong was arriving to pay his respects at court, presented themselves as his escort to the palace. Meanwhile, the ministers of state, in full convention, had resolved to have a hatchet man lie in ambush for Kiltong and cut him down the moment he came out of the palace.

Now Kiltong entered the court, made obeisance, and addressed himself to the king. "In spite of the grievous crimes I have dared commit, Your Majesty has bestowed his gracious benevolence on me, freeing me of my lifelong anguish. But now I must take leave of this court forever. I humbly pray Your Majesty may enjoy a long life."

So saying, Kiltong leapt traceless into the void and vanished, wrapped in clouds. At this sight, the king sighed.

"Indeed, Kiltong's marvelous talents would be rare in any age! Now that he has declared his intention to leave Korea, there will be no further cause for distress on his account. Although I may have had my suspicions, he has displayed the fine heart of a real man: there should be no cause now for worry." He then issued a command to the eight provinces pardoning Kiltong and ending the campaign to arrest him.

The story continues: Kiltong returned to his hideout and gave orders to his robber band.

"I must go somewhere for a while: I want you men to stay put here until I get back—no coming and going!" he commanded, and forthwith rose up into the air.

After traveling for a while in the direction of Nanking, he reached a place known as the Land of Lü-tao. Looking all about him, he saw that the mountains and streams were well formed and clean, the people prosperous, and the land capable of supporting comfortable life. From here he went on to see the sights of Nanking and thence to Chu Island, where he also toured about viewing the mountains and streams and examining the character of its people.

But when he reached Mount Wu-feng, he pronounced this scenery truly the most beautiful he had ever seen. The island, seven hundred *li* around, abounded in fertile fields and rice paddies—an ideal place for men to live. Kiltong thought in his heart: "Since I have now quit Korea, this is the place for me to live on in hiding, wherein I can lay great plans." With this, he abruptly returned to his home camp and addressed his men.

"On a certain day I want you to go to the banks at Yangch'ŏn on the lower reaches of the Han River and there prepare a good number of boats, whence you will proceed up the Han to Seoul on such-and-such day of such-and-such month and there await my further orders. I shall ask the king to give us one thousand bushels of unhulled rice, which I shall bring to you. Don't fail me!"

Meanwhile, the story continues: Now that Kiltong had forsworn his banditry, the former minister Hong was recovering his lost health, and the king, for his part, found the passing days free of the old concern. One evening, at about the full moon of the ninth month, the king was taking a stroll in his palace gardens, enjoying the moonlight. Just then a cool breeze sprang up unexpectedly, and he was startled to behold, descending from the void, the figure of a young piper playing an elegant melody on his jade flute.

The boy prostrated himself before the king, who exclaimed, "Child of another world! Why this descent into the human realm? Of what do you wish to inform us?"

Still prostrate, the youth answered, "I am Hong Kiltong, sire, Your Majesty's former Minister of War."

The startled king asked, "But why do you come here so deep in the night?"

Kiltong replied, "It would have been my wish respectfully to serve Your Majesty for eternity. But I was born the child of a lowly maid-servant and was denied the career a civil officer might enjoy in the Office of Special Counselors or that of a military officer in the Liaison Office. So it was that I took to roaming the country as I pleased, and it was only by raising havoc with government offices and offending the court itself that I finally succeeded in bringing my plight to the attention of the throne. Your Majesty deigned to grant my petition, and so I have come now to pay my last respects before quitting this court and land. I pray, sire, that you enjoy long life without end."

As Kiltong rose into the air and flew swiftly away, the king honored his prowess with unstinting praise. Thenceforth, with bandit depredations at an end, there was perfect peace in all quarters.

The story continues: Kiltong bade farewell to Korea and settled on Chu Island in the area of Nanking, where he built thousands of houses and strove to develop agriculture. Having taught his people the various skills, he set up arsenals and trained the able-bodied in the military arts. Indeed, his troops were well trained and well fed.

One day it happened that Kiltong was traveling toward Mount Mang-tang to obtain a certain herb to be applied to arrowheads when he arrived in the area of Lo-ch'uan. Now, a man living there by the name of Po Lung (White Dragon) had a daughter who was of uncommon talent and dearly beloved of her parents, but who had been inexplicably lost one day when a wild wind arose and wreaked havoc among them. Though the grief-ridden parents had spent one thousand measures of gold in a search that extended in all directions, there was not a trace to be found. The sorrowing couple let it be known: "Whosoever may find and restore our daughter to us, with him we shall share our family fortune and regard him as our son-in-law."

Kiltong was deeply moved when he heard of this, but since there was nothing he could do for them he continued on to Mount Mang-tang to dig up the needed herbs. It soon grew dark around him, and he was just wondering where to head next when the sound of men's voices arose and the bright glint of lamplight caught his eye. When he sought out the place whence it came, however, it turned out they were not men but monsters sitting about chatting with each other—the kind of monster called *ultong,* a sort that lives for many years and passes through infinite changes.

Concealing himself, Kiltong let fly an arrow and struck their leader, causing the monsters all to flee screaming. He propped himself up in a tree and after sleeping the night there returned to his search for herbs.

Kiltong's work was suddenly interrupted by three or so of the monsters who asked, "What is it that brings you so deep into our mountains?"

Kiltong replied, "I happen to be skilled in medicine and have come to find certain healing herbs. I consider it my good fortune to have come across you."

They were delighted to hear this. "Having lived here for some time, our king has now taken a bride, but just when he was celebrating at a banquet last night he was struck and seriously injured by some divine arrow. Since you are a knowledgeable physician, you would surely be rewarded handsomely if you could heal the king's wound with those wonderful herbs."

Kiltong thought to himself: "This king of theirs must be the one I wounded last night." When he had acceded to their request, Kiltong was led to a gate where he was made to wait while they went inside. Soon reappearing, the monsters asked Kiltong to enter. Lying abed within the spacious and elegant red and blue villa was the abominable monster, who groaned and twisted his body up in order to look at Kiltong.

"It has been my unexpected fortune to be struck down by a divine arrow and left so critically wounded. But having heard of you from my attendants, I bade you hither. This is a Heaven-sent salvation. Do not spare your skill with me!"

Kiltong expressed his thanks for the high trust and said, "I think it best first to give you medicine that will cure your inner distress and then, after that, to use herbs to heal the outer wounds."

When the monster agreed to this, Kiltong extracted some poisonous herbs from his medicine pouch and, hurriedly dissolving them in warm water, fed them to the monster. As soon as the potion had gone down, the monster let out a great cry and fell dead. At this, the other monsters flew into the room, only to be met by Kiltong's unleashed wonders. With great blows he felled them all.

Kiltong was startled then to hear the pitiful supplications of two young girls. "We are not monsters. We are human beings brought here as captives. Please save what is left of our lives! Let us go back into the world!"

Recalling what he had heard about Po Lung, Kiltong asked where they lived: one was Po Lung's daughter and the other the daughter of one Chao Che. He cleared away the bodies and took the two girls home to their parents, who were overjoyed to have their daughters back and received Hong Kiltong as their son-in-law. Kiltong took Po's daughter as his first wife and Chao's as his second.

Thus had Kiltong, in a day's time, gained two wives and two families—all of whom he brought back with him to Chu Island, to the pleasure and congratulations of all.

One day Kiltong was scanning the heavens and, startled by what he saw, broke into tears. People around him asked the reason for this expression of grief.

Kiltong answered with a sigh. "I have been divining my parents' health by reference to the heavenly bodies, and the configuration indicates that my father is critically ill. But I am saddened to think how far I am now from that bedside I cannot reach."

Everyone was saddened by his plight.

On the following day, Kiltong went into Mount Yüeh-feng to pick out a suitable grave site and had work started on building a tomb with stonework on the scale of a state mausoleum. He also had a large boat prepared and ordered it to sail for the banks of the West River and there await further instructions. Thereupon he shaved his head and, adopting the guise of a Buddhist monk, set out himself for Korea in another, much smaller, boat.

Meanwhile, the old minister Hong, who had suddenly fallen gravely ill, called his wife and son, In-hyŏng, to him.

"I am about to die and that itself is no cause for regret. But what I do regret is to die not knowing whether Kiltong is alive or dead. If he is alive, I am sure he will seek out the family now. In that event, there are to be no distinctions between legitimate and illegitimate, and his mother, too, is to be properly treated."

With these words, he expired. The entire family mourned grievously, but once the funeral had been carried out they were perplexed that it was so difficult to find a propitious site for the grave. Then one day the gatekeeper announced that a monk had come, asking to pay his last respects before the dead. The family was pleased to receive him, but when the bonze entered and began to cry in great wails, they did not understand any reason for this and so exchanged baffled looks among themselves.

After the monk had presented himself to the chief mourner and performed more sad cries of lamentation, he finally spoke.

"In-hyŏng, brother, don't you recognize me, your own younger brother?"

The chief mourner examined this monk carefully—it was Kiltong. He caught his younger brother by the hands and cried, "Is it you, dear brother? Where have you been all this while? Our father's final words were spoken in great earnestness—it is clear to me where my duty lies."

He led him by the hand into the inner chamber to greet the widow Hong and to see Ch'unsŏm, Kiltong's mother, who wailed, "How is it you wander about as a monk?"

Kiltong replied, "It is because I am supposed to have left Korea that I now shave my head and adopt the guise of a monk. Furthermore, having mastered geomancy, I have already selected a proper resting place for Father, so Mother need no longer be concerned over it."

The delighted In-hyŏng exclaimed, "Your talents are peerless! What further troubles could plague us, now that a propitious grave site has been found?"

The next day, Kiltong conveyed the old minister's coffin and escorted his mother and brother to the banks of the West River where, as instructed, boats were standing by. Once the party was all aboard, they sped off like arrows. Soon they arrived at a particularly dangerous spot where an army of men in tens of ships had been standing by for their arrival. As expressions of pleasure were exchanged, the flotilla and its new convoy proceeded on their solemn way. Before long, they had made their way to the mountaintop, and as In-hyŏng surveyed the majestic setting he was unrestrained in his admiration for Kiltong's knowledge and ability.

With the interment completed, they returned as a group to Kiltong's residence, where his two wives, Po and Chao, greeted their brother- and mother-in-law. Kiltong's mother, Ch'unsŏm, was unstinting in her praise of his choices and also marveled at the imposing stature to which he had grown. After several days had passed and it came time for In-hyŏng to take leave of Kiltong and Ch'unsŏm, he enjoined his younger brother to keep the grave meticulously tended, and then paid his own parting respects at the tomb before setting out.

When In-hyŏng arrived in Korea he went directly to see his mother, Madam Hong, and related every detail of the journey, all to her wonder and pleasure.

The story continues: Having conscientiously observed memorials both at the time of the funeral and on the two succeeding anniversaries of his father's death, Kiltong now once again called his braves together. He perfected them in the military arts and spared no efforts toward agriculture in order to create a well-trained and well-fed military force.

The island kingdom of Lü-tao to the south, with its many thousand *li* of fertile land had constantly held Kiltong's interest and attention as truly a country of Heaven-sent abundance. Calling his men together one day, he said, "It is now my intention to attack Lü-tao and I am asking every one of you to give his all in this effort."

The army set out the following day, with Kiltong himself in the forefront and General Ma Suk commanding the secondary force. Leading his fifty thousand select troops, Kiltong soon reached the foot of Mount T'ieh-feng in Lü-tao and there engaged the enemy. The local magistrate, Chin Hsien-chung, alarmed at the unexpected appearance of Kiltong's cavalry, notified his king and, at the same time, led his troops out to give battle. But in the engagement Kiltong cut down Chin Hsien-chung at the first encounter, took T'ieh-feng, and saw to the pacification of its citizens. Leaving one Chŏng Ch'ŏl to hold T'ieh-feng, he reassembled his main force and set out to strike directly at the capital city. First, however, he dispatched a declaration to the government of Lü-tao: "General of the Righteous Army, Hong Kiltong, addresses this missive to the King of Lü-tao. Let him be aware that a king is never the sovereign of one man alone but ruler of all men. It is I who have now received the mandate of Heaven and so raise armies against you. I have already destroyed the stronghold of T'ieh-feng and am now surging toward your capital. If the king will do battle let him join in it now. If not, then let him promptly surrender and look to his salvation!"

Upon reading the missive, the terror-stricken king said, "We had put all our trust in the T'ieh-feng fortress and now it is lost! What recourse do we have?" He led his ministers out to offer surrender.

Thus Kiltong entered the capital and pacified its people. When he assumed the throne, he enfeoffed the former king as Lord of Ŭiryŏng and appointed Ma Suk and Ch'oe Ch'ŏl as his Ministers of the Left and Right. When Kiltong had honored each of his other generals with appropriate rank and station, the full court convened to offer him congratulations and pray for his long reign.

The new king had reigned only three years but the mountains were clear of bandits and no man touched even a valuable left by the wayside; it was a nation of great peace. One day the king called in Po Lung and said, "I have a memorial here I wish to send to the king of Korea, which I must ask that you, my minister, spare no effort to deliver." In addition to the memorial, he also sent along a letter to his family.

Upon arriving in Korea, Po Lung first presented Kiltong's memorial to the king, who was greatly pleased to see it and praised its author, saying, "Hong Kiltong is indeed a man of splendid talents."

The king, furthermore, issued a warrant appointing Hong In-hyŏng a Royal Emissary. In-hyŏng made formal expression of his gratitude and returned home to relate these happenings to his mother. She, on her part, made clear her intention to join him on the return to Lü-tao, and In-hyŏng had no choice but to set out again with her.

After some days they finally reached Lü-tao, where the king came out to meet them and, ceremonial incense tables set before him, received the royal message. This accomplished, the king, rejoicing in the reunion with In-hyŏng and his stepmother, joined them in a visit to the old minister's grave and then spread out a grand feast that brought pleasure to all.

Not many days later, Kiltong's stepmother, Lady Yu, suddenly took ill and expired; she was buried together with her husband in the same tomb. In-hyŏng begged leave of the king to return to Korea and report to the throne. His Majesty, hearing of the mother's death, expressed his condolences.

The story goes on: When the king of Lü-tao had completed the three prescribed annual mournings, the Queen Dowager, Ch'unsŏm, passed away and was laid to rest in the royal tombs. Three mournings, once a year, were again observed.

Of the three sons and two daughters born to the king, the first and second sons were by Queen Po; the third son and the two daughters were by Queen Chao. He designated his first son, Hyŏn, as crown prince and enfeoffed all the others as princes and princesses.

The king had reigned thirty years when he suddenly fell ill and died at the age of seventy-two. His queens soon followed him and were laid to rest in the royal tombs. Thereupon, the crown prince ascended the throne and great peace reigned for successive generations on end.

TRANSLATED BY MARSHALL R. PIHL

POETRY IN CHINESE, I

Great Master Hambŏ (1367–1433)

RICE COOKED WITH PINE BARK

Clutching the clouds, astride the boulders,
    you grow old in the green hills.
When leaves flutter down from every tree,
    you alone brave the cold.
Ground into powder
    and matching human taste,
You make us learn
    The intent of pure cold.

Ŏ Pyŏn-gap (1380–1434)

WRITTEN ON THE WALL OF MY HOUSE

I return to my resting place,
A poor hut with one small room.
In rain and wind, my brothers chat,
Morning and evening, I see my parents.
Sound of two rapids by the gate,
A tower stands surrounded by mountains.
There is only loyalty between sovereign and subject;
May Milord not blame me for leaving him.

Ŏ Se-gyŏm (1430–1500)

CHRYSANTHEMUM

Chrysanthemum,
Chrysanthemum.
Your elder brother is the pine,
Your younger brother, the bamboo.
You hold the evening dew,
Receive the morning sun.
How beautiful and brilliant,
How fragrant and elegant!
Frost-laden blossoms glisten at night,
Rain-soaked leaves are like morning jade.
Out through the three paths,[1] I gaze at the southern hill.
Walking along a lake, I trace the sweet valley.[2]
Your sweetness and fragrance can stop old age.[3]
Your retiring nature is a cure to the frivolous.
Your fragrant undying soul retains your spirit.
Your color and form hold to the original self.[4]

Kim Chong-jik (1431–1492)

ON A PARROT PRESENTED BY THE LIU-CH'IU ENVOY

A single rare bird came to the eastern country.
How many days and nights have you sailed with common birds?
You weep, for this is not your home;
You are dumb as if imitating a foolish girl.
You love your emerald body in the mirror,
Your violet toes cannot fly from the jade lock.
How can you be a nine-hued phoenix from Cinnabar Cave
Which is silent but still betokens peace?

1. T'ao Ch'ien, "The Return."
2. *Pao-p'u Tzu:* "In the mountain of Li-hsien in Nan-yang, there is a sweet valley river."
3. T'ao Ch'ien, "In Double Ninth, in Retirement," 11.
4. Four lines omitted.

Kim Hŭn (1448–1492)

ON MY TRIP TO TSUSHIMA

Across the sea lies a different sky,
Around the island villages cluster.
The people are mostly fishermen,
Half of them saltmakers.
Even children wear swords,
The women know how to scull a boat.
Thatch is used in place of tiles;
Bamboo is split to make bows and arrows.
Crabs cling to the bamboo fences,
The stony fields grow meager grain.
With arrowroot they prepare broth,
Chicken feathers decorate their quivers.
Oysters and clams supplement their grains,
And the people trade with pepper and tea.
They burn maggots to cure illness
And heat bones to divine the wind and the rain.
They worship the Buddha with abundant offerings;
Their temples are a sanctuary for fleeing criminals.
They remove their shoes to show respect,
But eat at the same table with their fathers.
Their topknots are like mallets,
Their teeth, mostly blackened.
Hands clasped, they incline their heads
But an angry look betrays their fierceness.
Violent and fearless, they easily kill and plunder.
They start a sentence with *monono*
And shout *ya-ya* in a match.
At parties they laugh at strange words.
I am surprised by many dishes, quaintly prepared—
Oranges and citron served with drinks,
From the sea, chopped shark and crocodiles.
Talking, they twitter like birds,
Singing, they croak like frogs.
From behind a colorful curtain they emerge wearing masks,
They dance with glittering swords around them.
Our host shows unusual affection,

His guests are merry and joking.
A distant voyage is like chewing sugar cane,
Sweetness mixed with bitterness.
Return, soon I shall return to my home—
Though beautiful, this is not my land.

Ŏ Mu-jŏk (late fifteenth century)

UPON SEEING SOMEONE FELLING PLUM TREES

The world lacks true gentlemen,
Officials who enforce harsh laws are harmful as snakes and tigers.
Their cruelty extends to brooding hens,
Their harshness to young hornless rams.
When the people's bellies are full with rice,
Officials' mouths water and their anger stirs.
When the people are warm in fur coats,
Officials would seize their arms and peel off their skins.
Even if I burn incense for the spirits of the starved in the wilderness,
And scatter flowers over the bones of the fleeing people,
How can I express my sorrow
When my heart aches so?
Farmers, lacking common sense,
Humiliate trees with the axe.
You, trees, have suffered winds and the moon,
Who will summon your broken souls?

Linked Verse

Five young scholars at the Hall of Worthies—Sŏng Sam-mun (1418–1456), Yi Kae (1417–1456), Shin Suk-chu (1417–1475), Pak P'aeng-nyŏn (1417–1456), and Yi Sŏk-hyŏng (1415–1477)—were granted a leave of absence to study at the Chin'gwan monastery on Mount Samgak, where they composed a number of linked verses.

UPON LISTENING TO THE FLUTE (1442)

Where does it come from, the sound of a flute,
At midnight on a blue-green peak?   *Sŏng Sam-mun*

Shaking the moonlight, it rings high,
Borne by the wind, it carries far.   *Yi Kae*

Clear and smooth like a warbler's song,
The floating melody rolls downhill.   *Shin Suk-chu*

I listen—a sad melody stirs my heart,
I concentrate—it dispels my gloom.   *Pak P'aeng-nyŏn*

Always, ever, a lover looks in the mirror,
And amid vibrant silence, night deepens in the hills.

                   Yi Sŏk-hyŏng

Splitting a stone, limpid notes are stout,
"Plucking a Willow Branch" breaks a lover's heart.[1]

                   Sŏng Sam-mun

Clear and muddy notes come in order,
The *kung* and *shang* modes unmixed.[2]   *Yi Kae*

How wonderful, notes drawn out and released,
How pleasant, reaping waves of sound.   *Shin Suk-chu*

---

1. A "Music Bureau" song accompanied by a horizontal flute; so is "Plum Blossoms Fall," nine lines later.
2. The first two notes of the pentatonic scale.

Long since I played it seated on my bed.
Where is the zestful player leaning against the tower?

Pak P'aeng-nyŏn

Marvelous melodies recall Ts'ai Yen,
Who remembers Juan Chi's clear whistle?

Yi Sŏk-hyŏng

"Plum Blossoms Fall" in the garden,
Fishes and dragons fight in the deep sea.

Sŏng Sam-mun

First, the drawn-out melody startled me,
Now I rejoice in the clear, sweet rhythm.

Yi Kae

How can only a reed whistle in Lung
Make the Tartar traders flee, homesick?

Shin Suk-chu

On Mount Kou-shih a phoenix calls limpidly,
In the deep pool a dragon hums and dances.

Pak P'aeng-nyŏn

A wanderer is struck homesick over the pass,
A widow pines in her room.

Yi Sŏk-hyŏng

Floating, floating, the music turns sad,
Long, long, my thought is disquieted.

Sŏng Sam-mun

We were all ears at the first notes,
But can't grasp the dying sounds.

Yi Kae

A startled wind rolls away the border sands,
Cold snow drives through Ch'in park.

Shin Suk-chu

I don't tire of your music,
Should I rise and dance to your tune?

Pak P'aeng-nyŏn

Who is that master flautist,
His creative talent is all his own.

Yi Sŏk-hyŏng

Prince Ch'iao is really not dead,
Has Huan I returned from the underworld?

Sŏng Sam-mun

His solo—a whoop of a single crane,
In unison—a thousand ox-drawn carriages.   *Yi Kae*

Choking, choking, now a tearful complaint,
Murmuring, murmuring, now a tender whisper.   *Shin Suk-chu*

I beg you, flute master,
Hide your art, don't spoil it.   *Yi Sŏk-hyŏng*

Confucius heard Shao and lost his taste for meat;
I too forget to take my meal.   *Pak P'aeng-nyŏn*

I cannot help cherishing your art,
I set forth my deep love for you!   *Sŏng Sam-mun*

Hwang Chin-i (c. 1506–1544)

TAKING LEAVE OF MINISTER SO SE-YANG

In the moonlit garden, paulownia leaves fall;
In the frost, wild chrysanthemums wither.
The tower is tall as the sky,
Drunk, we keep on draining our cups.
Flowing water is cold as the lute;
Plum fragrance seeps into my flute.
Tomorrow, after we have parted,
Our love will be green waves unending.

Yi Hyang-gŭm (1513–1550)

TO A DRUNKEN GUEST

The drunken guest clings to my sleeve,
My gauze sleeve gets torn as I shake him off.
I don't mind the torn blouse,
I only fear the end of our love.

Great Master Sŏsan (1522–1604)

ON THE SOUTHERN SEA

The leaping sea blows up silver hills,
When winds lull, jade chips roll.
My skiff is a house atop heaven;
Sitting, I can gather stars and the moon.

THE DOZING MONK

In the deep recess a rain of pink petals,
The long bamboo emit emerald mists.
Frozen white clouds lodge on the peak,
A monk dozes beside a blue crane.

IN PRAISE OF THE PORTRAIT
OF MY FORMER MASTER

Your white robes are made of white clouds,
Your blue pupils, strips of water.
Your stomach cradles precious gems,
Your heavenly light pierces the Big Dipper.

Great Master Chŏnggwan (1533–1609)

AT THE MOMENT OF MY DEATH

The three-foot-long sword that can split a feather
I've hidden in the Great Dipper.
In the great void no trace of clouds,
Now you see its sharp point!

Sŏng Hon (1535–1598)

BY CHANCE

Forty years I've lived in the green hills;
Who will pick a fight with me?
I sit alone in a hut with the spring breeze—
How idle laughing flowers and dozing willows!

Yi I (1536–1584)

IN THE MOUNTAIN

Picking herbs I lost the trail,
Autumn leaves bury a thousand peaks.
A monk returns with a bucket of water,
At the grove's end steams the boiling tea.

Yu Yŏng-gil (1538–1601)

A GIRL POUNDING GRAIN

Up and down, how lightly moves your slender arm,
Snowy skin gleams through the gauze sleeve.
You pounded magic pills on the moon:
Now in exile perfect your art on earth.

Yi Sun-sin (1545–1598)

IN THE CHINHAE CAMP

By the sea the autumn sun sinks;
Startled by cold, the geese pitch a camp.
Anxious, I toss and turn—
Only a dawn moon on my bow and sword.

Im Che (1559–1587)

A WOMAN'S SORROW

A beautiful girl, fifteen years old,
Too shy to speak, sends her lover away.
Back home, she shuts the double gate
And sobs before the pear blossoms.

Yu Mong-in (1559–1623)

A POOR WOMAN

A poor woman at a shuttle, tears on her cheeks,
Weaves winter cloth for her husband.
Come morning, she tears a strip for a tax officer;
No sooner one leaves than another comes.

Great Master Soyo (1562–1649)

WONDROUS TRUTH

Flowers smile at rain on the steps,
Winds outside the rail make the pines sing.
Why do you seek wondrous truth?
There is a wisdom that pervades nature.

Hŏ Nansŏrhŏn (1563–1589)

POOR WOMAN

Till her fingers are stiff with cold,
She cuts the cloth with scissors
To make a dress for a girl to be married:
But every year she keeps to her empty room.

Kwŏn P'il (1569–1612)

UPON READING TU FU'S POETRY

The literary art of Tu Fu is
    honored throughout the world.
Every time I open his works and read
    I feel a great lift in spirits.
It's a divine wind murmuring,
    born in deep ravines,
Heavenly music pealing out,
    sounded by an ancient bell,
A speeding hawfinch crossing an azure sky
    after clouds have cleared,
A herd of dragons sporting in a blue sea
    when the moon is bright.
As before, setting out on a road
    to mountains where an immortal dwells,
I savor a thousand peaks
    and then ten thousand more!

TRANSLATED BY RICHARD J. LYNN

Cho Hwi (fl. 1568–1608)

IN PEKING TO A WOMAN WITH A VEIL

Shy, you veil your face on the street—
Clear moonlight through faint clouds.
Your slender waist, tightly bound, is a handspan.
Your new gauze skirt, a pomegranate color.

Yi Tal (fl. 1568–1608)

MOUNTAIN TEMPLE

A temple buried in white clouds—
But monks do not sweep them away.
A guest comes, the gate opens;
In every valley, yellow pine pollen.

Great Master Chunggwan (fl. 1590)

UPON READING CHUANG TZU

Give me wings, I'll reach to high heaven,
With scales, I can dive into a deep pool.
How silly, you dreamer within a dream,
Not knowing your body's in a melting furnace.

LATER YI ROMANCE

A Dream of Nine Clouds, written in Chinese and in Korean, is a seventeenth-century romance by Kim Man-jung (1637–1692), who wrote it to console his mother at the time of his exile. Set in ninth-century T'ang China, the story belongs to a tradition of stories bearing in their titles the word "dream," suggesting that even at its best life is no more than a dream.

The translator comments: "The prologue tells how a Buddhist monk came to transmigrate into a brilliant young Confucian scholar, and the epilogue tells how he became a monk again. The bulk of the story is the 'dream' of the successful career of his Confucian manifestation. The dream itself falls into two halves; in the first the hero meets eight women, in the second he marries them. He meets the women in different places, and the changes of locality, with a different woman as the center of interest in each place, give the first half a lively variety. The second half of the dream is an account of happiness and honor after the winning of glory and success. In contrast to the first half, there is little movement, but much conversation. Such psychological interest as the characters evoke is developed in this section, where the personalities of the women become more distinct.

"The fact that the book is good entertainment does not detract from its transcendental values, but transforms what might have been a philosophical parable into a genuine work of creative literature."

A Dream of Nine Clouds shares a number of features common to the romance; for example, the themes of descent and ascent, the vision of life as a quest, cases of coincidence, elements of fantasy and adventure, characterization by synecdoche, episodic structure, and a high degree of stylization and structural patterning. Our extracts give the prologue and epilogue of the story.

Kim Man-jung (1637–1692)

A DREAM OF NINE CLOUDS

[from *Kuun mong*]

HSING-CHEN BECOMES SHAO-YU

The five sacred mountains of China are Mount T'ai in the east, Mount Hua in the west, Mount Heng in the south, another Mount Heng in the north, and Mount Sung in the center. Mount Heng in the south is the highest of them. It has Mount Chiu-i to its south, Tung-t'ing Lake to its north, and the Hsiao and Hsiang rivers flow round it. Its five peaks, Chu-yung the Fire Spirit, Tzu-kai the Violet Baldachin, T'ien-chu the Pillars of Heaven, Shih-lin the Rock Granary, and Lien-hua the Lotus Peak, have their tops hidden in the clouds and wreaths of mist around their shoulders; on a hazy day it is impossible to make out their shapes.

In ancient times, the great Yü, after he had controlled the floods, climbed this mountain and set up a memorial stone on which he recorded his feats; the superb characters are still clear and easy to read. In the time of Chin, Lady Wei became a Taoist adept and by divine appointment came to live on this mountain with a troop of fairy boys and girls; that is why she is called Lady Wei of the Southern Peak. Here there is not space enough to tell of all the wonderful things that happened on the mountain.

In the time of the T'ang dynasty, an old monk from India came to China, took a liking to the Lotus Peak in the Mount Heng range and built a monastery for his five or six hundred disciples, to whom he expounded from his copy of the *Diamond Sūtra*. He was the venerable Liu-ju, known as the Great Master Liu-kuan. He taught the people and dispersed evil spirits; men said that a living Buddha had come to live on the earth.

Among his hundreds of disciples some thirty or more were advanced adepts. The youngest of them was called Hsing-chen. His complexion was pure as driven snow and his soul was as limpid as a stream in autumn. He was barely twenty years old, but he had mastered all the scriptures, and Liu-kuan loved him so much for his grace and wisdom that he intended him as his successor.

When Liu-kuan expounded the dharma to his disciples, the Dragon King from Tung-t'ing Lake used to transform himself into an old man dressed in white and sat in the lecture hall to hear the sermons. One day Liu-kuan said to his pupils: "I am growing old and feeble. I have not left the monastery gates for over ten years. I am no longer able to go out. Will one of you volunteer to go to the Dragon King's water palace and return his compliment in my behalf?"

Hsing-chen at once asked if he might be allowed to go. Liu-kuan was delighted and sent him off with his orders. He was dressed in a heavy robe and carried an official staff with six jangling rings attached to the top. Thus with high spirits he made his way toward Tung-t'ing.

Just after Hsing-chen had set out, the gatekeeper of the monastery came to the master and told him that the Lady Wei had sent eight of her fairy maidens, who were waiting outside the gate. He ordered them to be admitted. They presented themselves in due order where he was sitting and circled him three times, scattering fairy flowers, before they delivered Lady Wei's message:

"Sir, you live on the west side of the mountain and I live on the east. We are near neighbors, but I am so busy that I have never once had the opportunity to attend the monastery and hear your teaching. So I am sending some of my maids to greet you with gifts of celestial flowers and fairy fruit, and gems and silk brocade as tokens of my respect and devotion."

Then each girl knelt down and raised the gifts of flowers and fruit, gems and silks high over her head as she presented them to the old man. He handed them to his disciples, who set them out as offerings before the image of Buddha in the monastery.

Liu-kuan joined his hands in reverent greeting and said: "What has an old monk like me done to merit the favors of an immortal?" Then he entertained the girls appropriately and dismissed them.

They took their leave of him and left. Outside the monastery gate they began to talk among themselves about how the entire mountain had originally been their domain, but since Liu-kuan had established his monastery with its enclosure, there were parts where they could not go freely. It was a long time since they had had a chance to see the Lotus Peak. "Now that our lady has sent us here on this lovely spring day and it is still quite early, let's go to the top of the peak and loosen our robes, wash our ribbons in the waterfall and make up a few poems. Then when we return home to the palace we can tell our companions all about it!"

Joining hands, they strolled up to the ridge to see the source of the waterfall. Then they followed the watercourse down as far as the stone bridge, where they decided to rest for a while.

It was spring. The valley was filled with all kinds of flowers, surrounding them like a pink mist. A hundred species of birds sang as in an orchestra of pipes and piccolos. The vernal air was intoxicating. The eight girls sat on the bridge and looked down into the water. Streams from several ravines met there to form a wide pool under the bridge. It was clear as a polished mirror and their beautiful dark eyebrows and crimson dresses were reflected there like paintings from a master's hand. They smiled at their reflections and gaily chatted together with no thought of returning home and did not notice when the sun began to slip behind the hills.

At the same time, Hsing-chen had reached Tung-t'ing Lake and passed through the waves to the Crystalline Palace. The Dragon King had heard that a messenger was on his way from Liu-kuan and he appeared outside the palace gate with his entire retinue of courtiers to meet him. After they had gone into the palace, the Dragon King sat on his throne and Hsing-chen kowtowed before him and presented his master's message. The Dragon King replied graciously and ordered a banquet. Hsing-chen observed that the food, all made from fantastic delicacies, was entirely unlike what men eat. The king himself offered a cup, but Hsing-chen declined it: "Wine inflames the mind. It is a strict law of Buddha that monks should not drink it. Please do not force me to break a vow."

But the Dragon King replied: "Of course I know that wine is one of the five things that Buddha forbids; but my wine is quite different from the wine made by men. It neither arouses the passions nor befuddles the mind. Please do not refuse it."

Hsing-chen was not able to hold out against this, and he drained three cups before he took leave of the Dragon King and left the palace, riding on the wind to the Lotus Peak. When he came down at the foot of the peak his face was burning and he began to feel dizzy from the wine. He thought to himself: "If Liu-kuan sees me in this condition there will be no end to his anger."

So he went to the stream, took off his robe and laid it on the white sand while he swirled his hands in the water and bathed his flaming face. Suddenly a strange fragrance was carried to him on the breeze. It was like neither incense nor flowers. It entered his mind and intoxicated his spirit, like something he had never before imagined. He thought: "What wonderful flowers have bloomed upstream? Their scent has come down with the current. I must go and see what they are."

He put on his robe again, arranged it neatly, and then began to walk up the river. So it happened that the eight fairies sitting on the bridge came face to face with Hsing-chen. He at once dropped his staff, joined his hands and bowed deeply: "Gracious ladies, I beg your pardon. I am a disciple of the master Liu-kuan of Lotus Peak, and I have just been on an errand for him. Now I am on my way back. This bridge where you are sitting is very narrow and there is not room for a man to pass by if ladies are sitting there. Will you kindly step down for a moment and allow me to cross over?"

The fairies replied: "We are attendants of Lady Wei, and we are just on our way back from delivering a message to your master, Liu-kuan. We stopped here to rest for a little while. The *Book of Rites* says that men should pass on the left and women on the right, but this bridge is extremely narrow. Since we were here before you came, we suggest you find another path."

Hsing-chen said: "The stream is deep and there is no other path. Where else do you suggest I should go?"

The fairies said: "Bodhidharma is supposed to have crossed the sea on a reed. If you have really studied with Liu-kuan, you must have great powers too. Why do you dispute the right of way with a group of girls, instead of passing over this little stream?"

Hsing-chen laughed. "I see what you are after. You want me to pay some sort of toll. A poor monk has no money, but I have eight pearls and I will offer you those as a payment."

He snapped off a branch of peach blossoms and threw it to the girls. Eight flowers fell to the ground and immediately became sparkling fragrant jewels. The eight fairies each picked up one of the jewels, looked at Hsing-chen and, laughing gaily, at once rose in the air and rode away on the wind. Hsing-chen stood for a long while on the bridge looking in all directions, but he could not see where they had gone, and soon the shimmering mists had dispersed and the fragrance had faded away.

Hsing-chen was deeply troubled and could not quieten his soul. He returned and told Liu-kuan what the Dragon King had said. Liu-kuan upbraided him for taking so long to get back. Hsing-chen said: "The Dragon King detained me with his kindness and I could not refuse and get away. It made me late in leaving." Liu-kuan asked no more questions, but sent him away to rest.

Hsing-chen went to his cell. As he sat alone in the twilight, the voices of the eight fairies kept sounding in his ears and their beautiful forms kept appearing before his eyes as though they were there in the room with him. However hard he tried, he could not collect his thoughts as he sat distractedly trying to meditate. He thought: "If a man studies the Confucian classics while he is young and then serves the country as a general or a minister of state, he gets to wear a brocade coat and hang a seal of office on his jade girdle; he sees lovely things and hears wonderful things, he takes pleasure in beauty and leaves an honorable name for his descendants. That is the way for a man worthy of his name. We poor Buddhist monks have only a bowl for rice and a cup for water, volumes of scriptures and a hundred and eight beads to hang round our necks. All we can do is expound doctrine. It may be holy and profound, but it is terribly lonely. Suppose I do master all the doctrines of the Great Vehicle and succeed to the chair here on the Lotus Peak to carry on Liu-kuan's teaching, once my spirit and body have been parted on the funeral pyre, who will know that Hsing-chen ever existed?"

His troubled mind kept sleep at bay until deep into the night. If he closed his eyes he saw the eight fairies; if he opened them the girls would disappear without trace.

Then he pulled himself together: "The way of Buddha for purifying the heart is the highest course in life. I have been a monk for ten years and have avoided even the smallest fault. These deceitful thoughts will do my progress irreparable damage."

He burned some sandalwood, composed himself on his prayer-mat, and was concentrating quietly on the Thousand Buddhas while moving the beads of the rosary round his neck when one of the boys called from outside: "Have you gone to bed, brother? The master wants to see you."

Hsing-chen was alarmed and thought: "It must be something serious for him to call me at this time of night." He went with the boy to the lecture hall.

Liu-kuan had gathered all his disciples. He was sitting on the lotus seat, looking fearful and solemn. The lanterns and candles filled the hall with light. He rebuked Hsing-chen harshly: "Hsing-chen! Do you understand your sin?"

Hsing-chen, frightened, knelt at the foot of the dais and answered: "I have served you for more than ten years and I have never willingly disobeyed you. Now that you accuse me, I do not wish to hide anything from you, but truly I do not know what I have done wrong."

Liu-kuan grew angrier: "A monk has three things to study: his body, his speech, and his will. You went to the Dragon Palace and drank wine. That was sin enough. On the way back you lingered at the stone bridge and dallied in idle chatter with eight girls, then threw flowers at them and toyed with jewels. After that, when you got home you dwelt on their beauty and thought about worldly riches and honor and mentally rejected the pure way of life of a monk. You have sinned in all three respects at once. You cannot stay here now."

Hsing-chen wept and beat his head and begged: "Master! I have sinned, I know. But I drank wine in the Dragon Palace because I could not refuse my host's insistence. I talked with the fairies in the bridge because I had to ask them to get out of the way. I was tempted in my cell, but I repented and controlled myself. I have no other sins! If I have committed other sins, please instruct me and set me right. Why do you drive me away so cruelly and give me no chance to correct myself? I left my parents when I was only twelve years old to come to you and be a monk, and you loved me like your son. I respect and serve you as my father. The relation between teacher and disciple is sacred. Where can I go if I leave the Lotus Peak?"

Liu-kuan said: "I am making you go because you want to go. Why should I send you away if you wanted to stay? You say 'Where shall I go?' You must go where you wish to go."

Then he shouted: "Mighty Ones!" Immediately the commander of the yellow-turbaned constables of the underworld appeared and bowed to receive his orders. Liu-kuan said to him: "Arrest this sinner, take him to the underworld and hand him over to Lord Yama!"

When Hsing-chen heard this he broke out in a sweat of terror. Tears streamed from him as he put his head to the floor and implored: "Father, father! Hear me, please! When the holy Ananda slept with a prostitute, Śākyamuni did not condemn him, but admonished him. I sinned through carelessness, but I did not go so far as Ananda. Why are you sending me to hell?"

Liu-kuan spoke severely: "Although the holy Ananda slept with a prostitute, his mind was never shaken; you set eyes on female beauty only once and completely lose your heart. You cannot escape the suffering of transmigration."

Hsing-chen still wept, and did not want to move. Liu-kuan spoke to comfort him: "If your mind is not purified, even though you stay in a mountain monastery, you will never attain perfection. But if you remain faithful to the way of Buddha, even though you are buried deep in the dust of the world, you will surely come back one day. If ever you want to come, I will fetch you back. Go now, and trust me."

Hsing-chen then bowed to the image of Buddha, took leave of his master and brethren, and went with the constables to the underworld, past the gate and then the terrace of "Looking Back in Regret," till they reached the city walls of the underworld, where the sentries asked why they had come. The constables answered: "We have brought a sinner according to the orders given by Master Liu-kuan."

The demon soldiers opened the gates to let them in, and they went to the audience chamber where the reason for Hsing-chen's arrival was announced. Yama dismissed the constables and spoke to him: "Although you lived on Lotus Peak, your name was already written in the roster on the shrine before King Ksitigarbha, Guardian of Earth and Deliverer from Hell. I understood from this that you had already achieved perfection and would win grace and salvation for many souls. What is the reason you have come here?"

Hsing-chen was bitterly ashamed and hesitated before he replied: "I have sinned against my teacher by letting myself be misled by the South Peak fairies when I met them on the road, so I have been sent here. Do as you must."

Yama sent some of his attendants to Ksitigarbha with the message: "Master Liu-kuan of the Lotus Peak has sent his disciple Hsing-chen to the underworld for punishment, but he is not like other culprits. What should I do with him?"

The Bodhisattva replied: "A man seeking perfection must find his own way. Why do you ask me?"

But Yama was intent on judging the matter properly. At that moment, however, two demon soldiers came in and said: "The yellow-turbaned constables have come again at Liu-kuan's order, with eight fairies under arrest."

Hsing-chen was amazed at this news. Then he heard Yama say: "Bring them in!"

The constables brought the eight women in, and Yama made

them kneel before he asked: "Fairies of South Peak, indeed! You fairies have a boundless world of ineffable delights. How is it that you have come here?"

The fairies answered shamefacedly: "Lady Wei sent us to Master Liu-kuan with a message and on the way back we stopped to talk with the young novice Hsing-chen at the stone bridge. This made the master very angry. He said we had defiled Buddha's demesne, and sent a letter to Lady Wei telling her to send us to your Majesty. We implore you to be compassionate and send us to a pleasant place to live."

Lord Yama called nine messengers to stand before him and commanded them: "Take each of these nine people and lead them back to the land of the living."

Yama had barely finished speaking when a great wind suddenly arose in front of the palace and swept the nine people into the air and whirled them away to different corners of space. Hsing-chen was carried hither and thither on the wind behind his messenger until he touched down on firm ground. The noise of the wind died down and both his feet were steady. When he had collected his wits and looked about, he found he was closed in by thickly wooded mountains with clear streams flowing peacefully by. Here and there between the trees he caught glimpses of bamboo fences and thatched roofs, about ten houses altogether. The messenger made him wait outside one of the houses while he himself went in. While waiting, Hsing-chen heard someone in the next-door house say: "The wife of the hermit Yang is pregnant. She's over fifty years old. It's amazing! It's past her time, but I haven't heard the baby crying. I'm worried."

Hsing-chen realized he was to be born again in Yang's house and thought to himself: "I am going to be born into the world again. I have no body now, only a spirit. My flesh and bones have been cremated on the Lotus Peak, where I left them. I was too young to have any disciples and so there will be no one to keep my relics together."

He fell to thinking like this in considerable distress when the messenger came out and beckoned him to follow, saying: "This is the township of Hsiu-chou in the province of Huai-nan of the empire of T'ang. This house is the home of the hermit Yang. He will be your father. His wife's surname is Liu, and she is to be your mother. You were destined from your previous life to be the son of this family, so go in quickly and do not lose this good opportunity."

Hsing-chen went in and saw the hermit, wearing a kerchief of coarse hemp and a rough coat, seated on the wooden floor by a brazier stirring a medicinal concoction. The smell of it filled the house. The woman's moans could be heard coming quietly from the inner room. The messenger urged him to go into the room, but Hsing-chen hesitated, so the messenger pushed him from behind. Hsing-chen fell over and lost consciousness, calling out for help as he fainted. The sound stuck in his throat and would not come out as words: it was only the crying of a new-born babe. The midwife said: "It cries so loud, it must be a boy."

The hermit Yang was still stirring the medicine for his wife when he heard the baby cry. With mingled alarm and joy he hurried into the room, to find that she had already given birth to a son. Overcome with happiness he bathed the child in scented water, put it to rest and then attended to its mother. When Hsing-chen cried because he was hungry, they gave him milk, and as soon as his stomach was full he stopped wailing.

While he was very tiny he still carried traces of memory about the Lotus Peak in his mind, but as he grew and came to love his parents, he completely forgot all about his previous life. The hermit saw that his son had fine bones, and one day, stroking the child's forehead, he said to his wife: "This child is a heavenly being come to live among men." So he named him Shao-yu, which means "brief sojourner," and gave him Ch'ien-li, which means "a thousand leagues," for his literary name.

They loved him dearly and by the time he was ten years old his face was as pretty as a piece of jade, his eyes shone like stars, his character was gentle and strong and he was wonderfully intelligent. He was a model child, destined to become a great man.

The hermit said to his wife: "I was not originally a man of this world, but because I was joined to you by our karma, I have stayed a long time in this world of dust. A long long time ago I had a letter from my friends, the immortals of Mount P'eng-lai, asking me to go to them, but I could not go and leave you alone. Now that heaven has helped us and given you a brilliant son of more than ordinary ability, you have someone else to look after you. You will have riches and honor in your old age. So do not grieve when I leave you."

One day a group of immortals came to the house, some riding white deer, some on blue cranes. Then they departed toward the deep mountain valleys. The hermit Yang made a sign with his hand toward the sky, to summon a white crane which he mounted, and flew happily away. He had gone before his wife could utter a sound.

She and her son grieved beyond words. The hermit occasionally sent a letter through the air, but he never again returned to his home.

SHAO-YU BECOMES HSING-CHEN

So several years passed by. The sixteenth day of the eighth month was Shao-yu's birthday, and his family prepared a banquet in his honor. It lasted more than ten days. The business and bustle beggared description; when it was over everyone returned to his own home and peace reigned again.

Soon the ninth month came, the first buds of the chrysanthemums began to open, and the dogwood berries appeared. Autumn was in full splendor. To the west of Ts'ui-wei Palace there was a high peak; from the top of the pavilion a two-hundred-mile stretch of the Ch'in River could be seen like the palm of one's hand. Shao-yu particularly liked this view. On this occasion he had gone up there with the two princesses and the six concubines. Each had stuck a spray of chrysanthemums in her hair; they drank wine together as they enjoyed the autumn landscape. Gradually the setting sun made the shadows run down the mountain until they reached the wide plain. The brilliant colors of autumn were like a scroll painting unrolled. Shao-yu took out his jade flute and played a plaintive tune, as though composed of sighs and yearnings, of tears and reproaches. The women were all overcome with sadness; they did not like it. The two princesses said: "You have attained every honor, you have enjoyed riches for a long time, and everyone acknowledges it. Such a thing has hardly been seen before. Now in this lovely autumn weather, with a beautiful landscape before you, chrysanthemum petals floating in the cup, surrounded by beautiful women—what man could be happier? Yet the tune of your flute is so melancholy that it makes us all weep. You never played like this before; what is the matter?"

Shao-yu put the flute down, moved over to where they were and sat down by the balustrade of the pavilion. He pointed through the moonlight and said: "Look over there to the north. In the midst of the flat plain stands a single rugged peak. You can just see in the fading evening light where the ruined E-p'ang Palace, the vast palace of the first emperor of the Ch'in, stands among the weeds. Now look over to the west. A mournful wind stirs the woods where the mountain mist hides Mao-ling, the tomb of Emperor Wu of the Han. Over to the east, a whitewashed wall shines on the green hills, where a red-tiled roof stands out against the sky and the bright moon comes and goes between the clouds. Nobody leans now on the jade balustrade, because that is the Hua-ch'ing Palace where Emperor Hsüan-tsung dallied with his ill-fated concubine, the famous Precious Consort Yang. How sad: these three kings were all men of great renown in their time, but where are they now?

"I was a poor young scholar from the land of Ch'u but received the imperial favor and rose to the highest rank of the empire. I have married you all, and we have lived together in peace and harmony until our old age, and our affection continues to increase. How could this have been were it not a matter of karma fixed from our previous existence? After we have died, these lofty terraces will crumble and the lotus pools will silt up. The palace where we sang and danced today will be overgrown with weeds and wrapped in cold mists. Boys cutting wood and cowherds will sing sad songs, saying: 'This is where the Grand Preceptor Yang sported with his wives and concubines. All his honors and pleasures, all his wealth and elegance, all the pretty faces of his women have gone, have gone forever.' Those woodcutters and cowherds will look on the place where we have played just as I look on the palaces and tombs of the three emperors. Think of it—man's life is no more than a moment of time.

"There are three ways on earth: the way of Confucius, the way of the Buddha, and the way of the Taoists. Buddhism is the best of the three. Confucianism explains the working of nature, exalts achievement, and is concerned with passing on names to posterity. Taoism is close to meaninglessness, and even though it has many devotees, there is no proof of its truth. Think of the first emperor of the Ch'in and Emperor Wu of the Han and Emperor Hsüan-tsung. What happened to them is enough to make us understand. Since I gave up office, every night I have dreamed that I was bowing before the Buddha. This is clearly a matter of karma. I must do like Chang Liang, who followed the immortal Master of the Red Pine to the abode of the blessed. I must go to seek the Merciful Bodhisattva beyond the Southern Sea. I must ascend Mount Wu-t'ai and meet Mañjuśrī. I must put off the trammels of worldly life and obtain the way that has no birth or death. But because this means I must now say farewell to all of you, with whom I have spent such long and happy years, I feel sad. My sadness showed in my tune on the flute."

The women were deeply moved and said: "If you feel like this in the midst of your prosperity, it must be due to heavenly inspiration. We shall retire to our inner quarters and pray before the Buddha night and morning while waiting for your return. We shall pray that you will meet a great teacher and generous friends, so that you can attain the way, and return to teach it to us.''

Shao-yu, greatly delighted, said: "Since we are all agreed, there is nothing to worry about. I must leave tomorrow, so let us be merry tonight.''

They all said: "We shall each offer you a farewell cup.''

The cups were brought, and they were about to fill them when suddenly the sound of a staff striking the stone pavement was heard. Greatly surprised, they wondered who had come up there, when suddenly an old monk with long white eyebrows and eyes as clear as the waves of the sea, a man of strange bearing, stepped onto the terrace and greeted Shao-yu: "An old monk craves audience.''

Shao-yu realized that this was no ordinary person, so he rose quickly and replied: "Where have you come from?''

The old man smiled as he answered: "Don't you remember an old friend? I have heard that people in high rank have short memories; it seems to be true.''

Shao-yu looked more closely and thought he knew who it was, but was not quite sure. Suddenly it came to him; glancing at Po Ling-p'o, the daughter of the Dragon King, he said to the old monk again: "After I had defeated the Tibetans, I had a dream in which I went to the banquet of the Dragon King of Tung-t'ing, and on the way back I climbed Mount Heng, where I saw an old monk lecturing on the scriptures to his disciples. Are you not that teacher whom I saw in my dream?''

The old monk clapped his hands and said with a great laugh: "Right! Right! But you only remember seeing me in your dream; you do not remember the ten years when we lived together. And they say you have such a good memory! What a scholar!''

Shao-yu was perplexed: "Before I was fourteen or fifteen years old, I never left my parents' house. At sixteen I passed the government examinations, and ever since then I have held office in the state continuously. I went east as an envoy to Yen, and west to subdue the Tibetans; otherwise I have scarcely left the capital. When could I have spent ten years with you?''

The old monk said, still laughing: "So you still have not woken from your dream.''

Shao-yu asked: "Do you know how to awaken me?"

The old monk said: "That is not difficult," and raising his metal staff he struck the stone balustrade two or three times. A white mist arose, and enfolded the whole terrace, obscuring everything from view.

After a time Shao-yu, bewildered as though he were in a drunken dream, called out: "Why don't you show me the true way, instead of playing tricks?"

He was not able to finish his question. The mist disappeared. The old monk had gone. Shao-yu looked round, but the eight women had vanished. The whole terrace and its pavilions had gone too. He was sitting in a little cell on a prayer mat. The fire in the incense burner had gone out. The setting moon was shining through the window. He looked down at himself and saw a rosary of a hundred and eight beads around his wrist. He felt his head: it was freshly shaven. He was no longer Yang the Grand Preceptor, he was once more a young monk. His mind was confused, until at last he realized that he was Hsing-chen, the novice at the Lotus Peak monastery. He remembered: "I was reprimanded by my teacher and was sent to the underworld. Then I transmigrated and became a son of the Yang family. I came to the top in the national examination, and became vice-chancellor of the Imperial Academy. I rose through various offices and finally retired. I married two princesses and was happy with them and six concubines, but it was all a dream. My teacher knew of my wrong thoughts, and made me dream this dream so that I should understand the emptiness of riches and honor and of love between the sexes."

He washed himself quickly, straightened his robe and cap and went to the main hall, where the other disciples were already assembled. The master called with a loud voice and asked: "Hsing-chen, did you enjoy the pleasures of the world?"

Hsing-chen opened his eyes and saw his master, Liu-kuan, standing sternly before him. The lad bowed his head and wept as he said: "My life was impure. No one else can be blamed for the sins I have committed. I should have suffered endless transmigrations and pains in the vain world, but you have made me understand through a dream of the night. Even in ten million kalpas I could never repay your kindness."

The master said: "You went in search of pleasures, and came back having tasted them all. What part have I played in this? And you say that the dream and the world are two separate things, which proves that you have not yet woken from the dream. Chuang Tzu dreamed he was a butterfly, and the butterfly dreamed it was Chuang Tzu: and which was real, Chuang Tzu or the butterfly, he could not tell. Now who is real, and who is a dream—Hsing-chen or Shao-yu?"

Hsing-chen replied: "I am confused. I can't tell whether the dream was not true, or the truth was not a dream. Please teach me the truth and make me understand."

The master said: "I shall teach you the doctrine of the *Diamond Sūtra* to awaken your soul, but there will shortly be some new pupils arriving and you must wait till they come."

Before he had finished speaking, the monk who kept the gate came, announcing that the eight maids of the Lady Wei had arrived. The master allowed them to come in and they at once entered and bowed before him, saying: "Although we have been attending Lady Wei, we have learned nothing and are unable to control our wayward thoughts. Our desires go after sinful things and we dream the dreams of mortality. There is no one to waken us. Since you accepted us we have been to Lady Wei's place and yesterday took our leave of her. Now we have returned and beg you to forgive our misdemeanors and enlighten us with your teaching."

The master answered: "Your desires are good, but the Buddha Dharma is deep and difficult to learn. It requires steadfast and persistent effort before it can be attained. Think carefully before you decide."

The eight girls withdrew and washed the powder from their faces and showed their determination by cutting off their clouds of black hair. Then they returned and said: "We have changed our appearance and we swear that we will be diligent in obeying you."

Liu-kuan said: "Very well. I am deeply moved that you have made up your minds."

Then he went up to the lecture seat and began to expound the sūtra. Once again the light from the Buddha's brow shone forth on the world and celestial flowers descended like sprinkling rain. And he taught them the mantra from the *Diamond Sūtra:*

> All is dharma, illusion:
> A dream, a phantasm, a bubble, a shadow,
> Evanescent as dew, transient as lightning;
> It must be seen as such.

Eventually he finished his teaching. In due time Hsing-chen and the eight nuns all awakened together to the truth of the way without birth and death. Liu-kuan, seeing the faithfulness and spiritual maturity of Hsing-chen, called a general assembly of his disciples and announced: "I came to China in order to teach the way. Now there is someone else who can hand on the dharma, and I shall return whence I came."

He took up his rosary, his wooden rice bowl, his water bottle, his ringed staff, and his volume of the *Diamond Sūtra,* handed them all to Hsing-chen and set off toward the west.

From this time onward, Hsing-chen governed the community at the Lotus Peak monastery, and taught with great distinction. Immortals and dragons, men and spirits revered him as they had revered Liu-kuan. The eight nuns followed his teaching till they all became Bodhisattvas, and all nine entered together into Paradise.

TRANSLATED BY RICHARD RUTT

SIJO, II

This section of *sijo* begins with "Calling a Boy," a poem by Cho Chon-sŏng (1553–1627), and ends with a group of anonymous poems. The master of the form was Yun Sŏn-do (1587–1671), whose lyrics are diverse in mood and method and abound in finely chiseled phrases. No Korean poet suffered vicissitudes of public life more than Yun—he spent fourteen years in exile. His seventy-seven poems comprise "Dispelling Gloom" (1618); "New Songs in the Mountains" and their sequel (1624–1645); *The Angler's Calendar* (1651), a *sijo* cycle of forty poems written at his favorite retreat, the Lotus Grotto; and "The Disappointing Journey" (1652).

Riding happily in a solitary boat on the waves of flux, the speaker in *The Angler's Calendar* assumes the ethos of the fisherman as sage, a common topic in East Asia. He has renounced the world of chaos and absurdity and taken the stance of a recluse who finds joy and contentment in communion with nature. Built on a dialectical pattern of two modes of life and two views of world and self, the fisherman's self-discovery is shown to be the result of his renunciation of the world, the obstacle to final freedom and illumination. His poems celebrate his newly discovered values by depicting a simple and innocent landscape, a mirror of the contented fisherman.

Songs of the fisherman were popular at least from the fourteenth century, and were sung by male and female singers on festive occasions. Yun Sŏn-do's success lies in his mastery of the topics and techniques of older materials of China and Korea, but it is not so much the content as the manner—his virtuosity—that qualifies him as a discoverer of the beauty of the language.

Cho Chon-sŏng (1553–1627)

Boy, lead a cow to the northern village,
Let's taste the new-made wine.
Having drained it to the lees, I'll return home
On cow-back under the moon.
Hurrah, I am a Fu Hsi tonight,
The ancient glories at my fingertips.

Yi Tŏk-hyŏng (1561–1613)

The moon hangs in the sky, bright, full.
Since the dawn,
It has met wind and frost.
Alas, soon it will sink.
But no, wait, I say,
And shine on the gold cup of my drunken guest.

Kim Sang-yong (1561–1637)

Love is a deceit—
She does not love me.
She says
She comes to me in a dream:
It is a lie.
All night awake and restless,
Where shall I see her—in what dream?

*

Fierce beats the rain
On the paulownia's wide
Majestic leaves.
My grief awakes and twists my heart,
The loud rain beats on my sorrow.
Never again shall I plant
A tree with such broad leaves.

Shin Hŭm (1566–1628)

I would draw her face with blood
That lies stagnant in my heart.
And on the plain wall of my room,
I would hang it up to gaze.
Who has made the word "Farewell"?
Who causes me to love and wither?

   *

A rain came overnight;
Pomegranates are in full bloom.
Having rolled up a crystal screen
By the square lotus pond,
Can I unravel this deep, troubled self—
Ruled by whom? Who knows?

   *

Don't laugh, foolish people, if my
Roof beams are long or short, the pillars
Crooked. This snail shell, my grass hut,
The vines that cover it, the encircling hills
And the bright moon above
Are mine, and mine alone.

Kim Kwang-uk (1580–1656)

Bundle the piles of verbose missives,
Burn the scrolls of empty scribbles—
At last I ride home on a swift horse,
Whipping the autumn winds.
A bird newly freed cannot be happier,
I savor freedom, sup the rustic air.

Yun Sŏn-do (1587–1671)

from DISPELLING GLOOM

I myself know that sometimes
I was absurd and missed the mark.
My mind was foolish but
I only desired to honor you.
Beware, my lord, and reflect on
The words of those slanderers.

SUNSET

The mountains are more beautiful
After the sun has crossed them.
It is twilight:
Darkness settles.
Watch out for tigers now, boy;
Do not wander about in the fields.

SONGS OF FIVE FRIENDS

How many friends have I? Count them:
Water and stone, pine and bamboo—
The rising moon on the east mountain,
Welcome, it too is my friend.
What need is there, I say,
To have more friends than five?

They say clouds are fine: I mean the color.
But, alas, they often darken.
They say winds are clear; I mean the sound.
But, alas, they often cease to blow.
It is only the *water,* then,
That is perpetual and good.

Why do flowers fade so soon
Once they are in their glory?
Why do grasses yellow so soon
Once they have grown tall?
Perhaps it is the *stone,* then,
That is constant and good.

Flowers bloom when it is warm;
Leaves fall when days are cool.
But, O *pine,* how is it
That you scorn frost, ignore snow?
I know now even your roots are,
Straight among the Nine Springs.

You are not a tree, no,
Nor a plant, not even that.
Who let you shoot so straight;
What makes you empty within?
You are green in all seasons,
Welcome, *bamboo,* my friend.

Small but floating high,
You shed light on all creation.
And what can match your brightness
In the dark of night?
You look at me but with no words;
That's why, O *moon,* you are my friend.

TO MY FRIEND (1645)

Heart wants to sing, but cannot sing alone;
Heart wants to dance, but dancing must have music.
    Then lute shall play,
For none but lute can strike the secret tone
    My heart would sing
    So heart and song are one;
    Then lute shall play,
For none but lute knows what is heart's desire
    So heart may spring
    Into the dance
    And beat its rhythm out.
Welcome, sweet lute, my dear, my dearest friend,
There is no hurt thy music cannot mend.

from THE ANGLER'S CALENDAR (1651)

   SPRING

Is it a cuckoo that cries?
Is it the willow that is blue?
Row away, row away!
Several roofs in a far fishing village
Swim in the mist, magnificent.
Chigukch'ong chigukch'ong ŏsawa.
Boy, fetch an old net!
Fishes are climbing against the stream.

Let's return to the shore,
Twilight trails in the west.
Lower sail, lower sail!
How supple and sweet
Willows and flowers on the river bank!
Chigukch'ong chigukch'ong ŏsawa.
Who would envy three dukes?
Who would now think of caps and gowns?

Let's tread on fragrant grasses
And pick orchids and angelica.
Stop the boat, stop the boat!
What have I taken aboard
On my boat small as a leaf?
Chigukch'ong chigukch'ong ŏsawa.
Nothing except smoke when I set sail,
When I row back, the moon is my tenant.

   SUMMER

Wrap the steamed rice in lotus leaves,
No need for viands or delicacies.
Hoist anchor, hoist anchor!
I have already my blue arum hat,
Bring me, boy, my green straw cape.
Chigukch'ong chigukch'ong ŏsawa.
Mindless gulls come and go;
Do they follow me, or I them?

A wind rises among the water chestnut,
Cool, cool is the bamboo awning.
Raise sail, raise sail!
Let the boat drift with the current,
The summer breeze is capricious.
Chigukch'ong chigukch'ong ŏsawa.
Northern coves and southern river,
Does it matter where I go?

Lo, my snail-shell hut
With white clouds all around.
Bring the boat ashore, bring the boat ashore!
Let's climb the stone path
With bulrush fan in hand.
Chigukch'ong chigukch'ong ŏsawa.
O the idle life of an old angler,
This is my work, this is my life.

AUTUMN
Autumn comes to a river village,
The fishes are many and sleek,
Hoist anchor, hoist anchor!
Let's be free and happy
On myriad acres of limpid waves.
Chigukch'ong chigukch'ong ŏsawa.
Behind me the dusty world, but
Joy doubles as farther I sail away.

Silver scales and jade scales,
Did I have a good catch today?
Row away, row away!
Let's build a fire of reed bushes,
Broil the fat fishes one by one.
Chigukch'ong chigukch'ong ŏsawa.
Pour wine from an earthenware jar,
Filling up my gourd cup!

I want to admire the dawn moon
From a stone cave in the bamboo grove.
Bring the boat ashore, bring the boat ashore!
But the path in the empty hills
Is hidden by fallen leaves.
Chigukch'ong chigukch'ong ŏsawa.
Since the white clouds, too, follow me,
O heavy is the sedge cape!

WINTER
A snow settles over the night—
What new scenes before my eyes!
Row away, row away!
In front lie glassy acres,
Jade folding screens behind.
Chigukch'ong chigukch'ong ŏsawa.
Is it a fairy land, or Buddha's realm?
It can't be the world of man.

Red cliffs and emerald canyons
Enfold us like a painted screen.
Stop the boat, stop the boat!
What does it matter
If I catch any fish or not?
Chigukch'ong chigukch'ong ŏsawa.
In an empty boat, straw cape and hat,
I sit and my heart beats fast.

Day closes,
Time to feast and rest.
Bring the boat ashore, bring the boat ashore!
Let's tread the path where the snow
Is strewn with pink petals.
Chigukch'ong chigukch'ong ŏsawa.
Lean from the pine window and gaze
As the moon crosses the western peak.

Yi Myŏng-han (1595–1645)

Do not draw back your sleeves and go,
My own,
With tears I beg you.
Over the long dike green with grass
Look, the sun goes down.
You will regret it, lighting the lamp
By the tavern window,
Sleepless and alone.

*

If my dreams
Left their footprints on the road,
The path beneath my love's window
Would be worn down, though it is stone.
Alas, in the country of dream
No roads endure, no traces remain.

King Hyojong (1619–1659)

The rain that pits the clear stream,
                what has it got to laugh about?
Mountain leaves and flowers,
                why do they shake with joyous mirth?
They are right. Spring does not last many days.
                While we can laugh, laugh away.

Nam Ku-man (1629–1711)

Does dawn light the east window?
                    Already larks sing in the sky.
Where is the boy that tends the ox—
                    has he not yet roused himself?
When will he get his plowing done
                    in the long field over the hill?

TRANSLATED BY RICHARD RUTT

Yi T'aek (1651–1719)

O roc, don't ridicule the small black birds:
You and the little birds both fly way up in the clouds,
You're a bird,
They're birds.
Really, I can't see much difference between you!

Chu Ŭi-sik (1675–1720)

A boy stopped outside my window,
Told me it was the New Year.
So I look out my eastern window—
The sun rises as of old, unchanged.
Look, boy, it's the same old sun;
Don't bother me now, come back some other time.

Kim Su-jang (1690–1769)

What is black, they say is white,
             what is white they say is black.
Be it white, be it black,
             nobody says that I am right.
I had best stop my ears, close my eyes,
             refusing to judge things.

TRANSLATED BY RICHARD RUTT

Yi Chŏng-bo (1693–1766)

The Milky Way climbs higher, and
Wild geese are cackling overhead.
Last night, coming in out of the frosty air,
The hair below my ears looked gray.
A feeble and grizzled look in the glass—
Who is that? Alas, is that I?

*

If flowers bloom, we demand the moon.
If the moon lights up, we ask for wine;
When we have all these at once,
Still there is something missing.
O, when can I drink a night away,
Enjoying moon, flowers, and a friend?

Kim Ch'ŏn-t'aek (c. 1725–1776)

Having given my clothes to a boy
To have them pawned at the tavern,
Looking up to heaven,
I question the moon.
Who is Li Po, that ancient drunkard,
What is he compared with me?

Yun Tu-sŏ (eighteenth century)

A muddy piece of jade
                cast away beside the road . . .
Those who come and go here
                must think it's nothing but dirt.
But maybe someone will know better.
                Stay put there: look like earth.

TRANSLATED BY RICHARD RUTT

An Min-yŏng (fl. 1870–1880)

Speak, chrysanthemum, why do you shun
The orient breezes of the third moon?
"I had rather freeze in a cruel rain
Beside the hedge of dried sticks,
Than humble myself to join the parade:
Those flowers of a fickle spring."

Anonymous

In the wind that blew last night,
Peach blossoms fell, scattered in the garden.
A boy came out with a broom,
Intending to sweep them away.
No, do not sweep them away, no, no.
Are fallen flowers not flowers?

*

A horse neighs, wants to gallop:
My love clings to me, begs me to stay.
The moving sun has crossed the hill.
I have a thousand miles to go.
My love, do not stop me:
Stop the sun from setting!

*

The faint moon in a heavy frost;
A solitary goose flies cackling.
Love, I fancied it brought me news.
Was it a letter from my love?
No, I hear only the bird
Among the clouds, incredibly far off.

*

In the valley where the stream leaps,
Having built a grass hut by the rock,
I till the field under the moon,
Among the vast clouds lie down.
Heaven and earth advise me
To age with them together.

*

I have lived anxious and hurt.
Enough, enough, I would rather die,
Become the spirit of the cuckoo
When the moon is on the bare hills,
And sing with bitter tears
To him my forbidden hopes.

*

What was love in fact, what was it?
Was it round, was it square?
Was it long, was it short?
More than an inch, more than a yard?
It seems of no great length,
But somehow I don't know where it ends.

*

O love, round as the watermelon,
Do not use words sweet as the melon.
What you have said, this and that,
Was all wrong, and you mocked me.
Enough, your empty talk
Is hollow, like a preserved melon.

*

Deep among green valley grasses,
A stream runs crying.
Where is the terrace of songs,
Where the hall of dancing?
Do you know, swallow,
Cutting the sunset water?

KASA, II

This section presents three pieces from the late phase of *kasa* poetry.

"Grand Trip to Japan" was written by Kim In-gyŏm (1707–?), who, as third secretary, accompanied the Korean diplomatic mission to Japan, sent at the request of the Tokugawa shogun Ieharu (1760–1786). The party, consisting of some five hundred members, left Seoul on September 9, 1763. After some forty days of rest in Pusan, they resumed their journey, reaching Edo on March 18, 1764. They returned to Seoul on August 5, 1764. Although the work runs to some four thousand lines, it is full of entertaining episodes, marked by Kim's keen observation, criticism, humor and wit. The following selection attempts to show what was expected of a writer in a foreign country such as Japan. The scenes depicted occurred on February 23 and 24.

"An Exile's Life" is by An To-wŏn (*fl.* 1777–1800), also known as An Cho-hwan. He is said to have committed an odious offense and was exiled to the lonely island of Ch'uja, off the southeast coast of Korea.

Finally, "The Farmer's Works and Days" by Chŏng Hag-yu (*fl.* 1835–1849), the second son of Chŏng Yag-yong, a great scholar of practical learning, recalls the pattern of "monthly ordinances" in the *Book of Rites* for an agricultural society. Here the months are signaled by the twenty-four fortnightly periods *(ch'i)* which divided the twelve months of the tropical year, and which are still commonly used in East Asia. It touches on all aspects of the farmer's life, where heavenly bodies give signs and the cosmos is an almanac. The poem does not catalogue a variety of trees, vines, soils, and lands, as does Virgil's *Georgics,* nor does it deal exclusively with cereals, as does Hesiod; it emphasizes both hard work and the joy of country life. The selections give odd-numbered months in a slightly abridged form.

Kim In-gyŏm (1707–?)

GRAND TRIP TO JAPAN
[*Iltong changyu ka*]

On the twenty-third I fell ill,
lying in the official hostel.
Our hosts bring me their poems,
they are heaped like a hill.
Sickness aside, I answer them;
how taxing this chore is!
Regulated verse, broken-off lines,
old style verse, regulated couplets—
some one hundred thirty pieces.
Because I dashed them off on draft paper,
upon revision I've discarded a half.
If I have to work like this every day,
it will be too much to bear. . . .
The rich and noble in the city
bring presents, many in kind and amount.
But I return them all as before.
One scholar, his hand on the brow,
begs me a hundred times to accept,
rubbing hands together sincerely.
Touched with pity,
I accept a piece of ink stick.
When I offer him Korean paper,
brushes and ink sticks,
he too takes only one ink stick. . . .
Before dawn on the twenty-fourth,
they arrive in streams.
How hard to talk by means of writing,
how annoying to cap their verses.
Braving my illness,
and mindful of our mission
to awe them and enhance our prestige,
I exert myself for dear life,
wield my brush like wind and rain,
and harmonize with them.
When they revise their verses,

they put their heads together—
their writings bid fair to inundate me.
I compose for another round;
they respond with another pile.
I am old and infirm,
and the task saps my vigor.
I wouldn't mind it if I were young,
but they traveled thousands of miles
with packed food and waited for months
just to get our opinions.
If we deny them our writing,
how disappointed they would be!
We write on and on
for the old and young, the high and low.
We work as a matter of duty
night and day, without rest.

An To-wŏn (fl. 1777–1800)

AN EXILE'S LIFE
[*Manŏn sa*]

After a thousand miles over the sea,
At last I reach Ch'uja island.
I walk inland, a desolate place,
and look around in the four directions.
What I see is only the ocean,
what I hear, stormy waves.
After the flood water had receded,[1]
when this island of sand remained,
Heaven created hell,
its walls made of waves,
its gates cloud-capped hills.
Cut away from the world of man,
this is indeed Hades.
Where will I lodge?
Whose house shall I seek?
Tears blind my eyes,
and I stumble with every step.
I go to one house for shelter,
they say they're hard off.
I go to the next,
the master makes some excuses.
Who would like to put up
an exile as his guest?
Only because of court pressure,
they agree to take me in.
They dare not protest to an official,
but pour out their chagrin to me.
"Our family of three
live from hand to mouth.
How will our guest live?
What will we feed him?"
A hut lower than my head,
I crawl in and crawl out.

1. Literally, "Mulberry fields became a blue sea," referring to a cataclysm.

Their only room is for the husband,
the guest has no place to sleep.
With only a piece of mat,
I settle down under the
chilly, damp, and leaky eaves.
Vermin of all sorts swarm about,
snakes a foot long, green centipedes a span long.
They ring around me—
how terrible, how creepy!
After a sleepless night in tears,
I get cooked barley and thin soy sauce.
I push them aside after a spoonful.
Even that is scarce sometimes,
empty stomach on long summer days.
What I call my clothes
only draw a long sigh.
Under a burning sun and sultry air,
my unwashed quilted trousers
wring with sweat and grime—
a straw mat stuffing a chimney!
I wouldn't mind heat or filth,
but what about its stink?
Am I still alive?
Have I turned into a ghost?
I talk, so I must be alive,
but my looks are those of a ghost.
After a sigh come tears,
after tears, a sigh . . .
How absurd all this—
I drown my sorrow in laughter.
What has happened to me?
Has grief turned my brain?

*

What was right yesterday
has been proven wrong today.
Had I feared the growl of a tiger,
would I have entered a deep hill?
Had I known that I would topple,
would I have climbed a tall tree?

Had I known rolls of thunder,
would I have climbed a tower?
Had I known I would be a castaway,
would I have loaded a boat with grain?
Had I known I'd be guilty,
would I have sought name and fame?
I'm abused in no small way,
my host acts as if he were drunk,
his insults are hard to bear.
He mutters to himself and nags,
and gives me a long lecture. . . .
I can't fish, being a bad sailor,
nor am I strong enough to cut trees,
I never wove mats and sandals,
and have nothing to do but go begging.
A horsehair hat pulled over my eyes,
a broad-sleeved gown untied,
with sandals—only the frames left—
and shading my face with a fine-ribbed fan,
sucking on an empty pipe
as if to while away my time,
I walk leaning to one side,
every step provoking tears.
Foolish children, big young wives,
snap their fingers at me.
"Here comes a banished fellow!"
Unhappily, shame comes first,
so how can I ask for food?
I bow to a male slave,
use terms of respect to a servant,
and mumble as if talking to myself,
just like a mendicant monk.
One gets a hint and scoops out
a bushel of barley—
"Take it, your lot is bitter.
Exiles often come around."
When I receive it face to face,
I can't help thanking him.
Now that somehow I've got it,
how can I carry it without a slave?

My hat pushed down,
flapping sleeves wrinkled up
and tucked into my breast,
my gown becomes a sleeveless coat,
not a bad gait after all.
As if pulled from behind,
or pushed from the front,
however I bend, I tumble down.
After numberless hardships,
when I at last reach my hut,
as in a visit to a god or Buddha,
beads of sweat run down my back.
Look, how the host behaves—
He sneers, laughs in my face:
"What is a yangban for?
You've gone begging.
How vain to be a noble!
You've a load on your back:
What a disgrace for a plutocrat like you,
you've earned a big supper."
"I don't want your sniggers,
nor do I need a big meal.
Once is enough, mind you,
the first time in my life.
I cannot do it again.
I would rather starve
than play that kind of role."
What can I do next?
Let me make straw sandals.
I start with the four warps,
but I've never made even a paper string,
so how can I twist a rope?
Before I've done a foot,
my palms blister and swell.

*

At a frosty dawn,
a stray goose cries sadly.
The lonely traveler listens first,
it renews my longing for my lord.

A crane with outstretched wings—
I can then fly to his side;
A wind among tall pines—
I can then prevail on him;
An autumn moon among phoenix trees—
I can then shine on him;
A fine rain against the gauze window—
I can then scatter about him.
Autumn moons and spring breezes,
I served you night and day.
Now a sinner with myriad sorrows,
not a piece of news reaches me.
My liver is not iron, my innards not stone,
how can I endure this yearning?
I cannot forget my love for you.
With my dragon sword and a dagger,
even if I cut with all my might,
the blue stream among green hills
will not cleave but flow on.
No sword can cut the water asunder,
no dagger can cut off this love. . . .
I parted from you with tears;
I wish to meet you with laughter.
I ponder this way and that,
a fire rages within my breast.
My innards are all ablaze,
what water can put it out?
A heavenly water might quench the flames,
I know, but where can I get it?
My tongue scalds beyond words.
I'd rather die willingly
to forget my agony.
Slumped in a sandpit,
grieving the whole day,
I try to drown myself
more than once or twice.
I lock myself in,
giving up all lingering regrets,
resolved to perish of hunger.
A minute is like three years,

how can I end this hard life?
A dog barks at the wicker gate;
is it a letter of pardon?
I rejoice and go out—
It's a vendor of dace.
A boat glides over the sea—
is it an official boat for my release?
I start up and gaze—
it's nothing but a fishing boat. . . .

*

After clear autumn comes severe winter,
snow whirls over the riverside village,
north winds rage and turn
the tops and bottoms of hills
into a stretch of white jade.
I'm the one who sleeps out
with no stockings, no shoes.
Now, exposed to the cold,
I'll freeze to death in a moment.
Enlisting the owner's help,
I obtain a corner in the room,
its walls plastered, but not papered.
Every wall is gaping,
every crack full of insects.
I won't be afraid
of snakes and centipedes.
The host picks up larger ones,
and throws the small ones at me.
I weave a bamboo door
and cover it with an old mat. . . .
I rip open a straw sack—
it becomes a satin mattress;
I pull a dog skin over my face—
it becomes a dark red coverlet. . . .
Tears that soak my pillow
turn into monuments of ice.
How pleasant to hear a cock crow
after a windy, freezing night.
The eastern window pales,

the sun rises.
I get up lazily
and stretch out my legs—
my thighs split, joints creak.
Lighting a stone pipe
with kindling of cattle dung,
I sit on a sunny spot
and hunt lice in my rags,
my hair hanging about my shoulders.
I struggle to go on in this state,
how wrong it is to linger on.
Now I know how precious life is.
Some say time is medicine.
The longer my sorrow goes on,
the sooner it will turn into gunpowder.
Days pass, months hurry on,
it's already my first anniversary!
No gains without pains.
Heaven, I pray you,
grant my cherished hope!
One does not use again
the calendar which is a year old.
The royal displeasure may be lifted
following a good night's sleep.
Such are the affairs of the world,
my offense a matter of the past.
Please cleanse away my sins
and recall me to your side,
so that our old broken ties
will be bound again, my Lord!

Chǒng Hag-yu (fl. 1835–1849)

THE FARMER'S WORKS AND DAYS
[from *Nongga wǒllyǒng ka*]

In the first month it is early spring.
    The season begins with a rain.
On the snow-locked hills
    a valley stream crawls under ice.
But against the marshes and broad fields,
    clouds and hills look fresh and new.
Our king loves his people
    and respects husbandry;
he spreads to every village and house
    his teachings on agriculture.
Farmers, do not be ignorant fools, never
    put your own interests before his message!
We will till our patches:
    one half a field, the other half a paddy.
We cannot predict that the harvest will be good,
    but our hard work may dispel calamities.
Let's encourage each other,
    it's time to plan for the year. . . .
If you miss a chance now,
    failure ensues the whole year.
Let us keep farm tools in repair,
    let's feed the draft oxen,
spread manure in the barley field,
    work harder than we did last year.
An old man may lack the strength
    to do hard work, but he can
weave thatching during the day,
    or twist a rope at night,
and roof his cottage now
    to ease his fears of winter.
Peel the bark of fruit trees,
    plant stones between branches.[1]
At dawn on New Year's day,
    watch to see if new buds come.

1. To make the tree bear much fruit.

Daughters-in-law, don't forget
  to make good wine.
Let's get drunk when the blossoms open
  during the three months of spring.
On the fifteenth we watch the moon
  to divine flood or drought;
we read signs, we guess,
  as our fathers used to do.
Performing a New Year's bow
  is a simple, honest custom.
Put on your new clothes,
  join your relatives and neighbors.
The old and the young, men and women,
  children, too, walk about,
what a riot of colors,
  how splendid, how gay!
Boys fly kites,
  girls play on a seesaw,
the young bet on who will win
  the game of *yut*.
Worship at the ancestral shrine
  with rice-cake soup, fruit, and wine!
Put your scallion and parsley
  well spaced between the turnip.
How fresh they look,
  how succulent they taste!
Eating sweet rice on the fifteenth
  is a custom from old Silla.
We munch dried vegetables we boiled;
  they excel the flavor of meat.
Wine is good for hearing,
  chestnut keeps a boil away.
Sell the summer heat,² they say,
  lighting the torch to welcome the moon.
These are customs of long ago,
  and children have the best time.

*

2. A cup of cold wine drunk on the fifteenth will make one's ear become clear; also, at dawn the
girls shout to each other, asking if any will buy summer heat.

The third month is the end of spring,
    Clear and Bright and Grain Rain.[3]
When the spring days grow warm,
    everything is mild and pleasant.
Flowers bloom everywhere,
    birds of all sorts sing.
In front of the main hall,
    swallows return to their old nest.
Among the flowers butterflies
    flit here and there.
Now's the time for small insects
    to enjoy each other's company.
Visit graves on the Cold Food day,
    when white poplars begin to bud.
We repay with wine and fruit
    the ancestors' love and favor.
The farmers' hardest work is
    when the plowing starts.
Let's ready their lunch and snack,
    they need to eat their fill.
The family of helpers, too,
    come to share the meal.
Not to spare a bushel of grain is
    the farmer's generous custom.
We clear a sluice gate,
    clean out a ditch to hold the water.
One side is for rice seedlings,
    the rest for planting other seeds.
Every day we look, again and again,
    handle the tender plants like babies.
Among a hundred grains,
    rice requires the most care.
Millet in the field near the river,
    soybean and red bean on the hill.
Plant wild sesame early and hemp, too,
    the best seeds are for a second crop.
Weed the field of barley,
    plow the paddy over.

3. Begin on April 6 and 21, respectively.

Between work in the field
     look after your vegetable garden.
Grow pumpkin under the hedge,
     gourds under the eaves.
Plant winter melon along the wall;
     build trellises for vines.
Turnip, cabbage, marshmallow, lettuce,
     pepper, eggplant, scallion, garlic—
plant them, one by one, everywhere,
     make a fence from willow branches
to keep dogs and chickens out.
     Plant cucumbers alone, with plenty of manure.
What better side-dish in the summer
     than pickled cucumbers on the farm?
Mulberry leaves tell us when
     it's time to feed silkworms.
Ladies, they need your devotion—
     sweep and sprinkle the room,
check baskets, knives, and chopping boards,
     sieves and reed blinds, too;
make sure the room smells clean.
     Several days before Cold Food,
the grafting begins on
     apricot, peach, pear, and apple trees.
Peaches and plums with old roots
     should be transplanted to pots.
When the snow piles on your roof,
     you will have spring green in your room.
To grow plants indoors has no use
     but to bring indoors the amenities of country life.
One hard task remains: the
     making of soy sauce and bean paste.
Have salt ready, follow the recipe,
     stock red pepper paste and other spices.
Now that the rainclouds lift on the hill,
     let's gather scented wild herbs.
Aralia shoots, bracken, fern,
     bellflower roots and wild lilies.
Plait and hang one half to dry,
     mix the others for salad.

After sweeping away fallen flowers,
    when I have my jug of wine,
My wife seasons herbs as appetizers—
    nothing matches their flavor!

        *

The fifth month marks midsummer,
    Grain in Ear and Summer Solstice.[4]
The timely south wind blows,
    urging the barley to ripe.
Fields will turn yellow overnight;
    in front of the gate we mark the threshing floor,
we cut the grain stalks with a sharp scythe,
    and stack them in sheaves.
Standing face to face we flail,
    overwhelmed with joy.
On threshing day, a quiet household
    turns into a thriving place.
All but a few piculs of last year's grain
    are used up by now.
Now the new barley
    supplants the old.
Without our old stores, could we
    have managed throughout the summer?
Heaven granted us its endless favor.
    Cowherd, it's time to feed the oxen,
Mix their fodder with rice water,
    let them graze on the dewy grass.
We depend on them for our
    second sowing and replanting of the rice.
Dry the barley straw and stack the pine branches
    into faggots for a rainy season
to keep us warm in winter time.
    Now silkworms need human help—
put them on the frame to spin,
    spread the frames on a clear day,
dry them under the blazing sun,
    divide them by their color, then

4. Begin on June 7 and 22, respectively.

spin the snowy threads onto reels.
  How lovely the reels turn,
like music on the lute and mandolin.
  Ladies, it's the fruit of your labor.
On the fifth day of the month,
  we pick the first dew-laden cucumber;
and red cherries gleam in the sun.
  Girls, you there playing on a swing
in blue and pink skirts and iris hairpins,[5]
  you need to help on this festive day.
Don't forget to pick
  the medicinal mugwort between play.
The sky looks good, clouds rise up,
  you cannot stop a timely rain.
First it sprinkles the dust,
  then it comes in torrents during the night.
Sitting around the fire of pine logs,
  we will plan tomorrow's work:
who'll sow the back paddy,
  who the field in front?
Rain capes and bamboo hats,
  how many pairs do we have?
You will bring the young rice plants,
  I'll transplant them from the bed.
Servants, you will take care of the
  wild sesame and tobacco plants,
and you, daughters, the eggplants and pepper.
  Don't spend too much time, girls,
with cockscomb and balsam.[6]
  Mothers will mill the grain,
carry lunch to the workers—
  cooked barley and cold soup,
Red pepper paste and lettuce—
  count the mouths and provide enough!
As we leave the gate at dawn,
  the swollen stream rushes along;

5. On the fifth day of the fifth month, girls adorn their hair with a hairpin made of the iris stem.
6. Used to dye the fingernails with arum.

the farmers answer with a song,
    a song of peace and plenty.

*

It is the seventh month,
    Beginning of Autumn and End of Heat.[7]
The Fire Star moves west,
    Scorpio hangs in midheaven.[8]
Late heat may linger
    but can't deceive the season's round.
The rain clears lightly,
    the wind feels cool.
The cicadas, fed to satiety,
    still boast with their song.
The tears of the Herdboy and Weaver
    turn into rain on the seventh day.
After it falls far apart,
    the paulownias shed their leaves.
The moon like a moth eyebrow
    hangs in the western sky.
It is the end of the work season,
    but still much work remains!
Don't put your mind at ease,
    we still have plenty to do—
weed the furrows,
    sort the millet from rice,
with a sharp scythe mow the balk,
    and weed the ancestral grave.
Cut and pile the compost leaves,
    chase the birds from the young rice,
plant a scarecrow in the millet patch,
    level the path by the field,
strain the soil in the family acres,
    fertilize the turnip and cabbage patch.
Plant thorn hedges to protect our land.
    Ladies, use your judgment,
grasshoppers remind you of household chores.
    After the monsoon rain, dry your grain.

7. Begin on August 8 and 24, respectively.
8. The Fire Star is Antares, and Scorpio is the sixth of the twenty-four lunar mansions.

Gather silk threads
   and weave them into cloth.
The old folks' strength declines
   as the years run down.
Wash, starch, and pound their cloth,
   listen to the sound of pounding!
When greens and fruit are plenty,
   let us dry and store them.
Dry strips of pumpkin and gourd,
   salt cucumber and eggplant.
Then examine the cotton field,
   look after the cotton and harvest it.

*

The ninth month is late autumn,
   Cold Dews and Descent of Hoar Frost.[9]
Swallows are flying south,
   but wild geese have come back.
Their honking in the sky
   announces the coming cold dews.
Everywhere in the hills,
   maple leaves are scarlet-tinged;
yellow chrysanthemums under the hedge
   boast of the autumn sun.
Double Ninth is a festival day,
   let's offer flower cakes to the ancestral spirits.[10]
Following the fortnightly periods,
   we offer the ancestors a sacrifice.
The autumn view is good,
   but the crops must be in.
In the field and courtyard
   let's install threshing stands.
Cut and spread the rice in the paddies,
   thresh other cereals on dry fields.
Today we thresh late ripening rice,
   tomorrow awnless red rice and local breeds.
In the field heaps of millet,
   near the house soybeans and red beans.

9. Begin on October 9 and 24, respectively.
10. Made in the shape of a flower petal.

After the rice harvest we'll thresh
     sweet millet, cowpeas, beans—
Cut their ears first
     and keep the rest for seed.
Womenfolk scythe the sheaves,
     the young beat out the grains,
children tend the draft oxen,
     the old make straw sacks.
Neighbors come to help
     as if it were their own crop—
they winnow and dry the stalks,
     then pick up scattered grains.
To one side is the cotton gin,
     everyone is bustling about in groups,
and others press seeds for oil
     for the lamps and for the table.
On a chilly and long night,
     women pound rice in a mortar,
no time to look after their babies.
     Let's prepare chicken and wine,
salted shrimp and steamed eggs,
     cabbage soup and turnip salad,
seasoned pepper leaves, too—
     a table fit for a king.
Steam enough rice in a kettle,
     it's the season of plenty.
Why not invite the passing guests?
     Neighbors from our village
work in our yard,
     sharing labor and joy with us.
However busy you may be,
     don't forget the draft oxen.
They will soon be fat
     and repay our effort.

*

The eleventh month is midwinter,
     Greater Snow and Winter Solstice.[11]

11. Begin on December 7 and 22, respectively.

The winds blow, frosts fall,
  now it snows and now it freezes.
How much have we stored
  of our autumn crop?
We'll sell some, pay with some the taxes,
  some are for sacrifice,
some for seed, some to repay a loan,
  and some for wages.
Now that we've settled our accounts,
  not much remains for us farmers.
With bean sprouts and cabbage leaves
  we are happy just the same.
Ladies, make soybean malt,
  steam soybeans and pound them.
Winter Solstice is a holiday,
  the yang replaces the yin.
We eat red bean gruel with dumplings
  and share it with our neighbors.
The new calendar is out,
  let's see when are next year's festivals.
Days are short and
  nights are long and dreary.
No official harasses us,
  because we are paid up.
We have closed the brushwood door,
  the thatched cottage is idle.
Under the lamp mind your weaving,
  see the cloth stretch on the loom.
Youngsters study the classics,
  children are at their game.
Some chant, some chatter,
  this is the joy of family life.
The old have nothing much to do
  but plait the mats.
Boys, I say, go
  look in the cowshed.
Feed the cattle chopped hay
  and gather the dung from the straw bedding.

SATIRICAL STORIES

In "The Story of Master Hŏ" by Pak Chi-wŏn (1737–1805), a great champion of practical learning, the poverty-stricken scholar Hŏ breaks the mores of his class by becoming a merchant. His aim, however, is not to make profit but to show how money can be used. He pokes fun at the empty forms and pretensions of the upper classes and dreams of a society which is able to stand alone. Unlike Hong Kiltong, Hŏ is a pioneer. It is interesting to note that, unlike earlier examples, the story begins and ends with the description of his cottage.

"The Story of a Yangban" is a delightful vignette on the same theme, which trusts the reader's intelligence.

In "On Dismissing a Servant," Chŏng Yag-yong (1762–1836), another champion of practical learning and reform, casts a satirical eye on the psychology of the servant class.

"The Story of a Pheasant Cock," written in Korean, takes the form of a beast fable. The pheasant cock, the most loquacious and pedantic bird in Korean literature, represents the unreflexive male ego that demands conformity to the dominant culture shaped by the male ideology. The pheasant hen, in rejecting the traditional role of a passive and servile wife, exposes the social forces that limit the choices open to a woman. A product of the times, the anonymously written fable is a comment on the disparity and dilemmas of late Yi-dynasty life. References in the tale to the *Book of Songs, Historical Record,* and *Romance of the Three Kingdoms*—the most popular Chinese novel of the time—suggest the staple reading of the average educated person.

In these stories, the authors' views on the prospects of man and society are not melancholy; they do not distort reality in an attempt to make human follies more ridiculous than they actually are. Characterized by comic detachment, these compact and indirect stories exude humor and laughter.

Pak Chi-wŏn (1737–1805)

THE STORY OF MASTER HŎ

[*Hŏsaeng chŏn*]

Master Hŏ lived in Mukchŏk village. Those who went straight up the valley beside Mount South came to a well in the shadow of an old gingko tree. The twig gate to Hŏ's house, which faced the gingko tree, was always open, and his small thatched cottage was exposed to the wind and rain. But Hŏ loved to read books. His wife eked out a living by taking in sewing.

One day, no longer able to endure her gnawing hunger, Hŏ's wife began to weep out her dissatisfactions. "You've never taken the civil service examination. What's the use of reading?"

Hŏ laughed and answered, "I haven't finished my study yet."

"Couldn't you then become a craftsman?"

"How could I? I've never learned any kind of skill."

"Well, then, what about becoming a merchant?"

"How can I become a merchant when I have no capital?"

Her patience spent, Hŏ's wife shouted angrily, "How can I? How can I? Is that all you've learned from the books you've been reading day and night? You cannot be a craftsman, nor can you be a merchant. How about becoming a thief?"

At this, Hŏ closed his book and stood up. "What a pity! It was my plan to study for ten years; I have studied only seven years now."

Hŏ then went out of the house. But he knew no one else in town. He walked up and down Unjong Street, then finally asked in the market for the name of the richest man in town.

He was told that this would be a certain Pyŏn. Hŏ went to Pyŏn's house. When he was presented to Pyŏn he bowed low and said, "I am poor and have no money to start a business, but I would like to try out an idea that I have, if you would lend me ten thousand yang in cash."

"Fine," said Pyŏn and gave Hŏ the cash at once. Hŏ took the money and left without a word of thanks. To all Pyŏn's sons and guests gathered around, Hŏ appeared to be a beggar. His belt was threadbare, the heels of his leather shoes were completely worn down, his hat was battered, his coat was dirty, and his nose was even running.

"Do you know that man?" Pyŏn's friends asked, astonished to see him giving money to such a sort.

"No."

"You have given away ten thousand to a complete stranger without even asking his name. What are you going to do?"

Pyŏn answered, "You wouldn't have understood. A man who is trying to get a loan usually speaks at great length. He says that he will not fail to keep his word, that there will be no cause for worry on his account, and so on. He usually looks shamefaced and tends to repeat himself. But this man we have just met . . . His clothes and shoes may have been tattered, but he spoke to the point with no trace of shame. He is a man who is not interested in material wealth; he is content with his life. Therefore, what he has in mind in the way of a business deal must be something big, and I am curious to see what he does. If I hadn't given him the money I might have asked his name. But what's the use of asking his name when I have already given him the cash?"

Having so easily obtained the money, Hŏ thought to himself, "Ansŏng is at the border of Kyŏnggi and Ch'ungch'ŏng provinces, and all the roads to the three southern provinces meet there." Not even stopping at his house he went straight to Ansŏng and secured a place to stay. The next day he went to the market and began to buy all the fruit he could find—jujubes, chestnuts, persimmons, pears, pomegranates, oranges, tangerines and pomelo. He paid double to buy them all up, thus establishing a monopoly in fruit.

Before long no feasts could be held or sacrifices offered. Now, the fruit merchants came running to Hŏ to buy back what they had sold him at ten times the price he had paid. Hŏ sighed and said to himself: "What a pity that a mere ten thousand in cash can jeopardize the country's economy! By this we may easily gauge the shallowness of the country."

When he sold all the fruit, he bought knives, hoes, cotton, hemp, and silk. Then he crossed over to Cheju Island, where he bought all the horse tails he could find. "Within a few years no one in the country will be able to cover his head," he said. Before long, as expected, the price of horsehair hats rose to ten times the usual price.

One day, Hŏ asked an old sailor: "Do you know of any uninhabited island where men could live without hardship?"

"Yes, sir. Once, long ago, I was caught in a storm for three days and three nights. Finally I landed on an island. I believe it was somewhere between Samun and Nagasaki. There were flowers and trees everywhere, and fruit and cucumbers were ripening with no one to look after them. Deer strolled in herds, and the fish in the sea were unafraid of men.''

Hŏ was greatly pleased. "If you will take me there, I will share all my wealth with you.''

The sailor agreed. On a day with favorable winds they sailed due southeast and reached the island. Hŏ climbed a peak and gazed all about but he seemed dissatisfied: "The island is not even one thousand *ri* wide. What can be done with it? But since the soil is fertile and the water is sweet, here I could live a life of seclusion like a wealthy man.''

"Whom do you live with on a deserted island like this, with not a soul to be seen?'' the sailor asked.

"People will follow a virtuous man. I worry about my lack of virtue, not about the lack of people.''

At the time the area around Pyŏnsan was being plundered by thousands of bandits. The provincial government mobilized troops but could not root them out. As defenses became stronger, however, it became increasingly difficult for the bandits to plunder the towns, and they were finally driven back, without provisions, to their remote fastness. Only starvation awaited them in the end.

Hearing this, Hŏ went alone to the bandits' hideout and began to speak persuasively to the leader. "If you stole one thousand in cash and divided the take among the thousand of you, how much would each of you receive?''

"One yang, of course.''

"Does any of you have a wife?''

"No.''

"Do you own fields?''

"Why would we rob and endure hardships if we had wives and fields?''

"If you really mean that, why don't you marry, build a house, buy an ox, and till the land? If you do so, you won't be called a thief, you'll enjoy a happy marriage and you'll be able to go where you please without fear of arrest. How nice that would be! You'll have clothing and food for the rest of your life.''

"Who doesn't want that? It's just that we don't have the money!''

Hŏ smiled and said, "Imagine bandits worrying about money! If all you need is money, I will provide it. If you go to the seashore tomorrow, you will see boats flying red flags. They all will be loaded with money. Take as much as you want."

With that Hŏ made his departure. So fantastic had his words seemed to the thieves that they all laughed at him and called him mad.

Still, they did go to the seashore on the following day. There they saw Hŏ waiting with three hundred thousand in cash aboard his boats. Greatly amazed, they lined up and bowed to him. "We will do whatever the general orders us to do."

"Well then, try taking as much money as you can carry on your backs."

The bandits crowded around the money bags but were unable to carry even one hundred yang.

"How could you, who cannot carry so much as one hundred yang, be robbers? Now that your names are listed as thieves by the government, you cannot return to civilian life. You have no place to go. I have a good idea. Each of you take one hundred yang and get a woman and an ox. I will wait here."

The thieves agreed and dispersed in all directions.

Hŏ waited with provisions sufficient for two thousand people for one year. All the bandits returned on the appointed day. When all were aboard, the ships set sail for the island. Since Hŏ had shipped out all of the bandits, life on the mainland became peaceful again.

The island's new inhabitants began at once to cut down trees, build houses, and erect bamboo fences. The soil was so rich that the crops flourished even when Hŏ's men neglected them.

So abundant was the harvest that a surplus remained, even after three years' worth of reserves had been laid away. Therefore Hŏ's men loaded the surplus onto the boats, sailed to Nagasaki and sold it there. Nagasaki, a Japanese territory with 310,000 households, was at that time suffering from a great famine, so that Hŏ's men were able to sell all that they had brought, and they returned home with one million in silver.

"Now I have seen my idea realized." So murmuring, Hŏ called all his two thousand together and said, "When I came here with you, I planned to make you rich first, and then to invent a new writing system and new styles of clothing and hats for you. But the land is small, and my virtue is slight, so I am now going to leave this place.

When you have children, teach them to hold their spoons in their right hand and to eat after their elders." Then Hŏ had all the boats burnt. "If no one goes out, no one will come." Also, he threw five hundred thousand in silver into the sea: "Somebody will find it, when the tide is out. Not even on the mainland could one spend a million yang. Of what use would it be in this small place?"

Finally, he called forth all those who could read and bade them board the boat. "I'm plucking the roots of strife from the soil of this island," he said.

Thereafter Hŏ went around the country, helping the poor. Yet there remained one hundred thousand in silver. "I shall repay Pyŏn."

Thus, Hŏ finally called on Pyŏn. "Do you remember me'?" he asked.

Pyŏn was surprised. "Your complexion has not improved at all. You must have lost all of the ten thousand," he replied.

Hŏ smiled and said, "It is people like you who improve their complexions with money. How could ten thousand in cash nourish the Way?" Then he paid back one hundred thousand in silver and said, "I did not finish my studies because one morning I could no longer endure the hunger. Your ten thousand yang has brought me only feelings of shame."

Pyŏn was so astounded that he jumped to his feet, bowed to Hŏ, and said that he only wanted one-tenth interest.

"How can you treat me as a merchant?" Hŏ said. Shaking his sleeves he took his leave.

Pyŏn stealthily followed Hŏ, who went down the valley next to Mount South and entered a small cottage.

"Whose cottage is that?" Pyŏn asked an old woman washing clothes by the well.

"That is Hŏ's place. He was poor, but he always liked to read. One morning, he left home and did not return for five years. His wife lived alone and observed memorial services on the day of his departure."

Thus Pyŏn finally came to know the man's name. He sighed and turned back.

The next day, Pyŏn called on the cottage with all the silver he had received. Yet Hŏ would not accept it. "If I wanted to be rich, would I have thrown away one million to take one hundred thousand in its stead?" he asked. "Henceforth I shall rely on your supporting and looking after us. If you send enough grain for my family and enough cloth to clothe us, I shall be content all my life. Why should I wish to trouble my mind with money?''

Pyŏn tried in a hundred ways to persuade Hŏ, but Hŏ remained adamant. Pyŏn brought food and clothing to Hŏ ever after this, and always in good time. Hŏ was always glad to see Pyŏn but if he had brought too much, Hŏ would immediately show displeasure, and say, ''Why do you wish to bring evil to my house?'' If Pyŏn brought wine, however, he was given an especially warm welcome, and the two friends would exchange cups until they were drunk. Thus the friendship of the two grew deeper over the years.

One day, Pyŏn asked calmly, ''How did you make a million in five years?''

''This will make sense to you,'' Hŏ answered, ''because our country has no trade with other countries, and also because everything we use is produced and consumed in the same province. With a mere one thousand, you can't buy up everything in sight. If you divide that amount by ten you can buy enough of each of ten different items. If the goods are light they will be easy to carry, and even if you lose in one out of the ten items, the remaining nine are bound to make you a profit. This is how small merchants make money. But with ten thousand yang you can buy just about all of one particular item produced in the country. You can buy the whole lot, whether you load it on a cart or on a boat. It's the same with anything a country has a lot of. You just get the whole lot with one sweep of your net. Say you choose something that's produced on land and buy it all up, or else you choose a sea product or something they use in medicine; not one merchant in the whole country will be able to turn up even a hint of that item. However, this method is a plague to the people. If someday some official were to employ it, it would be bound to injure the country.''

Pyŏn asked, ''By the way, how did you know I would lend you the ten thousand yang?''

Hŏ replied: ''You were not the only one who would have lent me the money. No businessman that had ten thousand could have refused me. I might easily make ten thousand through my own ability, but one's fate is up to Heaven, and nobody knows for certain. Therefore, the man who trusts me is a lucky one. It must be because Heaven has ordained it that a man who is rich already becomes even richer. If so, how could he *not* give me the money? Once I had the ten thousand I was acting entirely under the aegis of that lucky man. And whatever I tried, I succeeded. If I had gone into business with my own money, who could tell what the result might have been?''

"These days, officials wish to avenge the shame of Namhan Fortress, at the time of the Manchu invasion. Now is the time for wise and able men to arise and serve the country. Why would a gifted man like you wish to remain obscure all his life?'' Pyŏn asked.

"Many have lived and died with their worth never recognized. Cho Sŏng-gi, who was worthy to be sent as an envoy to an enemy land, died in coarse hemp cloth. Yu Hyŏng-wŏn, who was expert in military provisioning, idly whiled away his time at Puan. That will give you some idea what sort of people are in charge of state affairs. As for myself, I had some talent in business, and I could have bought the heads of nine kings with the money I made. But I threw it all into the sea because I knew there was no way to use that money.''

Pyŏn gave a long sigh and rose to depart.

Pyŏn had long been acquainted with Minister Yi Wan, who was then commander in the Metropolitan Military Headquarters. The two friends were having a chat one day when the minister asked Pyŏn, "Do you know of an able and gifted man among the commoners that I could work with on behalf of a great cause?''

Pyŏn mentioned Hŏ.

Yi was greatly amazed and said, "How strange! Could there really be such a man? What is his given name?''

"I have known him for three years, but I have never learned his given name.''

"He must be a genius. Please take me to him.''

When night came Yi ordered his guards away and went on foot with Pyŏn to Hŏ's house. Pyŏn left Yi outside and went in alone to tell Hŏ the purpose of Yi's visit. Hŏ ignored him, saying only, "Open that bottle of wine you brought.''

So they drank happily. Pyŏn was concerned for Yi, whom he had left outside, and mentioned Yi's business over and over, but Hŏ would not listen.

It was not until the night was far advanced that Hŏ asked, "Shall we see the visitor now?''

Hŏ did not budge from his seat when Yi entered. For a time Yi did not know what to do, but he finally announced that the government had been looking for wise men.

Hŏ waved him to silence, saying, "The night is short and your words are long. It would be tedious to hear you out. What position do you hold?"

"I am a commander."

"Is that so? Then you must be a trusted officer of the state. If I were to recommend to you a recluse sage comparable to Chu-ko Liang, could you ask the king to thrice call on his thatched hut in person?"

Yi pondered briefly and then replied, "It would be difficult. I'd like to hear more of what you have in mind."

"I know nothing of second choices," said Hŏ.

When Yi begged again and again, Hŏ spoke: "As Chosŏn had been indebted to Ming in the past, the descendants of Ming generals and soldiers came eastward to our country. They are now living as vagabonds, homeless and unmarried. Could you ask the court to wed the daughters of the royal kinsmen to these men, and confiscate the estates of the meritorious and powerful to provide them with new homes?"

After a long silence with his head bowed, Yi said, "That, too, would be difficult."

"This would be difficult, that would be difficult! Well, what can you do? I have one rather easy proposal. Do you think you can do it?"

"I'd like to hear it."

"If one intends to rise up in a great cause, one must make friends with gallant men under Heaven. If one plans to attack another country, one cannot hope to succeed without using secret agents. Now, the Manchu, as the lords of all under Heaven, suspect that they have not been able to win the hearts of the Chinese. They regard us Koreans as their most trusted friends because we were the first to surrender. If we ask them to let our young men study in their country and serve in their government, as under the T'ang and Yüan, and to allow our merchants to come and go freely, they will be pleased with our gesture and will consent. Then we select the country's youth, have them cut their hair as the Manchu do, clothe them in Manchu dress, and send them to China.[1] The learned will take the examina-

1. After conquering China the Manchu required Chinese men to shave their heads and wear queues, and to adopt Manchu dress. However, they did not subject the Koreans to the same regulation. Even if the Korean upper classes despise the Manchu as barbarians and dream of the restoration of the Ming, Hŏ is saying, the Koreans must adopt Manchu customs if they are to achieve what they yearn for.

tion for foreigners; the merchants will go deep into the region south of the Yangtze to gather information and make friends with the most gallant men there. Only then will we be able to plan a great undertaking to wipe away the country's disgrace. Afterwards you can search for a member of the Chu house of the Ming and make him emperor. If no heir of the Chu is left, you and the gallant men of China can select a person qualified to be ruler. Then our country will be a teacher to China, or we'll at least enjoy the prestige of being China's elder uncle."

"With our scholar-officials adhering to the old ways as they are, who'd be willing to have his sons adopt Manchu hairstyles or dress?" Yi said with a sigh.

At this Hŏ shouted wrathfully, "Who are these so-called scholar-officials? How brazen it is to presume to call themselves so, when they were born in the land of the barbarians Yi and Maek! The white coat and white trousers you always wear are fit only for mourning, and you bind your hair and wear it on your head like a gimlet—just like the southern barbarians! How can you pretend to know about good manners? General Fan Wu-chi didn't spare his own head to avenge a personal grudge, and King Wu-ling of Chao wasn't ashamed to adopt barbarian dress in order to make his country strong. You say you want to avenge the Ming, but you still want to keep that gimlet-shaped topknot on your head. That's not all. You'll have to train yourself in horsemanship, swordsmanship, spear handling, archery, and stone throwing, yet you wouldn't part with those wide, flapping sleeves, and you speak only of good manners. I made you three proposals, but there is not one that you will carry out. How can you be a trusted officer? Is this all there is to a 'trusted officer?' Men like you should be beheaded!"

Hŏ looked right and left in search of a sword, as if he were ready to kill Yi then and there. Yi was so terrified that he threw himself through the back window and ran home.

The next day, Yi called at Hŏ's cottage again, but it was deserted. Hŏ had disappeared.

THE STORY OF A YANGBAN

[*Yangban chŏn*]

The word *yangban* is an honorific term for scholar-officials. In Chŏngsŏn county there was a yangban who was wise and who loved reading books. A new magistrate was wont to visit him to pay his respects.

The yangban was very poor; every year he borrowed grain from the county office. Over the years he had come to owe a thousand bags.

One day the governor made a tour of inspection. When he reached Chŏngsŏn county and examined the lending of government grain, he grew very angry and said, "What kind of yangban is he who borrows so much from military supplies?" He then ordered his imprisonment.

The magistrate pitied the yangban, for he knew that he had no means to restore the grain. He could not bear to jail the yangban but had no choice.

The yangban wept day and night but could find no solution.

His wife abused him. "You always love to study, but you're no good at returning government grain. A yangban you say, but your kind isn't worth a penny."

A rich man in the village heard of this and discussed the matter with his family. "The yangban may be poor but his standing is always high and prestigious. We may be rich, but we are always considered mean and low. We dare not ride horses, and when we see a yangban we lose heart and tremble. We scrape and bow before him in the courtyard, dragging our noses and walking on our knees. We have always been disgraced like this. Now, because he is poor that yangban cannot pay back the grain. Being in great distress, he will not be able, despite his prestige, to keep his title. I want to buy his position for myself."

He then visited the yangban and proposed to settle the account for him. The yangban was very pleased and consented. Thereupon the rich man sent the grain to the county office.

Astonished, the magistrate went to the yangban to find out how he had managed to repay the grain. Wearing a coarse felt cap and a hemp jacket, the yangban prostrated himself in the mud, referred to himself as a "small man," and dared not look up. Greatly astonished, the magistrate got down, raised him up, and asked, "Sir, why do you humiliate yourself like this?"

The yangban became even more afraid, bowed his head, and prostrated himself once more. He said, "I am terror stricken. Not that I dare to humiliate myself, but I have sold my title to repay the loan. The rich man is now yangban. How can I use my former status to honor myself?"

The magistrate sighed and said, "How superior the rich man is! How yangbanlike the rich man is! To be rich without being stingy is righteousness. To be anxious about another's difficulties is goodness. To despise the mean and desire the honorable is wisdom. That man is truly a yangban. However, a private sale without a contract may lead to litigation. You and I will call together the people of the county as witnesses and draw up a deed. I will sign it as magistrate."

Thereupon the magistrate went to his office and summoned the gentry, farmers, artisans, and merchants to his courtyard. The rich man was seated to the right of the deputy magistrate, and the yangban stood below the clerks. He then began to draw up a deed:

"On a certain day of the ninth month of the tenth year of Ch'ien-lung [1745], the following deed is executed because I have sold the title of yangban to pay back the official grain I borrowed. Its value is one thousand bags.

"Now the term yangban has many implications. He who studies only is called a scholar; when he holds court rank, he is called a great officer; when he has moral authority, he is called a superior man. The military corps stands to the west, the civil corps to the east; hence there are two corps. You may follow either of these courses, but from now on you must give up mean and base thoughts and imitate the ancients, with a lofty aim. You must always arise at the fifth watch, light the oil lamp, focus on the tip of your nose and sit with your buttocks on your heels, and recite from the *Critical Writings of Tung-lai* as smoothly as a gourd rolling on ice. You must bear hunger and cold and never say you are poor. You must tap your teeth and snap the back of your head,[1] swallow your spittle when you cough, brush your plush cap with your sleeves, and wipe away the dust that rises like waves. But you must not rub your hands too much when you wash or rinse to excess. You should summon your slave girls with a drawn-out voice, and walk in a leisurely manner, dragging your shoes. You should copy the *True Treasure of Classic Literature* and the *Anthology of T'ang Poetry* with characters like sesame seeds, one hundred to

1. To help circulation and invigorate oneself.

a line. Your hands should not hold cash or your mouth ask the price of rice. However hot it is, you must not take off your stockings or loosen your topknot at the dining table. You should not eat the soup first or slurp when sipping. Your chopsticks should not mash the food. You must not eat raw scallions or lap your mustache when drinking coarse wine or suck in both cheeks when smoking. You must not strike your wife in anger or kick utensils in irritation. You must not strike your children with your fists or swear at your servants or curse and kill your slaves. When scolding your oxen and horses, you must not insult their former owners. When ill, do not call a shaman; when sacrificing, do not invite monks. Do not warm your hands over a brazier; when talking, never splutter; and don't slaughter oxen or gamble. Should you act contrary to any of these precepts, the yangban can take this document and initiate legal action to rectify the wrongs.

"The magistrate of Chŏngsŏn county signs and the deputy magistrate and steward sign, as witnesses hereof."

Thereupon the attendant boy affixed the seals. The sound of stamping the seals clashed with the drum beats announcing the hour; the paper looked like a sky strewn horizontally with the seven stars of the Big Dipper and vertically with the three stars of Orion's Belt. Then the clerk read it.

The rich man stood in disappointment for some time but finally spoke: "Is this all there is to being a yangban? I heard that a yangban was like an immortal. If it means nothing more than this, I have been cheated. Please change it to read more profitably."

Thereupon the magistrate executed another deed which read: "When Heaven gave birth to people, it divided them into four classes, and among these the most honorable is that of scholar-officials, also called yangban. There is no profit greater than this. They do not till the soil or engage in trade. With a smattering of classics and histories, the better ones will pass the final examination, lesser ones will become doctors. The red diploma of the final examination is no more than two feet long, but it provides everything one needs—indeed it is like a purse. Even if a doctor gets his first appointment at thirty, he can still become famous on account of his father's name and fame. If he wins the favor of a man of the Southern faction,[2] his ears will become white from sitting under a sunshade,

---

2. A powerful political faction during the last quarter of the eighteenth century.

and his stomach full with the "yes" of servants. In his rooms he can tease female entertainers with an ear pick, and his grains piled in the courtyard are for the cranes to peck. Even a poor scholar in the country can decide matters as he wishes. He can have his neighbor's oxen plow his fields first, or use villagers for weeding. Who will dare behave rudely to him? Even if he fills your nostrils with ashes, catches you by the topknot, or pulls your hair at the temples, you cannot show resentment . . ."

When the deed was half written, the rich man put out his tongue and said, "Stop, stop. How absurd! Are you trying to turn me into a robber?"

Shaking his head he went away. And for the rest of his life he never mentioned the word yangban.

Chŏng Yag-yong (1762–1836)

ON DISMISSING A SERVANT
[Ch'ultong mun]

Once upon a time, Wang Pao [first century B.C.]drafted a labor contract for his slave. It was so severe and exacting that the slave could not sleep at night or rest during the day. Moreover, the rules were as numerous as the hairs on a cow, and Wang's nagging was as irritating as the droning of a mosquito. The slave toiled until his joints creaked and his bones ached. Tears and snivel flowed down his face, wetting his chin and chest. But to revile him because of momentary anger is not a gentleman's way.

Now in my servant's contract I made the terms generous. Its contents follow:

"Get up at dawn, sweep the yard, and dredge the mud from the drain. Quietly cook rice—only wash the chaff off and cook it well; you don't have to make it sweet and soft. After breakfast, hoe the garden. Cut down the dead trees, clear the plot of tangled vines, and plant peach or plum trees. Your work includes transplanting persimmon trees, grafting crab apple trees, separating the eggplants, thinning out scallions, picking mallows, plucking leeks, manuring the taro patches, heaping soil around the potato stalks, leveling the banks around the cabbage patch, and drying mustard seeds in the sun. Tend the cucumbers and water them, but take care not to hurt their stems. Sluice water through the tube to the lotus, plait straw mats to protect the plantains, and at times bank up the roots of the gardenia and pomegranate and water them. Mow the grass to clear the path and cut down trees to repair the bridge; chase away village urchins and keep haymakers away from my farm. But do not frighten them.

"You are not expected to do all this in a single morning, but to work at them throughout the seasons. In addition, you will at times deliver provisions to mountain temples, make trips to fishmarkets to buy fish and dry them, go to town to get pills, or run to a neighbor's house to borrow ginger or dates. In most cases, the distance will not be more than five to ten ri. When hungry, you may eat rice cakes and drink wine, but not to the point of falling down from drunkenness. If you have energy left, go to the mountains to cut down ailanthus and mangrove and store them as firewood for the rainy season. I will give you a patch of dry and paddy fields, where you can plant rice and beans. When harvest time comes, report to me promptly, but you are in sole charge of your own weeding and plowing. I will not take you to task if you have a bad crop. But if you don't follow my instructions, you will lose your job."

When I had read all this to him, the servant kowtowed, putting his hands to his brow, and said, "I am grateful to your honor for your favor." His face beamed with delight, and he repeated his oath of loyalty.

"I will not complain," he said, "even if I should become a pigmy or a cripple in your service. Flog my buttocks if I ever go back on my words."

His deeds, however, did not follow his words, like those of an official who neglects his duties once he gets his position. Wherever he went, he raised dust. As if confused, he did nothing right. He never fertilized nor watered. Mugwort grew thick and brambles ran wild. Snakes crawled about, and children ran away in fear. The vegetables and cucumbers were rotten, and flowering plants did not put forth their buds. He was in collusion with woodcutters and allowed them to fell trees. After breakfast, he sallied out only to return after dark. He prowled around the markets, drank much, and when he began to sober up, he snored under the tree. He wore fine linen and ate minced and pickled meat. He was not only stupid and dull, but arrogant and foolish. He giggled over nothing, bragged, and told lies. He committed crimes every day. When admonished with kind words, he did not reform.

At last, Master Yun called him in and rebuked him in a stern voice: "According to our country's rules of conduct, no one ranks higher than a minister. Yet, if he does nothing to earn his salary, he must be removed in order to accommodate the wishes of the people. If a magistrate is soft, weak, and unfit to uproot the villains and the rich local bullies, or if he is greedy and petty-minded and cannot comprehend the royal concerns, he must be dismissed so as not to squeeze the blood and fat of the people. But you are a mere servant in the kitchen. How dare you think to escape a similar punishment? Return your salary and don't presume to covet what is not due you."

Upon hearing this, the servant bit his fingers and pounded his chest with his fists in regret. His snivel flowed three feet long and his tears fell as heavily as an autumn rain.

Anonymous

THE STORY OF A PHEASANT COCK
[*Changkki chŏn*]

When Heaven and Earth came into being, all things prospered. Man stood above the animals below. There are three hundred species of winged creatures, and three hundred hirsute ones.

Observe the pheasant, plumed in five colors and called a gorgeous creature. In accord with the inborn nature of mountain birds and wild beasts, the pheasant lives far away from the world of man. Its arbor is the tall pine tree by an emerald stream in the dense forest; it pecks at grain scattered in the fields. All alone, it is often caught by official hunters and hounds to fill the stomachs of high ministers and rich old men in Seoul, and its feathers are used to decorate army banners and dusters at the shops—indeed, its contributions are many.

Young hawks fly up to the highest peak of White Cloud Terrace to scan the hidden valleys and magnificent scenery. Club-carrying hunters shout here and there, and hounds follow the scent between eulalia plants and oak leaves—alas, there is no escape. Byways, too, are encircled by hunters; where can this hungry bird escape the freezing cold?

In the hunting season, the pheasant cock is dressed in a purplish-red silk robe with yellow-green silk collar and white neckband, capped with a jade hairpin and twelve beautiful tail feathers. How grand he looks! Dressed in a finely quilted blouse and skirt, his mate walks behind her nine sons and twelve daughters, marching down the open field in a row.

"You peck in that row while we peck in this one. When we peck at beans, one by one, we need not envy what man provides. Living beings are not meant to starve. To eat our fill is only our fortune."

Then they espy a red bean in the very middle of the plain.

"It looks delicious," exclaims the pheasant cock. "How can I refuse Heaven's gift? I shall have it—it's my luck."

"Don't eat it yet. I see the tracks of men in the snow. It looks suspicious," warns the pheasant hen. "Upon looking closer, I see that the ground has been swept clean. Please don't."

"How foolish! Now it is the coldest month of the winter, with snow piled up everywhere. Birds have stopped flying over the mountains, and all roads are blocked. How can there be any human trace?"

"Your reasoning may be sound, but last night I had a dream that portends disaster. Please consider the matter carefully."

"Let me tell you my dream. I flew up to heaven on the back of a yellow crane to greet the Jade Emperor. He conferred on me the title of 'Retired Gentleman of Mountains and Groves' and granted me a bag of beans from his granary. This must be one of them. The ancients say that the hungry eat well and the thirsty drink easily. I shall fill my empty stomach."

"Your dream has been so, but I interpret mine as unlucky. At the second watch I dreamed that rain slashed the slopes of the North Mang hill, and a double rainbow in the blue sky suddenly turned into a cangue and cut off your head; it must portend your death. Please don't eat it."

"Don't worry about your dream. It predicts that I will come out first in the royal examination on the Ch'undang Terrace in Ch'anggyŏng Palace; I will parade through the streets of Seoul, with the two twigs of flowers that the king has granted me garlanding my head. I'll study hard for the examination."

"Let me tell you my dream at the third watch. You wore an iron cauldron weighing a thousand pounds and drowned in the deep blue sea, and I wailed alone on the shore—it must portend your death. Please don't eat it.''

"That dream is even better. When the great Ming is about to be restored and calls for Korea's help, I will be a general wearing a helmet and will cross the Yalu, restore order in the central plains, and return home in triumph.''

"That may be so; but listen to my dream at the fourth watch. An old man sat in the high hall and a boy was offering a cup of wine when the poles supporting the twenty-two-foot-wide awnings collapsed over our heads, a sign of bad luck. I had another dream at the fifth watch: towering pines filled our courtyard, and three stars guarded the purple forbidden enclosure, while the supreme sky god, the Great Unique, was surrounded by the Milky Way. Then one star fell before our eyes—it must have been a general's star. It is said that a similar star fell when Chu-ko Liang died on the Wu-chang plain.''

"Don't worry. The collapsed awning means that you and I will sleep together tonight on a floor of grass, with screens of flowery trees, a stump for a pillow, arrowroot leaves for a bed, and oak leaves for a quilt. The fall of the star means that the old mother of the Yellow Emperor has conceived a son with the help of the seven stars of the Great Dipper, and the Herdboy and Weaver will meet again on the seventh day of the seventh month. Hence you will have a wonderful son. Dream such a dream often.''

"At cockcrow I dreamed that, wearing a colorful jacket and skirt, I roamed the green hills and blue streams, when suddenly a shaggy blue hound bared his teeth, jumped on me and clawed me. Dumbfounded, I fled into a cluster of hemp plants—slender hemp plants fell down, and thick ones flew about, all tangled about my slim waist. This portends that I shall be a widow in mourning. Please, for my sake, don't take that bean.''

Fuming with anger and stamping and kicking, the pheasant cock retorts: "With your lovely face and graceful carriage, you will take a lover behind the back of your lawful husband. Hence the joints of your wings will be tied with a heavy orange rope, and you will be dragged through the streets and clubbed. That's what your dream forebodes. Never mention such a dream again or I shall break your shins.''

"A crying goose by the water carries a reed in its beak—that is the proper conduct of a gentleman. A phoenix that soars thousands of feet high does not peck a single grain of millet—that is a gentleman's sense of honor. Though a small creature, you should set your heart on noble deeds. Po I and Shu Ch'i shunned the grain of Chou, and Chang Liang of the Han retired because of his illness and ate with strict caution. You too should emulate them and be careful not to touch that bean.''

"How ignorant you are! As if I don't know the requirements of proper conduct, much less have a sense of honor. Yen Hui, a disciple of Confucius, died young, no more than thirty. For all their loyalty and integrity, Po I and Shu Ch'i starved to death on Mount Shou-yang. Because of his Taoist practices, Chang Liang joined the Master of the Red Pine. What good is a sense of honor? At the Hu-t'o River, Liu Hsiu, later Emperor Kuang-wu, ate a dish of cooked barley; at the Huai, Han Hsin, who later became general of the Han, was fed by an old woman bleaching coarse silk. Who knows but that I too will become like them after eating that bean?''

"I'll tell you what you will be. As a gravekeeper, you will be appointed a magistrate of the Yellow Springs, never to see the green hills again. Don't old books tell you how many stubborn men have brought ruin on themselves and on their families? The first emperor of the Ch'in never listened to the advice of his son Fu Su, and after forty years of disaffection and turmoil the dynasty was toppled by the time of his heir, Erh Shih. Hsiang Yü didn't listen to his aide Fan Tseng and had eight thousand of his men killed. Chased by the Han army, he fled to Wu-chiang and could not bear to return home; so he cut his own throat and died. King Huai of Ch'u rebuffed the advice of Ch'ü Yüan and decided to go himself to the land of his enemy, the Ch'in. When he reached the Wu-kuan pass, he was hemmed in by the Ch'in army and eventually died there. How pitiful and shameful must his spirit have been when it met the loyal soul of his banished minister, who had drowned himself in the Mi-lo River out of despair. Your stubbornness is bound to be your ruin!''

"Do you mean to say that everyone who eats a bean will perish? Read the old texts, and you will find that those whose names carry the letter *t'ai*[1] all lived to a good old age and became famous. The Heavenly Emperor of remote antiquity (*t'ai*-ku) lived 18,000 years; *T'ai*-hao Fu Hsi's heirs continued for fifteen generations; T'ang

---

1. *T'ae* in Korean. The author is punning on another Korean reading of the same logograph as *k'ong* (bean) *t'ae* and cataloguing those whose names contain the logograph.

T'ai-tsung quelled the rebels and helped found the T'ang. Among the hundred grains, the bean is the first. Chiang *T'ai*-kung was sought out by King Wen of Chou when he was eighty; the immortal poet Li *T'ai*-po went up to heaven on the back of a leviathan; and the *T'ai*-i [the Great Unique] in the north is a star among stars. After feasting on this bean, I too will live long like Chiang T'ai-kung, ride the heavens like Li T'ai-po, and become an immortal in the Great Unique.''

Utterly listless, the pheasant hen withdraws.

Observe the behavior of the pheasant cock as he moves toward the bean. Spreading out his twelve plumes, head nodding, hesitating, he advances. With his crescent-shaped tongue he pecks—and two pulleys fall over and strike his head, just as Chang Liang and his assassins tried with an iron bludgeon to assassinate the First Emperor but mistakenly struck the carriage of his attendants. Bang! Crash! He's caught!

''Haven't you realized what will become of you? A woman's word might ruin a family or bring disgrace.''

Observe the pheasant cock. In a flat field of gravel, he lets his hair down and rolls about, striking his breast. Now he gets up, heart-stricken, plucks the grass, stamps his feet, and cries his heart out. His nine sons, twelve daughters, and his friends all pity him and offer condolences. Only wailing resounds among the empty hills and bare trees.

''The cry of the cuckoo among the moonlit empty hills quickens my sorrows,'' the pheasant hen says. ''I read in the *General Mirror,* 'Good medicine is bitter to the mouth but benefits the sick, and loyal words offend the ear but are of benefit to one's conduct.' If only you had listened to my advice! How frustrating! What a pity! To whom can I lay bare the deep love between us? My tears become nails; my sighs, wind and rain. My breast is ablaze. What am I to do with my life?''

Lying under the pulleys, the cock still mumbles, ''Hush, you wretch! Who would climb a mountain if he knew what troubles lay ahead? If one is clumsy, one misses the opportunity. Have you ever seen anyone die without trouble? One can often tell by feeling the pulse if one is to die. Take my pulse and see.''

''Your pulse on the spleen and stomach has stopped, that on the liver is chilly, the yin and the yang pulse are gone, and your life pulse is slow. How sad! O you stubborn monster!''

"What about my eyes? Examine the pupils."

"Now you're done for. The guardian of one pupil left you this morning, and that of the other is about to abandon you. . . . I was born under an unlucky star. How often have I become a widow! My first husband was snatched away by a young hawk; the second was bit by a hound; the third, shot by a gunman. With you I have been happy, but before marrying off our nine sons and twelve daughters, you've been caught by the trap. Hunger drove you to your death. Am I possessed by evil spirits? How pitiable you look! Is it because of your age or illness? Or was it ill luck that brought you disgrace? Or the evil spirit of obstinacy? How can I make you live? Whom will our children marry? Who will help me deliver the one I am carrying? I planted magic herbs in a wide field thick with clouds and trees and hoped to share happiness with you for a hundred years. But before three years have passed, I must part with you forever. When will I find again one with your imposing stature? O sea-roses on the stretch of beautiful sand, don't resent the fall of flowers. Next spring you will bloom again, but my husband, once gone, will not return. I'll be nothing but a widow, a widow!"

"Don't give way to sorrow," he says, half opening his eyes. "It was my mistake to marry one who keeps on losing husbands. The dead cannot return to life, so it is unlikely that you will see me again. But if you are determined to have a last look at me, tomorrow morning after breakfast follow after the man who has trapped me. I might be hanging in the market of Kimch'ŏn or in some provincial storehouse; or as a dried pheasant presented by a bride to her in-laws. Don't mourn my death, but keep yourself chaste so as to be honored by the court. How wretched is my lot, how terrible! Don't cry, beloved, my innards are melting. However sad you might be, dying is sadder."

He puts up his last struggle—planting his legs firmly against the lower pulley and tugging at the one above. There is no escape; he merely loses some feathers.

Master T'ak the trapper has been keeping watch. With a mouse-fur cap and a stick, he walks swinging his arms, then jumps upon the trap and pulls out the catch. Rejoicing, he dances. "Hurrah, I'm happy. Did you come down to drink the blue-green water below Mount South? Or did you come to visit peach-blossom girls in the gay quarters beyond the mountain? Not knowing that greed invites death, you were driven by appetite. So I've caught you, who used to roam over blue waters and green hills. I'll offer a sacrifice to the mountain spirits and catch all your kin." He pulls out the bird's crooked tongue and places it on a rock and, pressing his hands together, prays: "May that trap also catch a pheasant hen. I put my faith in Amitābha and compassionate Avalokiteśvara!" Bowing again and again, he goes downhill.

Immediately thereafter, the widow goes to the rock and gathers the feathers; crying bitterly, she covers them with arrowroot leaves and buries them with honeysuckle. She inscribes the pheasant cock's name and rank on a flag of day lily and hangs it on a small pine tree; then she digs a grave close to where two sides of a field meet, and buries her mate. Then she offers a sacrifice to the mountain spirits and Buddhas. Offerings befitting the occasion include dewdrops of a fallen leaf, dishes made of Cheju chestnut shells, cups made of acorns, and spoons and chopsticks made of rushes. The well-dressed crane offers the first cup; the nimble swallow is the receptionist; the eloquent parrot is the protocol officer; and the crested ibis, kneeling, intones the prayer: "On a certain month of a certain year, your widow ventures to announce to you, my deceased husband, who were a retired gentleman, that your body has been buried and your soul has returned to become a spirit. I bow down and offer libations and hope that you will reject the old and follow the new. Please rely on this."

When they hesitate to clear the offertory table, a hungry black-eared kite looks down and asks, "Who is the chief mourner? I'll get you!" It pounces upon one of the young and flies up to the highest peak of the storied cliffs, but fumbles its prey: "I've been starving for more than ten days because of the cold. Today I have caught the favorite of man. The steamed octopus, abalone, and sea cucumber are the favorites of a bachelor. The peaches of immortality that ripen every ten years are the fruit of the Queen Mother of the West; the wine from Mount Yak is the favorite of the Four Whitebeards of Mount Shang; and puppies that have died a natural death and chicks are the favorites of the kite, the general. Large or small, it is a pheasant. Let me eat it to abate my hunger."

Swaying to and fro, it looks around and behold, the pheasant chick has fled downhill, leaving not a trace. He heaves a sigh, "For the cause of justice and humanity, Kuan Yü released Ts'ao Ts'ao in the narrow pass of Hua-jung, and out or kindness, even the suspicious kite has set his victim free. My children will enjoy a golden age.''

The jackdaw from the T'aebaek mountains, after an excursion to the north peak, comes down to allay his hunger and offer condolences to the widow. After feasting on the fruit, he sighs and says, ''With his stature and virtue I thought he would live long. But because of a single red bean he met with an untimely death. Listen, if there is a hero, there will be a fleet steed; if there is a writer, there will be a famous calligrapher. I see that we are destined to enjoy marital harmony. Would a butterfly have time to ponder fire among the flowers, and a goose to dread an old fisherman when it sees water? You know my lineage and prospects, so why don't we make our fortune and enjoy bliss for a hundred years?''

''Even though you're a creature of no account, in which book of propriety have you read that a widow can remarry before fulfilling a three-year mourning? 'Clouds follow the dragon, and winds follow the tiger.' And 'A wife should follow a husband.' Am I to follow every suitor?''

''How ridiculous,'' the furious jackdaw retorts. ''The *Book of Songs* says, 'We are seven sons, / And cannot compose our mother's heart.'[2] It suggests that the lady in question remarry even if she has seven sons. Much less should you, puny thing, talk about integrity and constancy. I've yet to see a chaste pheasant hen whose virtue is honored.''

Then an owl, after expressing his condolences, turns to the jackdaw: ''Your body is black, and your bill grotesque. You don't even stand up before an elder.''

''You bigoted and rude owl! If your eyes are depressed and your ears move, does that make you an adult? Don't laugh at my black body. My outside may be black, but not my inside. I happened to fly over Shan-yin and got smudged. Don't ridicule my bill. Kou-chien of Yüeh, whose mouth had the wily look of a crow's bill, polished his sword for ten years and succeeded in vanquishing his enemy, Fu-ch'a of Wu. How could you, unlettered as you are, pretend to be an adult? I won't let you go unpunished.''

As they quarrel, a lone goose happens to alight from among the clouds. Looking around, his body drooping, he attempts to cope

2. Poem 32.

with the situation. "Elders? When Su Wu of the Han was in captivity for nineteen years in the north sea, I carried his message and offered it to the Son of Heaven with my own hands. Take this into account; you'll know who the elder is."

A drake in the lotus lake in front, seven times a widower without an heir, has been seeking a mate for some time. Upon hearing the news, he intends to propose without a matchmaker—a honking goose carrying a pair of wooden geese,[3] an osprey bearing a box on its back, a lively stork following behind, and a graceful halcyon as a verbal messenger.

The halcyon asks, "Is the bride home? The bridegroom is here."

"You think you can handle a widow so easily—without even checking our fortune. Are you pressuring me?"

"What need to have a widow's and a widower's fortune told?" the drake asks. "A bride and a bridegroom sharing the same bed—that's marriage. Let's choose an auspicious day . . . Yes, tonight is the best. A union of two families is the source of all happiness. Cut out the chatter, let's go to bed."

"You think you can get away with such wicked words because you're a male?"

"Listen to what I can offer you. In a broad fairyland of water, with pink smartweed and white duckweed for our home, silver scales and jade bodies for our food, we'll wander about—the water is the best place to live between heaven and earth."

"How can you compare your life with mine on land? Listen. We stroll the flat plain and broad field, fly up to a high peak on a cliff, and view the four seas and the eight quarters. In late spring, when the willows are green by the inn, golden orioles flit among the willows; and when peach and plum blossoms brighten the night and the cuckoo calls sadly, even grass and trees and birds and beasts are moved to tears. In the season of yellow chrysanthemums, we pick a myriad of fruit and store them everywhere. The gorgeous attire and the belling of the manly pheasant are without parallel. How can your life match ours?"

The drake remains silent. By his side is a pheasant cock, another visitor bearing condolences: "A widower for three years, I have not been able to find a fit bride. Our ties are preordained by Heaven,

---

3. At the marriage rite (chōnan) the bridegroom presents a wooden goose to the bride at her parent's home as a symbol of conjugal love.

and by the grace of God, we'll become a couple and beget and marry off sons and daughters till we're buried in the same grave.''

"When I think about my late husband, it would be inconsiderate of me to marry again so soon. But I'm neither young nor old—I'm just at the age when I know the appeal of a man and how to keep house. When I look at your manliness, I've no desire to keep chaste, and lust stirs in me. I've rejected all other suitors. They say 'Birds of a feather flock together.' Indeed, it is meet and just for us to unite. Let's live together in any way we please.''

The pheasant cock billows and flaps his wings, and they are married. Ashamed, the crow, owl, and drake retreat, and the black bird, halcyon, greenfinch, parrot, peacock, goose, heron, stork, and crow-tit all return home.

With the new bridegroom in front and nine sons and twelve daughters behind, braving the snow and wind, they return to the emerald stream in the cloud-capped wood. The next spring, after marrying off their children and visiting famous hills and waters, on the fifteenth of the tenth month, they enter the great river and transform themselves into clams.[4]

4. An old Chinese superstition.

WOMEN WRITERS

Princess Hyegyŏng, daughter of Chief State Counselor Hong Pong-han, was born on August 6, 1735. At the age of nine she was chosen to marry the heir-apparent (Prince Sado, 1735–1762) and was officially appointed in the following year. The prince gradually began to develop symptoms of mental illness, and his stern and authoritarian father, King Yŏngjo, finally imprisoned him in a rice chest, where he died seven days later. Hyegyŏng's misfortunes did not cease even after her son became king (1776) and are recounted at some length in her memoir, *A Record of Sorrowful Days.*

As a focal point of the court and political intrigue of eighteenth-century Korea, she attempts to sift and shape the past and impose a pattern on her life. Here the truth of her feelings rather than the truth of facts receives emphasis. Keenly aware of the destiny to which she was born, she continues her search to find the meaning of her tormented existence throughout her experiences as a child, crown princess, widow, and queen mother. Although she wrote her *Record* to enlighten others, she must have discovered in it a sense of process and fulfillment as she imaginatively relives her life. She is at her happiest in the reconstruction of her all too brief childhood, as the following episode written in 1795 shows.

The author of "Viewing the Sunrise" accompanied her husband, Shin Tae-son, a staff supervisor in the provincial government, to Hamhŭng in the northeast. There she wrote travel records, portraits, and diaries. "Viewing the Sunrise" represents her vivid and lyrical descriptive style at its best.

"Lament for a Needle" is a delightful prose piece written in graceful language by an anonymous lady.

The author of "The Dispute of a Woman's Seven Companions," also nameless, takes a fling at the members of her own sex. Her little story is told with great simplicity, with art concealing art, to her friends gathered around a brazier on a winter night. It is interesting to note that she praises the perseverance of the thimble, portrayed as having mastered the secrets of life.

Princess Hyegyŏng (1735–1815)

from A RECORD OF SORROWFUL DAYS
[Hanjung nok]

That year [1743] an edict was issued, requiring families with eligible daughters to register them for selection. Someone said, "There will be no harm done if you don't register your daughter. A poor family like yours should be spared the burden of preparing the clothing required for the process." "No," replied Father. "We have been salaried officials for generations. I receive a stipend from the court, and my child is the granddaughter of the Minister of Rites. I dare not deceive the court." Father then registered me.

At the time, we were so poor there was no way for us to have a new wardrobe made. My skirt was sewn from fabric that had been stored away for the marriage of my deceased elder sister, and old material was used for linings. Even so, we had to borrow money. The image of Mother making every effort to complete the preparations still haunts me.

The first of the three sittings was held on the twenty-eighth day of the ninth month [November 13]. In spite of my inferior gifts, King Yŏngjo was extravagant with praise and the queen gazed steadily on me. The mother of the prince, Royal Consort Yi, beaming with happiness, summoned me before the ceremony and was very affectionate. When court women scrambled for seats, I was so embarrassed I could hardly think. When it was time to bestow royal gifts, Royal Consort Yi and her daughter, Princess Hwap'yŏng, noted my deportment and tried to correct my clumsiness, and I followed their instructions. I then left the palace for home and slept that night in Mother's arms.

Early the next morning Father came in and spoke anxiously to Mother. "What shall we do? Everyone seems sure our daughter will be the one favored." "We shouldn't have registered her," Mother whispered. "The daughter of a poor, unknown scholar." In my sleep I overheard their worried words and woke up crying. Recalling the kindness I had enjoyed at the palace, I was perplexed. Mother and Father tried to comfort me. "Do you think she understands?" they asked each other. I was deeply troubled in the period following the first sitting. Was it because I knew I would suffer many ups and downs at court? On the one hand I felt strange, but on the other this sensation seemed truly to forebode what was to come.

Word of my rating after the first sitting brought a large number of clansmen to our home. Servants we had not seen for years returned as well. This taught me much about our private and social life.

The second sitting was held on the twenty-eighth day of the tenth month [December 13]. I was terribly frightened. Mother and Father too were worried; they hoped that by sheer chance I would not be selected. When I entered the palace grounds, however, I sensed that the choice had already been made; my temporary quarters had been refurbished, and I was treated with a new deference and respect. I lost my composure as I ascended to the royal presence. The king did not treat me as he did the other girls, but instead made his way past the beaded screen and began stroking me affectionately. "We've gained a beautiful daughter-in-law. We remember your grandfather well. When we had your father in audience, we were pleased because we knew we had gained a capable man. You are indeed his daughter!" His Majesty was most pleased. The queen and Royal Consort Yi were also pleased beyond words and showered me with affection. The princesses gathered around me, holding my hands, and they did not want to let me go. I remained a long while in a building called Kyŏngch'un Hall, and there a luncheon was served to me. A lady-in-waiting tried to remove my green jacket. I did not want to take it off, but she coaxed and cajoled me until I relented. After she took my jacket off she measured my various parts. I was so startled I fought back tears of humiliation until at last I mounted the palanquin to leave the palace; then I cried. The palanquin was carried by palace servants. In the street the rows of black-robed women servants charged with delivering royal messages were an eerie sight.

When we arrived home, I was carried through the gate reserved for male visitors. Father raised the screen covering the palanquin and lifted me out. He had on his ceremonial robe and seemed uneasy treating me with deference. I clung to my parents and could not hold back the tears. Mother too was attired in her ceremonial robes, and the table was decked with a scarlet cover. Mother appeared somewhat awe-stricken as she kowtowed four times before accepting the missive from the queen, and twice before accepting one from Lady Yi.

From that day on my parents began to use honorific expressions with me, and the elders of the clan treated me with respect—all this made me feel uncomfortable and indescribably sad. Greatly apprehensive, Father gave me thousands of words of advice. I felt like a sinner who has no place of refuge. I did not want to leave Father and Mother. My heart felt as though it would melt away—nothing seemed to interest me.

Close relatives and distant clansmen wanted to see me before I entered the palace. Not a single relative failed to visit us. Distant ones were entertained in the courtyard. The important ones included my great-great-uncle from Yangju. One great-uncle remarked, "The palace is very strict. Once you enter its confines, we may not have the chance to meet again. Always respect your superiors and act with prudence. The letter *kam* in my name means 'mirror,' and *po* means 'help.' Keep this in mind after you have entered the palace." I seldom saw my great-uncle, so for some reason his words made me sad.

The third sitting was scheduled for the thirteenth day of the eleventh month [December 28]. With the passing of each day my grief grew more unbearable and I slept each night in Mother's arms. Father's sisters and his sister-in-law tried to comfort me; they stroked me tenderly and were unwilling to take their leave. Father and Mother caressed me night and day, losing several nights' sleep. Even today my heart chokes when I think of those final days.

Two court ladies appeared at our home the day after the second sitting. One of them was Lady-in-waiting Ch'oe, governess to the prince, and the other was Kim Hyo-dŏk, an overseer of the attendants. Unlike the others, Lady-in-waiting Ch'oe had a stern and imposing mien. Her family had served in the palace for generations, so she was conversant with the intricate court protocol and never made a blunder. Mother was cordial and made the two ladies feel welcome. They measured me for clothing and left. Lady-in-waiting Ch'oe returned before the third sitting, accompanied this time by Mun Tae-bok, another overseer. They presented me a gift of clothing from the queen —a formal dress jacket of green brocade, another of pine-pollen yellow with grape designs, and a third of lavender silk, along with a crimson satin skirt and a summer jacket of fine cambric.

I had never before owned such fine dresses and had never coveted the clothing of others. There was a girl my own age among our close relatives. Her family was wealthy and provided her with every possible item of clothing and toilette, but I never envied her. One day she came to visit wearing a gorgeous deep-red lined skirt with elaborate seams. Mother watched for a while, then asked me, "Would you like to have a dress like that?" "If I owned one, I would surely wear it," I answered, "but I don't want one if we have to have it made." "You may be the daughter of an impoverished family," Mother said. "But when you marry, I'll make you a beautiful dress like that one as a remembrance of the maturity you displayed today." Before the third sitting, when it became evident that I was fated to marry the prince, Mother came to me in tears. "We couldn't afford to give you beautiful dresses, but I never forgot my promise to you. Though you will soon be entering the palace, where common costume is not allowed, I dearly wish to fulfill that promise to you." She made the skirt before the third sitting came, and grieved. When I wore it, I dissolved in tears.

I felt that it would be appropriate to bid farewell to the ancestors of my clan and to Mother's family, and I made my desire known. My wish was conveyed through the sister-in-law of Pak Myŏng-wŏn, who was married to Princess Hwap'yŏng, to the mother of the princess, Royal Consort Yi. His Majesty was soon informed of my wish and commanded me to go.

Mother and I rode in the same palanquin and proceeded to the head house of the Hong clan, the house of a cousin of my father [Hong Sang-han]. Because he and his wife had no daughter, they had often invited me to come and stay with them. Their love for me was known to His Majesty, who ordered Hong Sang-han to help with the preparations for my marriage. After I was selected, he came and stayed with us. When Mother and I arrived at his home, his wife was delighted to see me. I was led up to the ancestral shrine to perform obeisances. Though it was customary for younger generations to perform the kowtows in the courtyard, I worshiped the spirits in the main hall of the house. I was stunned by the perquisites of my new status.

We then went to the home of Mother's family, where we were received by the wife of Mother's brother. She was pleased to see us and reluctant to let us go. On previous visits, my cousins took joy in giving me great hugs and in carrying me around on their backs. This time, however, they took pains to maintain a decorous distance and treated me with deference, which made me feel sad. I was particularly fond of one of my cousins, who later married into the Shin clan, and I was very sorry to take leave of her. On our way back home we stopped to pay our respects to Mother's two older sisters.

The days flew. Soon it was the twelfth day of the eleventh month.

That night Father's sisters led me outside. "Take a good look at your home, for it will be the last time," they urged me, as they led me by the hand into the bright moonlight. The chilly wind blew over the snow, and tears coursed down my cheeks. I lay awake the whole night.

The command summoning me came by messenger early the next morning, and I donned the formal dress provided by the queen. The wives of clansmen came to bid final farewells, and close relatives gathered to accompany me to the detached palace. We all went up to the ancestral shrine and performed a special service to inform the spirits of the great honor being bestowed on the family. Father struggled to hold back his tears as he intoned the prayer.

Parting was more than we could bear. I cannot find words adequate to describe the sorrowful scene.

I entered the palace compound, resting first at the Kyŏngch'un Hall before continuing on to the T'ongmyŏng Hall, where I was received in audience by the Three Majesties—the king, the queen, and Queen Dowager Inwŏn. It was the first time the queen dowager had seen me. "This girl is beautiful and looks very kind," she said. "She is a blessing to the kingdom." His Majesty patted me affectionately. "Our daughter-in-law is bright. We made a good choice." I cannot express in words the delight of the queen and the sincere affection of the Royal Consort Yi. Though of childish mind, I was grateful for the royal favor.

I freshened my makeup and changed into the ceremonial dress. After I had eaten, it was growing late; I performed the four kowtows to the Three Majesties and then left for the detached palace. His Majesty appeared in person at the place where I mounted my palanquin; he looked at me and took my hand. "We want you to be happy. We'll send you a copy of the *Lesser Learning*. Study it with your father and be happy until you return again to us." He favored me with his tender love.

Dusk settled and the lanterns were lit as I left the palace. Being surrounded by palace ladies, I was unable to sleep; I wanted Mother at my side. I was unhappy without her and could easily imagine how sadness must weigh heavily upon her heart. Lady-in-waiting Ch'oe, however, was strict and bereft of human feelings. She explained, "The laws of the kingdom do not allow you to stay on, My Lady," and with that, had sent Mother away, so that I was unable to get any sleep. There was no human being as inconsiderate as she!

The following day His Majesty sent me a copy of the *Lesser Learning*. I studied it every day with Father. The head of our clan was with us, as were Father's brothers, Hong In-han and Hong Chun-han, the latter a mere boy at the time. My oldest brother was also with us. The king sent a reader too, for me to peruse in my spare moments, one which His Majesty had written for Princess Hyosun when she married the former heir apparent.

My quarters were well appointed with furniture, curtains, folding screens, and toilette articles. Among these was a large Japanese pendant shaped like an eggplant. It was a gift from Royal Consort Yi and had once belonged to Princess Chŏngmyŏng—daughter of King Sŏnjo—who had married my great-great-grandfather. She had presented the pendant to her granddaughter, who had married into the Cho clan. Either the family sold it, or it had fallen into the hands of the family of a lady-in-waiting who attended the royal consort. Now I, a descendant of the princess, was again in possession of a family heirloom that had once belonged to her. Surely this was more than mere chance.

My grandfather was a lover of art and had owned an embroidered screen in four panels. After he passed away [1740], one of his servants sold the screen. Later, Royal Consort Yi purchased it from a relative of one of her attendants, had it remounted, and gave it to me to put up in my bedroom. When my aunt visited me she recognized the screen at once. "This is most strange," she said. "An object owned by your grandfather has found its way into the palace and now stands in his granddaughter's bedroom!"

Another gift from the royal consort was her own eight-panel dragon screen. Father was astonished when he saw it. "The dragon on this screen is just like one that appeared in a dream I had the night before you were born [August 5, 1735] . . ." The dragon's black scales were highlighted with gold thread so that the gold and black intermingled. Father mused, "This dragon is not completely black, but otherwise it's exactly like the dragon of my dream." Everyone marveled at the return of grandfather's screen and the similarity of the embroidered dragon to the one in Father's dream.

I stayed over fifty days in the detached palace. During that time I was often favored by visits from the lady-in-waiting sent by the Three Majesties to inquire after my welfare. On each occasion, at the wishes of the Three Majesties, my family was invited to visit me, and they were treated with hospitality. A visit by a lady-in-waiting was followed by the appearance of officials from the Ministry of Rites, who brought a table and wine cups. . . .

On the ninth day of the first month [February 21, 1744] I was invested as crown princess; the state marriage was scheduled for the eleventh. My separation from Father and Mother was nearing. I could no longer control my feelings and cried the whole day long. Father and Mother were sad and worried but managed to hold their composure. "When the daughter of a subject marries into the royal house," Father warned, "her family wins royal favor and her house flourishes. But when the family flourishes, disaster is sure to follow. Our house has enjoyed great favor for generations because my ancestor married a princess. Having enjoyed royal favor, I cannot shrink from boiling water or scorching fire. Still, for a lowly scholar to become overnight the father-in-law of the heir apparent—this is not a portent of happiness but the beginning of disaster. From this day on I will live in fear and anxiety, not knowing when I will die." Father instructed me in even the smallest aspects of my daily conduct. "Respectfully serve the Three Majesties and discharge your filial duties. Be helpful to the heir apparent with right actions and always be cautious in your speech. Add luster to the good fortune of your family and your kingdom." Though Father's exhortations on the last day ran to thousands of words, I listened with respect. But I could not keep back my tears. Even the trees and stones must have been touched by my grief!

After the marriage ceremony, Father and Mother continued their admonitions, which I heeded with respect. Father wore the deep-red official robes and cap of one who has passed the civil service examination. Mother wore her large ceremonial wig and the dress with the lime top and violet collar. All our kinsmen came to bid me farewell, and the palace was surging with guests. Every movement of Father and Mother conformed to the rules of propriety, and their deportment was grave and correct. Everyone said, "The kingdom has gained exemplary in-laws."

Lady Ŭiyudang

VIEWING THE SUNRISE (1832)
[from *Tongmyŏng ilgi*]

I was anxious lest I miss the sunrise, so I slept not a wink all night. I often called out to a servant and asked for the boatman. He reported that I was sure to have a view, but I was impatient and could not calm myself. At cockcrow I shook the kisaeng girls and servants awake. A petty official arrived and told us that a supervisor in the office thought it too early to leave. Undeterred, I pressed a maid to cook rice-cake soup, which I left untouched. Then hurriedly I climbed to the terrace.

All was bathed in the serene light of the moon. The sea was whiter than the night before, and a gale chilled my bones. Billows shook hills and valleys, but the stars gleamed brightly in the east. It seemed that daybreak was still a while off. A wakened child was shivering, and the teeth of the kisaeng and servants chattered. My husband was worried that I might catch cold. Uneasy, I remained silent and sat still, giving no sign that I was cold. Dawn was slow in coming, so I summoned a servant, who replied that I had to wait. Only the breakers pounded the shore. A cold wind slashed at us, and the attendants around me hung their heads and buried their mouths in their chests, shivering. After a while, the stars in the east began to fade, the moon grew dim, and I could make out a streak of red light. With a cry of joy, I alighted from my sedan chair. The kisaeng and servants about me did not look up.

At last day broke, and I observed a long red aura, rolls of red silk spread on the sea, myriad acres dyed crimson and filling the sky. The angry waves were majestic, and the water the color of a red carpet; the spectacle was magnificent! The color then turned dark red, dyeing the faces and dresses of the onlookers. The swelling waves last night had been jade-white, but now they stretched ruby-red to the horizon. What a splendid sight!

The red color spread and the sky and water were bright, but the sun had not yet risen. Clapping her hands, the kisaeng said anxiously, "Now the sun is behind the waves. The red will turn to blue, and clouds will appear."

Disappointed, I was about to leave, but my husband and daughter encouraged me. "Don't worry. You'll see it," they said. Then Irang and Ch'asŏm said derisively, "We're used to watching the sun rise, so we know. You might get a chill, my lady, so why don't you go in and wait?"

I went back to my sedan chair, but a maid stopped me: "The sun will be up any minute. How could you leave now? Those girls are only guessing." Irang laughed and said, "They don't know any better. Don't believe what they say. Please go back and ask the boatman again." When the boatman replied that today's sunrise would be spectacular, I came out of the sedan and noticed that Ch'asŏm and Pobae, who had seen me entering the sedan, were gone, as were the three maids.

The splendid redness seemed to leap skyward. When Irang cried out to me to look down, I saw a red skein was pushing through swirls of clouds underwater, and a strange object the size of my palm, glowing like a charcoal on the last night of the month. As its reflection rose in the water, it seemed round as a chestnut but amber like a jewel, only more beautiful and brighter.

Above the red sea the object spiraled in circles, casting a shadow about the size of half a sheet of paper. Then the chestnut turned into a fireball as large as a tray, square and level, bouncing about and spilling redness over the length and breadth of the sea. The color began to fade, and now the sun sparkled like a jar, gleaming in ecstasy, blinding my eyes. The air, tinged with red, was brisk and clear. I could count the first pink rays, and then the tray turned into a wheel of fire pushing skyward. No longer a jar, the rays that had earlier touched the sea now were like tongues of thirsty cattle about to leap into the ocean with a splash. The vast expanse of sky and water was dazzling, but the waves began to lose their hue, and the sun now was sharp and bright. Where else could one see such a spectacle?

When I think back, the first sight of the half sheet of paper came when the sun was about to emerge from the sea, its direct rays polishing the water. It resembled an amber chestnut when it was halfway above the horizon, seemingly half afloat, soaking up the red from the ocean. And when it was jar-shaped, the lovely object blinded me and more closely resembled a phantom. Ch'asŏm and Pobae, who had left earlier, came up to the sedan to congratulate me on viewing sunrise at the hour of the Hare [5–7 a.m.], while Irang, clapping hands, was pleased that I at last saw what I had longed for.

When I was about to leave, village women milled around to bid me farewell, asking for parting gifts. I gave them some money to share among themselves.

On the way back to my lodging, I felt as if I had found a priceless treasure.

Anonymous

LAMENT FOR A NEEDLE
[*Choch'im mun*]

On a certain day of a certain month in a certain year, a certain widow addresses a needle with a few words. To a woman the needle is an indispensable tool, though commonly people do not cherish it. You are only a small thing, but I mourn you greatly, because so many memories are connected with you. Alas, what a loss, what a pity! It has been twenty-seven years since I first held you in my hand. How could a sensitive human being feel otherwise? How sad! Holding back my tears and calming my heart, I bid my last farewell to you by hastily writing down this account of your deeds, and my memories.

Years ago, my uncle-in-law was chosen as the head of the Winter Solstice Felicitation mission to China, and upon his return from Peking he gave me dozens of needles. I sent some to my parents' home, some to my relatives, and divided the rest among my servants. I then chose you, and got to know you, and we have been together ever since. How sad! The ties between us are of an extraordinary nature. Although I have lost or broken many other needles, I have kept you for years. You may be unfeeling, but how could I not love you and be charmed by you! What a loss, what a disappointment!

I was unlucky, I had no children, but I went on living. Moreover, our fortunes began to fail, so I devoted myself to sewing, and you helped me forget my sorrow and manage my household. Today I bid you farewell. Alas, this must have come about through the jealousy of the spirits and the enmity of Heaven.

How regrettable, my needle, how pitiful! You were a special gift of fine quality, a thing out of the ordinary, prominent among ironware. Deft and swift like some knight-errant, straight and true like a loyal subject, your sharp point seemed to talk, your round eye seemed to see. When I embroidered phoenixes and peacocks on thick silk or thin, your wondrously agile movements seemed the workings of a spirit. No human effort could have matched you.

Alas! Children may be precious, but they leave when the time comes. Servants may be obedient, but they grumble at times. When I consider your subtle talents, so responsive to my needs, you are far better than children or servants. I made you a silver case enameled in five colors and carried you on the tie-string of my blouse, a lady's trinket. I used to feel you there whenever I ate or slept, and we became friends. Before beaded screens in summer or by lamplight in winter, I used to quilt, broad-stitch, hem, sew, or make finishing stitches with double thread, and your movement was like a phoenix brandishing its tail. When I sewed stitch by stitch, your two ends went together harmoniously to attach seam to seam. Indeed, your creative energy was endless.

I intended to live with you for a hundred years, but, alas, my needle! On the tenth day of the tenth month of this year, at the hour of the Dog [7–9 p.m.], while I was attaching a collar to a court robe in dim lamplight, you broke. You caught me unawares, and I was stunned. Alas, you had broken in two. My spirit was numbed and my soul flew away, as if my heart had been pulverized and my brain smashed. When I recovered from my long faint, I touched you and tried to put you back together, but it was no use. Not even the mystic arts of a renowned physician could prolong your life nor a village artisan patch you up. I felt as if I had lost an arm or a leg. How pitiful, my needle! I felt at my collar, but no trace of you remained.

Alas, it was my fault. I ended your innocent life, so whom else could I loathe or reproach? How can I ever hope to see an adept nature or ingenious talent like yours again? Your exquisite shape haunts my eyes, and your special endowments fill me with yearning. If you have any feeling, we will meet again in the underworld to continue our companionship. I hope we may share happiness and sorrow, and live and die together. Alas, my needle!

THE DISPUTE OF A WOMAN'S
SEVEN COMPANIONS

[Kyujung ch'iru chaengnon ki]

The lifelong companions of a woman are seven: a yardstick, a pair of scissors, a needle, blue and pink threads, a thimble, a long-handled iron, and a regular iron. The lady of a household is in charge of them all, and none of them can keep a secret from the others.

A certain lady who often used to work with the help of her seven indispensable companions one day felt sleepy and dozed off.

Brandishing her slender body, the yardstick said, "Friends, listen. I am so perceptive I can measure the long, the short, the narrow and the wide. It's because of me that my lady does not fail in her work. Don't you think my merits far exceed yours?"

Thereupon, the scissors grew angry. Shaking her long mouth, she replied, "Don't praise yourself so. Without my mouth nothing could be shaped or formed. It is only through my services that your measurements become reality. Hence my merits excel yours."

The needle reddened. "Don't argue, my two friends. However well you measure or cut, nothing is accomplished without me. So I am the first in merit," she retorted.

The blue and pink threads roared with laughter. "Don't talk nonsense. The proverb says, 'Three bushels of pearls have to be strung to become a treasure.' What could you accomplish without us?"

Then the old thimble laughed, "Don't quarrel, threads. Let me cut in. I cover tactfully the sore spot in the fingers of the old and young, so that they can finish their work easily. So how can you say I'm without merit? Like a shield on the battlefield, I help to get the work done, no matter how difficult it is."

The long-handled iron, fuming with rage, moved forward in a single stride. "You all want to show off your talents, but listen to me if you don't want to be called fools. My foot can smooth out wrinkles and correct what is crooked and bent. It's my work you're taking the credit for. Without me, you'd be ashamed to face our mistress no matter how hard you tried."

Choking with laughter the iron said, "How true the word of the long-handled iron. Were it not for our services, who could talk about rewards?"

Their wordy warfare woke up the lady, who suddenly rose up in anger. "What merits are you talking about? It is my eyes and hands that make you do what you do. How can you wrangle impudently behind my back and indulge in self-praise?''

The yardstick sighed and mumbled, ''How unkind and unfeeling is humankind. How could she measure anything without me? As if this is not enough, she uses me to thrash the maidservants. I've held out this long only because I happen to be strong, and it saddens me that our mistress takes no notice of this.''

The scissors joined in tearfully, ''How unkind my mistress is. Day after day she forces open my mouth and cuts thick and hard fabrics just as she pleases. But if I am not to her liking, she strikes my two cheeks with an iron hammer, accuses me of having thick lips or blunt edges and whets me. For her to talk like that after all she's done to me.''

The needle heaved a long sigh, ''I was made from an iron stick belonging to the fairy Ma-ku of Mount T'ien-t'ai and polished for ten years on a rock. She inserts thick and thin threads through my eye and makes a hole with my leg through all kinds of dress goods. What an odious chore! Overcome with fatigue, sometimes I pierce her under the fingernail and draw blood, but there's no relief.''

The blue and pink threads chimed in, ''How can we tell all our sorrow? Clothes of men and women, fine quilts, children's colorful dresses—how could one sew a single seam of these without us? When lazy ladies and girls pull us through the needle's eye too hard, or when we cannot pass through it easily, they curse us in unspeakable language. What is our crime, and how can we bear this grief?''

''My resentment is immeasurable,'' the long-handled iron complained. ''For what retribution am I stuck in a brazier day and night throughout the seasons? After children have used me sloppily to iron the clothes for their dolls, they stick me in any old way until some woman picks me up and scolds me for not being warm enough, or for being too light or too heavy. They make me feel there is no place for me in the world.''

''Your sorrow is like mine,'' the iron said, ''so there is no point rehearsing it. They put burning charcoal in my mouth; it's like the tyrant Chou's cruel punishments of roasting and branding. Only because my face is tough and hardened can I bear it. And that's not all. Lazy women will put off their work for ten or even fifteen days. Then they blame me for the wrinkles that will not come out.''

The old thimble leaped forward and waved her hand, saying, ''Listen, girls. I'm half dead from overwork too; stop chattering on and on. If our mistress hears, all your sins will be visited on me."

"What if she does?" all replied. "She cannot manage without us."

The lady finally scolded, "You dared to criticize my behavior while I was asleep," and dismissed them all. They were withdrawing in despair when the old thimble fell prostrate. "The young ones acted thoughtlessly. Please calm your anger and forgive them," she begged the lady.

Thereupon the lady called all of them together. "I forgive you for the sake of the old thimble," she said. She promised the thimble never to be parted from her, and to this day she cherishes her as her most intimate friend.

THE ART OF THE
SINGER: *P'ANSORI*

The *p'ansori* is a narrative verse form that flourished in the eighteenth and nineteenth centuries in Korea. It is performed by a single professional singer *(kwangdae)*, who both narrates and assumes the roles of his characters, accompanied by a single drummer. In addition to his superior voice and memory, the singer was expected to master narrative and dramatic techniques. The aspiring singer usually trained his vocal art near a waterfall, so that his voice could outreach the sound of the cascading water. Only when his singing was clearly understood by the people nearby was he ready to perform in public.

Around a core story comprising one or more folktale motifs, the plot of a *p'ansori* gathered fictional accretions during its long transmission. These accretions from different eras tend to be long, complicated, and often inconsistent, evincing a gradual accumulation of episodes created or reworked by the *kwangdae*. In a sense, a *p'ansori* is composed in performance. The late prose adaptations of the *p'ansori* works tend to smooth out textual and imagistic inconsistencies resulting from multiple authorship.

The *p'ansori* works comprise several layers of material: the archetypal pattern of separation–trials–return and the primitive ritual of human sacrifice; romance motifs of ascent and descent, usually to the underworld or the Dragon Palace; references to older classics of China and Korea; and reflections of indigenous beliefs. Core stories may have had their origin in the creative depth of the people; but classical allusions crept in when they were written down by the educated class. When they were sung as entertainment, native elements such as folk songs were added during the performance, often altering, abridging, or expanding the sequence of episodes. It is no wonder that such texts combine the learned and the folkloristic and are rich in song and drama. The text presented here, *The Song of a Faithful Wife, Ch'unhyang*, dates from the late nineteenth century and was written down by Shin Chae-hyo, the acclaimed master of the genre.

As the daughter of Minister Sŏng and a kisaeng, Ch'unhyang (Spring Fragrance) combines in her character the propriety of the nobility and the laughter of a female entertainer. Her resistance to force is remarkable: she confronts the evil governor's flogging with song. Likewise, at the governor's birthday party, the secret Royal Inspector reveals himself by indirection; as a knight of the brush, he strikes his adversary with the sword of poetry and finally redeems Ch'unhyang's love.

The realistic handling of the material, the local color—the setting is South Chŏlla province—the masterly narrative and characterization, the pervading humor even when the situation reflects the evils of insolent power—all these have made it the favorite story of the Korean people.

In reality, however, it is a satiric parody, a mock romance which assumes in the reader the knowledge of the values, conventions, and techniques of the romance. Its verbal brilliance is unmatched and difficult to render in translation—hence the translator presents the narrative in prose—but the native reader is often carried away by the charm, force, and rhythm of its verses.

This section begins with a *kasa* poem by Shin Chae-hyo, "The Art of the Singer," and the preface to the *Songs of the Kwanghan Pavilion* by Yun Tal-sŏn, who translated into Chinese verse *The Song of a Faithful Wife, Ch'unhyang*—both attesting to the popularity of *p'ansori* in the nineteenth century.

Shin Chae-hyo (1812–1884)

THE ART OF THE SINGER
[*Kwangdae ka*]

Poems by famous writers survive,
But they all seem to end in failure.
"Mount Kao-t'ang" and "The Goddess of the Lo,"
None believes in their tales of fantasy.
"The Ballad of Liang-fu" mourns the three brave warriors,
"The Return" sings of a recluse's peace and leisure.
"The Parting," "A Song of Everlasting Sorrow,"
"Lien-ch'ang Palace," and "Ballad of Fen-yin"—
Their sad stories grip our heart.
Fame and fortune are a spring dream,
And separation in life or by death draws a sigh.
Compare our happy wanderings on earth, our inn;
But a master singer is hard to come by.

His first requisite is to create characters,
The second, narrative art, and the third, musical knowledge.
Then comes his dramatic power.
Full of gusto and grace, he plays many roles—
Now a fairy, now a ghost—making us laugh and cry—
Romantics and gallants, men and women, old and young . . .
With musical taste he discerns five tones,
Handles the six pitches and sings by vocalization . . .
He narrates words of fine gold and jade,
Adding flowers to embroider, to adorn his story—
A lovely lady with seven jewels emerges from a screen,
The full moon appears from behind clouds—
He makes us laugh with beaming eyes!
Character is inborn and cannot be changed.
Such are the singer's infinite inner workings.

The prelude flows like a clear stream under ice,
Or a boat gliding with a fair wind.
Then comes the sound of falling water gushing forth.
His lifting voice soars like a lofty peak,
Rolling down voicefalls in a cascade—
Long and short, high and low, endless changes.
The "weaving" technique is a swallow's talk or a parrot's song,
He improvises from slow to quick tempo—
His rolling voice, the cry of a phoenix on Mount Cinnabar,
His floating voice, the whoop of a crane in a clear sky,
His plaintive voice, the lute played by Shun's consorts,
Sudden bouncing voice, a peal of thunder,
A resonant command tosses Mount T'ai—
Now it's a desolate wind among bare trees,
Sad as "Going Out the Passes" or the "Song of the Swan."
We change color and shed tears—
How arduous is the singer's art!

Let's forego great singers of the past,
And name the recent artists[1] praised by the people.
If we were to compare them with Chinese poets,

---

1. Most singers flourished in the first half of the nineteenth century, except for Kwŏn Sa-in (dates unknown) and Kim Kye-ch'ŏl (*fl.* 1777–1834).

The audacious Song Hŭng-nok, who rolls melodious words,
Is Li Po, king of poetry, who causes
Flowers to blossom and nature to exult in harmony.
Mo Hŭng-gap is Tu Fu, sage of poetry—
Now a moon-washed pass, a wind among trees,
Now the call of a crane in the farthest sky.
Kwŏn Sa-in is Han Yü, who revived the ancient prose style—
A waterfall thundering from a thousand-storied cliff.
Shin Man-yŏp is the drunken Tu Mu passing by Yang-chou—
He tilts the Milky Way from the ninth heaven,
In a voice lucent as the moon-white dew.
Hwang Hae-ch'ŏng may be Meng Chiao—
A pair of cuckoos calling to each other
In an empty hill flooded by moonlight.
Ko Su-gwan is Po Chü-i, who encourages husbandry—
He's a farmer who, with his wife and children,
Brings lunch to the southern acre and chats.
Kim Kye-ch'ŏl resembles Ou-yang Hsiu—
His boundless voice captures nature's forces,
A mountain's bright shadow or a cloud scudding by the moon.
Song Kwang-nok can be Wang Wei—
A boat under easy sail in the vast blue sea.
And Chu Tŏk-ki is Su Tung-p'o,
With numberless variations so elusive and wondrous!
Each enjoys fame with individual talent.
But who has mastered all the secrets?
I would attain perfection but cannot,
And that consumes my heart.

Yun Kyŏng-sun

PREFACE TO *SONGS OF THE KWANGHAN PAVILION*
[from *Kwanghallu akpu*]

The *p'ansori* is presented by one standing and one sitting. The stand-ing one is a singer, the sitting one a drummer. Among the twelve pieces in the *p'ansori* repertory, the "Song of Ch'unhyang" is the most important. When we listen to this, we must realize that it consists of three main episodes. The first starts when Yi Mong-nyong meets Ch'unhyang at the Kwanghan Pavilion, a story similar to that of Liu Ch'en and Juan Chao of the Later Han, who met fairies on Mount T'ien-t'ai.[1] The middle concerns the hardships of the imprisoned Ch'unhyang as she endures all kinds of trials but remains constant to the last. In the end Yi Mong-nyong returns to Namwŏn with honors and meets Ch'unhyang again. This third episode resembles the story of Hsü Te-yen of the Ch'en who, by putting together the two halves of a mirror, was reunited with his wife.[2] Although the story originated from a folk tradition and is in the vernacular, it is like the airs in the *Book of Songs,* and unlike the lewd music of the tyrant Chou of the Shang. Alas! Since the death of Ch'unhyang several centuries ago, there have been many talents among the nobility, but they have left it only as a performing art on the stage for the singer, and none has composed poems in Chinese to spread the story.

My friend Yun Tal-sŏn loved antiquities and read widely. He regretted that the story had not been handed down. Thereupon, on the basis of the song, he composed one hundred and eight cantos in Chinese and named them the "Songs of the Kwanghan Pavilion." Oh! The work magnificently recreates Ch'unhyang's complexion, expression, laughter, speech, cry, and tears. Indeed, there is nothing that does not capture her spirit. Its joyful scene recalls birds chirping after a spring rain has cleared, and it makes us happy. Its sorrowful scene makes us feel as if we listened to the sound of a sobbing stream and the cry of gibbons in the midst of a gorge, and its melancholy moves us to tears. Its cheerful scene can be compared with the great dancer Kung-sun, who brandished her sword like a rainbow and dodged the sun, as if the world seemed to go on rising and falling.[3] This illustrates the author's mastery of the craft of poetry. If Ch'unhyang saw it, she might smile but also secretly blush. Ch'unhyang is gone. Under the cherry blossoms you may offer a cup of wine to her soul and then drink it. Although we borrow the mouth of Ch'unhyang to sing this song, it can cleanse one's mind of lifelong sorrow piled up like a mountain.

In the twelfth month, the year of Imja [1852], the mountain dweller Okchŏn writes this preface at the Sleeping Lute Pavilion.

1. Li Fang et al., *T'ai-p'ing yü-lan,* chap. 41.
2. Meng Ch'i, *Pen shih-shih.*
3. Tu Fu's ballad, "On Seeing a Pupil of Kung-sun Dance the Chien-ch'i," line 4.

THE SONG OF A FAITHFUL WIFE, CH'UNHYANG

[from Yŏllyŏ Ch'unhyang sujŏl ka]

The servants and the yamen slaves went in a body to Ch'unhyang's house. Ch'unhyang knew nothing about their arrival; she was thinking night and day of nothing but her husband. Her sobs could be heard through the blinds. The voice of the deserted girl quivered with sad moans and wails; anyone who saw or heard her was wounded in his own heart. Her longing for her husband robbed her of appetite and sleep; the yearning drew her skin tightly over her bones and made her weak. She sang a mournful dirge:

> I want to go, I want to go,
> I want to follow my love;
> I will go a thousand miles,
> I will go ten thousand miles,
> I want to go to him.
>
> I will go through storm and rains,
> I will go over the high peaks,
> Where sparrow-hawks and peregrines fly,
> Beyond the Tongsŏl Pass.
>
> If he will come back,
> I will take off my shoes
> And carry them,
> So I can run to him.
>
> My husband is in Seoul
> And does he think of me?
> Has he forgotten me completely?
> Has he taken another love?

She was crying like this when the yamen servants heard her moans. They were not made of wood and stone, they could not help but be moved. All the joints of their bodies melted like spring ice on the Naktong River: "How pitiful! What sort of men are we who can do nothing to help a girl like that!"

Then one of the servants shouted: "Come on out!"

Ch'unhyang was surprised by the noise and peeped through a crack of the door. She saw the soldiers and servants gathered: "Oh, I had forgotten! Today is three days after the arrival of the new governor and they are doing the third-day inspection. What a row they are making!"

She opened the sliding door: "Hey, guards, come here, come here! We weren't expecting you. Aren't you tired after your journey with the new governor? How is he doing? Did none of you go to the old governor's house, and bring me a letter from the young master? When he was with me, I was very unwelcoming to you because I had to respect his position, but I didn't forget you. Come in, come in!"

She took Kim, Yi and several of the others by the hand, pulled them into the room and made them sit down. Then she called Hyangdan: "Bring in a tray of wine!"

When they had drunk and were slightly tipsy, she opened a box and took out five yang: "Please take this and buy yourselves something to drink on the way, and don't say anything about it afterward."

The men were befuddled with the wine. They said: "You mustn't give us money. Do you think we came for money? Put it away again."

"Kim, you take it."

"It's against the rules, but there are a lot of us . . ." He took the money; but as they were turning to go, the chief kisaeng came along clapping her hands: "Come on, Ch'unhyang, do as you are told! I'm as constant as you are! I'm as chaste as you are! Why are you making such a fuss about being chaste and faithful? Just for the sake of your virtue, you pretty little miss, the whole yamen is in trouble and everyone is likely to lose his job. Come on quickly! Get along fast!"

Ch'unhyang came reluctantly out of the gate, leaving her retirement: "Don't treat me like this, madam. You have your position and I have mine. We must all die once, and no one can die twice." So they hobbled along together to the yamen.

"Ch'unhyang's here."

When the governor saw her, he was delighted: "It is Ch'unhyang, indeed. Come up on the dais."

She went up and meekly sat down. The governor, entirely bewitched, gave an order: "Go to the office and tell the treasurer to come here." The little treasurer was already on his way in. The happy governor said: "Look at her now. That's Ch'unhyang."

"M–m . . . She's a pretty little piece. Very well formed. When we were in Seoul you kept talking about Ch'unhyang. She's worth looking at."

The governor laughed: "Will you play the marriage-broker?"

The treasurer sat down: "Oh, you shouldn't have called her yourself first. It would have been more proper to send a go-between. Things have been done a little carelessly. But now you have gone so far, there's really nothing you can do but marry her."

The governor enjoyed the joke, and then said to Ch'unhyang: "From today you must dress yourself properly and start to attend in the yamen."

"Your commands must be respected, but since I am married I cannot do as you say."

The governor laughed: "A pretty girl, a pretty girl! And a virtuous woman too! Your chastity is wonderful. You are quite right to reply like that. But young Yi is the eldest son of a famous family in Seoul, and do you think he regards you as anything more than a flower he plucked in passing? You are a faithful child and while you keep faith the bloom will fade from your face, your hair will grow white and lose its luster. As you bewail the vain passing of the years, who will there be to blame but yourself? However faithful you remain, who will recognize it? Forget all that. Is it better to belong to your governor or to be tied to a child? Let me hear what you have to say."

Ch'unhyang replied: "A subject cannot serve two kings and a wife cannot belong to two husbands; that is my principle. I would rather die than do as you say, however many times you ask me. Please allow me to hold to my ideal: I cannot have more than one husband."

The treasurer spoke to her then: "Look here, now; that lad is fickle. Life is no more than a mayfly, and men are all the same. Why should you take so much trouble? His Excellency proposes to lift you up in the world. What do you singing girls know about faithfulness and chastity? The old governor has gone and the new governor has arrived: it's proper for you to obey him. Stop talking strangely. What have loyalty and faithfulness to do with people of your sort?"

Ch'unhyang was amazed. She relaxed her posture and said: "A woman's virtue is the same for high ranks and low. If you listen I will explain.

"Let's talk about kisaeng. There are no virtuous ones, you say; but I will tell them to you one by one: Nongsŏn of Haesŏ died at Tongsŏn Pass; there was a child kisaeng of Sŏnch'ŏn who learned all about the Seven Reasons for divorce; Non'gae is so famous as a patriot that a memorial was erected to her and sacrifices are offered there; Hwa-wŏl of Ch'ŏngju had a three-storied pavilion raised in her memory; Wŏlsŏn of P'yongyang has a memorial; Ilchihong of Andong had a memorial erected in her lifetime, and was raised to the nobility; so do not belittle kisaeng.''

Then she turned to the governor again: "Even a mighty man like Meng Pen could not wrest from me my determination to stay a faithful wife and keep the oath, high as the mountains and deep as the sea, that I made to young master Yi. The eloquence of Su Ch'in or Chang Yi could not move my heart. Chu-ko Liang was so clever that he could restrain the southeast wind, but he could not change my heart. Hsü Yu would not bend his will to Yao; Po I and Shu Ch'i would not eat the grain of Chou. Were it not for Hsü Yu there would be no high-principled ministers; were it not for Po I and Shu Ch'i there would be many more criminals and robbers. I may be of humble birth, but I know these examples. If I forsook my husband and became a concubine, it would be treason as much as it is for a minister to betray his king. But the decision is yours.''

The governor was furious: "Listen, girl: treason is a capital offense, and insulting royal officers is equally serious. Refusing to obey a governor meets the same punishment. Don't put yourself in danger of death.''

Ch'unhyang burst out: "If the rape of a married woman is not a crime, what is?''

The governor in his fury pounded the writing desk with such force that his hatband snapped and his topknot came undone. His voice grew harsh: "Take this girl away.'' he shouted. The yamen guards and servants answered: "Yes, sir,'' and ran forward to catch Ch'unhyang by the hair and drag her away.

"Slaves!''

"Yes, sir!''

"Take this girl away.''

Ch'unhyang trembled: "Let go of me!''

She had come halfway down the steps when the slaves rushed up: "You stupid woman, if you talk to the officers like that, you'll never save your life.''

They pulled her down to the ground of the courtyard. The fearsome soldiers and yamen servants swarmed around her like bees and grabbed her hair, black as black seaweed, coiled like a kite-string on its reel in springtime, like a lantern on Buddha's birthday, coiled tightly. They threw her down on the ground. It was pitiful. Her white jade body was crumpled up like a figure six; she was surrounded by grim soldiers holding spears, clubs, paddles, and red cudgels.

"Call the executioner."

"Bow your heads, the executioner comes!"

The governor had recovered a little, but he was still trembling and panting: "Executioner, there is no need for any interrogation of this girl. Bind her to the frame immediately. Break her shin-bones and prepare the writ of execution."

See what the jailers do while they bind her to the frame? The noise they make as they pile the paddles and clubs in armfuls beside the frame makes Ch'unhyang faint.

Watch the executioner! He tries the paddles one by one, tests them for strength and suppleness, chooses one that will break easily and raises it over his right shoulder waiting for the governor's order.

"Receive your orders: if you pretend to beat her harder than you do, because you pity her, you will be punished on the spot. Beat her hard."

The executioner replied loudly: "Your orders will be obeyed. Why should we pity her? Now, girl, don't move your legs; if you do, your bones will break."

He yelled as he danced about her brandishing the paddle. Then he stood still and said to her quietly: "Just stand a couple of blows. I can't avoid it, but thrash your legs about wildly, as though it were hurting more than it does."

"Beat her hard."

"Yes, sir, I'll beat her!"

At the first stroke the broken pieces of the paddle flew through the air and fell in front of the governor. Ch'unhyang tried to bear the pain but ground her teeth and flung her head back, screaming: "What have I done?"

During the practice strokes, the executioner stood alone, but from the time he took the paddle to give the legal punishment, a servant stood facing him. Like a pair of fighting-cocks, as one stooped to beat, the other stooped to mark the tally, in the same way that ignorant penniless fellows in the wineshop mark on the wall the number of cups they have drunk. He drew a line for the first stroke. Ch'unhyang cried unrestrainedly:

One heart undivided,
Faithful to one husband,
One punishment before one year is over,
But for one moment I will not change.

All the townsfolk of Namwŏn, old and young, were gathered to
watch what was going on: "It's cruel! Our governor is cruel! Why
should he punish a girl like that? Why should she be beaten so? Look
at the executioner! When he comes out, we'll kill him!"

Everybody who saw and heard was weeping. Then came the second
stroke:

Two spouses are faithful,
Two husbands there cannot be;
Though my body is beaten,
Though I die for ever,
I'll never forget master Yi.

The third stroke came:

Three rules for a woman's life,
Three principles of behavior, and five relationships:
Though I am punished three times,
I will never forget my husband,
Master Yi of the Three Springs Vale.

Then came the fourth stroke:

The governor is father of the people,
But he ignores the four social classes;
He rules by force and power
And has no love for the people
In the forty-eight quarters of Namwŏn.
Though my four limbs are severed,
Alike in life and death
I'll never forget young master Yi,
My husband.

The fifth stroke came:

The five relationships remain unbroken:
Husband and wife both have their station;
Our fate was sealed by the five elements,
Sleeping or waking, I cannot forget my husband.

When the autumn moon shines on the paulownia where
   he is,
Will he send a letter to me?
Will there be a message tomorrow?
My innocent body does not deserve death.
Don't convict me unjustly.
Oh, oh, the pity of it!

The sixth stroke came:

Six times six is thirty-six,
And though I die sixty thousand times,
The body has six thousand joints,
All bound in love,
How can I change my heart?

The seventh stroke came:

If I have not broken one of the Seven Rules
Why should I receive seven punishments?
Take a seven-foot sword,
Cut me up and kill me quickly.
Executioner, do not spare me.
The seven jewels of my face must be destroyed.

The eighth stroke came:

The eight characters of my horoscope
Brought the governors of the eight provinces to meet me.
Are the governors sent
To rule the people well,
Or are they sent to do them evil?

The ninth stroke came:

In the nine organs of my body
My tears have made a nine-years flood.
The tall pine trees of the nine hills
Are cut and loaded on a riverboat
To go quick to Seoul
And lay my case before the king
In the ninefold palace.
When I leave the nine courts
I will go to the Three Springs Vale and meet my love,
To relieve my heart and refresh my soul.

The tenth stroke came:

> Though I live the tenth time
>   After escaping death nine times,
> My mind is made up for the rest of my days
>   And a hundred thousand deaths will not change it,
> But I cannot escape.
> Ch'unhyang at six and ten,
> Poor devil under the cudgels,
>   Is hardly alive.

Ten strokes were expected, but she was beaten fifteen times:

> The moon shines bright on the fifteenth night,
>   But is hidden in the clouds.
> My beloved is hidden in the Three Springs Vale.
> Moon, bright moon, do you see him?
> Why can I not see where he has gone?

Twenty strokes would have been enough, but they went on to twenty-five:

> Playing the lute of twenty-five strings,
> In the moonlight I cannot restrain my sorrow.
> Wild goose, where are you flying?
> If you go to Seoul,
> Take a message to my beloved,
> Who lives in the Three Springs Vale:
> See what I look like now;
> Take care you don't forget.

Her young mind craved to flee above the thirty-three heavens to the throne of the heavenly emperor. Her jade-white body was covered with blood, and she was bathed in tears. The blood and the tears flowed together, like peach petals in the water when the man of Wuling found the hidden vale.

Ch'unhyang cried in her bitterness: "Do not treat a girl like this. Better kill me quickly, and when I am dead my soul will become a cuckoo like the bird of Shu, crying in the empty hills on moonlit nights and breaking the dreams of young master Yi after he has gone to sleep."

She could not finish her words before she fainted. The officers and servants turned their heads and wiped their tears. The executioner who had beaten her also turned away, wiping his eyes: "No son of man should do such things."

All the onlookers and officials standing round also wiped their eyes and looked away, unable to bear the sight. "We shall never see anyone who takes a beating like Ch'unhyang. Oh, it's cruel, it's cruel! Her chastity is cruel; her virtue is from heaven."

Men and women, young and old, all alike were weeping, and the governor was displeased: "Now, girl, you have been beaten for insulting the governor. What good has it done you? Will you persist in your disobedience?"

Half dead and half alive, Ch'unhyang answered proudly: "Listen to me, governor; don't you understand an oath that binds till death? A faithless woman brings frost in summer weather. My soul will fly to the king and present its petitions. You will not escape; please let me die."

The governor was exasperated: "The girl is beyond reason. Put her in a cangue and send her to the prison."

The big cangue was fastened round her neck and sealed. The jailer took the weight of it and as they came out of the third gate the group of kisaeng saw it: "Poor Ch'unhyang! Keep hold on your senses! Oh, how piteous!" They stroked her limbs and offered her soothing drugs. They wept to see her. Just then the tall and stupid Fading Spring appeared: "What on earth is going on? It looks as though the board for a memorial gate is being brought in."

When she came closer and saw what it really was, she said: "Poor Ch'unhyang! How awful!"

While the commotion was going on, Ch'unhyang's mother heard these words, and rushed wildly forward to throw her arms round her daughter: "Oh! Why should this happen? What is her crime, and why was she beaten? Jailers! Chief clerk! What has my daughter done! Officers! Executioners! What enemy has ordered this? Oh dear, it's all my fault! I'm nearly seventy and I've no support. I have no sons and I brought up my only daughter so carefully and properly. I taught her to read and to study the rules of propriety for women, and she said to me: 'Don't cry, mother, don't cry. Don't be sad because you have no son. Can't my children offer sacrifices for you when you die?' Her great devotion to her mother was not surpassed even by Kuo Chü or Meng Tsung. Does social class make any difference to love for one's children? My soul will never rest. My sighs are wasting my heart away. Sergeant Kim! Sergeant Yi! Even though your orders were strict, why did you beat her so cruelly? Look at my poor daughter's wounds! Her legs were as white as snow, and now they are red with blood. If she had been the daughter of a well-born family, even a blind girl! But she is only the daughter of the kisaeng Wŏlmae. How can such things happen? Ch'unhyang, keep hold on your senses! Oh dear, oh dear, the pity of it!

"Hyangdan, go outside the yamen and hire two runners. I am going to send them to Seoul."

When Ch'unhyang heard that the runners were being hired, she said: "Mother, don't do it. What are you thinking of? If the runners go to Seoul and Mong-nyong sees them but does not know what to do about it, the worry will make him ill, which will make matters worse. Don't send them; I will go to jail."

She was carried on the jailer's back to the prison house, with Hyangdan bearing the weight of the cangue. Her mother walked behind. When they got to the door of the jail: "Keeper, open the gate. Are the keepers asleep?"

This is what the jail was like: the wooden bars were rotten, and a piercing wind came through them; through the cracks in the crumbling walls lice and fleas came in and attacked the whole of her body. . . .

*

Meanwhile Yi Mong-nyong was in Seoul studying poetry and composition night and day. He made himself master of a hundred authors; he was comparable to Li Po in poetry, and his calligraphy would compare with that of Wang Hsi-chih.

Soon there was an extraordinary examination, and he took his writing materials to the examination ground. Looking around, he saw a great concourse of people, crowds of scholars bowing before the king at one time. The royal orchestra was playing court music, and the parrot dance was being performed. The rector of the National Academy announced the theme appointed by the king, and the chief secretary posted it on the vermilion board. The subject for composition was: "Springtime in the examination ground is the same today as yesteryear." Mong-nyong found the subject to his liking. He spread out his paper and slowly ground his ink while he sought for inspiration. Then dipping his golden weasel-hair writing brush into the ink he began to write.

He wrote in the style of Wang Hsi-chih and according to the model of Chao Meng-fu. His brush flew over the paper, and he was the first to finish. When the chief examiner saw Mong-nyong's composition, every stroke was perfect and the couplets were like jewels on a thread. His calligraphy was strong, like dragons flying through the heavens. The verses had the rhythm of a flock of wild geese descending on the sandflats. He was the genius of his time. After the list of successful candidates had been announced, and he had received three cups of wine from the king, he was declared the top graduate of the examination. When he came out from the royal presence, he had the winner's sprays of pink paper flowers fixed on his hat, and he was wearing the yellow silk robe of his new rank, with cranes embroidered on the back and chest.

After the usual three days of celebration, with processions and games in the streets, he paid his respects to the family graves and then presented himself before the king. The king spoke to him personally: "The hopes of the court are set on you."

Then he called a royal secretary and appointed Mong-nyong Royal Inspector of Chŏlla province. It was the post he had always wanted. His embroidered robes of office, his heavy brass warrants and his brass yardstick were delivered to him. He left the royal presence and went to his own home. His official hat made him look awesome as a tiger from the mountain valleys.

He said goodbye to his parents and set off for Chŏlla. Outside the South Gate of the capital, at Ch'ŏngp'a post station, he mustered his scribes, agents and postmen, and mounted his horse.

When Mong-nyong and his men had parted for their several ways, Mong-nyong prepared himself for his journey. See what he looked like? No one would recognize him. His battered straw hat had no crown and was bound with wisps of barley straw; its hat strings were of the cheapest cord. The headband was all that remained of his topknot-cap. It had bone buttons, and was fastened with string. He wore a deceptively shabby coat, tied round the waist with a hank of yarn. Nothing remained of his fan but the ribs, and the two pine-cones hanging from its cords. It was his only protection against the sun. . . .

In every town, prefecture and magistracy he heard what was going on and tried to catch the feeling of the people, investigating the things that had been done by the authorities. All the yamens were in consternation. The minor officials were afraid, and those who had charge of public money were prepared to take flight, for it was known that the inspection teams were coming.

Eventually he came to Imsil, and in the fields at Kuhwa he found the farmers working. They were singing a farmer's song, and great was the din they made:

> Ŏyŏrŏ! Sangsadwiyo!
> Peace and prosperity reign through the land,
> High is the virtue of our king!
> Once again the children sing
> The songs that pleased the emperor Yao—
> Ŏyŏrŏ! Sangsadwiyo!

> The emperor Shun with highest power
> Invented the art of making brass dishes
> And plowed the fields of Li-shan—
> Ŏyŏrŏ! Sangsadwiyo!

> The Divine Husbandman made the hoe,
> And it has lasted from then till now.
> Wasn't that a mighty thing?
> Ŏyŏrŏ! Sangsadwiyo!

> Yü of Hsia, the gentle king,
> Brought an end to nine years' floods;
> Ŏyŏrŏ! Sangsadwiyo!

> T'ang of Yin, the gentle king,
> Suffered seven years of drought;
> Ŏyŏrŏ! Sangsadwiyo!

> We keep up the farmer's skill,
> Pay the king our tax in grain,
> Keep what's left to feed ourselves,
> Looking up to serve our parents,
> Looking down to wife and children.
> Ŏyŏrŏ! Sangsadwiyo!

So we set the hundred plants,
Tend them meetly in due season,
And they all bring forth their fruit—
  Ŏyŏrŏ! Sangsadwiyo!

What hope have we of rank and office?
What is finer than a farmer?
  Ŏyŏrŏ! Sangsadwiyo!

Tilling dry fields, plowing paddy,
We feed our mouths and fill our bellies.
  Ŏyŏrŏ! Sangsadwiyo!

Yi Mong-nyong stood leaning on his stick listening to them for a while: "It looks like a wonderful harvest this year."

But to one side there was a strange sight. Some wiry old men were banded together at work in a stony field. They were wearing reed hats, and as they raked the soil they sang the "Song of the White-headed Men":

Let's send up a petition!
Let's send up a petition!
Send a petition up to God
And see what he will say.
    Let the old men never die,
    Let the young men not grow old.
    Let's send God a petition.
Oh how hateful, oh how hateful!
White hairs are our enemies.
We try to stop white hairs,
With an axe in one hand
And thorns in the other,
But white hairs come round behind.
They take away our ruddy cheeks,
Bind us in blue cords,
Bind us so we can't escape.
    Rosy cheeks will fade away,
    White hairs will surely come,
    Wrinkles form beneath the ears,
    All our black hair will turn white.

In the morning fresh and bright,
In the evening white as snow,
Time is heartless in its passing.
Youth's a season full of pleasure,
But the days run swiftly by;
Time's nature is to fly.
    I want to ride a spanking pony,
    Ride the highway up to Seoul,
    I want to see the hills and valleys
    Just once more before I die.
    I want to meet a pretty maid
    And sit beside her at a feast.
Morning flowers, midnight moonlight,
All the glories of the seasons
Are things I cannot see or hear,
Because my eyes and ears are failing,
And there is no remedy.
    Oh how sad, how sad, my friend,
    Whither are you going now?
    Like the falling leaves of autumn
    Slowly, slowly you're declining,
    Like the morning star at daylight,
    You are ever growing weaker.
Where's the path that you are taking?
Ŏyŏrŏ! This work of tilling!
This life of ours is nothing
But the dream of a spring morning.

After a time one of the farmers straightened his back and said: "Let's have a smoke, let's have a smoke!"

In their pointed reed hats, they walked along the balks between the paddies, proudly holding their soapstone pipes. They took their leather tobacco pouches out of the back of their belts, spat on the tobacco and rammed it into the pipes with their thumbs. They lit a fire of chaff and stuck their pipes into the embers, drawing on them with a noise like the squeaking of baby mice. That is the farmers' way. Their cheeks swelled, their nostrils flared, until the pipes began to draw. Then they stood up to smoke.

Mong-nyong addressed them in familiar language: "Let me have a few words with you."

"What is it?"

"Is it true that there's a girl in this county called Ch'unhyang, who has entered the governor's household and takes so many bribes that the ordinary people suffer through misgovernment?"

A farmer grew heated: "Where do you live?"

"Oh, here, there and anywhere."

"Oh, you live anywhere! Have you no eyes and ears? Just because she won't go into the governor's household, Ch'unhyang has been beaten. You don't see many kisaeng's daughters make such faithful wives. Because some filthy beggar like you lusted after her white body, she can't eat and she's likely to starve. That young beggar Yi, who went and left her, has never sent a word of news to her. I don't care what rank he has risen to, he isn't worth the water in my chamberpot."

"Here, what do you think you're saying?"

"Why, what does it matter to you?"

"It doesn't matter, but you'd better watch your language."

"You don't know what you're talking about, you don't."

Mong-nyong broke off the conversation and turned away: "That's right, it's only a matter of disgrace and humiliation. You carry on with your work."

"Yes, sir."

*

Mong-nyong had barely turned the next corner after leaving the farmers when a youth came toward him dragging a stick and chanting a poem, half *sijo* and half *sasŏl:*

> What's the date today?
>> How many days will it take
>> To cover the thousand *ri* to Seoul?
> If I had the fine grey steed
>> On which Chao Tzu-lung crossed the river,
>> I might get there today.
> But, more's the pity, poor Ch'unhyang,
>> Always thinking of young master Yi,
>> Shut up in prison,
>> Hovering on the point of death,
>> Never gets a word of news
>> From that wicked gentleman.
>>> There's the gentry for you!

When Mong-nyong heard this, he said: "Boy, where do you live?"

"In Namwŏn."

"Where are you going?"

"To Seoul."

"What for?"

"To take Ch'unhyang's letter to the old governor's house."

"Let me look at it."

"You're a fine gentleman! You don't know your manners."

"What's that?"

"Well, just think: it's bad enough to want to look at a man's letter, but you are asking to see a letter from somebody else's wife."

"Now listen:

> The traveler about to set out on his way,
> I open the letter once again.

said the T'ang poet Chang Chi. Let me have a look. What does it matter?"

"You look bad, but your knowledge of books is extraordinary. Look at it quickly and give it back."

"You ill-mannered oaf!"

Mong-nyong took the letter and unfolded it. This was what it said: "I have had no news of you since we parted, but I pray that you and your parents are in good health. I have fallen foul of the governor and been beaten. Now I am more dead than alive. I expect I shall die soon and my soul will pass into the shades, but even if I were to die ten thousand times I could not serve more than one husband. Whether I live or die, I do not know what will become of my poor mother. Please be kind to her and look after her for me."

At the bottom of the letter was written a quatrain:

> Some time last year he left me.
> Winter has gone, and autumn has returned;
> Midnight winds and rain like snow—
> How have I become a convict in Namwŏn?

The letter was written in blood. It was as regular as a flight of wild geese landing on the sandflats, but every letter cried in pain. When Mong-nyong saw it his eyes filled with tears that dropped upon the paper. The youth said: "Why do you cry at somebody else's letter."

"You silly boy, even somebody else's letter, if it is sad, will make a man weep."

"Look what you've done!—pretending to sympathize, you've messed the letter up with your tears. That letter cost fifteen yang— you must repay it!"

"Listen. Young master Yi was one of my childhood friends, and he was coming down to the country with me, but on the way he stopped in Chŏnju. He promised to meet me tomorrow at Namwŏn. If you come with me, you will meet him."

The youth changed color: "Do you think Seoul is just over there?" He tried to grab the letter: "Give it to me!"

Mong-nyong resisted him. The other caught the edge of his coat, and saw underneath, that Mong-nyong was wearing a silk purse at his waist, containing something that felt like a flat dish—the brass warrant. The youth stepped back: "What's that you've got? Is that the way the wind blows?"

"You fool! If this matter gets out, I won't be answerable for your life."

Mong-nyong carried on toward Namwŏn. As he came over the Paksŏk Pass into the town, he looked around and saw the familiar hills and streams. He came to the South Gate: "Kwanghan Pavilion, how have you been? Magpie Bridge, is all well?"

The willows are green and fresh before the hostel
(That was where I tied the donkey)
The clear stream falls like a blue mist of water
(That was where I washed my feet)
The green trees line the road to the Ch'in capital
(That was the road I came and went on).

A group of girls were washing clothes under the Magpie Bridge: "You know . . ."

"What?"

"I feel very sorry for poor Ch'unhyang. He's a cruel man, our governor, a cruel man. He tried to force her to serve him, but her faithfulness is beyond belief. Did he really think that the fear of death would break her iron will? Oh, he's heartless, that young master Yi, he's heartless!"

As they squatted over their washing, chattering away, they might have been the Princess Ying-yang, the Princess Lan-yang, Ch'in Ts'ai-feng, Kuei Ch'an-yüeh, Po Ling-p'o, Ti Ching-hung, Shen Niao-yen, and Chia Ch'un-yün, all the girls of *A Dream of Nine Clouds,* but where was Yang Shao-yu, their hero?

Mong-nyong went up into the pavilion and looked around again.

The sun was going down in the west, and the birds were flying home to roost in the woods. Over there was the willow tree where Ch'unhyang's swing had hung: he fancied he could see it flying to and fro again. To the east in the green shade of Changnim woods was Ch'unhyang's house. The garden would be the same as ever, but beyond that high stone wall was the cruel prison where poor Ch'unhyang was languishing. The sun was dipping behind the hill and dusk was gathering when he arrived at the gate of her house. The gate-lodge was dilapidated and the main building was losing its plaster. The phoenix tree still stood in the grove, but looked sad and neglected in the wind. The white cranes inside the walls must have been worried by the dogs as they walked about, for their feathers were bedraggled and they were crying mournfully. The old dog lay feebly in front of the gate. It did not even recognize an old friend, but got up to bark.

"You silly dog, stop barking. I'm as good as your master. Where's your mistress gone? Why are you the only one to meet me?"

He looked up at the gate of the inner court where he had written and posted a Chinese inscription. The character for loyalty had lost its top part, so that only the bottom part, 'the heart,' remained. The inscription he had written for the name of the building, *The House of the Crouching Dragon,* and the spring mottoes had been torn by the wind and were fluttering sadly.

He went slowly into the house. Everything was quiet. See what Ch'unhyang's mother does? She was cooking gruel: "Oh, dear, it's all my fault! He's cruel, he's cruel, young Yi is cruel! My daughter will die, and he has forgotten her completely. He has cut her off without news. What grief is ours!

"Hyangdan! Bring some more fuel."

She came out, washed her hair in the runnel in the corner of the yard, combed it, and offered a bowl of clean water at the stone cairn in the garden, prostrating herself and praying: "Spirits of heaven and earth, sun, moon, and stars, unite to hear my prayer! I have nurtured my only daughter, Ch'unhyang, like a golden nugget, so that her children should remember me with sacrifices. Now she has been cruelly beaten and shut in the jail although she is innocent. There is no hope for her life. Heavenly spirits, exert yourselves, raise Yi Mong-nyong of Seoul to honor and glory, and save my daughter, Ch'unhyang!"

When she had finished praying, she called: "Hyangdan! Light my pipe for me."

She took the pipe and puffed at it, sighing. When Mong-nyong saw her devotion, he said to himself: "I thought my success was due to my ancestors, but now I realize it was due to my mother-in-law."

Then he said aloud: "Is there anybody in?"

"Who is it?"

"Me."

"Who do you mean, 'me'?"

He went inside: "It is Yi."

"Oh, young Yi! I see, the ward officer's son?"

"Oh, mother! Don't you know me? You're getting old—don't you know me?"

"But who are you?"

"A son-in-law is a perpetual visitor, they say. Do you still not know me?"

Wŏlmae was delighted: "My dear, my dear! What has happened? Where have you been? How have you come now? Have you been blown here by some great wind? Have you been carried on the clouds? Have you heard about Ch'unhyang? Have you come to save her? Come in, come in quickly."

She took him by the hand and led him inside. They sat down in the candlelight, and she looked at him closely, amazed to see that he looked like a beggar among beggars. She exclaimed: "What on earth has happened?"

"When a gentleman's fortunes change, the results are beyond description. I went up to Seoul, but lost all hope of advancement. The family fortune vanished, my father is teaching in a little school and my mother has gone back to her parents. We are all scattered, so I came to see Ch'unhyang in the hope of getting a little money, but it looks as though both our families are ruined."

Ch'unhyang's mother was astonished when she heard this tale: "You heartless man! After you left here you sent no news at all. What sort of manners are those? You were going to do so well in the examinations, and now see what's become of you! Your bolt is shot, you are like water poured out. I don't know who to blame. But what will become of Ch'unhyang?"

She leapt forward in a fury, bit his nose, and beat him.

"Is it my fault or my nose's fault? You can send me away. Heaven is heartless, and storms and thunder will always come."

She was sarcastic: "When a gentleman gets into trouble, he can always make light of it?"

Mong-nyong, deliberately trying to find out how she would react, said: "I'm very hungry. Give me a bowl of rice, please."

The woman answered: "There isn't any rice."

Of course there was rice in the house, but she was very angry with him. Just then Hyangdan returned from the jail. She heard her mistress shouting and rushed in without ceremony. She recognized Mong-nyong immediately and greeted him profusely: "I am so glad to see you back! Is your father well? How is your mother? You must be tired after your journey."

"Hello! You have been having a hard time."

"I am all right. Madam, please stop scolding him. He's come all this way to see us. You can't treat him like that. If Ch'unhyang hears about it, she will be terribly upset. Don't be so hard on him."

She went into the kitchen and put some green peppers and kim-ch'i and soy sauce with a little cold rice and a bowl of cold water on a table and brought it to him: "Eat this first, while I cook supper."

Mong-nyong said gratefully: "O rice, it's a long time since I saw you!"

He mixed all the food together and, ignoring the spoon, ate it with his fingers. The food disappeared as quickly as a crab draws its eyes in from the wind.

Ch'unhyang's mother said: "Yes, indeed! He's obviously learned to eat like a beggar."

Meanwhile, Hyangdan was thinking about Ch'unhyang's troubles. She could not cry aloud, but wept quietly to herself: "What can we do, what can we do? How can we save my lovely mistress? What shall we do? What shall we do?"

Mong-nyong saw her silently crying and said: "Don't cry, Hyangdan. It's hardly likely that your mistress will die. Anyone as good as her is sure to be all right in the end."

Ch'unhyang's mother heard him: "You're still the proud aristocrat. Why do you carry on like that?"

Hyangdan said: "Don't take any notice of what she says; she is old and her mind is feeble. Now all this has happened to us, and she gets so angry that she never speaks without raging. Please eat some supper now."

Mong-nyong took the tray of food. Suddenly he was overcome with anger and could not face eating: "Hyangdan, take the tray away."

Knocking the ash out of his pipe, he said: "Mother, shall we go and see Ch'unhyang now?"

"Yes, of course. What sort of man would you be if you didn't go to see her?"

Hyangdan said: "The gates are closed now. Let's wait until curfew rings."

At last they heard the curfew bell. Hyangdan carried a tray of gruel on her head and held the lantern. Mong-nyong followed behind. When they arrived at the gate of the jail there was no one about. All was quiet; not even the jailer could be found.

Ch'unhyang, either dreaming or daydreaming, thought she saw her husband coming. He had a guilded cap on his head, and wore a red court robe. They fell upon each other's necks and began to talk of their love for each other . . .

"Ch'unhyang!"

She did not answer. Mong-nyong said: "Try calling louder!"

"We can't do that: the garrison is nearby, and if we call too loudly the governor may hear about it and start investigating. We must wait a little."

"What do you mean? What sort of investigating? Wait while I call: Ch'unhyang!"

Ch'unhyang heard him calling. She was startled: "Is that voice real, am I dreaming? It's a strange voice."

Mong-nyong grew agitated: "Tell her I've come."

"If she hears you are here, she may faint from shock. Keep quiet."

Ch'unhyang heard her mother's voice. She was surprised: "Mother, why have you come? If you wander about after your daughter, you will fall over and hurt yourself. Please stop coming."

"Don't worry about me. He's come."

"Who's come?"

"*He's* come."

"I can't stand it. Tell me what you're talking about. I just had a dream that I met my husband and talked to him. Have you heard from him? Is there some news? Has he been gazetted? Tell me quickly!"

"Whether it's your husband or somebody else's, some beggar has come here."

"What are you talking about? Has my husband come? I was dreaming of him. Has he really come?"

She grasped his hand between the bars. She could hardly believe it was true. "Who are you, really? It must be a dream. After all this time, have you come like this? I can't take any more, I shall die. Why were you so heartless? Mother and I are ill-fated. Since you left I have passed the days and nights, waking and sleeping, thinking of you. I have been beaten till I was almost dead. Look at me now: have you come to save me?"

She was so glad to see him that she talked at length, but when she looked at him closely, how could she fail to grieve anew? "I don't care whether I live or die, but what has happened to you?"

"Ch'unhyang, don't grieve. Man's fate is decided in Heaven. I am sure you will not die."

Ch'unhyang spoke to her mother: "When he was in Seoul, I longed for him as people long for rain after seven years' drought: did he also long for me? Please don't knock down their own pagoda or trample on their own saplings. I am beyond help now.

"Mother, when I am dead, let there be no regrets. The silk coat I used to wear is in the inlaid wardrobe: take it out and exchange it for the best ramie cloth and make him a decent set of clothes. Sell my best white silk skirt and buy him a hat and headband, and some shoes. You will find my silver hairpin, my amber-handled knife and my jade ring in my jewel box. Sell them too and make him clothes of hemp. I shall die soon, so I don't need those things any more. Sell the wardrobes and the cedar chest for what you can get and use the money to buy him proper food. When I am dead, look after him as though I were still alive with him."

Then she turned to Mong-nyong: "Tomorrow is the governor's birthday. If he gets drunk, he will probably send for me. I am already so badly beaten that I shall hardly be able to stand. My head is dizzy and I shall stumble if I try to walk. I shall die of my tortures. Pick up my body like a bearer's load, and take it to the quiet Lotus Cottage where we spent our first night together. Lay me out with your own hands and comfort my soul. Don't remove my clothes, but bury me as I am in a sunny place. Then later, when you have achieved high office, come back and re-bury me in a fine linen shroud; have me carried in a decorated bier away from these hills and up to Seoul, so that I can be buried near your ancestral graves. On my gravestone simply write the eight characters: "Grave of Ch'unhyang, A Constant Wife, Unjustly Killed." That will be enough for me. The sun that sets behind the western hills will rise again tomorrow, but poor Ch'unhyang, once she has gone, will never come again. Requite my wrongs! Oh, the pity of it! My poor mother will lose me and all her belongings. She will become a beggar, asking for food from house to house, sleeping here and there out of doors. When her strength fails and she dies in some corner of the hills, the jackdaws will come from Mount Chiri, flapping their wings and cawing as they peck out her eyes, and she will have no daughter to stand by and scare them away.''

She wept bitterly. Mong-nyong spoke to her: ''Don't weep. Even though the sky should fall, there will be a hole to creep into. What do you think of me, that you should be so despairing?''

They left her and went to her house. Ch'unhyang, having seen her husband so unexpectedly in the darkness, was now left alone lamenting: ''When God created men, he made them all equal. What sin has brought my misfortune on me? I lost my husband at sixteen and lived in lonely misery; I was tortured and beaten, and brought to jail. Now for three or four months, day and night, I have waited for him to come back. At last I have seen his face again, but it has increased my sorrow. When I die and go to the Yellow Springs, what shall I be able to say to the kings who sit in judgment there?''

She wailed bitterly, exhausting her strength, more dead than alive.

*

Yi Mong-nyong came out of Ch'unhyang's house intending to spend the night in spying out the situation in the city. He went to the yamen and heard the chief clerk saying to one of the dispatch carriers: ''I have heard that Yi, who lives outside the West Gate of Seoul, has been appointed an Inspector, and a few minutes ago a suspicious character in ragged clothes and a battered hat was seen with Ch'unhyang's mother, carrying a light lantern. Tomorrow at the governor's birthday banquet we must have a special place prepared in case he comes. Make absolutely sure that nothing goes wrong.''

When Mong-nyong heard this he thought to himself: ''So they have guessed what's going on.''

Then he went on to the courts of justice. See what the commandant of the soldiers was doing: he was speaking to the guards: ''Just now there was a strange beggar hanging about near the jail. He may have been a secret inspector. Make a careful record of what he looked like.''

Mong-nyong said to himself: ''These devils know everything.''

He went on to the Office of Supply, where he heard the same sort of thing. After he had visited all six offices of the yamen he returned to Ch'unhyang's house.

The next day, after morning muster in the yamen, the officials from the nearby towns began to come in: the commandant of Unbong and the magistrates from Kurye, Koksŏng, Sunch'ang, Okkwa, Chinan and Changsu each arrived in turn. The military and civil officials were lined up on either side and the governor sat in the middle as host. He called an underling and said: "Tell the butler to send in the refreshments. Tell the butcher to kill a big ox, and the secretary of the Office of Rites to send the band; and get a servant to hang out the big canopy. See that the guards keep uninvited people out."

It was an animated scene. Flags and banners were waving, the air was full of the sound of music, and the kisaeng in their brightly colored dresses danced before him, their white hands and billowing gauze skirts moving to the rhythm of the music: *Chi-ya-ja, tungdong-sil!* The sound was deafening and Yi Mong-nyong was dazed by it all.

"Guard! Go and tell your officer that I am a beggar who has come a long way for this fine banquet. Ask him to give me some tidbits!"

See what the guard does:

"I don't care who you are, the captain says no beggars are to be admitted. There's no point in asking." He pushed Mong-nyong away; obviously he was hoping for promotion. The commandant from Unbong saw what was happening and said to the governor: "That beggar looks shabby enough, but he has a gentlemanly air. What about giving him a place at the bottom there and letting him have a cup of wine?"

The governor said: "Do as you like, but . . ."

The "but . . ." sounded reluctant. Mong-nyong thought: "Ah! You think I may steal something, but it is you who will be caught today."

The commandant ordered the guard: "Let that man come in."

Mong-nyong came in and sat down quietly. He looked around him and saw all the local magistrates sitting there with trays of wine and dainties in front of them. While they were performing the music, he looked at the table that had been put in front of him, and how could he but be angry? It was a broken little table with coarse wooden chopsticks; on it were plain boiled bean sprouts, pickled radish, and a bowl of cloudy rice-beer. He kicked the table over and pointed to the commandant's dish of beef-ribs: "I should like one of those ribs."

"Help yourself," said the commandant, and then went on: "On an occasion like this, music alone is not enough; we should have a verse competition. How if we were to compose a verse of poetry each?"

"A good idea!"

The commandant set the rhyme-words: *ko,* meaning "high," and *ko* meaning "flesh"; and they began to compose their poems. Mong-nyong said: "I studied a book of model verses when I was a boy; now I have come to a fine banquet and enjoyed the food, I can hardly depart without thanks. Let me try my hand at a verse."

The commandant was delighted to hear this, and had a brush and inkstone brought. Mong-nyong composed two couplets such as the rest of them could not match. He wrote about the people's feelings and the governor's style of administration:

> Fine wine in golden cups is the people's blood,
>   Viands on jade dishes are the people's flesh;
> When the grease of the candles drips, the people's tears
>   are falling.
> The noise of the music is loud, but the people's cries are
>   louder.

The governor was puzzled over the meaning of the verses, but when the commandant saw them, he thought to himself: "There's trouble brewing here!"

Mong-nyong left, and the commandant called the chief secretaries and said to them: "Be ready for trouble."

He called the officer of works to check the buildings, the commander to check the post-horses, the steward to check the catering, the jailer to check the prisoners, the executioner to check his equipment, the secretaries to check the documents and the captain to check the duty roster. When he returned after all this activity, the governor, who had noticed nothing out of the way, asked him: "Where have you been?"

"I went to relieve myself."

The governor commanded: "Bring Ch'unhyang here quickly!"

He was getting drunk.

*

Meanwhile Mong-nyong was collecting his troop. He made a sign to his scribes. See how the scribes and agents respond: they organized the post-horsemen, walking up and down between them. The men were wearing plain headbands and kerchiefs with new felt hats pressed well down, long puttees and new straw shoes. They had clean new hempen suits, and heavy cudgels hung from their wrists by loops of deerskin. Hither and thither they moved, swarming the streets of Namwŏn. See what the Ch'ŏngp'a postmen do: lifting high the round brass warrant, shining like a golden sun, they shouted: "The royal inspector comes!"

The mountains shook with the sound, and heaven and earth quivered. Trees and grasses, birds and beasts, all were afraid. At the South Gate, they said: "He's coming!"; at the North Gate, they said: "He's coming!"; at the East and West Gates, they cried: "He's coming!" till the blue sky reverberated with the noise.

"Summon the chief secretaries!" came the call. The whole yamen was terrified. Whips were cracking.

"I am ruined!"

"The officer of works!"

The officer of works heard the call and came in: "I was only doing what I was told. I dared not disobey."

The whips cracked.

"I am being torn to pieces!"

The lieutenants and the deputies went pale, the head clerk and the chief secretary were scared out of their wits. All the soldiers rushed about busily. The local magistrates took flight. See what they do: dropping their seal-boxes, grabbing the fruit, dropping their diplomas and grabbing rice-cakes, losing their scabbards and wetting themselves in fright. Lutes were broken and drums were smashed; the governor, fouling his trousers, ran into the yamen office like a mouse hiding in a roll of straw matting: "It's cold! The door's coming in! Shut the wind! . . . The water's dry—give me my throat!"

The butler dropped the tray and ran in with half a door on his head, the inspector's soldiers close behind him.

"Save me! This is the end!"

Then Mong-nyong gave orders to his men: "This town was once my father's responsibility. There must be no disorder. Withdraw to the guest house."

When he had set himself up in the yamen, he said: "Remove the governor from office and suspend the administration." He posted a board on each of the four great gates, saying: "The governor's administration is suspended."

Then he called the keeper of the jail: "Bring out all your prisoners."

When the prisoners were brought, he investigated their offenses and released those who were innocent.

"What has this girl done?"

The jailer said: "She's the daughter of the kisaeng Wŏlmae. She was jailed for creating a disturbance in the yamen."

"What did she do?"

The jailer replied: "The governor summoned her to serve in his household but she said that chastity and constancy prevented her, and she created a fuss in his presence. She is Ch'unhyang."

The inspector said: "Do you think that a person like you can create a disturbance in the yamen on the pretense of being faithful, and hope to live? You deserve to die. Will you refuse to enter my service?"

Ch'unhyang was in despair: "All you officers who come here are the same. I beg you to listen to me. Can the winds wear away the high rocks of a mountain cliff? Can the snow change the greenness of the pine and bamboo? Do not ask me to do such a thing. Have me killed quickly."

Then she turned to her maid: "Hyangdan, go and look for my husband. When he came to the jail last night he gave me hope for deliverance. I wonder where he has gone; he cannot know that I am about to die."

The inspector ordered her: "Raise your eyes. Look at me."

Ch'unhyang lifted her head and looked up to the dais. There was no question that it was her husband, who had come as a beggar, sitting up there now as judge. Half laughing and half crying she said:

> Wonderful, marvellous!
> My husband is the royal inspector.
>> Autumn had come to Namwŏn,
>> And now it is passing away.
> Spring has come to the guesthouse,
> Plum blossom and spring breezes have brought me to life.
>> Is it a dream or is it true?
>> I am afraid I shall wake up.

While she was rejoicing in this fashion her mother came in. What can express her happiness? Ch'unhyang's virtues now shone resplendent, and who would not be happy?

When Yi Mong-nyong had finished his work in Namwŏn, he sent Ch'unhyang and her mother and Hyangdan to Seoul. Their cavalcade was splendid, and everyone who saw it praised them. When Ch'unhyang left Namwŏn, although she was going to a life of honors, she could not help feeling sad at leaving her old home:

> Goodbye, Lotus Cottage,
>> Where first we loved and slept,
> Kwanghan Pavilion and Magpie Bridge,
>> Goodbye, Yŏngju Hall!
> The grass of spring grows green each year,
> But the sons of men cannot return.
>> That is true for me:
>> Everyone has his own farewells.
> And I bid you stay in peace—
> I know not when I'll come again.

TRANSLATED BY RICHARD RUTT

SASŎL SIJO

The following selections are examples of the *sasŏl sijo,* a variety of the common shorter *sijo* form. Breaking the conventions of the *sijo,* they are often extended in a chain and are characterized by an abundance of onomatopoeia, a tendency to catalogue, striking imagery, and bold twists at the end.

The growth of this new poetry, together with the rise of the novel, drama, genre painting, and popular entertainment such as *p'ansori,* reflects the rise of the middle class and changes in approach to life. Most of this new poetry is frank and humorous, often satirical and running to burlesque. Shorn of classical references, these lyrics gain extraordinary freshness by exploring the resources of language that is close to the soil. The *sasŏl sijo* gave back poetry —which had long been a monopoly of the lettered class—to the creative sensibility of the common people.

The reason for the survival of these anonymous poems, it should be added, is that they were song lyrics; their musical settings are still preserved.

The innovators of the *sijo* in the eighteenth century were Kim Ch'ŏn-t'aek, the compiler of the *Songs of Green Hills* (1728), the first anthology of *sijo,* and his junior colleague Kim Su-jang (1690–1769). The preface to the *Songs of Green Hills* pays tribute to Kim Ch'ŏn-t'aek as singer and anthologist.

Chŏng Yun-gyŏng

PREFACE TO *SONGS OF GREEN HILLS*
[from *Ch'ŏnggu yŏngŏn*]

In olden times, singers used poems, and poets composed poetry. Poems set to music became songs. Thus songs and poetry arise from a common source. The three hundred songs of the *Book of Songs* became poems of the old style, and "poems of the old style" became "poems of the modern style." Songs and poetry are therefore two distinct genres.

Since the times of the Han and the Wei, poems having tunes were called "Music Bureau" poems and were written by men of letters in the style of the anonymous folksongs collected by the Music Bureau [120–6 B.C.], but they are unfit for use in Korea. After the Ch'en and Sui a different style, the *tz'u* [song words], evolved, but it was not as popular as older poetry or the Music Bureau poems. The composition of songs requires not only lyrics, but melodies as well. Consequently, one who can write poems may not be able to write music, and writers of melodies cannot necessarily write lyrics.

Our dynasty does not lack poets who wrote lyrics, but few examples of their works survive; and existing ones are of recent origin. How can a country that reveres literature be so careless in preserving its music? Kim Ch'ŏn-t'aek is a talented and well-known singer, versed in both music and literature, compose new lyrics, and had the common people practice them. He has collected the works of famous scholars and poets, as well as popular lyrics written for *sijo* tunes. He has corrected errors in several hundred such lyrics and collected them into an anthology, to which he has asked me to write a preface. He has worked hard to disseminate song poems widely.

On looking at his work, I find the lyrics beautifully elegant, and well worth perusing. Their purport is peace and harmony. For the sad and the suffering, their subtlety and charm contain a warning. They stimulate and move us, and offer lessons that will help us shape our destinies. They differ little from poetry in their way of bringing social conventions under scrutiny. The texts not only express the writers' thoughts and feelings but stimulate the reader as well, and all this by implication and suggestion! Therefore when the texts are set to music, the people will be able to sing them and thereby will be morally uplifted. Though the texts may not compare in dexterity with the finest poetry, they will have considerable worth in public administration. Why then do gentlemen put them away and not adopt them? Why do lovers of music put them aside and fail to understand them?

Realizing this, Kim Ch'ŏn-t'aek has redeemed from oblivion the texts of several hundred lyrics and has recorded them so that they may be handed down to posterity. The authors of these lyrics, now in the underworld, will regard him as their best interpreter and friend.

A skilled singer, Kim is also able to compose new tunes. He made an agreement with the famous lutenist Kim Sŏng-gi. When Kim Sŏng-gi takes up his lute, Kim Ch'ŏn-t'aek sings harmony. So beautiful is his voice that it can move demons and gods and produce warm contentment. The skill of the two masters is unrivaled in their generation. Being ill, I am despondent, and nothing delights me. Kim Ch'ŏn-t'aek should come with Kim Sŏng-gi, bringing along this book. If they would allow me to hear them perform, I might be able to dispel my melancholy.

In the third month of the year Musin [1728], Hyŏnwa, Chŏng Yun-gyŏng, writes this preface.

SASŎL SIJO

"Come and buy my dainties!"
> "Vendor, tell us what you're selling,
> then we'll see what we will buy!"
"Bone outside and flesh inside,
> both eyes looking up to heaven,
> going forward, going backward,
> eight feet on the little legs,
> two feet on the big ones,
> oh so tasty with green soy sauce,
> buy my splendid crab meat!"
"Vendor, do not cry such nonsense!
> Simply say, come buy my crabs."

*

Mother-in-law, don't fume in the kitchen
> and swear at your daughter-in-law.
Did you get her in payment of a debt?
> Or did you buy her with cash?
> Father-in-law, tough as a rank shoot
> from a rotten chestnut stump,
> Mother-in-law, skinny and wrinkled
> as cowdung dried in the sun,

Sister-in-law, sharp as a gimlet poking
through the side of a three-year-old basket,
your son has bloody faeces
and is like weeds in a field of wheat,
a miserable yellow cucumber flower.
How can you criticize a daughter-in-law
who's like a morning glory
blooming in loamy soil?

TRANSLATED BY RICHARD RUTT

*

Middle- and small-sized needles
dropped in the middle of the sea.
They say with a foot-long pole
a dozen boatmen hooked the eye of every needle.
Love, my love,
don't swallow everything you hear
when they tell you a hundred tales.

*⌣

Let's put in a window,
Let's put in a window in my heart,
   a sliding screen,
   a latticed screen,
   the female section of a hinge,
   the male section of a hinge,
   hammer a lockbar for a ring,
   and make a window in my heart.
If my longing for him stifles me,
I'll open the window wide.

*

Cricket, cricket,
O sad cricket,
you keep vigil till the moon sinks,
with your long and short notes;
each sad note
of your lonely cry
wakes me from a fitful sleep.
Chirp on, tiny insect,
you alone know my misery
in this empty room.

*

You, wild hawk,
stop rending my innards.
Shall I give you money?
Shall I give you silver?
    A Chinese silk skirt,
    a Korean ritual dress,
    gauze petticoats,
    white satin belt,
    a cloudy wig from the north,
    a jade hairpin,
    a bamboo hairpin,
    a silk knife in an inlaid case,
    a golden knife in an amber case,
    a coral brooch from the far south,
    a gold ring set with a blue bell
    shaped like a heavenly peach,
    sandals with yellow pearl strings,
    embroidered hemp sandals?
For a night worth thousands of gold pieces,
give me one chance at your dimples,
lovely and fresh as a flower,
grant me only one night,
priceless as a swift steed!

POETRY IN CHINESE, II

Monk Ch'ŏnghak (1570–1654)

YEARNING

Layers of hills and waters increase my sorrow;
Twelve times I turn my head to sky's end.
In a desolate window the bright moon;
One thought calls another and another.

Yi Shik (1584–1647)

NEWLY RETURNED SWALLOWS

When myriad affairs begin to distress,
    I dismiss them with a smile.
When a spring rain comes to my grass hut,
    I shut the pine door.
But now how vexing! Outside the blinds
    the newly returned swallows—
They seem to be addressing the idle man
    with questions of right and wrong!

TRANSLATED BY RICHARD J. LYNN

Ch'oe Myŏng-gil (1586–1647)

IN THE SHEN-YANG PRISON HARMONIZING WITH A POEM BY KIM SANG-HŎN

Quietly I watch a crowd move,
Maybe I can get home safely.
Hot water and ice are made of water;
Fur and serge are both cloth.
Events may differ from time to time,
But can the mind go against the Way?
You well discern this truth—
Let's keep our secret silent.

Yun Sŏn-do (1587–1671)

EXILED TO THE NORTH

Madly I sing, sigh, and wail till hoarse,
But it's hard to ease my spirit.
At sundown, crows whirl about,
In the frosty north only geese cry.
The homeless traveler laments the passing year,
The border people dread the royal intent.
I would rather be blind and deaf
And spend my life buried in the woods.

Kim Ch'ang-hyŏp (1651–1708)

MOUNTAIN FOLK

I dismount and ask, "Anybody home?"
A housewife emerges from the gate.
She seats me under the eaves
And fixes a meal for the guest.
"Where is your husband?" I ask.
"Up the hill at dawn with a plow."
It must be hard to furrow the hill;
He isn't back even after sunset.
Not a single soul around,
Only chickens and dogs on tiered slopes.
"In the woods there are tigers,
I can't fill my basket with greens."
"What makes you live alone
Among rugged paths in the valley?"
"I know life is easier on the plain,
But I am afraid of the king's men."

Nŭngun (dates unknown)

WAITING FOR MY LOVE

He said he would come at moonrise;
The moon is out, but he has not come.
Perhaps he lives among high hills
Where the moon comes up late.

Kim Pyŏng-yŏn (1807–1863)

A SONG FOR MY SHADOW

You follow me as I come and go,
  No one is more polite than you,
You are like me,
  But you are not I.
On the shore under a setting moon
  Your giant shape startles me;
In the courtyard under a midday sun
  Your small pose makes me laugh!
I try to find you on my pillow,
  But you are not there;
When I turn around in front of my lamp,
  We suddenly meet again.
Although I love you in my heart,
  I cannot trust you after all—
When no light is there to shine,
  You leave without a trace!

TRANSLATED BY RICHARD J. LYNN

Pyŏn Wŏn-gyu (fl. 1881)

TO A FRIEND

Day after day I live, deer for company,
Bright moon on the waters and clouds on the hills.
Nothing except these in the crevice of my heart—
Shall I send you a painting of autumn sound?

Glossary

Adan Fortress: near modern Seoul, the mountain fortress Ach'a on the north shore of the Han.

Amitābha: the Buddha of Infinite Light, who presides over the Western Paradise.

Anthology of T'ang Poetry (T'ang-shih p'in-hui): compiled by Kao Ping.

arhant, or *arhat:* a person who has intuited the Truth and who will not be reincarnated; variously translated as saint, perfect man, or worthy one.

Assembly of One Hundred Seats: held on the *Jen-wang ching* (Sūtra of the Benevolent Kings) and to pray for the peace and prosperity of the country, i.e., to pray for the king's recovery from illness.

Avalokiteśvara (Kuan-yin in Chinese, Kannon in Japanese): "One who observes the sounds of the world," the bodhisattva of compassion.

"Ballad of Fen-yin": bý Li Chiao (664–713), on the theme of splendor and ruin. Translated in Stephen Owen, *The Poetry of the Early T'ang* (New Haven: Yale University Press, 1977), pp. 119–121.

"Ballad of Liang-fu": attributed to Chu-ko Liang, about the three heroes of Duke Ching of Ch'u, who were slandered and committed suicide.

Bamboo Ridge: the border between modern Ch'ungch'ŏng and Kyŏngsang provinces.

Blue Gate: when the dynasty changed, Shao P'ing, Marquis of Tung-ling under the Ch'in, had to live by raising melons; his melons were called Blue Gate or Tung-ling melons.

Bodhisattva ordination: the precepts of Māhāyana consisting of the ten major and forty-eight minor commandments.

Book of Changes (I ching): one of the five classics of the Confucian canon, consisting of a divination manual—short oracles arranged under sixty-four hexagrams—and commentaries. Translated by Richard Wilhelm, *The I Ching or Book of Changes* (New York: Pantheon, 1950), 2 vols.

Book of Songs: China's oldest anthology of poetry and one of the Confucian canon. The 305 poems are divided into: airs *(feng),* 1–160; lesser odes *(hsiao ya),* 161–234; greater odes *(ta ya),* 235–265; and encomia *(sung),* 266–305. There are at least three translations: Barnhard Karlgren, *The Book of Odes* (Stockholm: Museum of Far Eastern Antiquities, 1950); Ezra Pound, *The Classic Anthology Defined by Confucius* (Cambridge: Harvard University Press, 1954); and Arthur Waley, *The Book of Songs* (London: Allen & Unwin, 1954).

Book of the Yellow Court: the most famous of the Mao Shan texts of Taoism.

Chang Chi (768–*c.* 830): T'ang poet and a protégé of Han Yü.

Chang Liang (*d.* 187 B.C.): wise minister under Kao-tsu of the Han; later followed

Taoist practices. His biography is translated in Burton Watson, *Records of the Grand Historian of China* (New York: Columbia University Press, 1961), I, 134–151.

Chang Yi: minister of King Hui of Ch'in (278–272 B.C.).

changga: one of the four major poetic forms of traditional Korea, it is characterized by a refrain recurring at intervals, bespeaking its folk and musical origins and oral transmission. Consisting of pure onomatopoeia of drum sounds or nonsense jingles, the refrain helps to achieve a mood or tone which carries the tune and spirit of the poem.

Chao Meng-fu (1254–1322): a great painter and calligrapher of the Yüan.

Chao Tzu-lung: also known as Chao Yün, who helped Liu Pei (162–223) of Shu Han.

chapki: literally, "random notes" or "jottings"; translated as the literary miscellany. It is an encyclopedic form that flourished in Korea from the twelfth to the nineteenth centuries.

Chi Ch'ang-ju: governor of Huai-yang under Emperor Wu of the Han.

Chiang T'ai-kung: also known as T'ai-kung Wang or Lü Shang, he was the teacher of King Wen, the founder of the Chou, who discovered Chiang fishing in the Wei River.

Ch'ih-yu: a legendary rebel, ox-headed monster, or sea-dragon; inventor of metallurgy.

Cho Sŏng-gi (1638–1689): a scholar who devoted his life to reading and writing.

Cho Wen-chün: before becoming a famous poet at the court of Emperor Wu of Han, Ssu-ma Hsiang-ju (*c.* 179–117 B.C.) eloped with Cho Wen-chün, the young widowed daughter of a wealthy man in Lin-ch'iung; but they were so poor they had to open a wine shop. See Watson, *Records,* II, 298–299.

Ch'ŏnsŏng Island: location unknown.

Chosŏn: Land of Bright Morning, the designation used by Chinese historians to refer to Korea.

Chou: the evil last ruler of the Shang.

Chou Tun-i (1017–1073): a Sung philosopher and the author of the *Diagram of the Supreme Ultimate Explained.*

Chu-ko Liang (181–234): a great statesman and strategist of the Shu Han who served its first ruler as chancellor. While Chu-ko camped at Wu-chang-yüan in Wu-kung to engage Ssu-ma Yi of the Wei, he died. The episode is translated in C. H. Brewitt-Taylor, *San Kuo or Romance of the Three Kingdoms* (Shanghai: Kelly & Walsh, 1925), II, 459–465. As a hemp-robed commoner, Chu-ko used to farm the fields in Nan-yang.

Ch'ü Yüan (?343–278 B.C.): a loyal minister to King Huai of Ch'u (329–299 B.C.) who was rewarded with slander and banishment. Against his advice, the king of Ch'u set out for the Ch'in capital and was detained and died in captivity there. Shortly after the capture of the Ch'u capital by the Ch'in army, Ch'ü Yüan drowned himself in the Mi-lo River, a tributary of the Yangtze. His most famous poem is *Li sao,* comprising 374 lines. See Burton Watson, *Early Chinese Literature* (New York: Columbia University Press, 1962), pp. 231–254.

ch'uan-ch'i: one of the five forms of traditional Chinese stories; rendered as "tales of wonder" or "classical tales," it comprises love stories, historical stories, tales of knight-errantry, and of the supernatural. Twenty-six stories are translated in Y. W. Ma and Joseph S. M. Lau, eds., *Traditional Chinese Stories: Themes and Variations* (New York: Columbia University Press, 1978).

clay oxen: representing man's dualistic thinking, a hindrance to attaining enlightenment.

Cold Food: the day before Clear and Bright (about April 6) when no fire is lit and only cold food is eaten.

Critical Writings of Tung-lai (Tung-lai po-i): by a Sung philosopher, Lü Tsu-ch'ien (1137–1181).

cuckoo: the bird of Shu, alluding to the story of Tu Yü, a legendary ruler of Shu, who had an affair with his minister's wife and died of shame. After death his soul was metamorphosed into the cuckoo (or nightjar), which is said to shed blood while crying in late spring.

Diamond Sūtra (Vajracchedikā prajñapāramitā sūtra): sets forth the doctrines of *śunyatā* (emptiness) and *prajñā* (intuitive wisdom). There are six Chinese translations. See Edward Conze, *Buddhist Wisdom Books Containing the Diamond Sutra and the Heart Sutra* (London: Allen & Unwin, 1958).

Doctrine of the Mean (Chung yung): one of the Four Books (others being the *Analects, Mencius,* and the *Great Learning*), a primer of Confucian education, and a basic text for civil service examinations in China and Korea. Translated in Wing-tsit Chan, *A Source Book in Chinese Philosophy* (Princeton: Princeton University Press, 1963), pp. 95–114.

Fa-tsang (643–712): disciple of Chih-yen and considered to be the real founder of the Hua-yen (Flower Garland) school of Buddhism.

Fan Wu-chi (*d.* 227 B.C.): the Ch'in general who, after offending his king, escaped to Yen. When Prince Tan of Yen wished to avenge the humiliation he had suffered as a hostage in Ch'in, Fan cut his own throat so that Ching K'o, the famous assassin, could carry his head to Ch'in in his attempt on the life of the tyrant. See J. I. Crump, Jr., *Chan-kuo Ts'e* (Oxford: Clarendon Press, 1970), pp. 553–561, and "In Praise of Ching K'o" by T'ao Ch'ien, in James Robert Hightower, *The Poetry of T'ao Ch'ien* (Oxford: Clarendon Press, 1970), pp. 224–229.

Fang-fu: one of the five sacred mountains, east of the Gulf of Chih-li.

Flower Garland Sūtra (Avataṁsaka sūtra): an idealistic Mahāyana scripture. The founder of the school in Korea was the Great Master Ŭisang (625–702). See D. T. Suzuki, *Essays in Zen Buddhism,* Third Series (London: Rider, 1953), pp. 78–214.

fu: translated as rhymeprose or rhapsody, a Chinese poetic form consisting of a combination of prose and rhymed verse of unspecified length. It flourished between the second century B.C. and the sixth century A.D. See Burton Watson, *Chinese Rhyme-Prose* (New York: Columbia University Press, 1971).

Fu Hsi: a Chinese culture hero, who drew the eight trigrams and devised the knotted cords.

General Mirror: refers to *Tzu-chih t'ung-chien*, or *General Mirror for the Aid of Government*, compiled by Ssu-ma Kuang in 1084. It covers 1,362 years of Chinese history (403 B.C.–A.D. 959) in 294 chaps.

"Goddess of the Lo": a rhymeprose by Ts'ao Chih (192–232) about his encounter with a goddess on the banks of the Lo. Translated in Watson, *Chinese Rhyme-Prose*, pp. 55–60.

"Going Out the Passes": a Han Music Bureau song about Wang Chao-chün, who was carried off to the king of the Hsiung-nu in 33 B.C.

Great Unique, or Great One: the supreme sky god in Chinese mythology, elevated to a central position in the state by Emperor Wu of the Han in 113 B.C. It has a human form, represented as a venerable old man in a yellow robe, who resides in the palace at the center of heaven, marked by the pole star.

Han Hsin (*d.* 196 B.C.): while Han, a poor commoner, was fishing in the Huai River, an old woman nearby noticed that he was nearly starved, and fed him. Han was later made king of Ch'u for his services to the founder of the Han, but was executed on suspicion of having plotted a rebellion. See Watson, *Records*, I, 203–232.

Han-shan (Cold Mountain): early T'ang monk known for his poems of spiritual questing and attainment. Shih-te was a young contemporary of Han-shan. See Burton Watson, *Cold Mountain* (New York: Grove Press, 1962).

Han Yü (768–824): T'ang poet and prose master known for his reform of prose style. See Stephen Owen, *The Poetry of Meng Chiao and Han Yü* (New Haven: Yale University Press, 1975).

Herdboy and Weaver: constellations in Chinese astronomy, on both sides of the Milky Way; often invoked as a fit metaphor for the separation of lovers. Fated to a year-long separation, they meet once on the night of the seventh day of the seventh lunar month, when magpies form a bridge across the river of stars. The motif is as old as the *Book of Songs*, and was popular in the "Seventh Night Poem" in Japan and Korea.

Hsiang River: a large tributary of the Yangtze.

Hsiang Yü (232–202 B.C.): a rival of the founder of the Han. He is said to have cut his own throat when surrounded by Han forces. See Watson, *Records*, I, 37–74.

Hsiao River: a tributary of the Hsiang.

Hsieh Ling-yün (385–433): the father of the "mountain and water" school of poetry; Hsieh sought release from the world in visionary landscapes and loved to wander about the hills of Chekiang. On one occasion he "emerged at Lin-hai, to the great terror of the local magistrate, who mistook him for a rebel leader." See J. D. Frodsham, *The Murmuring Stream: The Life and Works of the Chinese Nature Poet Hsieh Ling-yün* (Kuala Lumpur: University of Malaya Press, 1968), 2 vols.

Hsü Yu: a legendary recluse. When Emperor Yao wished to make him his successor, Hsü was so horrified by the suggestion he went to the river to cleanse his ears.

Hu-ch'iu: NW of Wu, Kiangsu, one of the Buddhist centers east of Chien-k'ang, the capital of the Eastern Chin.

Huan I (*d. c.* 392): great flautist of the Chin.

Hui-yüan (334–416): eminent monk of the Eastern Chin, disciple of Tao-an

(312–285), and leader of the Buddhist community at Mount Lu. He initiated the Amitābha cult (402) and encouraged *dhyāna* (meditation) practices. He is the author of the treatise "A Monk Does Not Bow Down before a King."

hwarang: an ancient institution of Silla. Recruited from the nobility and trained in both the martial and the liberal arts (poetry and music), these young men were known for their patriotism and valor. They were also instructed in Buddhism by eminent monks. Their patron saint was Maitreya.

hyangga ("native songs"): the term for the twenty-five extant Old Korean poems. Of the three variants, the most polished and popular consisted of two stanzas of four lines plus a conclusion of two lines.

Juan Chi (210–263): a poet, musician, and lover of wine, one of the "Seven Worthies of the Bamboo Grove." Juan is known for his "Singing of Thoughts," comprising eighty-five poems. See Donald Holzman, *Poetry and Politics: The Life and Works of Juan Chi, A.D. 210-263* (Cambridge: Cambridge University Press, 1976).

kasa: one of the four poetic forms of traditional Korea, originating as song lyrics written to prevailing *kasa* tunes. It is characterized by a lack of stanzaic division and variable length, a tendency toward description and exposition, at times also lyricism, and the use of balanced parallel phrases, verbal and syntactical. Its norm is a group of two four-syllable words—or alternating groups or three and four syllables—which form a unit and are repeated in parallel form. Often likened to the Chinese *fu,* it emerged as a new genre toward the middle of the fifteenth century.

Kimch'ŏn: a market town in North Kyŏngsang.

King Adalla (154–184): the eighth ruler of Silla.

King Chinp'yŏng (579–632): the twenty-sixth ruler of Silla.

King Kaeru (128–166): the fourth ruler of Paekche.

King Kŭmwa: the son of King Haeburu of Fu-yü (Puyŏ) in southern Manchuria. Kŭmwa means "golden frog."

King P'yŏngwŏn (559–590): the twenty-fifth ruler of Koguryŏ.

King Suro (42–199): the founder of the kingdom of Karak or Kaya in the basin of the Naktong River; annexed by Silla in 532.

King T'arhae (57–80): the fourth ruler of Silla.

King Tongmyŏng (37–19 B.C.): the founder of Koguryŏ. His taboo name was Chumong ("able archer").

King Wu-ling of Chao (325–299 B.C.): ordered his people to adopt barbarian dress. See Watson, *Records,* II, 159.

King Yangyang (590–618): the twenty-sixth ruler of Koguryŏ.

kisaeng: Korean female entertainers. Trained in poetry, music, dancing, and polite conversation, they were an important part of the entertainment at royal banquets, receptions for foreign envoys, and other ceremonies. Official *kisaeng* were registered at court. Some such as Hwang Chin-i were accomplished poets. Some were known in China for their beauty and accomplishments and were eagerly sought by Chinese envoys.

Kuan Yü (*d.* 219): serving the Shu, he became the most revered hero in Chinese history. He released Ts'ao Ts'ao, who later became Emperor Wu of the Wei, at Hua-jung Valley. The episode appears in *Romance of the Three Kingdoms,* tr. Brewitt-Taylor, I, 525.

Kuo Chü: of the Later Han, one of the twenty-four paragons of filial devotion.

Kwanghan Pavilion: Kwanghan (Great Cold) is the name of a palace on the moon.

Kyerip county: modern Mun'gyŏng, North Kyŏngsang.

Lesser Learning, or *Elementary Education:* compiled by Chu Hsi (1130–1200) in six chapters. Its three main subjects are "the foundation of moral teaching," "making clear human relations," and "being serious about self-cultivation." King Yŏngjo translated it into Korean (1744). See Yves Hervouet, ed., *A Sung Bibliography* (Hong Kong: Chinese University Press, 1978), pp. 234–235.

Li Po (701–762): T'ang poet known in Korea for his poems on the moon and wine. See Arthur Waley, *The Poetry and Career of Li Po* (London: Allen & Unwin, 1950).

Li sao (Encountering Sorrow): attributed to Ch'ü Yüan (?343–278 B.C.). Translated in David Hawkes, *Ch'u Tz'u: The Songs of the South* (Oxford: Clarendon Press, 1959), pp. 22–34.

"Lien-ch'ang Palace": by Yüan Chen (779–813) and about the dismal years before and after the An Lu-shan rebellion (755–757). Translated in Wu-chi Liu and Irving Y. Lo, eds., *Sunflower Splendor* (Garden City: Doubleday, 1975), pp. 222–226.

Lin Pu (976–1028): lived on a hill near the West Lake and amused himself by keeping cranes.

Liu Hsiu: Emperor Kuang-wu of the Later Han. His subordinates served Liu a dish of cooked barley when he reached the Hu-t'o River with Wang Lang in pursuit (A.D. 24).

Lo-lang (Nangnang): one of the commanderies in north Korea established by China in 108 B.C.; annexed by Koguryŏ in 313.

Mahāyānasaṁgraha (Compendium of the Mahāyāna): a systematic exposition of the Consciousness-only system, by Asaṅga (*fl.* 310–390). Translated into French by E. Lamotte (Louvain, 1938–1939).

Maitreya: the future Buddha who resides in Tuṣita Heaven.

Ma-ku: a Taoist fairy.

Mañjuśrī: the bodhisattva of wisdom, whose abode was on Mt. Wu-t'ai in Shansi. In Korea Mañjuśrī resides on Mt. Odae.

Māra: the Destroyer, the Evil One, who tempts men to indulge their passions. Māra means "killing."

Master of the Red Pine: a legendary immortal at the time of the Chinese culture hero Shen Nung.

Meng Chiao (751–814): T'ang poet known for his harsh and intellectual imagery. See Owen, *The Poetry of Meng Chiao and Han Yü.*

Meng Pen: a Chinese hero during the Warring States period, who could pull the horns from an ox's head.

modern-style poetry: covers the forms *chüeh-chü* (broken-off lines), *lü-shih* (regulated verse), and *p'ai-lü* (regulated couplets). For a concise description, see Hans

H. Frankel, *The Flowering Plum and the Palace Lady: Interpretations of Chinese Poetry* (New Haven: Yale University Press, 1976), pp. 213, 215.

Meng Tsung: one of the twenty-four paragons of filial devotion.

Moon Goddess: Ch'ang-o or Heng-o, who stole her husband's elixir of life and fled to the moon.

Mount Heng: northern sacred mountain in China.

Mount Kou-shih: *see* Prince Ch'iao.

Mount Lu: a famous mountain in Kiangsi, celebrated by Li Po (701–762) in "Viewing the Waterfall at Mount Lu."

Mount San: location unknown.

Mount T'ai: eastern sacred mountain in China.

Naema: a title of Silla rank.

Namhan Fortress: in Kwangju, where the Korean king fled at the second invasion of the Manchu army; after standing a siege of forty-five days, he capitulated in 1638.

Nirvāṇa Sūtra: a Mahāyana scripture purporting to be the last sermon of the Buddha. It proclaims that all living beings can attain Buddhahood since they all possess the Buddha nature.

North Mang hill: a burial site near Loyang.

Old Man in the Moon: the matchmaker.

old-style poetry *(ku-shih):* consisting of lines of five or seven syllables. See Frankel, *The Flowering Plum and the Palace Lady,* p. 213.

Ŏm River: northeast of the Yalu.

Ou-yang Hsiu (1007–1072): Sung poet, prose writer, historian, and critic.

Pak Hyŏkkŏse (57 B.C.–A.D. 3): the founder of Silla, one of the three ancient Korean kingdoms.

p'ansori: Korean oral narrative sung by a professional singer *(kwangdae).* Flourishing in the nineteenth century, *p'ansori* resembles the Chinese chantefable *(chu-kung-tiao)* and the Japanese puppet libretti *(jōruri)* in the singer's improvisation of narratives. A singers' organization and the master-disciple relationship for the transmission of this art form resulted in a fixing of texts.

"Parting, The": by Li Po, on the sorrow of two widowed wives of the legendary emperor Shun. The spots on the bamboo leaves that grow on the Hsiang are said to have been produced by the tears of the two queens. Translated in Waley, *The Poetry and Career of Li Po,* pp. 36–37.

Peach Blossom Spring: the literary Chinese *locus amoenus* (pleasant place) created by T'ao Ch'ien. See Hightower, *The Poems of T'ao Ch'ien,* pp. 254–258, and my *Celebration of Continuity: Themes in Classic East Asian Poetry* (Cambridge: Harvard University Press, 1979), pp. 78–81.

Po Chü-i (772–846): T'ang poet known for his lucid style and narrative skill. See Arthur Waley, *The Life and Times of Po Chü-i* (London: Allen & Unwin, 1949).

Po I: together with his brother Shu Ch'i, he disapproved of the conquest by Chou of their overlord the Shang king, and retired to Shou-yang mountain; resolving "not to eat the corn of Chou," they died of starvation.

Potalaka: a sacred abode of Avalokiteśvara, off India's southern coast. In Korea the bodhisattva resides on Mt. Nak.

Prince Ch'iao (Wang-tzu Ch'iao or Wang-tzu Chin): said to have been a son of King Ling of Chou (sixth century B.C.), the noted player of the *sheng* (mouth organ made of thirteen bamboo pipes), who became an immortal on Mount Kou-shih.

Queen Mother of the West: a fairy queen who dwells on Jasper Terrace by the K'un-lun Mountain. Her peaches that ripen once every three thousand years confer immortality.

"Return, The": a poem by T'ao Ch'ien (365–427); one of the prototypical and influential poems in Korea. Translated in Hightower, *The Poetry of T'ao Ch'ien*, pp. 268–270.

ri (Chinese *li*): a measure of distance, about one-third of a mile.

śāla: the tree under which the Buddha had his enlightenment.

samādhi: concentration.

Samantabhadra: the bodhisattva representing the Buddha's teaching, meditation, and practice. He made ten great vows. His name means "universally worthy."

Samgi Mountain: north of Kyŏngju.

sasŏl: narrative verse.

Shen Nung: the Divine Husbandman, a Chinese culture hero and the inventor of agriculture.

sijo: the most popular, elastic, and mnemonic poetic form of Korea, dating from the fifteenth century; it is a three-line poem and the typical *sijo* is said to follow the pattern of theme–development–antitheme. The *sijo* was sung and orally transmitted until the texts were written down from about the beginning of the eighteenth century. It is an oral art even today for both the lettered and unlettered.

"Song of Everlasting Sorrow": by Po Chü-i (772–846) and about the T'ang emperor Hsüan-tsung's love for Precious Consort Yang (*d.* 756). Translated in Cyril Birch, ed., *Anthology of Chinese Literature*, I (New York: Grove Press, 1965), pp. 266–269.

"Song of the Swan": said to have been composed by Kao-tsu of the Han to console his favorite concubine, Lady Ch'i. Translated in Watson, *Early Chinese Literature*, p. 286.

"Spring in Jade Pavilion" *(Yü-lou ch'un)*: the name of a *tz'u* tune.

Ssu-ma Ch'ien (*c.* 145–90 B.C.): Grand Historian of the Han, the author of *Shih chi* (Records of the Historian, completed *c.* 90 B.C.) in 130 chaps. See Watson, *Early Chinese Literature*, pp. 92–103.

Su Ch'in (*d.* 317 B.C.): a political theorist and adviser to the states of Yen, Chao, and others.

Su Shih (Tung-p'o; 1037–1101): Sung poet, prose master, calligrapher, and painter. See Burton Watson, *Su Tung-p'o: Selections from a Sung Dynasty Poet* (New York: Columbia University Press, 1965).

T'aebong: a site associated with Kung Ye (*d.* 918), who raised a rebellion against Silla.

Taehyŏng: a title of Koguryŏ rank.

Taesa: a title of Silla rank.

T'an-hsüan chi: Fa-tsang's commentary in 60 chapters on the first Chinese translation of the *Avataṁsaka sūtra* by Buddhabhadra (359–429).

T'ang: the founder of the Shang or Yin dynasty.

Tangun: the mythological founder of Korea. Tangun means "Sandalwood Lord."

Tathāgata: "He who is thus gone or come"; who has trodden the same path as all other Buddhas to supreme enlightenment. An epithet for a Buddha.

Tattvasiddhi: also *Satyasiddhi* (Treatise on the Completion of Truth), by Harivarman (*c.* 250–350).

Tripiṭaka (The Three Baskets): collection of Buddhist scriptures, rules of discipline, and treatises. The Chinese canon is known as "Great Scripture-Store."

True Treasure of Classic Literature (Ku-wen chen-pao): an anthology of Chinese verse and prose compiled by Huang Chien.

Ts'ai Yen: the daughter of Ts'ai Yung (133–192) and a skilled musician.

Tu Fu (712–770): often considered to be China's greatest poet, he is revered as "the sage of poetry" in China and Korea. See William Hung, *Tu Fu, China's Greatest Poet* (Cambridge: Harvard University Press, 1952), 2 vols., and A. R. Davis, *Tu Fu* (New York: Twayne, 1971).

Tu Mu (803–852): a late T'ang poet known in Korea for his quatrains on wine, women, and his fun-loving life south of the Yangtse.

Tung-t'ing Lake: in NE Hunan.

Tuṣita ("satisfied"): one of the Buddhist heavens, where the Buddha lives before his last rebirth on earth.

tz'u: song words or lyrics; poems in irregular meters, "written in fixed patterns to go with new or old musical tunes." See Frankel, *The Flowering Plum and the Palace Lady,* p. 216.

Ubal Stream: south of the mountain range of Changbaek on Korea's northern border.

Vairocana: the Brilliant One or the Illuminator, who lives in the Land of Eternally Tranquil Light.

Vajrasamādhi Sūtra: the scripture translated into Chinese during the Northern Liang dynasty (397–439) that expounds the "diamond meditation," that of the last stage of the bodhisattva, characterized by indestructible knowledge, penetrating all reality.

Wang Hsi-chih (303–*c.* 365): famous calligrapher of the Chin.

Wang Pao (first century B.C.): Han poet and the author of "Slave's Contract" *(T'ung-yüeh);* translated in C. Martin Wilbur, *Slavery in China during the Former Han Dynasty, 206 B.C.–A.D. 25* (Chicago: Field Museum of Natural History, 1943), pp. 383–392.

Wang Wei (701–761): T'ang poet, musician, and landscape painter, known for his visual imagery ("In his poetry there is painting and in his painting there is poetry"—Su Shih) and nature poetry. See Pauline Yu, *The Poetry of Wang Wei* (Bloomington: Indiana University Press, 1980).

Wei Yen: T'ang painter.

Wen T'ung (1018–1079): Sung painter of bamboo and a friend of Su Shih.

Witches' Mountain: refers to Sung Yü's (third century B.C.) "Kao-t'ang fu," which narrates King Hsiang's amorous encounter in a dream with the goddess of Witches' Mountain, who appeared to him as clouds and rain. "Clouds and rain" is a euphemism for sexual intercourse. See Lois Fusek, "The 'Kao-t'ang Fu,' " *Monumenta Serica*, 30 (1972–1973), 392–425.

yang: ancient Korean monetary unit; a tael of silver.

yangban ("two corps"): civil and military; as a class term it refers to the scholar-officials.

Yang-tu: capital of the Ch'en, modern Nanking.

Yellow Springs: also Nine Springs, the Chinese underworld.

Yü: Chinese culture hero and the sage-founder of the Hsia.

Yu Hyŏng-wŏn (1622–1673): advocator of reform in institutions, agriculture, and taxation.

yut: a popular Korean game played with four sticks which are thrown in the air; the score depends on how they land.

Bibliography

The bibliography is in two parts: Korean sources include primary sources, standard modern editions and reprints, annotations, and translations. Unless otherwise noted, all books are printed in Seoul. Western sources are selected translations and studies in English.

Korean Sources

FOUNDATION MYTHS

Iryŏn. *Samguk yusa* [Memorabilia and Mirabilia of the Three Kingdoms]. Ed. Ch'oe Nam-sŏn, 1954. Tr. Yi Pyŏng-do, 1972.

Yi Kyu-bo. *Tongguk Yisangguk chip* [Collected Works of Minister Yi of Korea]. Photolithographic reprint. 1954. Chap. 3. See Minjok munhwa ch'ujinhoe (National Culture Promotion Society), *Kugyŏk Tongguk Yisangguk chip* (a modern Korean translation of the *Works*), 1978.

OLD KOREAN POETRY: *Hyangga*

Chŏn Kyu-t'ae. *Nonju Hyangga* [Hyangga Annotated]. 1976.

Hong Ki-mun. *Ko kayo chip* [Collection of Ancient Korean Songs]. P'yongyang, 1958.

Iryŏn. *Samguk yusa*. Ed. Ch'oe Nam-sŏn. 1954.

Yang Chu-dong. *Koga yŏn'gu* [Studies in Old Korean Poetry]. 1957.

BIOGRAPHIES

Iryŏn. *Samguk yusa*. Ed. Ch'oe Nam-sŏn. 1954.

Kakhun. *Haedong kosŭng chŏn* [Lives of Eminent Korean Monks]. *Taishō Tripiṭaka*, 50, 1020c–1021c.

Kim Pu-sik. *Samguk sagi* [Historical Record of the Three Kingdoms]. Ed. Yi Pyŏng-do. 2 vols. 1977.

POETRY IN CHINESE

Sŏ Kŏ-jŏng et al., eds. *Tongmun sŏn* [Anthology of Korean literature in Chinese]. Photolithographic reprint. 3 vols. 1966–1967. Chap. 19. For a translation, see National Culture Promotion Society, *Kugyŏk Tongmun sŏn*, vol. 2, 1968.

KORYŎ SONGS: *Changga*

Chŏn Kyu-t'ae. *Koryŏ sogyo ŭi yŏn'gu* [Studies in the Popular Koryŏ Songs]. 1976.

Pak Chun, ed. *Akchang kasa* [Words for Music]. A reprint. 1957, 1972, 1973.

Pak Pyŏng-ch'ae. *Koryŏ kayo ŏsŏk yŏn'gu* [Studies in the Vocabulary of Koryŏ Songs]. 1968.

Siyong hyangak po [Contemporary Korean Music]. Photolithographic reprint of the pre-1500 text. 1954.

Yang Chu-dong. *Yŏyo chŏnju* [Studies in Middle Korean Poetry]. 1961.

PROSE ESSAYS

Sŏ Kŏ-jŏng et al., ed. *Tongmun sŏn.* Chaps. 65, 69, 96, 107.

Yi Che-hyŏn. *Ikchae chip* [Collected Works of Yi Che-hyŏn]. Photolithographic reprint. 1959. Chap. 6.

Yi Kyu-bo. *Tongguk Yisangguk chip.* Chap. 21. *Hujip.* Chap. 11.

POETRY IN CHINESE

Ch'oe Cha. *Pohan Chip* [Critical Essays by Ch'oe Cha]. A reprint. 1909. For a translation, see Yi Sang-bo, *P'ahan chip, Pohan chip, Nagong pisŏl,* 1975.

Sŏ Kŏ-jŏng et al., ed. *Tongmun sŏn.* Chaps. 4 and 19.

Yi Kyu-bo. *Tongguk Yisangguk chip. Hujip.* Chap. 4.

POEMS IN CHINESE BY ZEN MASTERS

Yi Wŏn-sŏp. *Koryŏ kosŭng hansi sŏn* [Anthology of Poems in Chinese by Eminent Koryŏ Monks]. 1978.

SONGS OF FLYING DRAGONS

Ch'oe Hang et al. *Yongbi ŏch'ŏn ka.* Photolithographic reprint. 2 vols. 1937–1938. For textual commentary, see my *Songs of Flying Dragons: A Critical Reading* (Cambridge, Mass.: Harvard University Press, 1975).

EARLY YI ROMANCE

Kim Si-sŭp. *Maewŏltang chip* [Collected Works of Kim Si-sŭp]. Photolithographic reprint with translation. 3 vols. 1977–1978. The text is in the *Maewŏltang woejip,* 9b–19b; translation on III, 316–336.

Sijo, I

Chŏng Pyŏng-uk, ed. *Sijo munhak sajŏn* [Dictionary of Sijo Literature]. 1966.

Sim Chae-wan, ed. *Kyobon yŏktae sijo chŏnsŏ* [The Complete Canon of Sijo Poetry with Textual Variants]. 1972.

Yi Ki-mun, ed. *Yŏktae sijo sŏn* [Annotated Anthology of Sijo]. 1973.

PROSE PORTRAITS

Ŏ Suk-kwŏn. *P'aegwan chapki* [The Storyteller's Miscellany]. A reprint. 1909. A variant text is in *Yasa ch'ongsŏ ŭi ch'ongch'ejŏk yŏn'gu,* 1976.

Kasa, I

Chŏng Ch'ŏl. *Songgang chŏnjip* [Collected Works of Chŏng Ch'ŏl]. Photolithographic reprint. 1964. *Songgang pyŏlchip* contains all his poetry.

Im Ki-jung. *Yŏkchu haesŏl Chosŏnjo ŭi kasa* [The Annotated Kasa of the Yi Dynasty]. 1979.
Kim Ki-dong et al., eds. *Han'guk kojŏn munhak chŏnsŏ: kasa* [Collection of Classic Korean Literature: Kasa]. 1972.
Kim Sa-yŏp. *Kyoju haeje Songgang kasa* [Collected Poems of Chŏng Ch'ŏl Annotated]. 1959.

A TALE OF ADVENTURE
Chang Chi-yŏng, ed. *Hong Kiltong chŏn, Sim Ch'ŏng chŏn.* 1964.
Hŏ Kyun. *Hong Kiltong chŏn.* Photolithographic reprint of the Wanp'an woodblock edition. 1971.

POEMS IN CHINESE, I
Hwang Pyŏng-guk, ed. *Yijo myŏngin sisŏn* [Anthology of Chinese Poems by Yi Dynasty Writers]. Ŭryu mun'go 28. 1975.
Kim Chi-yong, ed. *Yŏktae yŏryu hansimun sŏn* [Anthology of Chinese Verse and Prose by Korean Women Writers]. 1973.
Literary Works Compilation Committee, ed. *Han'guk yŏktae myŏngsi chŏnsŏ* [Anthology of Famous Chinese Verses in Korea]. 1959.
Ŏ Suk-kwŏn. *P'aegwan chapki.* 1909.
Sŏng Hyŏn. *Yongjae ch'onghwa.* A reprint. 1909. Translation, 1975.
Yi Chong-ch'an, ed. *Chosŏn kosŭng hansi sŏn* [Anthology of Poems in Chinese by Eminent Yi Monks]. 1978.
Yi Pyŏng-ju, ed. *Han'guk hansi sŏn* [Anthology of Poems in Chinese], 1968.

LATER YI ROMANCE
Chŏng Kyu-bok. *Kuun mong yŏn'gu* [Studies in the Kuun mong]. 1974.
———. *Kuun mong wŏnjŏn ŭi yŏn'gu* [Studies in the Original Texts of Kuun mong]. 1977.
Kim Man-jung. *Kuun mong.* Ed. Chŏng Pyŏng-uk and Yi Sŭng-uk. Han'guk kojŏn munhak taegye [Classic Korean Literature Series; hereafter *HKMT*]. Vol. 9. 1972.

Sijo, II
Yun Sŏn-do. *Kosan yugo* [Works of Yun Sŏn-do]. 1791, 1798. Addenda, chap. 6B contains his poetry.
(See also sources for *Sijo,* I.)

Kasa, II
An To-wŏn. *Manŏnsya.* Manuscript copy in the Karam collection, Seoul National University Library.
Chŏng Hag-yu et al. *Nongga wŏllyŏng ka, Hanyang ka.* Ed. Pak Sŏng-ŭi. *HKMT.* Vol. 7. 1974.
———. *P'ungsok kasa chip.* Ed. Yi Sŏng-nae. Sin'gu mun'go 2. 1974.

Kim In-gyŏm. *Iltong changyu ka.* Photolithographic reprint of a manuscript copy. 2 vols. 1973.
———. *Iltong changyu ka.* Ed. Yi Min-su. T'amgu sinsŏ 105. 1976.

SATIRICAL STORIES

So Chae-yŏng, ed. *Han'guk p'ungja sosŏl sŏn* [Anthology of Korean Satirical Tales]. Chŏngŭm mun'go 102. 1975.
Yi Ka-wŏn, ed. *Yijo hanmun sosŏl sŏn* [Anthology of Yi Dynasty Stories in Chinese]. *HKMT.* Vol. 17. 1975.

WOMEN WRITERS

Princess Hyegyŏng. *Handyung rok.* Ed. Yi Pyŏng-gi and Kim Tong-uk. *HKMT.* Vol. 14. 1961.
Lady Ŭiyudang and Yi Hŭi-p'yŏng. *Ŭiyudang ilgi, Hwasŏng ilgi.* Ed. Kang Han-yŏng. Sin'gu mun'go 3. 1974.
Yi Hŭi-sŭng. *Yŏktae kungmunhak chŏnghwa* [Essence of Korean Literature]. 2 vols. 1953. See vol. 1.

THE ART OF THE SINGER: *P'ansori*

Ch'unhyang chŏn. Ed. Ku Cha-gyun. *HKMT.* Vol. 10. 1976.
Kim Ki-dong et al. *Han'guk kojŏn munhak chŏnjip: kasa.* 1972.
Shin Chae-hyo. *Shin Chae-hyo p'ansori sasŏl chip.* Ed. Kang Han-yŏng. *HKMT.* Vol. 12. 1974.

Sasŏl Sijo
See sources for *Sijo,* I.

POEMS IN CHINESE, II

Hwang Pyŏng-guk, ed. *Yijo myŏngin sisŏn.* 1975.
Literary Works Compilation Committee, ed. *Han'guk yŏktae myŏngsi chŏnsŏ.* 1959.
Pak Yong-gu, ed. *Kim Ip sisŏn* [Selected Poems by Kim Pyŏng-yŏn]. Chŏngŭm mun'go 156. 1971.

Western Sources

Cho Oh-Kon. *Korean Puppet Theatre: Kkotu kaksi.* East Lansing: Michigan State University Asian Studies Center, 1979.
Kim Han-kyo, ed. *Studies on Korea: A Scholar's Guide.* Honolulu: Univeristy Press of Hawaii, 1980. See chap. 6, "Literature and Folklore."
Kim So-un. *The Story Bag.* Rutland, Vt., and Tokyo: Tuttle, 1967.
Korean National Commission for Unesco. *Traditional Performing Arts of Korea.* Seoul: Korean National Commission for Unesco, 1978.
Lee, Peter H. *Lives of Eminent Korean Monks.* Cambridge, Mass.: Harvard University Press, 1969.

———. *Poems from Korea: A Historical Anthology*. Honolulu: University Press of Hawaii, 1974.

———. *Songs of Flying Dragons: A Critical Reading*. Cambridge, Mass.: Harvard University Press, 1975.

———. *Celebration of Continuity: Themes in Classic East Asian Poetry*. Cambridge, Mass.: Harvard University Press, 1979.

McCann, David R., ed. *Black Crane: An Anthology of Korean Literature*. Ithaca: Cornell University East Asian Papers, 14. 1977.

Pihl, Marshall R. "The Tale of Simch'ŏng: A Korean Oral Narrative." Ph. D. dissertation, Harvard University, 1974.

Rutt, Richard. *The Bamboo Grove: An Introduction to Sijo*. Berkeley: University of California Press, 1971.

Rutt, Richard and Kim Chong-un. *Virtuous Women: Three Classic Korean Novels*. Seoul: Korean National Commission for Unesco, 1974.

Index

Production Notes

This book was designed by Kenneth Miyamoto
and typeset on the Unified Composing System
by University of Hawaii Press.

The text typeface is Garamond No. 49
and the display typeface is Benguiat.

Offset presswork and binding were done
by Vail-Ballou Press. Text paper is Writers RR
Offset, basis 50.